I Hope This Finds You Well

I Hope This Finds You Well

A Novel

NATALIE SUE

wm

WILLIAM MORROW

An Imprint of HarperCollins*Publishers*

I HOPE THIS FINDS YOU WELL. Copyright © 2024 by Natalie Sue. All rights reserved. Printed in the United States of America. No part of this book may be used or reproduced in any manner whatsoever without written permission except in the case of brief quotations embodied in critical articles and reviews. For information, address HarperCollins Publishers, 195 Broadway, New York, NY 10007. In Canada, address HarperCollins Publishers Ltd., Bay Adelaide Centre, East Tower, 22 Adelaide Street West, 41st floor, Toronto, Ontario, M5H 4E3, Canada.

HarperCollins books may be purchased for educational, business, or sales promotional use. For information, please email the Special Markets Department at SPsales@harpercollins.com, or in Canada at HCOrder@harpercollins.com.

FIRST EDITION

Library of Congress Cataloging-in-Publication Data has been applied for.

Library and Archives Canada Cataloguing in Publication information is available upon request.

ISBN 978-0-06-332036-9
ISBN 978-1-4434-7025-4 (Canada)

24 25 26 27 28 LBC 5 4 3 2 1

For Joanne. Thank you for everything you did.

I Hope This Finds You Well

This Could've Been an Email

THERE WILL BE questions. Ones I don't have socially acceptable answers for. I know because today is my birthday, and a last-minute meeting has appeared on my calendar. A poorly disguised office cake party will be my supposed reward for turning thirty-three six and a half hours ago. Half the office will cram around a conference table, against our will, to eat dry sheet cake and force polite smiles.

The questions will be about my life and how I plan to celebrate. Answers: I don't have a life, and I will likely celebrate by drinking alone and going down Reddit rabbit holes researching random and upsetting things like fecal-matter transplants, or the Golden State Killer, while making myself regret everything. I'm not sure that's relatable, so I'll say I'm having dinner with friends. Oh, the lies I am forced to tell just to fit in at the western regional office of Supershops Incorporated.

The meeting reminder flashes on my monitor again, persistent as a pesky cold sore. My fingers tingle, and I take a few slow breaths, but I can't get air to settle in my lungs. So many office situations show no regard for people with anxiety, yet we're the bad guys if we can't cope.

I should just walk away from it all.

My eyes dart to the flimsy wall of my cubicle where my name card still faintly reads *Jolene Smith* after years of sitting beneath violently fluorescent lighting. Three pushpins pierce the industrial fabric; they've always been there, even though I've never felt the urge to pin anything up. My workspace remains bare and beige in a sea of personalized cubicles. Yet those pins sit reassuringly in their same formation, day after day.

And I don't think I could ever leave them.

A new email appears in my inbox. It's from Rhonda, whose official title is "lead accounting administrator," but really she's just our boss Gregory's assistant, a role she's held for a thousand years.

Reminder, I've booked you for a meeting in boardroom 435 that starts in one minute. You don't want to be late.

This meeting has automatic reminders set up, yet she's emailing me from seven feet away. I peer over the half wall of my cubicle toward hers, which boasts a shelf lined with an assortment of dusty trinkets, inspirational quotes printed on crinkled yellow paper affixed to the wall, and a file box I know is filled with medications, tea bags, and biscuits that expired in 2012. It's as though she anticipates being trapped here one day and not only surviving the ordeal, but thriving.

I don't mean to lock eyes with Rhonda; I blame her excessive eyeliner and the green eyeshadow that could direct traffic. She notices and breaks the stare first, lowering her head so I can see only the tips of her spiky grey hairdo. Then her mouse clicks, pointedly.

Technically, she's to blame for this entire mess. She doesn't usually pay much attention to me, and when she does it's often paired with a scowl and a pointed gum-snap. But Rhonda runs the morale club, and with Brendan Fraser as my witness, there's nothing more demoralizing than the Morale Boosters. Her morbid obsession with birthday tracking, cake buying, and forcing people to sit through off-key renditions of the "Happy Birthday" song can't be out of love.

Planning these thirty-minute-long office parties and telling people about the mundane interactions she's had with service people are big portions of her personality, but her primary passion is her "grown-ass son," whom she visits every weekend. He's some rich dick who supports her. In her eyes, he is on the brink of curing all human ailments, keeps the transit running on time, and has about a million matches on Tinder. Although, judging by the framed picture of him on her desk, he could be the stock model used in advertisements for plain bread and mayo.

I keep my expression deadpan as I turn back to my keyboard and type:

Hello Rhonda,
Thanks very much for reminding me about the meeting. I must say, your reminder is so much more personal and well received than the default

one that the computer gives. I almost feel that one is pointless when I've got you in my corner.

Best regards,
Jolene

Adding extra sugar to the part that's visible helps make the invisible part so much more satisfying. I change the font to white and type the stuff that's just for me:

P.S. Deep in my core, I find you insufferable. There are times, when you're on the phone fake laughing or retelling someone the same story about your toenail surgery, that make me consider joining a cult as a preferable alternative to staying here with you. Also, I'm fairly certain you can't legally brag about your son since you named him "Carl."

As I click send, I halt my breath. The rush of adrenaline hits as a flutter in my abdomen. It's a safe high, since she won't actually *see* the message. The knot in my chest loosens. This is truly the second-best coping mechanism to survive the peril that is my colleagues.

I creak out of my chair to begin the walk to the boardroom. Rhonda's shimmery nails continue to clack across the keyboard as she peeps up at me from beside the corner of her screen. I smile politely in her general direction.

As I pass behind Caitlin's desk, the scent of the vanilla-icing hand cream she applies seventeen times daily wafts my way, microdosing my irritation. The same scent always transfers to the documents and envelopes she handles, like a dog marking her territory. She tilts her chin toward me and gives this little brow raise but doesn't look directly at me. Something uncertain bubbles in the pit of my chest. She's been watching me all day, and I trust her less than my Wish.com recommendations.

Caitlin and I have worked adjacent to each other for three years in the same admin role. We were destined to be best friends, but because of who we are as people, our years of forced proximity have instead culminated in a specific form of petty hatred. The problem is Caitlin tries *way* too hard. She's still talking about how this job is a "jumping-off point" for her to step into a larger role at Supershops, while I gave up on that notion after less than a year here. Her violations include: cc'ing Gregory when she notices any of my errors "in case it becomes a relevant pattern" (which is a good point, and I've made sure to include him when calling out her mistakes too), forgetting to add my mug when she runs the dishwasher (I can never find space for hers either), and interrogating me when her yogurt goes missing from the office fridge (as if blueberry Dannon is something I'd mess with). It's reached a healthy point where our only communication is via curt emails, and we gleefully mix up anything the other sends to the printer. It's unfortunate because I like to think I support my fellow women in the office, or at least I stay out of their ways as much as everyone else.

More lifeless eyes seem to pull toward me from each cubicle I pass. I curl my arms around myself, to limit how much I'm perceived. I catch my reflection in a glass door and jolt at my frizzy brown hair and puffy eyes. I may be entitled to compensation for that. It's not that I'm a terrible-looking person, but I haven't slept well this week, and I always seem to look my worst when I don't expect myself.

And it's not like I care about making a great impression here. This is not one of those cool places to work with free snacks or standing desks or nap pods. My office is sort of like a recent time capsule. If someone wanted to travel seven to nine years into the past, they could come view our poster of men eating lunch on a plank, the fax machine still plugged into the wall, and the sagging yoga ball chairs. We politely ignore the decade-old coffee stains on the industrial carpeting near Larry's coffeemaker and the fact that Larry sleeps here a few times a year.

When I reach the dusty bird of paradise plant that Rhonda snuck into the office five years ago that's both plastic and dying, a familiar dread sets in. I take a breath and open the door to the boardroom.

Seated closest to the entrance is my boss, Gregory. He's got the same hair as a golden retriever and dresses in clothes that were likely issued by someone who got them during a rushed grocery shop, and at least once a month he mentions that he championed getting the complimentary dollar store tampons placed in the bathrooms. He's not just a regional manager; he's an ally. The single most notable thing about him is that he often discreetly touches his penis (via his pockets, but we can all see the movements) and then openly touches the door handles, printers, and Nespresso buttons, leaving his penis dew that seeped through the pocket fabric everywhere. Because he's the boss, there's no stopping his dick fingers, and that's why no workplace is ever truly equal.

Next to him is Anna, our office manager. She's frowning at her phone and stabbing at the screen with a French-manicured finger. She's all business and sharp angles with her black pantsuit and blunt bangs.

But she doesn't normally come to these gatherings.

And at the end of the table is a guy I don't recognize—a guy who is openly sketching a small doodle onto a faded yellow legal pad. Beneath his trimmed beard I can see the beginning of a smirk. He's wearing a hoodie that says *Warhammer*, which would not be my weapon of choice in a war. The sleeves are pushed up, and I take the obligatory tenth of a second to appreciate his forearm flexing, as is my right.

I glance back toward the open door, but Rhonda isn't trotting in behind me balancing a cake against her bosom. There aren't even discount decorations in here—no wispy paper streamers absently taped under the buzzing light fixture or silvery birthday sign that is well past retirement. I take another tentative step inside the room, visibly stirring up the dust in the stiff air.

My mouth dries and my brain starts to swim. Just three hours ago, the office stress case, Larry Goodwin, was all sweat sheened and breathy in the copy room as he warned some guy in payroll that massive layoffs were on the horizon.

But I shrugged it off.

The doodling man lets his pen fall onto the notepad and he grins uncertainly at me. I don't know why they decided to invite a high school gym coach to help fire me—unless the goal is maximum shame? Maybe he'll yell at me about my three-croissant lunches and have me attempt a push-up.

"Please have a seat." Gregory's voice is stern, absent of its usual shameless bubble.

My heartbeat jumps into high gear as I plonk into a seat across the table from the three of them.

Gregory broadens his shoulders in this showy way before speaking. "We wanted to discuss a concern that was brought to our attention." He scrapes a single piece of paper across the plastic-top table, driven by his callused fingers. Caitlin's pink cursive email signature flashes from the bottom corner.

My heart stops.

Gregory continues: "I'm sure you're aware of our corporate policies about interpersonal communication."

I nod, realizing my neck has gone stiff. A shuffling motion to my right distracts my attention. The gym coach is writing something down on his pad.

"Did you include additional text in your April seventeenth email to Caitlin Joffrey?"

Three sets of eyes bore into me as realization dawns. I try to think of what to say, but my mind can only race through random thoughts that blur together, garbled and incomplete.

"So no cake is coming" is what ends up coming out of my mouth. They glance at each other in confusion. "Never mind," I mutter, as I look down at the paper in front of me. My heartbeat overtakes the sound of Gregory's mouth breathing.

Hello Caitlin,
Per my last email, reports are due Wednesday.

Regards,
Jolene

We always choose the most violent form of business casual communication with each other.

Gregory leans across the table to tap his finger on the page. "Right there, can you please review the additional text on the bottom?"

I blink rapidly as the words come into focus.

P.S. What is wrong with you? You're eating that puke soup to deliberately torture us, and you left a trail of destruction from the microwave to your desk.

Sincerely,
Everyone

Admittedly, when I scribed it, I was having a particularly shit day and Caitlin had been getting to me all morning. But she was the one with the gall to microwave an actual bowl of fish vomit and slurp it in front of us with no regard for the fact that I was nursing a hangover. Writing that note was the only form of therapy I could afford.

All the joints in my fingers stiffen.

All I can think up as a defense is "I don't understand how that got there?"

Except I do. I messed up bad.

Until now, I've never forgotten to change the font color to white before hitting send.

The gym coach's mouth twitches again before he turns his gaze to the window. I'm here dealing with an actual nightmare, and this guy has the audacity to laugh.

"Maybe I left my computer logged in?" I mutter.

Nobody on the panel will look directly at me.

My ancestors overcame plagues, poverty, and war so that I could be here. My mom separated from her family and risked everything to emigrate from Iran to Canada without even knowing English, because she wanted more for me. All those sacrifices, all those brave acts, just so this could happen. All of it leading up to this moment, to this boardroom at my very *meh* job, so my managers can address how much of a fucking weirdo I am.

My legacy was taken down by a bowl of trout soup heated for one minute and thirty seconds on high.

An unfortunate phlegm sound tears through the silence as Gregory clears his throat. "We know you wrote it, Jolene." His jaw ticks twice. "And as this was an alarming message, we considered having our IT coordinator track your computer activity for instances of threatening behavior."

"What?" I blurt out. "That wasn't a threat. You can't search my—"

I cut myself off, probably my first wise move since I entered this meeting. I've always felt like someone at corporate was watching everything I did on my work computer anyway. I imagined they could see my search history and were plotting little dots on some graph to show the higher-ups how absolutely disturbed I am.

I never expected it to be true.

A chair creaks as Anna, who has never been one to show solidarity, adjusts herself and stares stonily at my forehead. Maybe it's some type of corporate head office protocol on how to look at an employee you're about to fire.

Gregory rubs his chin, every scratch of his nails against his stubble audible. "Our new HR analyst has looked things over, and although the letter contains a threatening tone, he agrees that it isn't a threat." I now understand the presence of the coach, who flashes another small grin my way. His smile has far too much sympathy tinting the edges. In his line of work, he should be as unfazed as a three a.m. Uber driver.

I nod automatically like a keen employee engaged in an important business discussion, instead of whatever the hell this is. Gregory slides the printed email away from me and shuffles it back into a manila folder as he winces the next words out. "We know you don't often, uh ... socialize with other employees, and that you aren't one to participate in team-building activities."

Heat rushes up my neck, my humiliation hitting new peaks.

"But when you start to engage in actively inappropriate behavior," he continues, "we have to get involved for the comfort of all."

I nod again. Now would be an appropriate time to inquire if NASA has any rockets scheduled to launch, so I can hitch a ride directly into the sun.

Anna shifts higher in her chair. "Miss Joffrey came to us feeling quite jostled and rightfully emotional."

I'll bet. I focus all my energy into controlling my ocular muscles, as my body is physically overcome with a need to roll my eyes. The only emotion Caitlin felt was glee over an opportunity to get me in here.

Something shifts behind me, so I turn slightly toward the still-ajar boardroom door. I catch Armin, the other accounting admin, darting out of view as he pretends to scan something at the printer. He is the fourth member of our cubicle pod, sitting next to Rhonda, Caitlin, and me. The very fact that he's standing at a printer and repeatedly pushing buttons gives him away. The guy is a serial printer breaker who walks away when faced with any adversity from IT equipment—or any minor challenge, really.

Gregory continues where Anna left off. "We want this to be a comfortable environment for all." A fresh wave of bitterness washes over me. If Caitlin had shown the most basic regard for communal microwave etiquette, we'd all be sitting at our desks right now, trying to ignore our thoughts for the rest of the afternoon.

Gregory was right. I'm not one to engage with these people. I haven't spoken to anyone in the office unless absolutely necessary for most of the eight years I've worked here. I spend more time with them than anyone else in my life, yet I remain hardly visible, like my name plate.

"Since this is your first incident of this nature, you won't be terminated as long as you meet certain conditions." My head swims with his words, trying to decipher their meaning. "There will be mandatory security restrictions on your computer, including flagging of emails with certain key words, and"—he glances toward the coach—"Clifford will assist with your progress through an anti-harassment course."

The Clifford guy gives a small wave, which accidentally knocks his pen out of his hand. It rolls onto the floor, and he disappears under the table to retrieve it.

Gregory lets out a heavy breath. "If you agree, the restrictions will take place immediately upon your signature, and you'll be scheduled to attend five sessions with Clifford over the next few weeks."

"Do you agree?" Anna pipes in with a breathless monotone.

I try to steady my hands into fists on my lap.

I can't lose this job—I'm barely making rent as is.

And my lifestyle can't take another hit. I'm down to seven-dollar wine and one single *macro* fiber towel. I can't move in with my parents and become the shame to my worldwide network of aunties. There will be a tongue clucking heard far and wide.

But it's more than that. If I have to live under my parents' roof again, it could literally end me this time.

The room and the world compress in on me as the panel of shame stares me down.

I nod stiffly. The only one to smile is Clifford.

Gregory claps once. "Great."

Anna pushes a small stack of papers secured with a binder clip across the table, then offers me a silver pen. The cool pen is too heavy for my shaking fingers, but I manage to flip straight to the last page of the packet, which is marked by a Post-it flag, and sign on the line.

Gregory and Anna shuffle out of their seats as Clifford waits behind me, collecting the documents. Gregory pauses and leans against the doorframe, his pants creased in all the wrong ways, his left hand *very* anchored in his pocket. "Clifford, you're going to have to set up Miss Smith's computer security today. Our IT service is on a work order. We'll show you the way." Then he marches out the door, Armin scurrying from his post at the printer in his wake.

Oh my god. They're doing it now? In front of everyone? My mouth sours, and Clifford, who is still arranging my paperwork, scrunches his shoulders guiltily toward me, which I don't buy. His whole career is shame centered.

I peel myself out of the chair and head toward the exit, but my feet stop at the doorway, once again contemplating leaving for good and becoming a shepherd, or moving into a wax museum and pretending I'm a figurine.

Clifford shifts the papers in his arms and says, "I noticed here that it's your birthday. Happy birthday! You're thirty-three. Same as me."

I force a smile. What is it with HR people always being so . . . in people's business? Like you have to be part sociopath to go into that line of work.

"Thanks," I reply, and dryly add, "This is exactly how I pictured it."

His laugh is way too loud, and I try not to encourage it with a smile. His notepad is tucked under his arm, and the doodle he was working on presses heavily into the page.

"Nice cat," I say. "Glad you found the time for some artwork during my professional misconduct meeting."

His mouth drops as his eyes slip away from mine.

I'm out of the room before he looks up.

May the procession of shame to my desk commence.

Walk of Shame

I FOLLOW GREGORY LIKE a scorned child. Clifford strolls behind me, whispering chipper hellos to the tilting heads we pass.

Eight years of doing everything I could to remain invisible here, and this is what it comes to. There were days when not one person said a word to me. I'd come in, put on my headphones, have a lunch-hour cry alone in the bathroom, then clock out.

Eight years, and now it's like I've lost a layer of skin.

As my desk pod comes into view, Garret crouches over Caitlin's cubicle wall and mouths something that draws Caitlin's stare toward me. I focus on my breathing, on my footing.

Garret is Caitlin's best friend, and not by coincidence. As the head of business development, he's Gregory's second-in-command, and he is always sharing insider information with Caitlin. As a person, he's like the human embodiment of an internet comments section. Caitlin can't suppress her grin when she spots our parade. I get it; this situation is her big break. I live for this from the other side of it. But right now, I'd love to remind her about the time she got drunk at our Christmas party two years ago and rubbed against the guy who was cutting ham slices at the buffet. Also, the party took place here in the office at three p.m. The highlight of the event was the secret Santa. Some legend, in a brazenly genius move, took a piece of crappy office stock art off the wall outside of Gregory's office and wrapped it up for him. Nobody knows who it was, but I'd have paid a month's rent to see Gregory's face when he opened it again.

Gregory halts and loudly proclaims, "Everyone, this is our new HR analyst, Cliff. He'll be shadowing some of our processes to learn more about what we do here." Then he nudges Cliff in the side, who doesn't hide his flinch. "Don't worry. He won't be spying on everyone *that* much."

Cliff's eyelids droop to half-mast, which I appreciate, as whispers creep over the cubicle walls. He clenches his jaw before saying, "I'm here for any concerns you might have, so please feel free to come by and say hello."

And I don't know if I want to hug him for diverting some of the attention away from me or jab him in the kidney for drawing more looks in our general direction.

When we're finally at my cubicle, Gregory huddles closer. "I'm not needed for this part." He places his hand on my shoulder—I've lost track of how many times I've been touched against my will by this man—and nudges Cliff once more. "You'll take it from here? She can wait there." He points at a spot right next to my garbage bin.

Blinking eyes are peering over all the cube walls like owls. The new HR guy. My computer. It's too much for these people.

Clifford sends me another apologetic smile. Pointless. I stare at some unknown beige stain on the seat of my chair that I never much minded until now.

Then Gregory's gone, and Cliff, who seems to dwarf my entire desk area, covers the mouse with his hand.

After thirty seconds or twelve hours, Cliff says, "So, any big plans for the birthday weekend?"

No. Not the questions. Not from this HR *analyst*. I try to keep any emotion from my voice as I reply, "Can we not?"

"Sure." He nods as his grin evaporates. I force my attention on a loose plasticky thread pulling up from a seam in the grey office carpet. Guilt is pointless right now.

The office drifts back into silence, aside from a few throats clearing and chairs shuffling and too-rhythmic clacking on keyboards, all the noises someone makes when they're fake working. Eventually Cliff lifts himself from my chair and says, "You're all set. Would you like to see what I've done?"

Because I know everything, I mutter, "I'm good," and shrink further into the collar of my sweater.

"Okay. I feel like I need to warn you that if your emails contain certain words, they'll be flagged and sent to management—so tread lightly." His smile curls up, all cheeky, as he leans in conspiringly. "Also, your browser will block certain searches and websites."

His fresh-linen scent lingers past his words. He's speaking in low tones, but still, he needs to keep his voice down. I cannot physically crouch further into myself, and all the stares are churning my stomach.

I don't respond. Instead I focus on some random child's demented art that a magnet holds to a filing cabinet behind Rhonda. This place really is in a sad state. The first red flag should have been during my interview, when Gregory said the company was "like family."

Cliff lingers. "For what it's worth," he whispers, "I will try and work with you where you're at, to make this as painless as possible. It'll just be constructive ways to get along with people." He grins again, like he's already laughing at the joke he's about to make. "I gotta change the rep us HR guys have."

My smile isn't that forced. "Thanks."

Finally, he walks away, leaving me alone with an hour of work still to go and a dozen eyes burning against my back.

I need to plot my revenge on everyone.

Because this has sparked joy in their hearts. The thing about working in a regional office for a big-box retailer that sells corn by-products, camping things, and cream for various types of rashes and boils is that not one of us is living our dream. They'll talk about starting a sandwich truck, even though they aren't even qualified to roast a marshmallow, or fleeing to Belize to teach surfing lessons. But every one of them shows up on Monday, until the weeks turn into a life sentence.

My situation is the only beauty left in life for them.

The suggestion that I need to get along with people here is actually bonkers. Because that was exactly what I wanted when I first joined this so-called family eight years ago. I was so optimistic that this job would be a fresh start and I'd make friends, move up the ladder, and do what any person would do while working at a place like this. Even when Rhonda showed me to my new pod—the stained chair, while *hers* was brand new—I didn't take the hint that I was entering a stupid game in which the rules are unclear and the prizes are yet unknown. I didn't factor in my anxiety and my complete inability to be a casual person about anything. I failed miserably during my first six months.

I had no idea yet about things like: working faster than everyone is bad, actually; not talking about your private life with colleagues is suspicious; and you have to be fake nice to powerful people even when they treat you horribly. When I finally realized that the same situations that caused me so much anxiety in high school had followed me here, I had a panic attack and took four sick days. I almost didn't make it back.

I returned because I needed to survive, and this job was the only way I knew how to do that. So I figured out how to keep a low profile, working in silence while everyone hung out around me. I've survived this long, even though I've seen a lot of turnover. Four years ago, Armin's desk used to be occupied by a guy named Harold. And I've seen three other people in Caitlin's role before her: two who moved up the ranks, and one who transferred to another city.

I've spent more time with these people than anyone. We're forced to work together in close proximity every day, which really means we're forced to live together. And it's the *living* involved. The sheer humanity of that, which could never be professional, or even normal. We're all dry flecks of skin turning to dust and breathing each other up. It's too much.

I never talk to them, yet I know things about them. Every day I put on my headphones, but I listen. Rhonda may brag that her son poops at exactly nine thirty a.m. Eastern Standard Time, but she also steals coffee creamer from the fridge on the sixth floor.

Armin is slowly and intentionally killing Joey, Rhonda's fern that sits between their desks. I've seen him pour blue Gatorade into the soil at least a dozen times. I have a theory why he's committing plant murder (possible revenge for the high crime of unwarranted kabob disposal), but the behavior is still unhinged.

Mel Elliot has an outfit routine that is disturbingly precise. Blue cardigan and beige skirt every Monday, painful-looking shoes every Friday.

Ron McDowell lost access to the shared drive last month and has opted to try to live without it by simply working way less. Nobody has noticed.

And Mary Perkins has a literal plank and hammer in her office that she crushes walnuts with. It sounds like she's doing a murder every afternoon, yet we all zombie-stare at our spreadsheets of data without flinching at the batshit noises.

I didn't choose a single person here and never would've, yet I'm spending my life with them.

"Where's the accounts paid doc?" Armin asks Rhonda, breaking me from my thoughts.

"It's not in the accounts folder?"

"If it were in that folder, I wouldn't have asked."

With that, our office clicks back into its mundane rhythm. My drama has already dissolved.

I'm invisible once again.

Birthday Party for One

S HE WASN'T WAITING at the bench by the corner when I got off the bus, but I can still sense her. I walk slowly up the pathway, which boasts several cracks and a variety of weeds, to my apartment complex.

"Jolene!" Miley calls.

My stomach drops. Damn, I should really learn to climb the fire escape. I could've spent all these years figuring out parkour or becoming a master of disguise.

She's twelve years old and lives in my building, one floor above me, and she's always so . . . *needy*. Always looking for someone to talk to about her life, trivial stories about her homework and friends. She just started middle school this year, and I already know how those stories will go. Any day now somebody will laugh at her or somebody else will betray her, and she'll figure out what the world is really about.

She skips closer, her mousy hair bouncing on her shoulders, before standing in a way that blocks the entire path. "Guess what? I got a new phone. What social media do you have? Facebook, I bet."

And she's always rude like that. I'd wave her off, but my hands are full of grocery bags, which are full of bottles of wine I bought to properly celebrate my birthday.

"No, I *don't* have Facebook," I say quickly. "I see enough ugly babies IRL."

"Really? I thought all old people had it. How do you stalk your friends from your glory days of high school?"

A jolt pushes through my abdomen. Not flinching is the only way she won't notice.

"Do you have Instagram?"

I shake my head, the bottles clinking against each other in the bags.

Her gaze drifts over me, eyebrows scrunching together. "What are you doing tonight?"

Why are people so obsessed with asking about other people's plans? Has anybody ever wowed someone with their answer? My answer will always be that I spend my days off recuperating and forgetting my days *on*.

But because she's a technical child I say, "I'm just watching a movie or something."

She scrunches her face, disappointed. "Isn't it your birthday today?"

"Who told you that?"

Miley curls her fingers uncertainly. "You did–last week during your tarot reading."

For fuck's sake. I nod in recognition over this conversation I have no recollection of. The thing about Miley is that she spends most of her time in the common areas of the building that people aren't supposed to actually hang out in. She's always trying to rope someone in to chat. Last week, she was sitting there playing with some tarot cards while I was heading to the liquor store for a top-up. The event is blurred, but I remember mentioning my star sign and sitting on the bench for a bit saying who knows what else. Bottom line: I have to be more careful avoiding her when I've been drinking. She tracks everything, and I'm bound to say something that'll scar her.

"Right," I mutter, taking another step up the path. I'm only a few feet away from the door.

"And are you having a party?"

Miley isn't subtle about how she investigates the grocery store bags. I shake my head quickly and step around her. "I prefer my quiet times."

"But it's your birthday." Her brow knits. "Last week you said you wanted to celebrate a new era of Jolene."

Shit. The child may have seen too much at this point to ever lead a productive life. I need to cut things off with her while it's safe. When I drink, it makes me feel less trapped inside myself. But sometimes, after a few too many, I'll remember why the cage was built in the first place.

"When you get older, birthdays aren't such a big thing," I tell her.

"That's not true. My mom's thirtieth birthday was so big that I had to go to my cousin's 'cause they couldn't fit us all in."

My heart constricts against my will. There's a reason Miley is always in the hallway or sitting on the stoop of the building, much as I try to pretend not to notice. Ever since she was six, her mom would send her outside to play alone. Then she started sending her out to eat dinner alone. When she was younger, she used to draw outlines of bodies on the walkway and insist on playing this portable piano for every passer-by's displeasure. Lately, though, she's inconveniently become chattier. It's like she's suddenly become aware I'm a person with a whole life—in theory.

I take another step, almost past her.

"Can I come over?" Miley blurts out of nowhere. Her eyes are so round.

I shake my head before noticing the way her shoulders drop.

But there's no way.

Miley shuffles her feet. "I'm running low on data, and I'm learning how to crochet from YouTube."

"Don't you have Wi-Fi?"

Miley's eyes droop. "Yeah, but my mom's working a double and she changed the password."

I only ever notice Miley's mom coming and going in scrubs at odd hours and occasionally leaving in makeup for the evening.

It's the croak in her voice. I could just let her in, have a glass while I let her watch videos without interacting. The thing is, she'd never leave. And I can't be a thirty-three-year-old woman hosting a twelve-year-old child in my apartment after the worst day of my career. A terrible plan. The bottles of wine twitch in my hands.

I shake my head. "Sorry."

"Yeah, it's a weird ask I guess." She sighs. "But you took longer than the others to say no!"

Clearly, I need to limit my interactions with her even harder.

At last, I haul open the heavy metal door that's supposed to stay locked but is constantly propped open with a hunk of wood. Its hinge creaks as I pass through. The drab, musty air of the room that is theo-retically the lobby greets me.

My building is one of those rental company specials, the target de-mographic being us folks who have no room to be picky about vibes with the rent we pay, which means the design is void of personality in favor of cheap durability.

The envelope is taped to the outside of my suite door. Freaking Marty, the landlord, always has to leave his threatening letters the same way. I tear it down and stuff it in my bag. My rent is always three days late due to my pay schedule and tight budget, and these letters won't change that. Just another piece of clutter to add to the vivid tapestry of life, I suppose.

I unlock my door and am greeted by a counter of take-out boxes, half-filled glasses of water piled on every surface, and clothes that hang from the corners of every piece of furniture, like a whole party of sad people disappeared a few minutes prior.

I can't believe I briefly considered letting Miley in here. I must *never* let anyone in here.

And something breaks deep inside me, like my whole day, or life-time, is catching up with me at once. I blink through the prickle in my eyes. I know what life I'm supposed to live; I have Pinterest. Obviously, this isn't it.

When I first moved to Calgary, seven years after high school and long after most of my classmates moved away from our town, it was all so easy. Sure, my job wasn't going perfectly, but it paid. I was finally free from my parents' home—free from the years of them trying to control me and force me back into being a person. This meant I could finally do more than hide from them in my room reading epic fantasy and crying.

But most crucially, I could be anonymous.

Friday nights were magic. I went to bars and hung out with strangers who didn't know who I was. Drinking snuffed the usual tightness in my chest I felt around other people, and I could say anything because nobody knew me. I even made friends, or at least a group of drinking buddies. At one point I was tagged in a picture where the group of us regulars were celebrating some birthday. I had a real smile. There was sex and laughing, and sometimes the wrong song would play and I'd order a round of shots that would cost a month's rent. Yes, during those first years here, everything seemed cured.

It worked, until it didn't. Because their sob stories would always slip in. And I couldn't unsee their void stares that never found a place to land.

Because every now and then, I'd say something like, "We're all going to be dead and we'll forget we ever existed, someday." And they'd look at me like they recognized something inside me too. Then they'd ask me if I was okay, or they'd suddenly realize they didn't even know where I was from. Rather than letting things get messy, I settled into my Netflix and nothing routine.

It meant I had lived through it. Plus, I survived everything before.

Except there's nobody really living here.

The problem is people eventually want to know more and more about you. And with time, they'll find out enough to see what's always been there. I've had one real friend my entire life, and she's not here anymore. It always hits like a brick wall: Ellie technically doesn't exist anymore.

Yes, when people find out enough about me, they stop wanting to know anything at all.

Nothing bad happens when I'm alone. I have YouTube and my little projects. I like to replay the greatest arguments of my lifetime and win them, research child actors and what their families look like, and disassemble things like the remote control.

I drop my bags on the counter and pour myself a healthy glass of wine, then head to the couch with my phone and open my creeper Instagram account. This is one of my favorite pastimes while drinking: checking in on what people I used to know are up to.

My heart almost drops out my butt when I spot the newest post. They're all together, sitting at a picnic table with a tent in the background.

Camping.

The hashtags may be ironic, but they're also *not*: #highschoolreunion, #friends5eva.

They're not wallowing or hiding in their apartments drinking alone. They've all moved on with their lives.

They can look back on everything with a smile.

It makes sense. I pinch at the photo, zooming into every pixel, studying it like an archaeological dig.

Something about it feels off, uneasy even, but I can't pin exactly why. I stare at it like it's a Magic Eye poster, and still nothing.

I let my phone drop onto the faded beige couch cushion. There's a line of grit tucked into the corner of the case that could kill someone if they were to lick it.

I shouldn't do this anymore. I should be able to focus on my own life by now, instead of cyberstalking people who don't matter. They moved out of their parents' houses, and so did I. They have jobs, and I do too.

But I should have a *real* Instagram.

I pour myself another drink and resolve to change my profile picture to my face. I take a few selfies, only they all look weird. I'm either smiling too much or not smiling enough, looking too hard at the camera or not at all.

Finally, I settle on one that seems okay. I change the picture. Then I upload my real name.

Gregory said I should make friends with my coworkers, and I have to start somewhere. I type their names into the search bar—some are already in my recent history from previous creeping.

I hit follow on so many.

I go to pour myself another glass, but somehow the bottle is empty.

That's okay. I'm ready for gin anyway.

The olives are all the way in the fridge—I'll have to go without.

The most depraved thing I do when I'm drinking is search for men who are #lookingforlust. I don't do it for actual sex reasons, but to judge the countless men posting underwhelming pictures of themselves. Their lone penises sit sadly between their legs, not so much a prize as a participation trophy. I know looking at them doesn't make me any better, but it does *feel* that way.

A banner appears on my screen, notifying me that Armin has followed me back. Maybe he and I could be work friends. He's also Persian, and I'm pretty sure we're similar ages. Maybe, if I think back to when he started at the office four years ago, there were a couple times that he tried to be friendly to me. Unfortunately, I was already deep in my rut. Once, he came over to my desk and asked if I'd tried poutine from the shop across from our building, but I was too nervous to start a conversation because Charlie—the person who used to hold Caitlin's job—was listening in, which made it all so embarrassing. And one afternoon he pointed at my headphones and asked what I was listening to, but I was caught off guard because the true answer would've been an audiobook about souls. I didn't have it in me to explain that I'm not, like, into souls in a weird way, more just unhealthily obsessed with what *other* people think happens when we die, but also too logical to believe any of it, yet still hopeful that I'll find some explanation that will make what happened feel okay. So I replied, "Just a random thing," and, unintentionally, had a tone in my voice.

I do know that both of our moms come from Tehran. Unfortunately, this discovery was unveiled during a diversity initiative that Gregory organized for the office. We were both quietly enraged that Gregory lumped us and a few others into a token group for a Q&A session to "educate the office." After the ordeal, Gregory praised himself for personally hiring us both, even though I'm certain during my interview he had no idea I was anything other than white. After that, Armin and I never mentioned anything about our Iranian backgrounds again.

And I'm not even sure we *should* speak about it, or if Armin even believes me. I grew up with so little contact with anything Persian outside of my family, I have a hard time telling which parts of my upbringing are cultural and which are just *my family*. I remember how seen I felt when I was twelve and we visited another Iranian family, and they also had a watering can on their toilet tank. I can't exactly go through the logistical nightmare of bringing Armin to see my bathroom to prove it.

I scroll through his account: photos from concerts in crowded bars, some of his impressive sneaker collection, and a few Twitch clips of some video game.

I turn on the TV to play *The Bachelorette* in the background. I like feeling like I'm part of Bachelor Nation. I'm a part of something.

I realize I'm not. It happened so fast the way I made my life.

A banner appears on my phone again: Caitlin Joffrey would like to follow me. Maybe things are actually okay then? Maybe we're not the enemies I thought we were. I scroll through her grid, drinking in all her wannabe influencer vibes: her at the beach with an Etsy blanket cape and mug, her monthly goals written on the page of an open journal in sparkly cursive, smoothies topped with artfully sliced pieces of fresh fruit, her boyfriend's hand holding hers. Always just his hand or torso. That's for the best; this way I can picture him having a mild Guy Fieri aesthetic. As I go deeper into her timeline, I find photos of her friends. They do trips together, nights out with matching shirts, spa days, wine and paint nights.

Do they just, like, text each other whenever? I swallow to dislodge the thing caught in my throat.

Another notice: Garret would like to follow me. Somewhere beneath my brain's cozy booze blanket, a needling thought worms its way to the surface. This timing might not be coincidence.

But I'll just post a picture to my story of myself laughing. I can be fun.

I'm zooming in on a picture Armin posted over a year ago of art he commissioned for the gamer fandom he's into. I accidentally hit the heart. And oh my fuck with the deep like.

Maybe it was meant to be? I'm sure it's fine. This is how people make friends. I should write him a message.

I type: Looks like you have a lot of fun with that game.

I unsend. Weird shit to say to someone.

I type: It's my birthday and I'm lonely.

I pass out.

Hangovers Are a WIP

THE DAY AFTER my thirty-third birthday, I wake up with a stiffness in my limbs so intense I'm certain I actually died and my body has begun rigor mortis. The sun is far too bright, and my brain bangs against my skull. Pain seems to reach into me from another realm. It's like everything–all the booze, the workdays, and a lifetime of angst–has taken literal bites out of me.

In short, it's not a great way to wake up. I clear my throat in a failed attempt to clear the sawdust coating the inside of it.

Then last night comes rushing back.

I remember running into Miley. Did I scar her? Again?

I roll sideways, and the cool corner of my phone presses against my temple. I try not to think about all the cancer waves it must've seeded in my brain as I slept. The damn thing looks like a little shit; fingerprints dance all over it like it's been partying. On the inside, I'm sure it's laughing at all the things it's seen me do. It deserves to.

When I grab it, the screen lights up and displays the message I sent to Armin. Shit. I fly into an upright position and blink the screen into focus. Five minutes after I sent it, he read it, yet there's no reply.

I should get rid of my phone. I should drag my body into the tub and hate myself there for a while, but the cool comforter between my legs is all I have left.

I stare at the wall, at the power outlet that seems to be making a "wow" face at me, when my phone chimes with the noise that means my mom wants to FaceTime.

If I ignore her, she'll just show up in person. So I hold the phone up to my face and hit accept.

Mom's already scowling as the call connects, and in the corner of the screen, I can see why: my eyes are bloodshot and ringed with smudged mascara. I tilt the camera away, but it isn't fast enough.

"Why don't you wash your face anymore? This will give you wrinkles, and you're getting older now."

"I forgot." My voice is gravelly and worn. "I was having dinner late with friends." It's not lost on me that there was once a time I would lie to my mom that I was "staying in," and how pathetic this new brand of deception is.

"I hope you didn't drink and drive. Stop showing me your ceiling—I call to see your face." There's a hollow hitch in her voice. She's no stranger to wine herself. People underestimate how traumatic it is to leave a country because it dramatically changed overnight. How messed up it is to start a new life in a place where a good portion of the people will hate you for simply *being* there.

My mouth and tongue sour against themselves. "I don't drive."

"Did you do kosbazi with someone? Is that why your makeup is on?"

The hope in her eyes is the worst.

"No, Mom, my kos was empty the whole night." We only use Farsi words for the sex talk.

She tsks me again, but through a feat of great restraint, she doesn't push the issue. "How's work?" she asks.

"Good, good!" My voice is too pitchy. To drive it home, I say, "My job seems very secure."

There's nothing more important to my mother than my financial security. For years I've been sugarcoating everything about that job to make it seem like a bigger deal than it is.

"Good. Maybe you'll get a promotion."

"If one comes up, I can't see why not."

I don't dwell on how far outside the realm that is. I'm once again thankful I didn't lose my job yesterday. The trauma that would cause my mom would be too much. When I was a child and we were shopping for school supplies, she told me I didn't need an eraser, I just shouldn't make mistakes.

My gaze drifts to the wall again, thick and milky from several layers of paint meant to wash over each previous tenant's emotional baggage. Maybe it doesn't look that great to an outside observer, but the life I've built here in my apartment is *everything* compared with what it was when I was living with my parents. Here, I'm free to drink and watch whatever I want and not be perceived with disapproval 24/7. I don't have to feel like a failure all the time, and when I do, it's on my terms.

But if I lost my job, those threatening letters from Marty would become actionable in a matter of just a few days. I'd have no choice but to move back in with Mom and Dad.

"Keep working hard and they'll notice." Mom smiles, though the top half of her face remains still due to a healthy dose of Botox. But she seems to look deeper into the camera. "You sure you're okay?"

"Oh yeah." I nod way too hard. "Where's Dad?"

Her gaze shifts. "Putting on his shoes. The ugly man drove his car over a curb, so he has to get it fixed—"

"Happy birthday, Jolene," he pipes in from the background, followed by a throat clearing. A hand holding one shoe appears to wave on the screen.

"Thanks." I wave back, my hand as stiff as his voice. Speaking to him always leaves me hollow and splintered. Ever since I overheard him seven years ago: "She's twenty-five and she's a dependent still. She doesn't have a life yet; she won't even make friends." Shame flushed every inch of my skin, and a few weeks later I moved out. If Mom wasn't around, we'd only see each other for a sad Christmas dinner.

As the screen shifts back to Mom's face, there's a moment of silence that nobody can fill. Here is the part where I should ask about the aunties. Except there are usually at least two whom she's not on speaking terms with at any given time and mentioning the wrong one could set the mood off.

"Well, thanks for calling."

"Happy birthday. Once Daddy fixes the car, we take you for dinner tonight? I'll come pick you up."

I practically yell, "No!" There's no way they're coming here. I need twenty business months to make it presentable.

She huffs. "I'll only come for a minute. I have to meet Kumar near you. I need more saffron."

My stomach clenches as I take in the mess of bottles and clothes strewn around the apartment. "I thought your saffron dealer was in

Inglewood?" Even though there are quite a few Persian markets in town, Mom gets most of her specialty groceries via a network of dealers sprinkled across the city due to "better pricing and quality." It's all very tough to track.

"I stopped going to Peyman. He's cheapskate and his saffron is no good anymore."

It's best not to get into it. "Mom, I'm really not feeling well and won't be good for a visit. I think I'm getting a migraine."

Her disapproving gaze churns the acid in my stomach. "You haven't let me see you in very long time. I didn't move to not see you and only visit my same old relatives, when Minoo is always bitch."

My parents are social people, and after high school, while I stayed holed up in the basement, Mom and Dad were still attempting to venture into our too-small town. But they were disgraced by proxy in every way. Dad worked as a chemical engineer at the same company as my friend Ellie's dad. In fact, my dad reported directly to Mr. Wong. And after everything happened, Dad's career crumbled at the same rate the wall between me and him solidified. Two years later, he retired in shame, and for seven years we were the town pariahs, living in purgatory under one roof. When I finally took the online courses for business administration, finally got an interview at Supershops, and finally moved two hours away from that town, it became obvious that my parents would leave too. There was nothing holding them there anymore. They came to Calgary, and Mom's been trying to convince me to move back in with them ever since. It always sounds innocent—"Save money for a house or wedding"—but the real tone of it all is that I'm supposed to *want* a house and wedding. The guilt of everything I did to them would be enough, but add to that the pressure of the life they want for me, and every conversation we have is *the worst*.

"We can have dinner another night, I promise, when I'm better," I say before thinking too hard.

The twist in Mom's smile sends a shudder through me. "Oh! Why not come to dinner with the aunties this week? They all can wish you happy birthday."

That would be entering the lion's den. Every Monday, my mom

meets some local Persian ladies for half-price kabob and even cheaper gossip. As soon as my parents moved to town, Mom's social life somehow became livelier than mine. They try to convince their kids to come, but rarely will one of us cousins be emotionally stable enough to agree to such a thing.

I'm about to pull out the excuses, but Mom's eyes glint back, hopeful. "Okay," I blurt out.

Her smile wrinkles her whole face. "Ey jan. Remember to do your makeup pretty. I want to be proud that you came out of my kos."

"Will do, and thanks for that birthday image. I should tidy up."

"Good girl. You should leave the apartment and make sure you get some sun on your skin." She makes a gesture to look behind me. "It's so dusty and dark, I don't know why you need to live there."

Just like that, guilt is replaced with a deeper irritation branded specifically for her. "Talk soon."

"Eat some fruit," Mom says as a goodbye.

After letting her go, I spend a good ten minutes zoning out on my phone. I end up watching a disappointing proposal video with cue cards and then reading a clickbait mess of different ways people were caught in lies.

Finally, I'm disgusted with myself enough to shuffle unsteadily off the couch, my every move heating my head. I peel off my dad's old company shirt and shimmy out of my underwear. The cool porcelain of the empty bath softens the wooziness. I twist the tap with my foot, and as the bath fills, I search YouTube, and then the whole room is filled with the song that was playing when Ellie died.

I sing along.

It's a sick thing I don't know how to stop forcing myself to do.

Before I can even finish a thought, giant tears stream down my face and glob at my cheeks.

And they feel like home.

I didn't even go to her funeral. It was the right move.

When the song ends, I hit play again.

Because if Ellie hadn't been friends with me, there wouldn't have been a funeral at all.

Bcc Bcc'ident

T HE BUZZ OF one forever-dying fluorescent light mixes with the saddest scent in the world: burned hazelnut coffee. And another dreadful week begins.

Caitlin eyes me as I approach our pod, and her smirk makes my head pound. Rhonda looks up and then quickly diverts her gaze to mark my arrival. I wish there was a way to stop people from looking at your face.

It's the sheepish grin Armin's directing at me that does it. Heat creeps into my neck as the events of Friday pour over me for the millionth mental replay.

Caitlin's keyboard smashes as I pass. I'm too distracted by my need for death to care, when a little yellow box in front of my computer catches my attention.

I stand over it protectively as I subtly slip the box open, and I'm greeted with a gourmet-looking rainbow sprinkle donut. Taped onto the inside lid, a sticky note reads: *Welcome to thirty-three.–Cliff.* There's a tiny cat smiling on the bottom.

What's wrong with this guy? He's supposed to be the example of professional behavior?

Although . . . I suppose this is not, like, illegal, or wrong even.

I ball the note and shove it in the bottom drawer, where I file things that are likely garbage but don't feel *quite* ready for the bin.

I eye the box again. It seems illicit. The only solution to this donut disaster is to hide it on my lap, underneath my keyboard tray, and break off pieces until it disappears.

A rush of pillowy soft sweetness hits. It's the best donut in the world. But I can't enjoy it.

Gregory pounds through the office door, all jolty and happy. He nods and names everyone he passes like the damn president of Clown Town.

I fake dragging my mouse across the screen as he approaches, the acid in my stomach creeping up to overpower the taste of sugar on my tongue. I shouldn't have drunk more wine again last night. I should've learned my lesson from Friday. But I had one bottle left to finish, and now my head is like a pressure cooker.

That's it. This week—and, more important, this weekend—no more drinking for me. I'm thirty-three now. Time to grow up.

I log in to start my usual routine, but the number on my email icon halts me. How can fifty-six new emails have arrived already?

A new record. I need coffee for this.

I stand up, careful to keep my focus on the rubbery grey baseboards as I make my way toward the copy room. I hear Caitlin whisper something to Rhonda under her breath as I pass.

Must not focus on anything human.

Far too many people are gathered in the kitchen. Their conversation dies off immediately upon my entry, but they don't put much effort into hiding their smirks behind their coffee mugs. I know the kinds of things they talk about. I once overheard someone saying, "She's so weird. I think she might come here and shoot us all. People do that."

They're all crowded around the coffee machine staring at their toes—several of them are members of the Coffee Club—which means I can't steal their product right now. I fill a mug with hot water from the cooler instead, sweat gathering in my cleavage as their conversation continues in muted tones. The tea bags from 2017 in my desk drawer will have to do.

Back at my cubicle, I take an underwhelming sip of grassy tea as I click the first email: an office-wide notice about some tax form coming.

There's no way this reality was the intended human experience.

The hollow splash of Barry Goodwin refilling his thermos-sized water bottle sounds from the cooler behind me. I hate that my cubicle is positioned where people are always walking past. Always on display while alone.

The next email is from Armin. My chest plummets. He never emails me directly. Is this about my drunk message?

Hey,

So I got an odd IG message from Jolene on Friday. Did you know it was her birthday? Shouldn't the Morale Boosters have gotten a cake party together? I'm not the best person to point this kind of oversight out to Rhonda, but I think she forgot. Jolene said she was lonely, and I didn't know what to say but it felt . . . sad. I'm terrible with this kind of thing. It's awkward.

Armin

My heart almost falls out my vagina. Oh god. Oh no. I reread the message again as I slowly, but thoroughly, turn to stone. Anxious tingles shoot through my fingertips and earlobes. I'm pinned to my chair.

The email header draws my gaze. It's addressed to Caitlin but not me. He must have accidentally bcc'd me.

Another email appears in the chain.

FROM: Caitlin Joffrey
TO: Armin Habib
SUBJECT: Re: Jolene's Birthday

Oh! Shit! Garret and I were at the bar when we saw she started an Insta. We were roasting the shit out of the weird stories she was posting.

I can't believe she slid into your DMs! Imagine being 33 and messaging some colleague you hardly know and saying that you're lonely. Maybe she was hitting on you?

Also, Rhonda didn't want to throw a party given the situation with the email she wrote me. She's so unstable. Tread lightly or you'll end up chopped up and sewn together different.

—C

I want to both scream and never make another sound. If it weren't for Rhonda's leaning back and forth in her desk chair stirring up the air, I'd be certain I was dead.

But how did I manage to get bcc'd again?

And if I were going to murder Armin, I wouldn't chop him up. I'd find some kind of industrial liquid to dissolve his body. Only a true imbecile wouldn't understand that's the best way.

My heart stops completely as another email pops in the chain. I'm somehow bcc'd *again*.

FROM: Armin Habib
TO: Caitlin Joffrey
SUBJECT: Re: Jolene's Birthday

She wasn't hitting on me. Anyway, I feel bad for Jolene.
Armin

I slump so low in my chair the plasticky metallic scent from the wiring under my desk tinges my nostrils. Pity from Armin, a guy who once reheated a day-old hot dog (bun, ketchup, and all) in the toaster oven, is too much to bear.

The quiet calmness within the office narrows in on me—I'm trapped. I need to run away. But if I run to the bathroom now, it'll be a free-for-all to comment.

Then the worst thing happens. Garret lets out a cackle that carries all the way to my desk.

I can't help it. I'm an absolute masochist. I peep in his direction—he's looking toward Caitlin, whose shoulders are silently shaking as she looks back. She must have just messaged him.

I stare at the floor, wishing I could dig myself to the core of the earth. I used to think everything would be fine so long as I didn't interact with the humans I work with. Maybe I didn't try hard enough. Now I'll never leave my desk. I'll come into work before anyone and leave after they've all gone home. I'll eat at my desk and get special glasses that block my peripherals. I'll drown out everything with murder podcasts.

This will be a good life.

Except I already chugged my whole mug of tea, and the water bottle I had on the bus isn't helping either. By ten a.m. I can't hold it any longer. I'm thinking through the logistical possibility of keeping a pee bucket under my desk when it fully hits me that I'm considering peeing. In a bucket. Under my desk. As a way to remain incognito? I push out of my worn chair and head to the washroom.

I'm washing my hands with the cough-syrup-pink liquid soap when I truly notice my face, how pale, dry, and puffy it is. I'd put on eyeliner and clumpy mascara this morning, but they only make me look worse at this point.

It's been a progression, my life here. When I first started, this place had appealed to me because it seemed like an easy place to just exist in. During month one, I signed up to bring drinks to a potluck Rhonda was managing. I bought a bunch of soda, but then I worried about the people who don't drink soda, so I went back to the store to buy loads of juice and various kinds of milk. I dented my second paycheck pretty hard from the drama of it, and the whole thing kept me up at night. The day of the event, Rhonda laughed when I showed her all the drinks. She said, "Most people just end up drinking coffee." And fuck me when Garret was like, "Where is all this milk from—did we get a cow?"

Minor, and yet the idea of being laughed at stopped me from breathing properly. After that, I decided that limiting my interactions was the best way to keep people from hating me. But over time, embarrassment became resentment. I was annoyed that Rhonda had me buy drinks if coffee and the watercooler would've done it. That was the first step down a road. The thing about annoyance is that once there's a spark, you can find more things to stoke it. It grew and amplified between me and them. And eventually the abyss stared back.

Tears prickle my eyes. I quickly blink and wipe and suppress. The soft skin under my eyes is so familiar with the scratch of a hard beige paper towel.

I harden my stance and step out of the bathroom. I'm passing the copy room, eyes on the floor, when a cry—"Oh, happy belated birthday, Jolene"—comes from Rene Salinger. Her smile protrudes into her cheeks, fake and proud of it—she thinks she's funny. But so do Marla and Garret, who snigger next to her.

"Thanks!" I try to keep my own smile solid wood.

I hate everyone here.

Back at our workstations, Caitlin holds her phone in the way she does to take a selfie from above: some strategically placed, color-coordinated folders in the background, and she tilts her head and does the lip thing. Soon her story will read #backtothegrind, and it'll gravely misrepresent the aesthetic of our office into something not depressing.

When she first started, I thought she might be nice. She offered to help me with some data analysis sheets. Only, as she turned them in, she mentioned to Gregory that it was because I had trouble managing them on my own. She plays with Rhonda too, acts like she gives a shit about every detail of her tedious weekend errands. She joined the Morale Boosters and is very helpful, of course. But I overheard her calling Rhonda an "old lifer" to Garret one day. She said the idea of ending up like her, "an assistant forever," scared the shit out of her. And she stared at my desk pointedly as she said it.

I make it back to my computer and tap my mouse to awaken the screen. A few new emails are already waiting for me. The first one is a notice from Cliff in HR about my computer update. It's sent to Gregory, not me. How can I be bcc'd on that one as well?

But the following email is from Jared to Brenda, two people who work in sales and hardly know of my existence. I cross paths with Brenda only when she's sitting silently in the bathroom waiting to do a number two at the same time as me, which devolves into a standoff of who can wait in the bathroom the longest. And like any other war, nobody wins.

Next is one from Rhonda to Gregory, asking for a replacement company credit card as she misplaced hers and had to cancel it.

Brandy and Josh are discussing some account that they mutually handle.

They keep going—email after email, none of them meant for me. I close out of my inbox and stare at the three pins on my cubicle wall.

Something is happening. Bcc'd in error this many times? A lot of freaky things would have to align for that to work.

Are they all in on it?

I click on Jared's email again and try to hit reply. But all the emails are marked "read only."

Then I see it. Directly beneath my main inbox folder, there's a new one. I click on it, and it expands. Listed in alphabetical order are the names of everyone in the office. I click on one at random, and it's as though I'm in their inbox. I can even see their sent items.

But whose account am I in? I click compose, and there's a new option to expand in the "From" box. I can email from either Jolene Smith or Supershops Administration.

Oh my god.

Another email pops into my inbox. I hastily click to check it.

Then I vomit to death, resurrect myself, and vomit to death once more.

Because this one is to Gregory from who must be his wife—it's an outside account. The words that pop out are "hard" and, curse it all, "cock."

Right. His marriage still has spice—and that's good, I suppose. I'll just need to drink a nice glass of bleach to remedy the visuals I'm dealing with.

Deep breaths. He probably just has a chicken coop in his backyard. He's having a hard time with the rooster. That's all.

I click out of the email and briefly contemplate how my entire existence could have possibly led me to this.

Right. It's time to talk to Cliff.

HR Stands for: Helpful Rarely

CLIFF'S OFFICE IS located on the fourth floor, down a remote hallway mostly used for storage and utility rooms that remain undisturbed and lifeless as I pass their droning hum. But then I catch the music—something acoustic and maybe whimsical—coming from what must be his office.

I reach his open doorway and spot his plaid-shirted back first. His arms are stretched behind his head as he leans back in his chair. He's resting his actual feet up on the desk.

A rush of butterflies swoops through my chest. I'm reasonable and considerate enough to know you don't just *walk up* behind people when they're trapped at work, but Clifford is the only person to fix this situation—the one who messed things up in the first place.

I knock my knuckles against his open door because *I* still have some etiquette.

"What's up, Jolene?" he says, without even turning around.

"I . . . How did you know it was me?"

He lowers his legs, swiveling his chair to give me a half grin. "I was pretty sure you'd pop by today."

It's the way his expression is so relaxed and certain—it throws my footing. I square my shoulders before I speak. "Oh, so you knew about this? A fun little joke you cooked up with the other HR buddies at the old HR mill?"

"The wha—?" His forehead wrinkles and his hands drop to his lap.

I take another step into the room. Crossing the threshold is like being wrapped in a warm blanket. The shelves are filled with video game trinkets, '90s movie posters overtake the walls, and there's a sugary scent wafting toward me from an identical donut box to the one he left me. I stop in my tracks and narrow my eyes at him. "Didn't you just start here?"

"Been here for six business days. Why?" But he follows my gaze to the windowsill of framed pictures and bobbleheads. His mouth twists into a smirk. "I like to settle. Birds need a nest."

"I see that."

How can he feel so comfortable being himself here? I shake the thought away and continue. "The changes—the IT thing you did to my computer."

"Ah." He pulls a pen from a Luigi mug and twists it in his hands. "It'll take some getting used to, but don't worry. We'll get you back on track so the computer can be normal again. That's my job."

I can't even with this. "What are you talking about? My emails are messed up. I'm seeing things I shouldn't, and it's a huge privacy breach."

He nods. "Yeah, I know it seems less private—like someone's watching you with all those restrictions, but I promise that's not the case. Your internet access has been limited some, but that doesn't mean we're tracking you."

Again, this man smiles.

"That's not what I'm talking about." I could do without the panicky lilt in my voice, but my words are fumbling en route from my head to my mouth. "It's all a big...a big mess-up!"

Cliff's eyes soften. "I know, Jolene."

When did I start breathing so loudly? I must look manic from his angle.

He continues: "It feels like a mess, but my hands are tied. I can't make any changes until we've gone through the course."

"But I'm seeing . . . everyone. Like, they're talking about me. I can show—" I stop myself just in time. The idea of showing Cliff what my colleagues are writing about me makes me want to crumble into more pieces than any of the Lego figurines on his desk.

He nods, way too chill. "Working alongside your colleagues after that difficult meeting may feel awkward, but we're going to work on ways to cope so issues of discomfort don't affect you as much. Right now, you're a tiny boat in the sea being pushed by every wave, fighting the current. We're going to help you become a sailboat who flows with things."

I absolutely give up on Cliff right then. I break my eyes away from his to stare at all his trinkets, from the video game merch to the little warrior army toys, and nod in understanding. Obviously this Cliff is not a serious person. And obviously, there's been some kind of mistake. It's like instead of having any restrictions added, I've been given some unauthorized top management access to everything on the server. But if Cliff's more concerned with boat metaphors than hearing about his masterful fuck-up, then why should I fight him on it? This is what's wrong with the world right here.

"Hey," Cliff says, cutting through the silence when I don't reply. "I get it. This isn't enjoyable for me either. But I have a dog that needs fancy kibble and several low-stakes addictions that I need to fund, including the butter pretzel I'm about due for." He pulls himself up and grabs a jacket from the hook on the door that somehow already has two other hoodies hanging from it. "Come on, I'll buy you one too."

I give him a shitty staredown.

"Or not." He combs his fingers through his bangs to push them away from his eyes; his hair is kind of unique, sort of a shiny golden-honey hue. As soon as he drops his hand, the strands fall back over his temples. He exhales softly. "You seem like an agreeable person. I know this is a tough situation, but I think we can make it fairly painless. Maybe even nice. After all, I'll be doing the course with you."

But I've stopped listening to him. No point, if he won't listen to me.

I follow him out as he says, "Thanks for coming by. It gets pretty lonely down here, as you can see."

I'm about to say something snarky about this not being a social visit, but when his gaze locks on me, it's like the ground softens below me. All these things he's surrounded himself with, the tilt in his head, the tiny hitch in his voice. I think he means it, that he's lonely.

"Oh, and thanks for the donut," I blurt out, trying to say it like a farewell as I half turn in the opposite direction than he's going.

He gives a small grin. "Thought you could use one. How was your birthday, by the way?"

The details of that night flash through my mind. No way can I lift the veil for this man.

I fully turn away from him, stepping down the hall.

I must not have heard him.

Real Talk

RHONDA IS PICKING at Joey Tribbiani, her fern. She named him that a few weeks after she adopted him. And she adopted him from my desk (without my consent) not long after I started here, because "somebody needed to water him."

No matter how carefully she tends to him, his leaves continue to yellow and wither. As she crunches off the dead pieces, shaking her head, she announces, "I think it's the negativity around here." She sprays Joey and gently massages the mist into the soil. "Plants die when they sense their environment isn't loving."

She directs her gaze toward me as she says this, and I guess she doesn't remember that I was his original mom. Makes sense. Rhonda's also somehow missed the ten thousand eye rolls Caitlin has powered toward her over the years, choosing only to notice her random compliments. Rhonda thinks Caitlin is her little pet too.

Rhonda also doesn't know that Armin is the one killing Joey. Just yesterday, I saw him pouring light blue Gatorade into the pot.

The timing works out: about a year ago, Rhonda took Armin's joojeh kabob out of the fridge and threw it away. When he asked her, she said she thought it had gone bad because of the smell. Joey's mysterious decline began soon after.

I thought I had these people figured out. I thought I knew their ticks, their habits, what bullshit made them laugh. Turns out I was making up stories about everyone around me in my head.

Now I know that, when given the opportunity to read shit that's personal and that I have no business reading, I will absolutely do it. I've spent the past hour digging through all their inboxes.

And they're all so much worse than they let on.

Every email is either a complaint about another person not doing their job right or a rebuttal to protect their own ass. Nobody actually *does* anything nice, or helpful, or even interesting.

It's like opening a curtain. I've never known any of them, never seen the faces behind the masks, and there's something super fragile about breaching this.

A new email for Caitlin appears as Rhonda goes to retrieve her flower-shaped watering can from the top of an ancient filing cabinet. It's from an outside account: kyle@electriansplus.com. This is Caitlin's Kyle! Based on the heart-shaped gifts he occasionally sends to her at the office, he's also a potential serial killer. I've learned about a thousand useless facts about this mediocre man over the years—and now he emails!

I shouldn't read it.

Hey hon,
Hope work isn't too busy. Not sure if my messages are coming through so I'm trying you here. Just letting you know I can pick up dinner and wine. How bout your fave?
    I also have a surprise for you.

Love you,
Kyle

Nice enough. A tad boring, really. An odd sensation swoops through me, like the earth isn't quite below me. I knew I shouldn't have read it. Caitlin's retying her bun, focusing on a printout on her desk. She hasn't even seen the email. Such a comfortably intimate email, probably the kind she receives daily.

She glances up to check the calendar pinned to her wall and I search her face. I need to see something recognizable inside her—something to help me understand what it's like.

Finally, she turns back to her screen and clicks. She stares for a moment and, like a switch, her expression softens. She pulls out the silver pocket mirror that she keeps next to her lotion bin. She's tacked up a bunch of pictures of her friends who look so similar to her behind it. It occurs to me there are no pictures of Kyle there. I guess a weird, distant part of me thought her life with him was fictional.

Her gaze crawls my way, and I jolt hard enough that my chair squeaks.

Damn it, I was staring way too hard.

She gives me a micro-glare for courtesy.

An instant message pops up. The sound rattles through my monitor. I quickly mute.

So, all jokes aside, it seems like Jolene didn't get in shit for any of the stuff she did. They're sending her to some harassment meetings with the new HR guy, but that's nothing. What does one have to do to get in actual trouble here? Short of murder, can we just do whatever we want?

My skin cools.

Caitlin sent that message to Rhonda and Armin. I'm even getting instant messages. This is dangerous.

Armin's reply comes first:

Armin: She got that sensitivity training, so it's not like she got off scot-free.

Caitlin: That's not a real punishment. All she has to do is sit there for a few sessions and then all's forgiven. That's only going to show her she can get away with anything. We're essentially training her that she can do what she wants.

Armin: She's our coworker, not our pet.

Rhonda: They also did something to her computer. Gregory had me note it down.

Caitlin: I know, but I guess I still don't feel . . . comfortable. After that email to me, and the message she sent Armin, and all the other things she's always doing, I just feel like she's too unstable to work so near to us. Armin, I think you should report her message to HR—say it made you worried. We're in these pods with her day in and day out, fully vulnerable. If we all went to Gregory and that new HR guy and stated our concerns, they'd have to at least move her.

Armin: I mean, the message she sent me was weird, but trying to get her in trouble again? Might be best to just leave it. Live and let live and all that.

Rhonda: I've sat next to Jolene for eight years. She's rude, sometimes, but I can manage that myself.

Caitlin: I think you've both just gotten so used to her abuse that it doesn't faze you. Armin, what did she say to you when you asked for pledges during your Bike for Cancer?

Armin: Ha, right. She said she didn't understand why she'd pay for me to bike around in a circle a bunch.

Caitlin: See? Miserable.

I almost break my neutral expression as I peek at each of my colleagues. Their faces are all tilted toward the light of their screens like tropical plants to sunlight. When I asked Armin about the bike pledge, I simply wanted clarification on what I'd be getting for my dollars. I was broke, late on rent, and confused about how his biking would help anyone.

I lay a hand over my forehead like a visor. Sure, Caitlin and me have a bad thing going, but with the other two . . . I always got the sense I was giving off quiet vibes and nothing more.

I startle when Penny Johnson appears behind me. She's looking at the communal bulletin board with the schedule for when the next blue jeans week is. She must have big plans to rock her perma-wedgie Wranglers for us all. I wheel back toward my screen just in time. A new message is flashing orange. I try to puff out my shoulders to hide my monitor.

Caitlin: And Rhonda, remember how she wouldn't let you decorate for Christmas? She took down the tinsel that breached her cubicle. What is that?

Rhonda: Ridiculous. I was only trying to spread holiday cheer. She's very unpleasant, but it's common these days.

Caitlin: That's what I'm saying. We've gotten conditioned to think it's normal. She's been warring with us for years.

I always knew they didn't like me, but to see it summarized so concisely—it's like being slapped from the inside. I blink and blink and blink some more. I couldn't handle Rhonda's tinsel because it was covered in some type of glitter that would fleck all over my desk and attach to my clothes. If I wanted to wear the same office pants two days in a row (or, being real, three), I needed to mitigate the mess, so I moved it to the other side of the wall.

I didn't mean for everything to become a fight. Every petty thing I did was small, but they slowly compounded, and now it's who I am to them. It's my whole life here. The hollow feeling from before expands.

Another message from Caitlin appears. I don't want to read it, but it's like I don't have a choice.

> **Caitlin:** She doesn't even have friends. Work people were the only ones she added when she started her Instagram.
> **Armin:** Exactly, her life is sad enough. We don't need to involve ourselves in making it worse. She's got it covered lol.

The back of my throat hitches. Yeah, I'm a general mess, but I didn't realize how much of a joke I am to them.

They don't know that I did have a friend, once. At least.

> **Caitlin:** The elephant in the room is there's going to be layoffs. If she passes that HR course, it's like, on paper, the bad actions didn't even happen. Hopefully she's not taking one of our spots when the layoffs come. Maybe then you'll wish you'd said something earlier.
> **Armin:** So what are you suggesting, getting her fired?
> **Caitlin:** I'm saying you should at least consider going to HR about the message she sent—it made you uncomfortable, didn't it? I think it's almost sexist if you don't. Us women have to fight harassment all the time. If they choose to terminate, it'll be her fault. But if you don't say anything and then something happens, what then?

Heat swoops over my cheeks. Armin shakes his head as he types.

> **Armin:** Uncomfortable? Yes, a little. But not enough for me to go to HR about. If something else happens, I'll start to consider. But if she has

no friends, this shitty job is all she has. I can't ruin her life over a likely harmless message.

Rhonda: With nothing left to lose, she could retaliate!!

Rhonda: She doesn't seem violent, mind you. But she might steal a wheel from our chairs or destroy my singing Santa decoration.

Rhonda: I need to get a lock for my festive decor closet ASAP!

Armin: Well, this is getting unhinged, so I'm out. If all this is because you're worried about our jobs, don't be. Those rumors always happen, and they always stem from Larry Goodwin. He's paranoid because of that new HR guy, but not exactly on the cutting edge of office news. Next week, he'll be scared if the watercooler moves one inch away from his office. Besides, Rhonda and I are in accounting—a different department.

Armin Habib has left the conversation.

Caitlin and Rhonda exchange a look. I do my best to freeze my expression as my insides implode.

Armin's chair squeaks. He stretches up and grabs his hoodie from the back. He catches me peeping before I can divert my gaze. His eyes flash with something that might be anger for a quick second, before they glaze over with an unreadable expression.

Shit.

I duck behind my cubicle wall, heart beating into my temples as I stare at my dusty keyboard. All I had to do was keep him from thinking I'm unstable. A herculean feat.

After a beat, I peep at my screen. Another message awaits.

Rhonda: Don't tell Armin, but the rumors are true. I saw a memo on Gregory's desk. They may be reorganizing.

Caitlin: See! Why couldn't they have fired her yesterday then?! Jolene gets out of jail free if she passes the course, and I still have to worry about my job security when she's the clear choice.

Rhonda: I know it's hard for us nice people to work with some of the less friendly folks, but don't worry, I'm sure if they have to let one of you go, they'll pick her. I've been around long enough to see all the bad eggs get taken out.

Caitlin: I'm not sure. She's been here for years longer than me. She'd be the easier one to keep. Plus, not to give too much credit to Larry Goodwin, but what if he's onto something with the new HR guy? Like now Jolene gets to work closely with the guy who might be helping with the firing choices?
Rhonda: You took all those leadership courses a few years back. Gregory knows you see a future here.
Caitlin: Jolene took them too. She only did them to get out of regular work, I'm sure. But I remember because she stole my pen.

I stifle a groan. Yes, I did take the leadership courses to get out of regular work. And I passed—but so did everyone who attended. Larry's certificate is currently framed in his office; he's essentially advertising that he sat in a room and possibly stayed conscious for three days. And when Caitlin lost her pen during the lunch break, she asked me if I'd accidentally taken it. I shook my head, and she said it was so weird because hers looked just like mine. As she walked away after yet another accusatory stare, I muttered, "Maybe the company decided to manufacture more than *one pen* to increase profits." She glared at me, which made me realize I didn't mutter low enough, and that was our first petty party.

Another message from Caitlin pops up.

Caitlin: Maybe you could put in a good word for me with Gregory?
Also can you give me the leg up again this month? That way I can stay hanging with you and still help with the Morale Boosters.
Rhonda: Of course, dear.

A chime sounds from Caitlin's desk phone. It's that double ring that means the call is coming from inside the office. She hauls the receiver to her cheek. "What's up, Ron? Nope, sent them yesterday."

Her head tilts my way out of nowhere and she catches me staring again. I quickly frown at my screen, but I'm a second too late. I'm sure my face is flaming red; I'm about to combust. What in the world is the "leg up"? And how long has Rhonda been giving it to her?

Caitlin rolls her shoulders as another message pops up.

> **Caitlin:** Ugh, I have to track something down for Ron that's probably right in front of his face. Can we talk more at lunch?
> **Rhonda:** Sure :)

As Caitlin marches off, I'm left with nothing but Rhonda's horrible little smiley face staring at me. Who knew that, while we all sat in our cubicles, lifeless as depressed zoo animals, these messages were being flung through the cages like invisible crap, tainting it all?

Across the pods, Caitlin's all giggles and plastic smile as she enters Ron's office. It's so easy for her, yet nobody sees through it.

I can't just sit here while they conspire against me. Those fuckers are colluding, and I need any advantage I can to stay afloat. I can't afford to lose this job, but I *won't* lose it because of Caitlin. I'm clicking through her folders, looking for something, anything useful. Her sent folder has a new email from ten minutes ago.

FROM: Caitlin Joffrey
TO: kyle@electriciansplus.com
SUBJECT: Re: Hello my love

That sounds good. I'll text when I leave.

Her cackle sounds from Ron's office. Every day Caitlin leaves this place and has dinner and wine with someone who loves her.

My throat is thick, and that hollow feeling in my chest won't subside. I'm sure it's only because I'm worried about getting fired and not because it's recently come to my attention that this shitty admin job is truly all I have.

Aunt: Another Four-Letter Word

EVEN THOUGH THE promise of mountains of kabob could normally make me do questionable acts, dread sits heavy in my chest. After I left work, my head was tight and hot. I drafted a cancellation text to Mom, but right before hitting send, an image of her explaining my absence popped in my head, and I couldn't pull the trigger.

When I pull open the brass handle of the creaky wooden door of House of Shiraz, I'm greeted by the savory smell of dozens of khoobideh skewers roasting over a flame grill. A mix of affection and angst builds inside me as their signature big hairdos and bright blouses draw my gaze. Dinner with my mom and all my aunties is sort of like being in a hospital: you don't want to be there, but you could die if you leave. I normally try to limit my interactions with the clan to five mandatory occasions a year, making this visit rogue and dangerous.

I inhale as I make my way over to their lively table. My first mistake was not packing a change of pants. The ones I'm wearing are wrinkled from a day of sitting in an office, and as I make my way over it's like a runway of shame to a row of harsh judges. Aunty Miriam spots me first and gives me a look that's somehow proud and disapproving at the same time. Aunty Miriam is the only aunty here who's *actually* my aunt. In the Persian aunty network, there's a series of women in every corner of the world who are either vaguely related to me or close family friends. If I were to vacation in Antarctica, my mom would tell me to check in with an aunty there or face certain public shaming. Today Aunty Miriam is sporting aggressively dark eyeshadow and a designer handbag that's so sleek and sharp, it could be wielded as a weapon. She nudges my mom, who is seated beside her, and mutters something—a lovely comment about me, I'm sure. Mom yells, "Jolene, come sit," as if I were planning on going to the kitchen and showing my nips to the chef if not for her direction. Roya, the one Mom can stand the least, raises her newly threaded eyebrows as she spots me. The ground below me seems to warp as I make my way over to the one available chair at the head of the table.

Silence sweeps over the party. Mom is sitting on my right, Parvin on my left, then Miriam and Roya beside them, respectively. A waiter is heading to the table beside us, but before he can get there, Mom directs him in Farsi to get me a mint yogurt drink, her lips sticky with thick, waxy lipstick. His helmet of shiny hair bobs in acknowledgment, yet his hands ball into little fists as he heads back to the bar.

"Mom, I could've waited. I don't want my food to come with spit."

She flicks her perfectly manicured nails my way. "It's okay, we're Persian."

This is Mom's defense for most things that my dad and I question. The waiter places the drink down in front of me. As soon as the cool, perfectly salted, minty perfection hits my tongue, something in my soul lights up. All the women at the table stare at me, not unlike predators stalking their prey.

Parvin speaks first. "It's nice to finally see you, Jolene joon." Crow's-feet pull at the corners of her eyes. She's my favorite aunty. She lived with us when she first moved from Iran. She'd watch stuff like *Jersey Shore* to learn English and write down the words she didn't understand. The ones my mom couldn't translate would often be my job. Spending my early teen years explaining words like "quiff" to an innocent older lady may have affected my development in some way. She continues: "Have you been busy? How come you never talk in the group chat?"

"Oh, I think I need to update my app." I chase the straw with my mouth. If there's some FBI guy assigned to monitoring that group chat, his life has likely lost all meaning. All day long, aunties and cousins send each other: Hello Beautiful. I love you. [Heart GIF] [Teddy bear holding roses picture that sparkles for some reason] I don't believe there's a place for me in there, but I'm stuck and terrified that if I mute, they'll somehow sense it.

Aunty Miriam frowns. "You look tired." That's the first bite.

But Roya goes in for the kill. "How can she be? No kids, no husband, and her job . . . Well, she's not a doctor." She mixes her stewed tomato into her rice and continues. "Fereshteh comes to see all of us twice a week, and she's running a big engineering project, and her kids are both in very demanding extracurriculars."

Damn, Roya, fire right out the gate. I should've expected this. When I lived with my parents during my frozen-in-time years, I did everything my mom told me to do, yet I was still a big disappointment. Roya was always my loudest critic. Truthfully, I think she enjoyed making Mom feel bad that she had messed up her only child. Because according to the Aunty Way of Raising Kids, I'm a glitch in every way possible. When I lived at home, they wanted to know why I couldn't move out. When I did move to the city, Roya shifted her criticism to me leaving my family for a dead-end job, which broke a different, and slightly worse, Persian daughter code.

Mom, who knows that any criticism of me is also a criticism of her, flashes me a disapproving look that lasts a millisecond, then pipes in with: "Jolene's very successful at her job. It's big national corporation, and she's about to get a promotion."

Silence drapes the table as they all pause their eating to process this. The messages my colleagues sent today flash through my mind, followed by the pang of shame that I'm starting my mandatory training tomorrow. Oh, the ammo Roya would have if she only knew I was about to be laid off from a place that has a one-pancake limit during its annual rodeo breakfast.

"What's your promotion?" Aunty Parvin asks. "Aren't you a secretary?"

I mean, if the Supershops Apricot Body Wash gift pack Gregory gives me every Administrative Professionals' Day is right, then yeah, I'm technically a secretary. I'm not about to admit that to Parvin. Her son is an actual doctor who specializes in something like noses and ears.

Mom looks at me, pleading. So I say, "I'm currently an administrative technician, but will likely be given a supervisory position."

Mom beams. "She's been getting more and more responsibilities, and a lot of people rely on her."

I try not to let the plastic smile I've put on crack. "Yeah, I believe I'll soon be designing how we run certain departments, once I'm given my new role."

Mom smiles. Well, it's a very quick pull of her lips, but it's there. And as she stirs her cucumber yogurt into her rice, head just a little higher, I really wish my words were true. Me actually getting a promotion, and her actually being able to brag to this bunch, would make her entire decade.

Aunty Miriam lowers her brows as she finishes her bite of joojeh. "It's not good to only worry about work. You're thirty-three now. Time is running out for kids. Are you seeing anyone?"

I cough into my drink. There's no way I'd ever be able to take care of a tiny human life when I've killed plants faster than Armin without trying—Rhonda was right to kidnap Joey.

Mom's knuckles are white from balling her hands into fists around her napkin. If these dinners are painful for me, they're even worse for her. But I know why she keeps coming. Back in Mountain Valley, before everything with me happened, she'd fought hard to climb up the ladder of the Horticulture Society, which was no small feat in a small town in Alberta, Canada, in the '90s. She even won Best Front Garden two seasons in a row. With that many old white ladies in charge, she was hanging on only by a thread. Then our lives imploded, and she was basically ghosted by them all. I heard her complain to Dad that she'd go to meetings, and they'd literally ignore her when she spoke. She even had somebody she'd conversed with hundreds of times comment that her accent was too thick to understand. That was when her gardening stopped.

At least here in Calgary she has friends again, even if all the aunties talk about is their kids—every single one happy, with real career-type jobs and actual families, houses, cars, and alive plants. My mom needs a community, just like she needs a better daughter.

All the aunties shift sideways to glance between me and Mom. I practically crumble when I say, "I haven't been focused on dating much, but will start to soon." I can't actually imagine dating anyone for more than one night. But unfortunately, all the aunties' eyes widen.

Aunty Miriam claps her hands, clacking all the rings and her fancy old-lady watch together. "Your mommy has been waiting for this. There are so many eligible bachelors." Good god, I've set off a terrible alarm. The aunty dating arrangement call is possibly the most precarious situation to be in.

But the worst offender, my mom, calls over the waiter again, and her Farsi is too fast for me to track. Maybe she's ordering champagne to celebrate me saying I want to date? It's when Mom points at me that my heart stops. Roya laughs and says, "Oh, your mom's so excited she's asking the waiter if he's single."

"She isn't?" I ask, even though I know the answer. All the guilt I had about hurting Mom dissolves like it always does at some point in our interactions, and I remember exactly why I moved away. I shouldn't have come here. As the waiter leaves, I pretend to take a bite of food as I grit through my teeth, "Mom, you didn't just ask the waiter out for me, did you?"

Mom keeps her lips even: "He's in school for engineering, and his mom owns this restaurant. He's very good catch."

The small bite of perfectly tender chicken in my mouth turns dry. "Did he just turn me down?"

Mom pats my hand. "Don't worry, I asked him if he had friends who would like you. He promised he'd let me know."

I'm obviously not interested in him either, but I could've done without the unsolicited rejection.

Roya laughs. "Oh, Leila, when my Fereshteh was looking for a husband, she didn't have to look, there was line around the block."

"That's great," I say, wondering if I can dissolve into this gold-painted chair. What else could one really say to that?

Miriam pipes in: "You're very beautiful and a very nice lady. We just need to show people how pretty you are. I can give good makeovers, huh?" She closes her eyes and proudly displays her eyeshadow that's more Beetlejuice than juiced beetles. "Want me to help you with your makeup?"

Mom leans in closer and whispers, "You didn't take your time on your eyeliner. It's crooked. I told you to make sure to do good job."

The conversation switches to heated Farsi. Arguing fingers point at my face, my hair, my boobs—and based on the expressions, they're assessing how dire my desirability is. This isn't meant to be as hurtful as it feels. It's honestly just the weirdest display of love. But I need to pull in the reins. "I can't commit to any makeovers. I have to focus on getting this promotion before I can do anything else."

"Good girl." Mom pats my shoulder with one hand as the other reaches for the bowl of sabzi. "A stable job is very important. And you can always move in with me if you want to save money for a wedding one day."

They all smirk in agreement while the walls close in around me, powered by the heat of their stares. "Once you get promoted, we can work on finding you a husband," Parvin says, and they each give a single nod like they've concluded this meeting of the Sad Niece Society.

In my peripheral vision, I spot the waiter and a colleague crouching together while pretending not to look at me. I take another skewer from the platter since I'll never be eating here again.

At least I can leave this restaurant. At least when I walk out the door, this specific misery will end, and I can get myself a family pack of Kit Kats and go home and be alone. If I lose my job, I'll have to move in with Mom again, and there'll be no escaping any of this.

Conveyor Belt Artist

THE "GROCERY SHOP of shame" is a form of modern art that peaks in its grandeur at the conveyer belt. My post–aunty dinner angst may have influenced what went into the basket. Plus, the signature sky-blue color painted all over Supershops—the same shade that brands everything in our office—triggers something in me that can only be cured by processed foods.

All the items that I plan to purchase and consume are splayed out and slowly gliding toward the cashier, a visual representation of the state of my mental health. The weeks when I get the marshmallow strawberries and the Corn Nuts are particular cries for help.

The key to a successful grocery shop of shame is all about timing. Eight p.m. on a Monday is usually the safest hour if you want a little discretion, but somehow there are two people behind me tonight. Worst of all, the one closest to me looks to be the juicing type. We wait in meditative silence as the cashier scans the items in hollow beeping intervals.

I add the Flamin' Hot Cheetos—was that a gasp? The guy behind me winces as he eyes my treats, and he looks like he might shit his high-end sweatpants. He clearly doesn't understand my craft. He's perfect and sinewy and could make it as a time-share brochure model if he desired. He glances at his teal Apple Watch, grunts, then lifts his basket of produce from the ground and storms away.

If only I could leave this situation too.

The guy behind him shuffles forward and grabs the last bag of All-Dressed peanuts I'd been eyeing. My stomach twists as he adds it to his pile. It's him. *Him* as in Clifford HR guy. He's dressed like a British gangster in an Adidas sweatsuit, and his basket is filled with puffy bags of chips with reckless flavors made for eating alone: pickled onion, chilly and chive.

Solidarity.

His gaze shifts from the conveyer belt to me. He jolts in surprise, then a genuine smile overtakes him. "Jolene, what the hell? So good to see you."

"Nice to see another patron of the arts." I look pointedly at his snacks, and his grin tugs a little wider. Only it's too much—what is he doing here, after everything today? Maybe Supershops hired him to monitor me at all company locations. Maybe this is a social experiment on how to break a person in one day. "You're doing a good job acting surprised," I say.

"What?" He raises a brow, but he's still smiling. He's a stark contrast to the scuffed floors and depressive Supershops-branded endcaps.

"Are you saying this *isn't* some kind of HR undercover op then? Gregory isn't hiding in the store, dicking up the produce with his fingers as we speak?"

He lets out a startled chuckle. "What did you just say?"

I should probably be embarrassed that I said that out loud. But running into him here is the cherry on top of my surreal day. This feels like a glitch in the matrix or a dream. So I poke some more. "I'm off work. This is my time; I can say 'peen-hole' if I want." I stare him down like this is a dare. After all, he spent my performance meeting doodling cats, so he's not the paradigm of professionalism either.

"That's fifty-six seventy-three," the cashier chimes in neutrally.

I tap the machine to pay and thank her, but I keep my eyes on Cliff.

His brow crinkles. "I was referring to the part about Gregory. I would *never* bring him on an undercover operation. He doesn't have what it takes."

I try not to laugh in surprise, but it feels like he passed some kind of test. To hide my amusement, I narrow my eyes at his groceries. His eyes follow my gaze.

"As you can see, I'm just here for my essentials." He nods toward the front entrance. "I just live a few blocks away."

I take a step back. "So do I. I shop here all the time for our employee discount. I've never seen you before."

"Well, you wouldn't have recognized me. We only met a few days ago."

"I suppose." I nod politely to the cashier as she hands me my receipt. "Well, bye," I mutter as I grab the frayed handles of my Supershops reusable bags and hope for peace.

"See ya," he calls, and holds up his keys in a wave. I'm already walking through the automatic doors, too far gone to wave back.

I trot across the asphalt parking lot with slightly heavier than planned shopping bags. The sun has gone down and things are turning shadowy. The creaky squeal of a retirement-aged car trying its darnedest sounds too close behind me. I turn sharply to face a golden sedan that could be considered vintage if the world didn't want to forget this model ever existed.

"You're not walking home with that many groceries, are you?" Cliff calls from his rolled-down passenger-side window.

I shrug as best as I can with the pounds of sugar weighing them down. "It's how I keep my fitness levels optimum." Although, if we're being honest, the Alphagetti cans were a poor choice.

"I'll give you a ride," he says, without hesitation.

"Nah, we're good," I say back, also without hesitation.

"You sure you're okay walking home in the dark?"

As if on cue, the streetlamp above me flickers on, casting a creepy fluorescent sheen over the tar lot.

Cliff stretches himself over the passenger seat and opens the side door. "Come on, it's no trouble." He nods toward my grocery bags. "Anyone can see your spicy Cheetos; you're going to get mugged."

For the second time this evening, I find myself biting back a smile. I stare at the sidewalk ahead. Admittedly the neighborhood has been on the sketchier side after dark these days. But would getting mugged be as bad as him seeing where I live?

The interior light in his car clicks on, like a moth lamp beckoning me in, so I accept my fate. "Just so you know, I've been doing this route for eight years sans incident," I say as I unload my bags into the passenger-side footwell. The tang of relief in my forearms is almost too much. "But thanks."

The interior of the car smells about how you'd imagine. There's a New Car Smell air freshener hanging on the rearview mirror that must

be ironic, because I'm picking up old-dog vibes. Music is quietly fil-
tering through the crackly speakers, but it's instrumental and low and
sends a soothing warmth into my chest.

"Sorry," Cliff mutters. "I don't have too many guests in here. But I
think you should know that I realize how bad it is."

"It's nice," I say. I don't mean it to sound sarcastic. Because even
though it's obvious his dog spends many happy a moment in here, the
vibe is still good.

"So, what's on your docket now that groceries are sorted?" he asks.

"See, if you don't want to sound like an undercover HR guy, you're
doing a terrible job."

He chuckles, and we pull out of the lot. "Okay, now for the obtaining
your address part of my covert operation, so I can bug your place and
expose your secrets."

"Is that an inappropriate joke?" I lower my lids at him accusingly.

He shrugs. "I thought it was funny."

"It was," I say evenly. "I live at Sixty-Fourth and Bow-West Road. My
building's called the Riviera."

"Seriously?"

I nod and brace for his impending judgment. I'm not sure how many
more knocks I can take today. "Yeah, the Riviera boasts interiors that
haven't been updated since the seventies, questionable stains throughout, and ambient views of public urination."

"I meant 'cause that's literally a block away from me." He lifts one
brow. "But they had to add the last brag once you moved in, didn't they?"

This time I can't catch it fast enough—a chuckle escapes me. "I didn't
think you had it in you to make a decent joke."

"Hey, I'm off the clock too."

His right arm is resting on the center console, and I swear I can feel
the warmth of it radiating through the car's interior. It feels cozy.

"You know the white-and-blue-trimmed building across the street?
I've been there for like a year. I'm surprised I never see you around.
Where do you normally hang out?" He nudges the air beside my arm
playfully, and the world tilts. "Other than Supershops and the office,
of course."

"Oh, you know..." The liquor store, mostly. "Just around."

His gaze briefly flickers from the road toward me as he cranks the stick shift. All the warmth that surrounded me has turned clammy.

"And like you said, you wouldn't have recognized me."

"True." He nods and his gaze returns to the road. I take a steadying breath. "You don't have a car? There aren't any trains running out here; how do you get to work?"

"The lovely transit system."

"Isn't that, like, three bus transfers?"

I shrug. "We can't all be blessed with fancy corporate parking spaces... or cars."

"Yeah..." Cliff stiffens a little. I realize how that must've come off, like I was shaming him. Shit. This is why I shouldn't speak.

"How long have you been in HR?" I blurt out.

"Oh, about a year or so." Is there an edge to his voice?

"And is it everything you hoped it would be?"

"And more." He smiles, but it's not as natural as before. "Hey, Jolene, since I'm driving every day anyway, I could pick you up."

"Oh no. Cliff, it's okay—I swear I wasn't trying to pressure you to offer."

"Nah, I know you weren't. Well, maybe there's some carbon footprint pressure—it's common sense. We're both heading to the same place at the same time, and I wouldn't mind the company." He says all this so casually, like it's a totally normal thing for an HR guy to offer an employee who is currently on probation. His hands weave over the wheel as the car turns the corner. "But I get it if you prefer the bus. They still hosting those public masturbation matinees?"

I cackle against my will, sharp and loud. How has this guy managed to break my cool twice in one night? While he focuses on the road, I dare a longer stare, as though his face will reveal what's hidden inside his head. "To be fair, that show gives a lot of bang for your buck," I quip back. "But honestly, it's fine. I'm sure us pleb employees aren't allowed to carpool with HR anyway."

"Believe it or not, management has determined that HR bots are allowed to be friendly with employees. We just can't date them." His hands go tense around the wheel, and his eyes flash toward the exterior mirror. "Sorry, I didn't mean—that's not going to be a—"

"Oh god, *definitely* not," I interrupt.

His knuckles loosen. "You flatter." But then his eyes soften. "Totally don't want to make things awkward, though. The offer's there, but no pressure. I get it could be weird."

He obviously offered only out of obligation because of my weird comment about his parking spot, but I can't carpool with a corporate cop, anyway—no matter how much he wants to act otherwise. Besides, if we commuted together, he'd just ask tons of questions, and we'd get to know more and more useless shit about each other, and then we'd get to the useful parts and . . . I shake that train of thought away. "Thanks, I appreciate it, but I'm good."

Yes, it's only because he's HR that we can't carpool.

He pulls up to the curb of my street—or, I guess, *our* street now—soundless but for the clicking of the turn signal. I hold my breath as my building comes into view, with its broken sign and the empty shopping cart leaning sideways on the front lawn. Those things were invisible to me just yesterday. Why did I have to tell him where I live? This is too much. What if I leave the hall light on, the one I always forget about, and he sees my colossal dish pile through the window? What if he deems my apartment unsafe for human life and has to make a report to headquarters about me? What if Miley's there and she tells him about my tarot reading? He can track my comings and goings if he wants to, can inspect my garbage if he so desires.

All the calm vibes have dissipated. My seat belt pulls tighter across my chest. I rush to unclip it and open the door. "See you tomorrow."

"Hey, I'll help with your—" I grab the grocery bags in a rapid swoop and slam the door shut before I can hear him finish.

It's just that HR people aren't our friends. Nothing else.

Power Move

I FLASH MY BADGE, and the door to my office floor buzzes open, welcoming me with a charred plastic scent. The big clock in front of my desk tells me that it's not even 8:15, yet some shithead has already burned popcorn and tainted up the office.

My feet grow heavier with each step. I just need to make it through another cursed day.

Rhonda's removing the teal tissue paper she'd pinned to the backdrop of her cubicle and replacing it with purple. A tedious process, but she changes her "color scheme" on the first of each month, saying, "It's only a couple of dollars to brighten up a place we spend our waking life in."

This place could easily be a case study.

With Armin's desk still sitting empty, Caitlin's the only one who marks my entrance by locking eyes with me and then abruptly looking away. She's poured her Tim Hortons coffee into a speckled artisan mug and is snapping no fewer than five pictures of the situation. Her backdrop is the corner of her cubicle with her open bullet journal. *May Goals* in fancy lettering. There's also the creepy heart-shaped wooden box she keeps the Post-it notes her boyfriend puts in her lunch. It'll make a beautiful, slightly motivational picture, that. To think, if her phone was angled slightly more to the left, she'd capture Larry Goodwin scratching his wrinkle-resistant khakis while struggling to bend over and refill his water bottle.

I log in, and just to be sure I wasn't hallucinating yesterday, I click into my email to confirm I still have admin permissions. The only message actually addressed to me is the office-wide memo Rhonda sends monthly asking for more Morale Boosters volunteers, even though the lady hasn't had a new recruit in years.

I click into Rhonda's inbox before I can think too hard about it. It's all boring stuff, confirmations for Gregory's appointments and budget grids. There's one odd thing sitting there, though:

FROM: Rhonda Staples
TO: Rhonda Staples
SUBJECT: Summary for Month

April 1: Late by 7 minutes
    April 5: 12-minute phone conversation with Elite Sneakers
    April 16: Returned from lunch 1:16 pm
    April 17: 27-minute conversation in copy room: various
people
    April 20: Spent 17 mins staring at screensaver. Also 14 mins staring at
his own hands.
    April 25: Morning researching all-season tires
    April 27: Detoured on way to bathroom to have 12-minute conversation
with Larry Goodwin

Is she tracking someone's schedule? As if on cue, she turns abruptly, sweeps her hands together, and declares, "There, so much fresher." She riffles through the Rolodex she's been using since Bob Barker was a baby, a dreadful indication that she's about to make a loud phone call that most certainly should be an email. And of course, Rhonda yells into her receiver, "Hello, Marianne! How's things?"

She cackles at whatever Marianne's response was, then narrows her eyes as Armin stumbles to his desk. He's all giant headphones, bass blaring, with hair still wet and some generic "fresh" men's body wash scent stinking up the air around us. His eyes are red and puffy, like he just opened them from a sleepless night two seconds ago.

Rhonda looks him up and down, leans over her computer, and starts typing something.

And oh my shit, Rhonda's tracking every time Armin dicks around. Unsettling, yet painfully on brand.

I sip my gas station coffee, which I'm sure tastes just the same as

Caitlin's even if it hasn't been jazzed up by a mug or backdrop, when a DM pops up from Caitlin to Garret.

> **Caitlin:** I'm going to commit murder—is it too early for that?
> **Garret:** You're asking the wrong guy for legal advice. Who's the victim?
> **Caitlin:** Larry Goodwin just refilled his water bottle, and when he realized the cooler needed changing, he walked away. Am I supposed to do a menial task to stay hydrated?
> **Garret:** I see. Yes, you could murder him and see if that helps?
> **Caitlin:** Haha. Btw, do you know what the deal is with the new HR guy? Larry told Armin he was some corporate spy.
> **Garret:** TBH I don't know too much at the moment, but Gregory said to "expect change." And we might have meetings with him.
> **Caitlin:** Meetings? For what?
> **Garret:** Usually it's to review roles and hear how people work as a team. Off the record: it's a good time to bring up any interpersonal issues. That usually helps their . . . "process."

I stare straight forward at the screen, but I physically feel Caitlin's eyes draw to me, the heat of them burning against my cheek like lasers.

> **Caitlin:** Well, that is good to know! I certainly have a long list.
> **Garret:** I wouldn't bring up the Jolene email thing since it's been dealt with. It may give off the wrong tone for what you want to present.
> **Caitlin:** Ugh. I guess. We gotta convince Armin to talk. It's crazy her DM wasn't enough to sufficiently creep him out.
> **Garret:** Oh, speaking of! That Cliff guy asked me where I was headed when I was leaving for Friday drinks. Was sort of sad looking—even mentioned having no plans that night.
> **Caitlin:** YIKES!
> **Garret:** Yeah, it's like, dude, nobody's drinking with you—you're HR.
> **Caitlin:** No, we need to invite him next time! Convince him to keep me on.
> **Garret:** No! Sorry, babe. Not worth it.
> **Caitlin:** Haha, can you imagine?

The problem is I *can* imagine. Cliff's a nice enough guy, and Caitlin and Garret will probably spin their fake bullshit on him like they have everyone else.

Garret: I wouldn't worry too much—just keep up the good work. Your evaluations are always decent. But I just peeped. Gregory is going to send out a multi-unit meeting request for next Wednesday.

Caitlin: Ugh, so that's when I'll murder Larry. Every meeting he holds us hostage with his parade of questions. During the last one, I wished for lightning to come through the roof and end it all. Like, my dude, some of us have things to live for, we can't endure your sad man voice anymore.

A chuckle bubbles up from my chest, but I catch it before it can find its way out. I thought I was the only one wishing for death during that meeting.

Garret: Greg plans on doing one of those round tables at the end and asking for efficiency strategies.

Caitlin: Okay, that's good to know . . .

Caitlin suddenly leans back in her chair, clicking her monitor to turn the screen off, and stands with a huff. As she marches off in the direction of the bathroom, my heartbeat pounds in time with the dull click-clacks of her heels against the carpet.

I think again about what Garret said about Cliff—about him looking sad. Instinctively, my mouse moves through the server folders in my mailbox list until it lands on his name: *Redmond, Clifford.* I admit, after he drove me home last night, I spent an unfortunate amount of time considering what his deal might be while in that fake-it-till-you-make-it phase of trying to fall asleep.

His emails are minimal, which is to be expected since he started only a week ago. But there is one notable exchange.

FROM: Gregory Hall
TO: Clifford Redmond
SUBJECT: Org Chart

Cliff,

Now that you've settled and gotten to know our team, I'd like to discuss the goals for your busy first month with us.

Head office would like your recommendations to go along with the new org chart they've prepared (attached) by June 1. That gives three weeks to assess each employee's role here and one week to draft the report. I will schedule an employee conference within that time for you to better assess the group's dynamic and their contributions. I believe the employee's mandatory training will also be wrapped up by then, and their progress in that course (or lack thereof) could be used for a termination with cause.

Regards,
Greg

I scan the area for onlookers. So the gossip is true. Apparently, if you want information to travel at lightning speed, you better make it confidential.

And what kind of person acts all buddy-buddy with his coworkers when his first task for this company is eliminating long-term employees? I can't believe I felt bad for him.

I click download on the org chart before I can overthink it.

Caitlin's high-pitched laugh grates through the room behind me, and I nearly skyrocket out of my chair. She's still leaning against Larry's door and giggling far too loud. She needs to calm down—Larry's about as amusing as a survey.

I jot down the date of the meeting on a blank piece of printer paper. Not that I'll be speaking. Gregory's meetings are designed for maximum intimidation: he makes us voice brainstorms in front of the whole group, and he accepts or rejects them on the spot. I'm sure he credits the ideas he likes as his own for the head office. Usually, my only goal is to move as little as possible so he can't see me, but this time I'll need to keep an eye on whatever Caitlin's planning.

I realize I'm staring too hard into her back when I sense something to my right. I turn to catch Armin watching me watching Caitlin—*shit*. I jolt against my will, which makes me look guilty of something, so I try smiling at him, which probably only looks more manic—*shit again!* I focus on dulling the corners of my lips into a more neutral, innocent expression.

He raises an eyebrow at me as he slides his chair back toward his computer, disappearing behind the cube wall.

It shouldn't be this hard to convey normalness to a person.

I return to my computer as well. The org chart download link is sitting temptingly at the bottom of my browser, and my fingers are itching to open it, but I can hear Garret and Marla Singer gathering in the boardroom behind me, their voices far too animated for this place. The traffic around my desk is too high.

Armin pokes his head back over the cubicle divider toward Rhonda this time, peeling his headphones away from his ears to announce, "I've gotta grab a coffee. I'll be back in ten."

"No problem, dear." Rhonda's smile is as thick as syrup. As soon as his back turns, she glances at the wall clock, opens a document, and types.

Everyone here is so fake.

And that pang of anger is all it takes for my finger to tap twice on the org chart and hit print. Except as soon as I do it, I realize someone else might already be at the printer. What was I thinking?

I almost knock my chair over to stand. Rhonda looks up, mildly curious. I force myself to slow down as I head with purpose toward the copy room.

The burned popcorn smell is twice as pungent in this area, but at least it's keeping people out. The incriminating evidence in question is just pushing itself out of the printer. I grab the still-warm page before it can land on the tray. There's a box of maroon folders sitting on the supply table, so I grab one and stuff it inside.

As I round the corner back to my desk, I nearly collide headfirst with Marla. "Hey, Jolene, another day in paradise, eh?" Her smile pushes her cheeks into her glasses. I nod shakily, lowering the folder and casually half hiding it behind me as I pass.

Back at my desk, I assess my surroundings. The door to the conference room has closed, and no one's at the watercooler. My heart is pounding against my ribs, my fingers tingling from where they pressed against the folder. This must be exactly what a spy feels like when committing espionage.

I carefully open the folder, keeping the cover propped to protect its contents from wandering eyes. There's a simple grid listing our team's names and job titles alongside any credentials and courses, and little symbols like x's and check marks sit lifelessly on the page. Beneath it, there's the usual corporate mumbo about desirable cuts to be made.

As I read through it, I realize what it is I'm looking at. They're planning on folding certain roles together. Essentially, either Armin or Rhonda will be fired, and the one who remains will be promoted. Next to Rhonda's name is a note: "potential to mandate early retirement, savings of $5–10k."

This shouldn't do anything to me. How many times have I silently cursed Rhonda out for not just retiring already? But when I glance her way and see her shuffling through her ancient Rolodex yet again, I wish the C-suite executive who designed this chart could see her brand-new purple tissue paper on the cubicle walls, or her Morale Booster emails she fills with actual clip art.

Then I find my own name, sitting just above Caitlin's. Where do we fit into this master plan? Just like with Rhonda and Armin, there's a mark indicating that our roles will be folded into one. The remaining employee's title will be changed to "Document Lead," whatever that means. Both our names have leadership course credit and years of working experience listed. But next to mine is a note that reads: "potential for dismissal with cause, should employee not pass course."

I already knew this, but seeing it written there in Times New Roman sends a sharp bite through my ribs. I try to shake it off and focus on the silver lining this paper reaffirms: my dismissal *isn't* guaranteed yet.

I close the folder and go back to my computer, heading to the Supershops employee portal. I search for the document lead position, and motherfucker, the salary range would be a minimum 15 percent increase in pay. It would mean I could move to an apartment that doesn't require me to dodge mousetraps every time I do laundry. I scan the credentials and I'm surprisingly qualified. I could actually get this, so long as I don't fuck up the course and get fired, of course.

It's dangerous to dream. But getting a new job title that sounds like a *job* job—something that means I'm actually progressing. I could even mention it in the aunty group chat and be rewarded with a heart-eyed mouse GIF. I could take Mom to dinner and offer to pay the check, and she would look at me without that curl in her lip for once. Best of all, Caitlin would be gone, and I could come to work every day without worrying about her making fun of or sabotaging me.

But there's only one problem with this fantasy: they'd have to pick me over Caitlin. Let's be real. Next to her name, there's no disclaimer about potential dismissal with cause.

A reply from Cliff appears in Gregory's inbox. I click it open, my fingers rattling with the beat of my computer fan.

Hi Gregory,

While that timeline is on the tighter end, I can make it work. I understand there was concern from HQ about my process, so I want to reiterate: I need to evaluate employee potential and personality for certain roles. I find the benefits of on-site evaluation and getting to know employees beyond their written reports far outweigh any other inconveniences these meetings may cause.

Also, as the head of the office, I trust that you'll be able to provide a more comprehensive overview of the personnel and assist with suggestions one may not find on the page.

Best,
Clifford

And there it is. Cliff, the fucking doodler with his donut birthday gift who pretended not to be like other HR guys, colluding with Gregory, the guy who can't even rotate PDFs so he instead twists his monitor. Of course these two will be deciding our fates. Typical.

I absently scroll Gregory's email, judging his terrible grammar, offensive jokes, and boomer overuse of ellipses. Why do men like him always get so far? It should be impossible if the world were serious.

A new email at the top of his mailbox catches my eye because the subject line reads: "Is Papa Bear Hungry?"

I know it's a bad idea even as I click it open, but it's like I have some cursed reflex.

> Papa Bear was so hungry for the honey pot last week. I'll be sure to make him another helping tonight.
> Leave work on time tonight.
>
> Love,
> Cutie Bear

I grab my coffee cup and hold it against my lips just to do something other than scream. The liquid makes its way down my throat with a burn. I wish I could pour it on my eyeballs. I spend several minutes staring blankly at my cubicle wall. Is there some sort of authority you call in situations like this to reset Earth from the beginning, just to stop the sequence of events that led to that email being written next time around?

Gregory's office door clicks open and he barrels out, shaking me from my mental vortex of doom and back into this terrible reality. He passes my desk, still adjusting his dick, which is a form of harassment to us all, and I try my best not to look at him. He's about to clear my area when he stops and turns abruptly toward me.

"Miss Smith, has your interpersonal training started?"

He says it loud enough for half the floor to hear, which means Caitlin and Larry, who are walking toward the pods, look my way—wide-eyed imbeciles.

"I have my first session today," I mutter.

"That's wonderful." Gregory smiles like the proud Papa Bear he is.

"We want you to do as well as possible. Soon this whole nonsense will be behind us."

"Yes," I reply, still staring straight ahead. I'll never be able to look this man in the eye again.

He takes a few strides forward, then stops and says, "Have you seen that email?"

I stop breathing. My skin becomes ice. I shake my head way too hard, ready to shout every excuse I can possibly come up with, when it clicks that he's actually talking to Rhonda. He continues, leaning over her shoulder: "We, um, won't be able to send you another replacement credit card."

"What?" Rhonda huffs. "But I use it for your—"

"I know you use it a lot. However"—he crouches even lower to whisper—"head office red-flagged that you lost three cards in one year. With this latest one being stolen and used—well, it's unusual. Maybe they think you're running some kind of embezzlement scheme."

His chuckle doesn't pair well with Rhonda's sudden stiffness, the way her face goes pale white beneath her cakey makeup.

"But don't worry, hon, I defended you. What is it, twenty-odd years you've been here? We'll sort it out." He claps his palms together, and Rhonda visibly jolts.

Three lost cards in one year? How does that happen? Other than arguing with employees at Jo-Ann fabrics, I can't imagine Rhonda gets up to that much. She's lived alone since her husband died of a heart attack over a decade ago, and she never seems to have plans aside from visiting her son on the weekends.

Armin makes his way back to his desk, a Starbucks coffee in hand, yet somehow looking even more tired than before. Gregory calls out, "Nice of you to come in, my guy. Lunch is in five minutes."

Armin's face drops, but he manages an even response. "I'm sorry, I had to step out briefly." He drops his hoodie on the corner of his desk as he sits down.

"No sweat," Gregory says, his pompous grin violating every bulletin on the board. "It can't be easy being in estrogen alley all day." He pauses for laughter. Nobody says a word. After a long beat, he raises his hands in protest to god knows what. "I kid, I kid. I know I'm not allowed to joke these days!"

He's in that category of people who should be ashamed of themselves, yet he's never had to confront guilt because the world always tells him that he's the fucking papa bear.

Caitlin practically leaps into her cube at the sight of Gregory and gives him a big-eyed smile. "Happy first of May, boss."

Gregory nods as he walks off. I watch Caitlin turn to her computer and innocently run her hands across the keyboard.

A DM pops up to Garret:

> WTF, he wants Jolene to pass now? This is mad. I'm going to talk to Rhonda again. She can say something to Gregory about how awful Jolene is.

I knew these people were fake and cruel, but I didn't realize they're all playing a game. If I hadn't read their emails and DMs, I never would've understood the rules. Now I see where I truly sit on the chessboard.

I should probably be freaking out, but instead a weird lightness takes over. A tiny spark of new possibilities.

If this is a game, I can play just like everyone else. Except now I have the cheat codes. Thank Zeus Cliff didn't understand his mistake with my emails. Now I have a candid view of their weak spots, their insecurities, and everything they'll try to hide and exploit about me, themselves, and one another.

Rhonda stands up to reach for the tea box on her shelf. "Unpleasant," she called me in her DMs. Well, I can prove her wrong.

I lift myself up and say, "Hey, Rhonda, how are you?"

She glances over at me, and I let myself smile, nice and casual.

Her eyes widen. "I'm fine. How are you, dear?" she asks, her voice hesitant. Across from us, Caitlin and Armin have fallen completely silent at their desks.

"I saw your email about the Morale Boosters. I'd be happy to help."

For a second she just stares, like I'm the Sphinx and just offered her a riddle. Her shimmery eyeshadow glints beneath the fluorescent lights as she blinks. Finally, she says, "Of course, dear, that would be great! I'll email you the details. We have Gregory's twentieth work anniversary party in just about three weeks."

I focus all my energy into not letting my grin falter. One doesn't simply plan a party for Gregory out of want or desire. One plans one out of a specific need to hurt themself and others. This is the kind of evidence that convinces me Rhonda is part evil.

But I manage to hold my head high because I can feel Caitlin's eyes boring holes into me. Her keyboard is clattering, just like I'd hoped. "By the way," I say to Rhonda, "I love the new purple theme you have here." Though I wonder if Rhonda will be around next month to change the tissue paper again.

This time her smile is genuine. "Oh, thank you."

Caitlin's DMs are waiting for me as I lower myself back into my seat.

Caitlin: What even was that?

Armin: Jolene wants to join the Morale Boosters.

Caitlin: Yes, I can see that, but be careful. She's obviously up to something.

Armin: Right. Okay, thanks for the warning, detective.

It's like walking into a room and worrying everyone was just talking about you; the real power is knowing that they were.

They can't bully me when I have the power this time. After everything they've put me through, I deserve this promotion. I deserve to move on. I, at least, deserve to be here.

I open the maroon folder and flip over the org chart to the blank side. My plan crystalizes and I write it all out, like goals for this quarter:

—*Do everything better and faster than Caitlin*
—*Win over Gregory via his tolerable proxy, Rhonda*
—*Convince Armin I'm normal/give him no reason to talk to HR about me*

The list stares back at me, simple and tidy. This is doable. I could actually do this.

I glance at Caitlin, who is blotting her maroon lipstick with a tissue, one eye on me. When she notices me looking back, her lips curl around the paper into a sneer.

And then I almost smile at her, because I realize there is one more piece on the chessboard I can take control of, and she dropped the idea right into my lap.

I open a new email.

Hey Cliff,
If you were serious about carpooling, I'd actually love to take you up on that. Although I would want to pitch in on gas.

Thank you,
Jolene

I hit send, the tips of my fingers crackling with anxious energy. His response comes too fast.

Of course! I can't tonight, but how about you meet me after work tomorrow and we'll go from there? P.S. nonsense with your gas money—I'll be driving anyway and you're helping me into the carpool lane, which is more than money can buy lol.
See you later for meeting.

Caitlin accused me of using my extra time with Cliff to get ahead, so it might as well be true.

I pick up my pen again and add one more item to my list:

—Get Cliff to like me

It's weird, this power I've tapped into—what nobody counted on, what even I didn't expect. I'm willing to fight to keep my job, and they don't realize how much. I've eaten enough poison that it can't kill me anymore, and now I'm here to win.

This might even be fun.

But Who Will Watch Me Watch the Movie?

A S I MAKE my way down the lone and darker corridor that leads to Cliff's office, my mind races. I have a bit of heavy lifting to do today, since my first few impressions weren't great.

Entering Cliff's office is like emerging from a cave. The blinds are pulled back to let in the sun, which twinkles against all his plastic action figures. Something in my peripheral vision catches me: a cardboard cutout of Bob from *Bob's Burgers* is leaning against the back wall. It wasn't here when I came to talk about my email problem yesterday, which means, between then and now, he put it in his car, walked it through the parkade and up the elevator, unfolded it, and set it up.

What is wrong with this man?

I find the maniac in question leaned over his desk, scribbling on a notepad. His gaze pulls up as I cross the threshold. "Hey, it's my carpool buddy." He follows my gaze toward the new decoration. "I see you're interested in Bob?" He grins, and I notice that the shades of brown in his eyes catch in the light like a kaleidoscope.

Get Cliff to like me, my list said. I gotta relate on this guy's level. I nod enthusiastically. "Oh, yeah," I reply. "Super interesting cartoon. One of my all-time faves."

He's still smiling, but his eyes narrow suspiciously. Shit, how can he see through me so fast? "I'm going to choose to believe that and not ask anything specific about it."

"Probably for the best." I smile back and scan for something better, something I actually like, but hardly anything in his office, despite the clutter, is something I recognize. It's like we're from different realities. He's the pampered HR rep with millions' worth of fandom crap, and I'm the admin who loves reality shows and early 2000s repeats where I've memorized all the plotlines.

He clears his throat and gestures to a box of Timbits. "Please, help yourself."

I take a tentative step toward his desk. "Are any of those jelly filled?"

He shakes his head aggressively. "Why would I ever get jelly filled?"

I try not to let my pleasure at his correct answer show. "Because, Cliff, some people are just born evil."

"Too right." He grins, and I can't help it when my mouth twitches too. And as I take the first bite of the chocolate donut, the sugary glaze cracking against my lips, my gaze draws to a framed poster of some *Star Wars* thing. Cliff notices and nods pointedly at it. "That's a remake, but still really limited."

I nod as if those words make sense to me and take a step closer. "That frame is huge. It must've cost a fortune."

Cliff crosses his arms, a bit bashful. "Yeah, I like the..." He provides some explanation about "novelty" and "community," but all I can think about is the amount of effort it must have taken to get a framed poster that heavy hung on these paper-thin walls.

Maybe this whole office arrangement is some psychological move on his behalf. Everyone who comes here will think he's relatable and just like you or me with these irreverent vibes. This could be a whole operation from head office to get people to think of him as a normal guy.

"It's so nice." I try to sound more convincing this time, but the words feel weird and loose on my lips.

"Right." His hands smack together and pull a plastic chair from the corner of the room, wheels squeaking and resisting their journey. "Have a seat there. It's time for you to watch a video."

"And what will you be doing while I watch the video?" I ask.

"I have to watch you watch the video." His wince is the only clue he's actually serious.

As I sit down, he goes to adjust the blinds, cutting off the sunlight and plunging the room back into the drabby greige shadows that should really be the Supershops brand colors. My palms start to sweat. "But who is going to watch you watch me?"

His eyelids droop to half-mast. "Nobody."

"So they're just going to take your word for it then? Must be nice."

"I have taken an oath." His smirk suggests otherwise, but he walks over to his office door and pushes it shut. This whole lights-off, door-closed thing feels a little too covert. "This video can touch on some sensitive and intimate topics," he says, "so please let me know if you're feeling uncomfortable at any point."

"Sorry, but my doctor says I'm not allowed to watch any more porn at work." I laugh at my joke, but the way his body goes still stops me. Shit. Why oh why would that be the thing I say?

"Excuse me, Jolene?" His head shakes once. My stomach drops. Why did I not practice before I interacted with another human today? "That doesn't sound like medical advice at all. I think your doctor should stay in their lane."

I have severely underestimated him.

Every time he quips back, it's like we're in on something together. Like we could be friends...

Except we can't be. Not really.

He pulls up his chair beside me, and I pick up his soft bar soap scent. I try not to picture him using the soap as a professional courtesy to us both.

He clicks on a remote, and the bulky '90s television monitor crackles to life. The video begins with dreary music as the title flashes across the screen, likely made by an early version of PowerPoint: *HARASSMENT AT WORK: DON'T BE PART OF THE PROBLEM.*

Next plays a scene where a manager slaps an employee on the butt. I can't help but chuckle. "This is what they're still peddling over at the old HR mill?"

Cliff gives a curt nod without looking at me. "There's no need to comment on the video. There will be a quiz."

I shrug. "Let me take it now, then. Contrary to popular belief, I'm actually fantastic at not being a harasser. I mostly keep to myself while I'm out there." I nod pointedly toward the hallway.

He clicks the remote to pause the video and turns to me, resting his hand on the arm of his chair. "I haven't actually had the opportunity to observe any form of reservation from you." He raises a teasing eyebrow, then becomes more serious. "But ignoring your colleagues can cause issues too."

"Fair." I nod and stare straight ahead. "I'm working on that too."

He restarts the video. We spend about eight minutes facing the monitor, but all I can hear is the hum of the VCR and the sound of his every breath.

Kissing ass shouldn't be this difficult. I need to focus on the goal here.

But then the video shifts to a scene of two colleagues pointing at someone who spilled coffee on themselves. And it's funny the things that seem like they should be nothing. It's just a subpar production with bad acting. But all the air in the room turns heavy. Then my hands close in on themselves and I realize I'm not breathing. It's their laughter—when it's at someone's expense, it always sounds the same. The fuzzy outline of another scene, one I've replayed a million times in my mind, takes shape: Ellie, running farther into the woods, stumbling and angry.

This room is too small and much too hot.

"Stop," I croak. I grab the remote from the arm of Cliff's chair and jab at the pause button.

Cliff's eyebrows draw together. "Everything okay?"

"Sorry," I mutter, immediately aware that I am not being normal. But the intensity of his stare is not helping me control the heartbeat pounding against my eardrums. "I just—it's fine—sorry." The second apology feels like too much.

Cliff creaks out of his seat and makes his way to an actual minifridge I hadn't noticed before. From it he pulls a Supershops brand water.

I crack the cap and let the liquid flow into me and cool me from within before resting the bottle on my overheating forehead. I shouldn't have actually focused. I should have just zoned out and not have been thinking thoughts and feeling things all the time. That's the life hack everyone else has tapped in to.

"Was it something in the video?" His eyes are still darting across my face with concern.

This can't be how this is going. I'm trying to get him to like me, not pity me. I shake my head too hard. "I'd like to challenge the test now. As fun as it is to see this company's productions, I have quite a bit of work I'd like to get to."

"It doesn't work that way. I have to sign off on you watching the video." He smiles sheepishly. "This isn't high school."

And those words hit something deep inside me too. I don't think I physically respond to it, but somehow he must sense my reaction, because he stops what he's writing—literally puts down his pen—and leans closer to me.

"Are you sure you're okay?" His voice is soft. It makes me feel like I'm one of those butterflies museums pin under glass.

"Yes," I tell him. "I think I'm just . . . This week is not me at my best, and I'm feeling guilty about everything. I just want to do well." I can't quite look him in the eye.

Cliff's mouth forms a line. Then he goes to his desk and shuffles some papers until he produces a pamphlet. He holds it out for me so I can read the title: *Anxiety and the Workplace.*

I cross my arms so the pamphlet has no place to land. "I don't need that."

"I'm just trying to help." His voice is gentle. I remind myself that this is fake corporate concern, which can so easily be turned against me.

"If you're implying I have some masked issues, everyone in this office does. I mean, you have a pretty high toy-to-adult ratio going on in your office here, but I was polite enough not to point it out."

"Until now." He raises a brow, but a smirk starts at the corner of his mouth. It gives me hope that we can brush this off as a joke.

"Right. I'm just saying, one might think you have a Peter Pan issue or something, but I doubt you have any pamphlets about that."

Redness spreads from under Cliff's beard, moving to his temples, and his gaze falls to the floor.

It's so odd to regret words the moment you've spoken them. There's just something he brings out in me. It feels too comfortable.

"Sorry," I say, and I try to convey just how sincere I am. "I didn't mean that. I just meant . . . Let me put it this way: If you were seeking mental health advice, would you really source that information from Supershops Incorporated? I mean, would any employee want their employer helping them with their mental health when they've done so much to harm it?"

A single chuckle escapes him. "As a representative of Supershops Incorporated, of course I believe this is the best company in the world. But let's say, theoretically, I agreed with you that it's not the greatest with benefits." He's still trying to meet my eyes, but I avoid him by staring at the Lego Bowser on his desk. "I get it if Supershops has let you down in the past, but you've never worked with me before."

His words hang between us, simple and true. He's asking me to trust him.

Trust can be dangerous.

But, I remind myself, it will only be for four weeks. For now, I need to focus on doing whatever it takes to keep my job.

"That's fair," I say. And then I force a smile. "Thanks. Could you, uh, not tell anyone about this—"

"Not tell anyone what?" He winks. "And since none of this happened, I guess we should finish the movie. If you're up for it?"

I nod, so he leans over me to grab the remote back. The warmth of his body radiates toward me for a brief second, before he's back in his seat and the light of the TV flashes on once more.

I try to watch with full concentration, but my fingers keep jittering against my leg and I keep peeking his way. Next time I encounter Cliff, I need to be more careful. Most important, I need to stay in control.

Because with him, it's too easy.

Dos and Donuts

THE MORNING HAS just settled after the chaos hour of people marching around to caffeinate, put lunch bullshit in the fridge, and pretend to care about Marsha's opinion of the TV show she watched last night with her husband. Armin slipped in about fifteen minutes late, with bloodshot eyes and a pale forehead, all recorded by Rhonda.

I take a long swig of coffee and swish it around in my mouth to warm my tongue, still cottony from the wine last night. I tried not to, but it was the meeting with Cliff. Every time I closed my eyes on the bus home, I saw *her*. Specifically, her face when she realized my lie...

I need to focus. Today is a new day. Today will be better.

When I passed Caitlin's desk this morning on the way to my own, I saw she had several documents open; she's probably working on ideas for the multi-unit meeting. I should be doing the same, but this particular battle might already be lost. Coming up with ideas is the easy part. It's the speaking-in-front-of-the-group piece—all their beady eyes and dry expressions zooming in on me—that always sends me into a panic and trips me up.

I'm just going to have to beat the system from the side.

As if on cue, a DM dings onto my screen from Caitlin to Rhonda, and I am all too eager to read it.

> Hey, remember to send me the May inventory data today and then Jolene tomorrow?

Understanding dawns on me. No wonder Caitlin's been so fast lately! "Can you give me the leg up again this month?" Caitlin had asked Rhonda yesterday. I couldn't figure out how she was managing to complete her spreadsheet only an hour after the data arrived, but holy shit, Rhonda's been giving her a sneak peek. What a sad, petty little place this is.

At least I have a leg up of my own this round. I switch to Gregory's inbox—with caution this time, as I am not mentally prepared for the depravity I might cross—and sure enough, the data from all the branches arrived last night. He hasn't even sent it on to Rhonda yet!

Caitlin's responsible for A to M in this grid, and I, L to Z. It's going to be glorious when I complete mine first, even with no "advantage."

I just can't believe they've stooped to this flat-out method of sabotage. And Caitlin was so brazen about asking; clearly, they've been doing this for a while. If they're keeping the monthly inventory grids from me, what else could they be hiding?

I click into Rhonda's inbox. And holy hell, it's awful here. It's a sea of red flags marking emails as "to-do," but aside from that, there's barely any organization whatsoever. It's appalling how much vital information she has access to that she hasn't shared.

There is one subfolder with a curious title: *Things to Figure Out*.

I click it open.

Every email is from Gregory. A whole collection of requests, some dating back months. And she hasn't done them. He asked her to digitize several archives and to create online versions of common documents. She's replied to him, On it :), but I can't find any evidence that she's touched a thing.

I peer over my cubicle wall. She's filling out a hard copy of the EAE schedule with a pencil as she munches on an apple. "Drat," she says, as she picks up the only physical eraser in the office.

Back in her inbox, I see last month's corporate credit card statement has come through for the card she reported missing. I have to stifle a giggle. Whoever stole Miss Rhonda Staples's company card somehow managed to charge $64.12 to the Supershops Liquor Depot the day before the account was closed. Bold of them to use it where you can get a company discount. No wonder HQ flagged it as suspicious. Did Rhonda accidentally charge a personal expense and then report it stolen? Maybe that's why she seemed a bit cagey when Gregory asked.

Beneath her emails is a folder that contains her desk phone's log records. She's on that thing all day long, so I quickly skim through it. Mostly she's talking to other department heads or to Gregory. But one odd pattern draws the eye. Every day, like clockwork, she calls the same outside number at least four times. And every single time, it's marked as unanswered. I scroll back at least seven months and it seems almost ritualistic—like she's calling a ghost.

It's probably nothing, but I pull a Post-it from my drawer and write the number down.

I shift to Caitlin's inbox next. Unlike Rhonda, she's got folders for *everything*. And subfolders inside of those folders. I start to wonder if she makes a new folder for every piece of mail she receives. Then I come across one with the title *Passwords*.

I open that bitch up so fast—and *ding ding ding!* It's a freaking folder full of her passwords for work. She emails them to her personal box monthly. Her most recent one from April 13 reads:

WORK EMAIL AND LOGIN: Iamworthy44
INVENTORY SPREADSHEET: Iambeautiful19*
WORK FOLDER: Iamagoddess19*

Please let me hold it together. Let my cackling at her expense stay inside my heart. My mouth twitches, threatening a chuckle. She's actually typing this stuff to herself several times a day? No wonder she's so cocky. Then my excitement withers; obviously I can't use her passwords to actually *send* anything. She would definitely notice that, and the goal is to not get fired. But now I can at least log in to her locked folders.

I quickly add the passwords to the Post-it note, while glancing from side to side to make sure no one sees. Not all spies get the glamour of one Jean Adler heavy breathing outside Gregory's office while wiping dandruff from his glasses.

"Hello again, everyone."

I nearly vault out of my seat from shock, half shoving the Post-it under my keyboard. Cliff is striding around the corner with a familiar yellow box in his hands. He's wearing a blue plaid shirt that looks really soft. His smile is not quite bright enough to counter the furrowed brows and frowns he's getting in return. "I brought some mini donuts from my favorite place," he proclaims.

Crickets in response.

Cliff's smile is hesitant and small. "Just wanted to say hi again. I'm looking forward to getting to know you all."

A message flashes on my screen, from Caitlin to Garret:

Please lord, let me hold my cringe.

"I'll just leave them over here." Cliff's voice loses its spark with each word. His shoulders round as he places the box on the communal table near the pods.

Finally, Caitlin breaks the silence. "You got us little donuts, aww! You're so sweet."

Cliff looks up sharply, clearly delighted. Too bad. I thought he might be beyond falling for Caitlin's fake bullshit.

"I hope you enjoy them." He tilts his chin toward the name plaque on her cubicle. "Caitlin, is it? Glad to meet you." Then he raises his voice a little and turns in a half circle so he's not got his back to anyone. "I'm going to be booking meetings with each of you over the next week. I just want to get to know more about you and your roles here. It's really an open mic for you to share anything." At the blank stares, he clears his throat. "So, just wanted to come by again, so you know the meeting request isn't spam or anything bad." He points to himself. "I'm a real guy on the fourth floor and my door is always open."

Expressionless sets of eyeballs, including my own, peer at him like emojis.

"And these donuts are real too," he adds. His chuckle mixes with the sound of keyboards frantically typing—and so the gossip mill begins. I feel pain in an unknown part of my body on his behalf. But then Cliff locks eyes with me and his expression brightens. "Jolene, hey!"

All my pity for him vanishes in an instant.

I catch Caitlin smirking, and she shifts her gaze from Cliff to me. My skin tightens as more eyes tilt in my direction.

I give Cliff a small, curt nod. I can't even muster a smile. He doesn't seem to register the vibes I'm giving off, because he makes his way to my desk and leans an arm against my cubicle wall. The sweet scent that permeated his office has followed him here, and everything in me seems to liquefy.

"Can you meet me by my office after work? We can take the parkade elevator from there."

A nod is all I can muster as I sink farther in my chair, willing it to absorb me like another random mucus stain. Cliff should know that you don't give the fucking vultures anything while you're in the ring. At best, he's reminded everyone that we know each other because of my mandatory training. But at *worst*... The last thing I need is my fellow professionals picturing me having sex, which is a thing people do when they think two people are dating.

Then he leans over a touch more into my cube's space and points a finger toward my desk. "Hey, can I have that Post-it?"

My stomach nearly drops onto the carpet. My head whips toward my keyboard, where the incriminating yellow paper I'd shoved under it is poking out.

Then I realize Cliff's finger is actually pointing at the block of unused notes. I shove the whole thing toward him, too relieved to trust myself to speak. He takes a piece from the top as well as the pen that had nearly rolled off the corner of my desk and holds them up to my cube wall so he can scribble a quick note.

"Well, it was nice to see you all," he announces to the room. "I'll go back to my cave now." He holds his head high, but his shoulders have a slump to them as he walks over to the donut box and presses the note on top of it.

More crickets as he disappears down the hallway, the blue jeans schedule sheet on the bulletin board flapping in his wake.

A split second after he's cleared the room, it's like someone's hit the on button. Chairs push back, footsteps descend upon the box. Rhonda,

Armin, and Caitlin are the first to arrive on the scene, pulling the lid back and tearing into the little gourmet treats.

Heat burns through my stomach as I watch them pick the box clean like hyenas. Jean Adler scrunches his face so close to the box that I'm sure there's a powdered dandruff flavor being made before our eyes.

"These are from that new place," Armin says as he pops one in his mouth. "I'm not saying they're good, but I've just found the will to live."

Caitlin places a hand on his shoulder. "You have to stop pulling all-nighters. You're too old to be gaming like that."

He blinks through his puffed eyes. "I wasn't online last night."

"Has he booked a meeting with you yet?" Marla asks Caitlin.

Caitlin huffs. "Not yet, but I've got plenty to say." The insistent way Caitlin glances at Armin makes acid burn in my stomach. But both their gazes draw to me too quick. I drop my eyes, but not in time.

Caitlin makes a big show of taking her hand off Armin's shoulder as she hardens her stare at him. She continues. "What's weird is he's trying to act like he's our friend, when we all know what he's really here for."

But they don't know the half of it. I stare, imploding inside, when a message from Cliff appears on my screen.

Cliff: Hey, sorry if I assumed—no pressure if you don't want to carpool today. I should've confirmed via email.

The pit in my stomach hardens as I picture him, typing to me alone from his trinket-filled office after that embarrassing display. He's the only person who's been nice to me for no reason here. And I'm a venti-sized pile of shit.

Jolene: *I still want to! Sorry if I seemed off.*
Cliff: No need to apologize. See you later then.

I type: Cool. Hit delete. Type: Thanks. Hit delete. Rotate between the two twice more until *not replying* becomes my only option with the time that's passed.

The swarm is beginning to dissipate from the donut box, so I stand up and head over. However, there's nothing left—these animals have picked it clean.

The Post-it Cliff left on top reads: *Not Poison ;)*

I peel it off. I take it back to my desk and stuff it in my locked drawer along with the more incriminating one containing the passwords.

Caitlin finishes off the last bite of her second donut and says, "He could've sprung for full-sized ones."

Bunch of dickheads.

Music Taste Is Raunch Rock

CLIFF'S ALREADY GOT his coat on when I meet him at his office, and he's shutting his computer down. "Ready?" he asks with a strained smile as he marches up to where I'm lingering just outside the threshold.

I nod and force a smile back, stiff and unnatural on my lips. We make our way to the parkade wordlessly, our footsteps echoing off the concrete that encompasses the stairwell.

Great. This awkward-as-shit vibe wasn't exactly the point of my agreeing to carpool.

Inside his car, the scent of dog has been replaced by something tropical. The tree that was hanging on the mirror last time I was in here has been replaced with a bright yellow one. But more important, the console doesn't have the dust or trash it did on Monday either. Oh my god, Cliff tidied his car for me—my throat thickens, and I try to swallow around it—and I was a whole asshole to him today.

The car starts in a swift churn. "Off we go." His forced brightness hollows me out. It takes him three frustrated grunts as he taps his corporate card against the gate pass before the barrier finally opens.

As it pulls upward, a honk sounds behind us. I glance over my shoulder and see Rhonda staring back from above her fuzzy zebra-print steering wheel.

I can't help the laugh that escapes. It's like she's a satire of herself in a parkade.

Cliff's mouth twists. "I've only been here for eight days, and she's already honked at me twice. I love her consistency."

I raise a hand to my chest and clutch my fake pearls. "Are you giving out HR secrets? I'm honored."

Finally, he flashes the first real grin I've seen since the donut incident. "Au contraire. Rhonda's horn trigger is no secret."

I chuckle again, and the air loosens between us. "All right," I say.

"More shop talk. I've always wanted to know—and this is probably going back to your HR schooldays—how often does the average employee spend moaning about the thermostat?"

"It's like you knew that thermostat moaning was the topic of my grad school thesis." His hands shift on the steering wheel as he flashes a grin.

"I mean it was sort of obvious," I reply.

"But, hey—while we're still talking shop . . . I wanted to bring this up. I'm sorry if I acted too familiar in front of everyone today. I know it's sort of weird, me being HR. Especially since you're also trying to work things through with your colleagues." His arm flexes as he changes gears, but he keeps he gaze on the road. "I guess I was thinking it would be good if more people in the office knew it's okay to be friendly with me, like you are. But I should've thought about how that would affect you."

"Oh." I look at him sincerely. Sure, I was short with him, but it's that he saw how uncomfy I was—understood why. This guy may be more perceptive than the average bear. "Cliff. Thank you for saying that. But I also didn't need to be such a dong about it. I mean, you're doing me a favor, reducing my exposure to bus-bound fecal matter."

"Even still . . ." He shakes his head. "I guess, I worked for a long time in a job where I was really close with my coworkers. It's weird, suddenly feeling like Freddy Krueger whenever I walk into a room." His brows fold together. "Not a fair excuse, I know. So I was at least a partial dong today. A weenie." His flashes me an entreating grin, and I accept it. It seeps through my warming skin. "Being colleagues and carpool buddies is a little trickier than imagined."

"True," I agree.

"Maybe we need some ground rules," he offers. "Like, nothing we discuss here should influence how we do our jobs there."

"So in here I'm allowed to be myself, raw and uncut?"

"That's encouraged."

"Thank fuck," I say, and he chuckles. "Just making sure. I'm big on following rules to a T, so if there are any exceptions, beyond the normal ones, let me know now."

"Fair enough," he smirks. "Maybe we should make a list?"

I break eye contact as I remember the list I already have stashed in my desk drawer, particularly the last item on it: *Get Cliff to like me*. My plan seems so obvious now.

I clear my throat to stifle down the guilt. "By the way, I haven't met too many HR people, but you seem like the very best one in the world—insert other miscellaneous compliments here."

He laughs again.

I put my hand to my chest, even though he's watching the road. "Cliff, that was super genuine. Did you always know this was your life's calling, or was it a fallback career if you didn't make it as a professional Warhammer guy?"

The car comes to a stop in front of a traffic light, and he looks directly at me, lids narrowing into a probing stare. It's hard to know what he's thinking, so I lean back an inch and raise a questioning eyebrow. His mouth curls as he draws his gaze back to the road.

"What exactly do you think Warhammer is?"

"Something that involves pelts?"

He shrugs. "Actually, that's not totally wrong."

I nod once. "I glanced into a mall store once that had the Warhammer sign above some figurines, so I'm basically an expert."

"It's really hard to tell if you're making fun of me or being sincere."

I grin. "I actually mean it. It's cool how you're into things. So many people don't have anything they like and they just walk around making life miserable." I stare out the window.

"How about you? What's your dream?"

"I stopped dreaming," I blurt out, too quickly—too honestly. He doesn't respond right away, and I internally wince. How can someone just casually ask that kind of question to someone? Why did my answer have to sound so heavy? So *specific*.

I dare a glance at him, and he's looking at me with the same soft expression from his office, and no—no way are we repeating my meeting breakdown. "Jolene—"

"When I was a little girl in a small mountain town," I interrupt loudly, "my father and maman took me to the most wonderful place on Earth. It had just opened up in our area, and people lined up from miles away. There were sandwiches made to everyone's specifications. Candy in bulk. A makeup counter filled with possibility and reinvention." I sigh wistfully, for maximum effect. "If that little girl had known that one day she'd work in that very place's western regional office, she would've shed tears of joy to fill a river."

"Okay." Cliff sighs. "That was quite the display."

"Thank you." I nod once. "Feel free to report my dedication back to headquarters."

His grin falls flat like a stack of cards, and he shoots me an exasperated stare. "Another rule: there will be no favoritism for my carpool buddy. No matter how hard you ass kiss."

I nod silently as a new wave of guilt hits. Cliff might be too honest for me—certainly too honest to be successful. And here I am, just as full of shit. It should be perfect.

"On that note…" He grabs his phone off the console between us and hands it to me. "As passenger, you get to pick the music."

I dutifully take it, even as dread begins to bubble in my gut. I don't know enough for this task. These days, I tend to avoid music altogether. Even if there's just one song in the world you can't listen to in public without panic taking over, it's surprising how much it can sneak into your life. Malls, bars, even offices, play music, and the odds of that one song playing go up every time I leave the house. I'm aware people judge you for what sounds you like to hear, but I'd rather jump out the window than have Cliff know this specific weakness of mine.

I scroll through a random playlist and pick an album cover that looks neutral and socially acceptable. Hold my breath as I hit play and hope for the best.

A high voice screeches, *"I need you to come deep into me."*

… I've made a terrible judgment call.

Cliff's knuckles whiten on the steering wheel, and I'm pretty sure he's looking at me but can't confirm since I refuse to look at anything other than my hands.

The lyrics reach: *"Make it deep and messy."*

My insides dissolve. I fully believe in my heart that I've lost the will to go on and my body has turned to ash.

Cliff belts out a deep roaring laugh that shocks the dust pile formerly known as me. "Okay, you almost had me. Nice HR test. But again—not going to rattle me."

I chuckle, but it's obviously forced. Thankfully, he's laughing too hard to notice. "Just keeping you on your toes." I look out the window and see we've reached my road. "Oh, by the way, could you pick me up at seven tomorrow? I have to make coffee for everyone."

Cliff's gaze lands on me. "Yes, that's nice of you."

"It's no biggie, just joined the Coffee Club."

I gather my purse and lunch bag. He eyes my laptop. I pretend I need it for paperwork, but really, I've been using it to watch Netflix. Another thing HR guys shouldn't know, off duty or not. "Can I help with your stuff?"

"Oh god, no. I have, like, two things. Plus, we should probably draw the line at going into each other's apartments."

Cliff nods. "Good point. I'll add it to the list."

I slide out the door. "Thanks again." I wave.

Miley spots me as soon as I'm through the building door. I give her a head shake—not having it today. Futile.

The tap on my back causes instant dread. "Is that man your boyfriend?"

I sigh as I turn around. I'm about to kindly tell her to mind her business, when I notice her fisted hands and how messy her hair is. But worst of all is her face. Her eyes are wide, and it's like nobody has properly looked at her at all today.

"He's sort of a coworker," I say, and immediately regret placing such an elusive answer in Miley's hands.

"What's his job? Do you like him? Is he your boss?"

The stairwell door shuts and rushed high-heeled steps click toward us. Miley's face drops in a flash.

Miley's mother rounds the stairwell and doesn't look up from the phone she's stabbing with pointed-nail clicks. Her outfit is entirely black: leggings, thigh-high boots, and an oversized sweater that hangs off one shoulder. Her makeup would make my mom proud with its drama, and it smells like she just applied an intense coat of hair spray to keep her dark bun in place.

Miley watches her but doesn't speak. She walks halfway past us—and is she not going to acknowledge her daughter? But then she turns toward Miley and says, "I have to head out. Please don't spend the night bothering the neighbors with your problems again. I got you a phone." She then smiles at me apologetically before continuing onward. At the same time, Miley's chest drops, like she's a deflating balloon.

I have no idea what to say or do, so I end up blurting out, "Hey, Miley, the other day you asked my favorite animal. I thought about it, and I'm going with zebra."

"That's a weird choice, Jolene." She steps toward the stairs. "I'm going to watch TikToks on the stoop." She pauses to give me a cheeky grin. "You can fill me in on this work man another day."

I roll my eyes, but I can't hold back the huff of laughter. "Night, Miley."

Armin & Rhonda EFFs

BEFORE WORK EVEN starts, the morning is already going decently. I got in early with Cliff, and during the ride I managed to get him to explain the history of Warhammer and how measuring tape is somehow involved. He was focused enough on driving that he didn't even notice my eyes glazing over.

In the office I made the coffee without burning it. It didn't smell great, but it worked, and both Jean Adler and Joy Chan, the other early birds, have already enjoyed a cup, or at least consumed a cup.

More important, I've prepared three documents to share with Rhonda. With the morning ready, I move on to my private audits. I check Caitlin's emails first, but nothing notable appears. Armin has a note from Cliff asking him to schedule a check-in. Shit, I hope Caitlin hasn't actually convinced him to turn on me.

Next, I check on Rhonda. There's a new note from Gregory, requesting that she make a virtual logbook for the quarterly reports—or, to be more accurate, a follow-up on the request he sent last month. I double-check and find the original note sitting in her *Things to Figure Out* folder.

At this rate, there might be no saving her in time.

One other new message in her inbox pops out:

Congratulations Rhondabear1960,
You're ready to start meeting people in the area. Welcome to Silver Timings.
 We've added some exciting profiles for you to explore.

I close out immediately upon seeing three of the same type of red-faced man in a too close/low profile. One of them has his knee on a canoe to show he's outdoorsy, but his shorts sit tucked around his junk to show he's violating as well.

Enough of that, I tell myself. But I am a masochist, I guess, because less than two seconds later, I head to the website and search for Rhondabear1960.

Her profile picture shows her with a big golden brooch on her blouse, pink blush smeared like sharp lines on her cheeks, and her hair curled out with even more bounce than usual. The background looks familiar, and I flash back to the work conference three years ago where the photo must've been taken. There was a banquet and a dance floor. I ended up at a table with people from Ontario whom I didn't know, since I didn't get invited to sit with others from our office. When the DJ played a Drake song and way too many office-panted men with tucked-in shirts started toward the dance floor, I got the fuck out of there and retreated to my hotel room with the two queen beds: a drinking bed and a sleeping bed. That's where Rhonda's profile photo is from.

Her caption reads: I'm the self-sufficient single mom of one very busy adult son. Looking for someone to fill my evenings and weekends with. I like to converse, sew, and plan parties. No sex freaks! I want someone to spend time with me for me. The sex will come after.

Whoa. Rhonda said the quiet part of dating profiles out loud. I stifle a giggle, even though the office is still pretty much empty. But just below it reads:

Companionship is all I want. Looking for someone willing to spend time with me. We can shop, go to movies, and all the other things life has to offer. Would be able to spend the holidays with you and your family. Grandkids very welcome. I would love to cook a big meal for them or do crafts together! I'm serious! Last Christmas I had too much food and no mouths.

Last Christmas, all I recall is Rhonda's relentless bragging about her festive plans. She said Carl had booked her and him a week in Banff, where he took her to the fancy fondue restaurant on Main Street. At the time, it sounded a little *American Psycho,* but did she actually make it up?

I almost miss Rhonda pounding into the room behind me with her giant embroidered bag while her profile's papering my screen. I snap the page shut just in time.

"Good morning," I say, way too brightly.

For a moment she hesitates, odd expression on, before a smile forms on her face and she replies, "Good morning." She takes a folder and heads to the copy room.

The manual clock strikes 8:15. Caitlin and Armin trickle in and settle into their desks, giving my turned-on monitor and nearly empty coffee mug a double take as they pass me, like me being early is some marvel.

Rhonda returns holding a stack of freshly photocopied papers. She goes over to Armin and proffers them.

"Morning, dear. I've finished the Q2 forms for you."

Armin frowns as he takes the pages. "Rhonda, we talked about this. Can't you just send me this grid in an email? When you give it to me like this, I have to retype everything and it takes twice as long."

"It's easier for me to work on a hard copy," Rhonda says, nonplussed.

"Easier for you, maybe. Is it easier for all of us, though?" Armin splays out his hands toward Caitlin like he's garnering support.

No support comes.

His gaze crawls toward me. I hunch lower in my chair, glad that I have my earphones on even though I'm not playing anything, and do my best impression of a focusing-on-work worker.

When I peep at him next, he's riffling through another stack. "Why are you printing so much anyway? Why did you need to carbon copy this email from Marsha in finance, when we already have the digital version? Can't you see this madness? The environment suffers when you don't stop yourself from printing."

"Oh, stop." Rhonda squares her shoulders. "You young people talk about saving the environment but then don't do anything but send a tweet that's all for show."

Caitlin nods way too hard. "That's such a good point."

Rhonda's chest puffs up. "Thank you, dear." She returns her focus to Armin. "You kids today spend more time trying to make people miserable online than making yourselves happy in real life. My son's your generation, but he hardly ever touches his phone."

Every time Rhonda and Armin disagree, it always devolves into a debate about generational differences. We then hear about how great Rhonda's son is.

And we all suffer.

I pretend to stare at my screen, stone-faced.

Armin grates his bottom lip with his teeth. "But seriously, why are you printing so much?" He gestures at the many, many stacks of papers on her desk. "All this information exists online, and it would be easier for everyone if it stayed that way."

"Not for me. Everything came printed before. That's what I'm used to," she mutters as she twists her erasable pen between her palms.

"If you aren't able to keep up with the office, maybe it's time to consider—"

"*Retiring?* Is that what you want?" And oh shit, now Armin has done it. Rhonda splays her hands out on the desk, the five pounds of costume jewelry rings clinking on her fingers as she pushes herself into a standing position—her jaw set, eyes wide as she can make them.

"Goodness, no," Caitlin chimes in, a sickly-sweet smile on her face. "No one wants that."

Armin winces. "Rhonda, I didn't mean—"

"I'd love to," Rhonda interrupts. "My Carl's been *begging* me to. He wants me to have more time to travel and help him when he starts a family. But just because I prefer working on a printout, that doesn't mean I need to be put to pasture. Besides, the tires would fall off this place without me."

Rhonda pushes back her shoulders and takes a heavy breath. Her gaze flows to Caitlin, who still has that fake grin plastered on her face, then to my area. My first impulse is to cower from her attention. Work shouldn't involve the constant danger of other people noticing us.

Then I look down at my desk—at the drawer where my secret list sits inside.

Two of the goals:

—Win over Gregory via his tolerable proxy, Rhonda
—Convince Armin I'm normal/give him no reason to talk to HR
  about me

An idea jangles through my nerves. This could be a good two-birds-with-one-stone situation.

I bolt out of my seat and rip my headphones off. "I can retype the grid for you," I squeal.

Everyone stops. Armin's and Rhonda's wide eyes draw to me at the same speed. Caitlin's smirk slides right off her face.

My pulse pounds as the room blurs. Only their stares glom to me perfectly clear.

"Pardon me, dear?" Rhonda's brows narrow.

Heat rushes through me. Why did I have to do that? "Just . . . I'm sort of caught up with work, so I could retype the grid and Armin can work off that, if it's helpful," I croak. My hands ball into fists as my pulse pounds.

Caitlin inserts, "Yeah, that's a good point. Jolene doesn't have anything going on, really."

I blink as I force my face to remain neutral. My knees feel like Jell-O as I stand pathetically, pinned by their shocked expressions.

"That's very nice of you," Rhonda begins slowly.

Armin shakes his head. "You shouldn't have to do more work, Jolene." He won't quite look at me as he speaks. "Updating the grid is my task."

"It's no trouble! I was actually thinking about archiving all the quarterly reports virtually anyway."

Rhonda's eyebrows dart together. "Did Greg ask you to do this?"

I shake my head. "No, in fact, I was hoping you'd bring up the change to digital logbooks to Greg since he trusts you so much. Why?"

I struggle not to flinch as she searches my face. I have a theory that when you get to be her age, you can smell bullshit better than a fly.

"I just wanted to make sure you'd be on board," I continue quickly. "And if you want, we could make the schedules like that too. Everything, eventually."

She stiffens as my words land. "But how would I ever use them?"

"Well, if you wanted, I could sit down with you and go through it? Like during a quiet time—or I could email you step-by-step instructions." Again, she stiffens, her fingers clenching into little bony fists at the bottom of her blouse. "I'm not trying to overstep. I was already doing it with some of the docs Caitlin and I use, and it just seemed like a good moment to bring it up."

"That would work for me." A tiny threat of a smile creeps into the corners of her lips. "Thank you, Jolene."

"Glad we could find a resolution," Caitlin says, narrowing her eyes at me. With the match officially declared over, we all lower back into our seats. I practically fall into my chair, my skin still flushed.

The DM to Rhonda and Armin appears in an instant.

Caitlin: So tell me that wasn't creepy??

I can't breathe.

Rhonda: Jolene? She's trying to help.
Caitlin: Yeah, maybe.
Caitlin: But when has she ever offered to help, or even joined a conversation? I feel like she's been watching our every move lately.

I feel Armin's eyes tick toward me and my skin goes taut. Admittedly, the creepy factor wasn't something I considered when I tried to enact my plan, and the optics were unfortunate in that sense.

His reply finally flashes across my screen.

Armin: She was just being nice.
Caitlin: Yep. Anyway, I've got lots of work. Best of luck with the nice stalker. You should probably report her before you end up tied up in her apartment, though.

Caitlin clicks the chat closed and starts toward the copy room.

I should log in to her email now and send a message to herself that reads: You are a goddess. It would be the only time getting fired might be worth it.

But at least I've achieved one small victory here. Armin hasn't totally been swayed by Caitlin to join the firing squad against me. I don't think.

Yet, even as the office returns to its normal beat, I still jitter from it all. I do a quick scan of Armin's emails. He still hasn't replied to Cliff's meeting request, but I'll have to keep an eye on that. I've bought myself some time, but not much.

I check Rhonda's again next. She's pulled one email out of the *Things to Figure Out* file and responded to Gregory: Will have this ready by the end of the week :)

When I glance at her, I expect her to look pleased. But instead, she's slouching, staring at the inspirational sayings pinned along the border of her cubicle. After a beat, she picks up her phone. I silently hiss through my teeth. What if she's calling Gregory, or even Cliff in HR, because she believes Caitlin and thinks I'm plotting something?

I quickly click into her phone log and check the number. It's not internal; it's that same number again. This is it: the Ghost Call.

A few moments pass; presumably she is listening to a ringtone. I hold my breath and wait. Only it's like a balloon deflating. Just as her phone records predicted, every time she calls this number it goes unanswered. I hear her receiver placed down with a solemn click.

The curiosity is too much. So before thinking too hard, I grab my desk phone and dial the number from her log.

I make sure my earbuds are plugged into the phone about twenty times, my heartbeat picking up with every drawn-out ring. I check behind me for no good reason. After four rings, the automated voicemail lady voice comes in: *You've reached the mailbox for: Carl Staples. Mailbox is full.*

My heart plummets, matching the drone of the punishing dial tone.

I put down the receiver.

Minor Distractions

AFTER A LUNCHTIME spent eating a ham sammy while solo people-watching at Prince's Island Park, clashing with the crowds of laughing families, ball-busting businessmen, and brightly colored runners, I return and confirm that Rhonda has officially shared my half of the inventory data grid with me, even though Caitlin received her piece yesterday evening. No matter, because I already finished it. Now I just have to wait a believable amount of time to return it.

Caitlin is throwing a plastic container, half full of browning Caesar salad, into the waste bin under her desk. Typical. There's a whole recycling center in the lunchroom, yet she chooses to leave it up to the members of the cleaning service to properly dispose of her mess.

I log in to check if Caitlin's already returned her part of the grid. Instead, I find another email from Cliff asking to schedule a meeting. Unlike Armin, Caitlin's already responded and offered to see him tomorrow.

Fuck.

A DM appears from Caitlin to Garret.

Caitlin: I am so ready for this HR meeting. Have all my talking points prepped.

Caitlin: I don't want to be too obvious, but I have plenty of examples of why I'm a better fit here than Jolene.

Garret: Yeah, be careful to not go overboard. What are you going to say?

Three dots bounce across the screen as Caitlin types. I lean in, my skin cooling, the goose bumps on the back of my wrist matching the ones continuously dancing on the screen.

Before any message appears, the accessible door beeps open, followed by a sleek stroller. "Helloooo!" calls the stroller pusher, also known as Celeste Laird, who is supposed to be on maternity leave for another six months. And unless that baby knows how to file, she must be bringing it to meet us.

Caitlin and Garret both instantly rise from their seats, leaving me in the dark.

The office is a blur of oohs and bright, tender faces, all rushing toward Celeste. I also notice a few stragglers, like Joy and Armin, who are hiding the screen guard and wrist support they each respectively looted from her desk as soon as she'd left.

I sit frozen, still staring at my screen. The three dots in the chat have disappeared. I was *so close* to knowing exactly what she had in store. Why can't we normalize telling babies and the people who love them to fuck off in some polite way?

Rhonda leans over my cubicle wall and says, "Celeste brought her little guy in, isn't that sweet?" She stares pointedly from me to the group of baby fans in case I've lost all six of my senses. Caitlin's already at the stroller, front and center. I smile stiffly but make no move to stand and join them.

Then Gregory stomps out of his office, coffee in hand, rocking his chino fucking pants, and nods directly at me. "Let's go see the baby!"

And it's certain: *not* looking at this little asshole will cost me something.

So much of what I do here has nothing to do with my actual job, yet these little interactions matter *so* much. I trudge out of my seat and make my way toward the shit show. As soon as I reach the coffee-breathed group of people, I lock eyes with the baby and it, predictably, begins to wail.

Celeste picks it up and pats it on the back to soothe it while people continue to ask her boring questions about motherhood, her sleep schedule, and laundry. This little human doesn't even realize the greatness of this: the only time in your life when people will simply ignore your public outbursts. The rest of us must cry without *actually* crying. This child, I learn as Celeste continues to soothe it, is named Thomas. I watch his little eyes dart around the room, taking it all in. Maybe Thomas is just now realizing that eventually he will grow up to spend all his daylight hours under fluorescent lights and water-stained ceiling tiles.

I don't mean to chuckle at that depressing thought, and I stifle it as soon as I can, but that doesn't stop a few eyes from drawing my way while I pretend I didn't just cackle at a technically crying baby.

Then Thomas begins being passed around like a hot burrito. I curl my hands close against my chest and try to back away. When Caitlin takes said bundle, it stops crying in an instant, and her face softens in a way that makes me realize how hard it's been lately. She inhales the top of the baby's head—which is a choice—then smiles and says to Celeste, "So how is being a mom?"

Celeste starts describing things that sound dire as shit. Rhonda, who has taken up a position behind Celeste's left shoulder, nods along while intermittently agreeing or interjecting about how it was with her sweet baby Carl.

Gregory randomly pokes the fucking baby in the belly, and the cries start again in a screeching pitch.

Has anyone ever punched him in the face?

"How was the birth?" Stu for some cursed reason has to ask. I take a step back in order to avoid sticking around for Celeste's answer.

Rhonda flashes me a disapproving stare. Why is it so socially acceptable to discuss a human getting pushed or cut out of a body, yet somehow, it's unprofessional for me to simply *work* rather than hold the tiny person I don't even know, while it's wearing something designed to catch any fecal matter that comes out of it?

I quietly take another step away. And another.

I pass Joey and am almost in the clear when Caitlin loudly says, "Don't take that personally—it's her. We need to catch up about *that* as well."

I lower into my chair, and her fractured message chain greets me on my screen. Who does she think she is? Her cackle rattles with the flash of the burning-out fluorescent above her. It's the cackle of someone who believes herself a goddess.

And that's it!

I check to make sure nobody is around, and thankfully, they're all still at the infant show. I flip to her document folder and type Iamagoddess19* when prompted. I try to stop myself from shaking as my heart pounds into my eardrums.

I click, and in an instant her inventory report covers my screen. It's almost complete. I move a decimal, such a tiny thing. I change a 63 to 64, an easy typo to make if one's not focusing.

My finger hesitates before clicking. I can't *actually* sabotage—it's a different line. Deniability, even to myself, won't be an option.

But as she passes the baby to Garret, I realize there's no telling what she's going to say to manipulate Cliff tomorrow. And there's no telling what else she's done over the years—how much my reputation has been messed with in silent conversations and quiet sabotage.

This is the only thing I can control.

I save the changes and close out.

Milkshake Brings Nothing to Nobody

As I settle into Cliff's car at the end of the day, I can't help but wonder if we'll be doing this again tomorrow, after Caitlin turns him on me and tells him every horrible thing, real or invented—it makes no difference sometimes.

Cliff shoulder checks me as he turns onto the main road. "You all right there?" he asks.

I nod. "Yeah," I say, voice shaky.

I bite the inside of my lip. Now is not the time to act sketchy. He's the fucking HR guy with a unique set of skills to detect if someone is up to no good. He might have taken a course on detecting facial expressions of people who broke into emails. Or maybe he'll determine that I sabotaged Caitlin's grid just by spotting my twitching fingers.

I need to be chill.

Besides, this might be my last chance to convince Cliff I am normal, and worthy of this job, and incapable of any of the awful things Caitlin will undoubtably accuse me of tomorrow.

But once I get myself into a doom spiral, there's no easy way out. It's going to be an Evening of Angst, and I will need booze to survive.

I lean my cheek against the window. After tomorrow, if Caitlin's testimony doesn't get me fired immediately, at the very best Cliff will have to stop this carpooling agreement and I'll be back on the bus. A shame, because this was a pretty nice arrangement, however short-lived. I take a deep breath and soak in the tree-lined streets and small businesses: little cafés and restaurants, boutiques, and a bookstore.

I can sense that Cliff's eyes are still on me, so I think of something to say. "Oh, that's a cool-looking store." I point to a building that's painted bright purple with rainbow accents and an ice-cream-cone-shaped door. It's like a beam of sunshine between the other redbrick storefronts.

"Yeah, Angels," Cliff says as we stop at the intersection beside the building.

A couple of beats of silence tick by, and then Cliff suddenly slaps the steering wheel with his palm. I look at him abruptly.

"Wait." Cliff raises a brow suspiciously, and my heart stops. What the hell? Have I said the exact combo of words for him to know I'm a liar who read his private emails? "You aren't shitting me, are you?"

"What do you mean?" I croak, every cell in my body tense.

"You've never been to Angels? *Never* had one of their shakes?"

Relief floods through me. I almost melt into a puddle in his cushy car seat, but I try to pass it off as a shrug. "I don't drink things unless they'll alter my mood."

"This will alter any mood. If you're telling me you've never tried one, that's unacceptable."

I shake my head. I should've kept my mouth shut.

"The fucking pillar of this city. The best milkshakes in history. You, Jolene Smith, have never been?"

Honestly, I've never been to most places. But that's not normal, so I mutter, "I didn't grow up here. I'm sure they lure most of their customers young."

"Technically, I grew up in the neighborhood just behind there, but the first time I went was as an adult. I never would've gone as a child."

His shoulders tense, and it's the way he says "never" that feels like something more lives behind it. The neighborhood he grew up in is the one my bus drives through: lots of run-down duplexes for former military housing—paint chipped, siding missing. Something swells inside me.

"It's been way too long since I've had a milkshake from Angels," he says wistfully. "We should fix this immediately. What are you doing this evening and can you do ice cream instead?"

I try to picture myself walking into a place like that—bright and sugar scented, music playing in the background, lots of people crowding around tables. I try to picture myself sitting at one of those tables with another human, then with Cliff specifically. "I don't, uh, I don't do . . . things," I blurt out, my words turning into confusing garble against my will.

He lowers his chin, bashful. "Oh, sure, no worries." And I instantly regret my words. It's the softness in his voice that grates me, like he thinks he's the one who overstepped.

Great. That could've been my only opportunity to neutralize the meeting tomorrow.

So I plaster on a fake smile and dial up the charm. "That was a joke. If you, a grown-ass man, would like a milkshake, then I think that's a wonderful idea."

Except I can't charm for shit.

Still, he chuckles, and there's a softness in his gaze that lightens something inside me. "Wonderfully put."

"But I'm paying."

Cliff parks and we make our way inside. The place is a retro wonder, with metal-rimmed tables, a real jukebox, and a checkered floor. As we walk up to the counter to order, Cliff pulls a well-stamped Frequent Shaker card out of his wallet with his head held high.

At the register, Cliff cheats his way into paying by insisting it's because he's a member. I roll my eyes and go to grab a booth while we wait. It all feels so normal—*I'm* being so normal. But then I take a breath, and the scent of fake cherry mixed with deep fryer hits my nostrils in such a specific way that it bowls me over.

And just like that, I'm back in middle school. Ellie's holding a mint chocolate chip cone and telling me we have a whole weekend ahead where we don't have to see anyone from school, and we can watch *Buffy* and stay in our own little bubble with *Mario Kart*.

It's so strange, being caught in a memory like this: I want so badly to go back there and stay, but also to run away. Because I know what happens to those girls. My skin tightens with unease, and I'm sure I'm the worst person to ever sit in this booth.

"Hey," Cliff says as he slides into the booth across from me. I blink, and I'm back in the present, hands clenched around the edge of the table like I'm trying to shatter it. "I know it's a weird vibe, but I swear, the ice cream is worth it."

I shake my head quickly. "I think I'm just thirsty."

He stands to get me a cup of water, and I use the opportunity to stare at my hands and will myself to hold things together. This is getting old. I should be able to do this. I can be a person.

Cliff comes back with my water and I take a grateful sip. "So," I begin, "you grew up here? Are your parents still in town?" I can ask friendly, nonthreatening questions.

He shifts, though, like I've asked something hard. "I mean, maybe. I don't really know much about them."

"Oh," I say, unsure what to do with this information.

Cliff shrugs, an attempt to brush away the tension, but it's not convincing. "My grandma raised me. She actually worked at the gas station right over there." He gestures out the window toward the Fas Gas across the street. "I'd get free hot dogs when they were on the spinners too long to sell, so it wasn't too shabby, as long as you don't care about meat temperature danger zones."

I try to imagine a child-sized Cliff with messy golden-honey hair and skinned knees, sitting across the street with his grandma eating expired hot dogs. My chest swells, pressing against a space that's typically hollow.

"What?" Cliff kicks the edge of his foot against mine.

I force a smile. "Just picturing child HR Cliff telling people at the playground they need to display positive communication cues and drawing org charts in chalk."

"Wow, that's exactly accurate. How were you able to do that?"

"Just a hunch." I take another sip of water. "Did you go to college here?"

He nods, and I wait for him to elaborate, but he just taps idly at the table with his pointer finger.

"So have you ever lived anywhere else?" I try again.

"Yes. Vancouver." It's not rude, exactly, but he still doesn't offer more, and I get the sense I'm prying where he doesn't want me.

And this is starting to feel like a bad date, even though neither of us wants it to be. It feels like I won't know what to say ever again. How can anyone be comfortable with another person when their brains are also always working? I rack my mind for something safe. "So, tell me more about Warhammer stuff."

His eyelids droop. "Jolene, you can stop the fake Warhammer routine. I know you zone out when I talk about it." Then his expression turns cheeky. "This morning, I slipped in that we should plot to murder someone, and you nodded aggressively."

"That's not fair." I put my palm to my chest. "I *was* listening, but I didn't want to make you feel weird for having a murder plan, since you're new and all." Our eyes lock, and I can see the silent laughter in his. I internally breathe a sigh of relieve that we are on safe ground again. "Anyway, now we're talking. Who of the people at work would you kill?"

He coughs, eyes going wide. "What the hell?"

"I know, I know, you're new—hardly know us. But just go with your gut. Might be fun to compare answers after a while working there."

"I just—" He swallows hard. "I don't want to kill anyone?"

I point a finger at him. "Okay, but say it was for a billion dollars. And you don't have to do the killing. You just pick the person who needs to go."

He leans closer, flattening his hands on the table to look right at me. His bar soap scent wraps around me like a hug.

"I don't care that much about money," he says. "I have what I need."

I can't help the disappointed sigh I let out. "Oh. You're one of those."

"One of what?"

"People who are full of shit."

A sharp bark of laughter escapes him. "No, it's true. If I were to kill someone, it wouldn't be for money."

"Okay, be boring," I declare, leaning back into the booth seat. "But I think we need to normalize being comfortable roasting people. Everyone is way worse than they pretend to be. We should start discussing it openly—it might be a good way to connect people."

"Maybe, but I don't think I can add that idea to any team-bonding flyers."

"Coward."

His stare lingers. I let it.

"Fine." He sighs. "I'll give you an answer, but only if we never speak of it again."

"Deal," I agree, not even bothering to hide my delight.

He pulls a pen from his shirt pocket and grabs a napkin from the dispenser on the table. "I will write my opening choice below. But then you must destroy it."

"I never noticed you carry a pen."

"A gift from my grandma that's surprisingly useful."

I wait patiently as he scribbles something onto the napkin and then pushes it toward me like we're making an illegitimate deal. I flip the napkin, look at him, look back down, and shake my head in wordless disappointment.

He splays his hands defensively. "What? Robin Winters is a legitimate choice."

I stare evenly. "There are so many better options. He's so unnoticeable. How can he be your choice?"

"Come on. He's perfect. He's already sent three reply-alls to the office-wide emails that are just 'Thanks.' You don't need to acknowledge every email. He stares me down when I walk by. And worst of all, he sits on the can and reads a newspaper for a whole hour with his pants down, and the stall door is open a bit like it's his personal bathroom. He just sits there, and we all have to see it."

My jaw goes slack. "Brilliant."

Cliff winces. "I shouldn't have said all that."

"I loved everything about what just happened." I reach across the table, then suddenly catch myself—was I going to touch his hand? That would be very weird. I turn the motion into grabbing the napkin to look at the name again. "I think that we can be friends after all."

"This is a terrible way to start a friendship," Cliff moans.

"Order sixty-four," the cashier calls.

He instantly brightens. "Okay, no more murder talk in front of the innocent milkshakes."

He shifts out of the booth, leaving me to wonder how the hell my plan to convince Cliff I'm normal led us there. But he was smiling, and I can feel the corners of my own lips pushing up too.

He returns holding two glasses of Tiger-Tastic ice-cream shakes. Large scoops of creamy orange ice cream peek from the tops of the cool metal cups, with whipped cream surrounding all the orange in fluffy bursts.

He waits and watches as I take my first sip. And shit, I have to look at the ceiling, because this is the best thing I've ever tasted.

"What the hell is this? It's amazing."

He claps his hand against the table. "It's good, right?"

"It's the sweet nectar that has just renewed my every hope and dream. I feel like I just got my billion-dollar colleague-offing payout."

He gives me the most mischievous grin, and oh, I like this side of him. "See, you just had to trust me."

And my core freezes—not just from the shake. Trust needs to be two ways for it to work. I take another sip, and when I look up, Cliff's staring at me with a curl in his lips. "What?"

"I realized what it is about you. I almost never know what you're going to say—a surprisingly rare trait."

"You say that like it's a good thing." I lower my chin.

"It is." His stare deepens and his elbows slip a millimeter closer to me on the table. "Makes life so much more interesting. I'd love for you to accompany me to the DMV or something normally unbearable just to Jolene it up."

This makes me laugh for real. "Cliff, I'm the least exciting person I know, but thanks, mate." I bite my straw.

He taps his fingers on the table. "I can't see how that's true."

"See it," I huff.

And I realize that he's been looking straight into my eyes through this whole conversation, and normally that would make me feel uncomfortable, but I forgot to be insecure. Maybe things are easier with him because I know what the point of this friendship is. Maybe it's easy because I know it will be over soon anyway.

My stomach churns at all the things I'm hiding from him. It would be different if he wasn't so genuine, so open with me.

"So," I say, to drown out my thoughts, "tell me, why are you so against leaving stall doors open in bathrooms?"

He shakes his head. "Please, I want to be able to eat."

We do eat, and I continue badgering him about his choice, and as the evening progresses and our conversation flows, I forget to worry about Caitlin, the grid, the meeting, any of it.

I forget to worry about what's going on in his head.

Or mine.

Missedcakes

I STARE DOWN THE scratched-up door to our office floor, willing myself to open it. Each dent tells the story of someone knocking it with the paper cart on a different version of the same old day. My hand is heavy as I pull the handle and drag myself into the sterile air that hasn't seen the light of day.

As I make my way to my desk, nobody looks up. The drone of the computer fans matches the blank stares the humans give the machines in return. I'm invisible, until Rhonda's gaze drifts to me—it's just a small nod, but that's more than I usually get.

I give her a small grin in return.

Armin is zoning out, presumably still working on the same accounting grids he's been staring at but hasn't altered in a significant way for days. If you don't look too closely, he appears to be the busiest unconscious guy around.

Caitlin marches out of the copy room to her desk. She's in high-rise tailored pants with iron-pressed lines my mom would be impressed by. I suppose she wanted to look good for her big meeting with Cliff today.

I tried really hard on the drive in with him this morning, hoping to keep up our vibe from last night. I asked him about some trading cards he had in his car's console, and it was like setting off a firework, how animated he got. I nodded in all the right places, enthusiastic as a clam this time. But the damage Caitlin will do today is out of my control. All I can do is deal with the shrapnel.

I conduct some quick email audits, but it's clear nothing new or notable has happened. Rhonda doesn't even have a single new match on her dating site.

I expand my reading into other departments. It's kind of addicting to read work-related emails about tasks I know nothing about. It's like a bizarro-world version of my department, a puzzle made of several different shapes. And it's also mad how the same tasks get volleyed around departments, going nowhere or being repeated unnecessarily. If I ever suspected my work was pointless, I now can provide evidence.

The wildest part of it all is that it doesn't have to be this way. I follow a trail into some supply chain memo and open some shared documents to track how it's being implemented and—

"Quick question for you, my dear."

A startled gasp escapes me as I register life away from my screen. Holy crap—I somehow missed Rhonda approaching my workspace from behind. I rush to click the window closed.

Her gaze jumps to my monitor, clumps of eyeshadow already gathering in the wrinkles of her eyelids.

She crouches closer. "Is now a good time?"

"Now is great!" I reply, while Caitlin's posture perks toward us in my peripheral vision.

"Great." Her voice lowers. "The digital grid . . . there are a few things I'm not sure how to . . ."

A pang tightens in my chest at her timid stance, her fiddling hands. "Let me come to your desk and we'll go through it together."

As we make our way to her workstation, Caitlin's eyes bulge, somehow still on her screen yet watching us.

I walk Rhonda through navigating the document, and I can tell she's really trying to learn. She asks good questions, does things twice to be sure she gets it. I'm going over the formatting tool when I feel it. Rhonda has rested her hand on my arm, warm and kind. Both our eyes dart to her hand as she says, "I think I have it from here, dear." Her voice is quiet, like she's afraid to really speak the words out loud. "Thank you." It's the faintest smile, barely even there, but every crumb of it genuine—enough to make me forget why I started helping her, for just a second.

"Of course," I croak.

Predictably, as I sit down again, a new message from Caitlin pops up.

Caitlin: What's happening? Is Jolene giving you computer lessons?
Rhonda: She's helping with that project I'm doing for Gregory. Nothing exciting, dear, mostly account archiving.

Caitlin: If you'd like more help, don't be afraid to ask me. I can even look things over for you—make sure Jolene's leading you on the right track.
Rhonda: Thank you. I'll keep that in mind.
Rhonda: And if you'd like me to double-check your inventory reports before submitting to Gregory, I'd be happy to. Make sure no future errors.

The gasp I let out. The grin that stretches across my cheeks. I smack my hand over my mouth to hide it. I always knew Rhonda had sharp knives, but not these razors. I dare a peep at Caitlin; her eyes are locked hard on the screen, typing double speed. Caitlin continues to type furiously, but I don't see any bouncing dots in the chat. I double-check her DM history; she's not chatting with anyone else either. She must be crafting a new email. I can be patient.

But after forever, or eleven minutes, her email to whomever still isn't complete. What is she even writing?

I stand up and grab my coffee cup to fill it at the watercooler. As I pass, I tilt just enough to catch her screen open to a giant email filled with a messy clump of text.

"Well," Caitlin finally says, "I'm off to speak with the HR guy."

As she walks away, I immediately go into the server and search her sent folder. But whatever she was writing, she didn't send it.

Time ticks onward. I try not to think about Caitlin and Cliff sitting in his trinket-filled office, discussing how horrible I am. Right now, I am being slandered beneath the gaze of several plastic Marios and Storm Troopers. I contemplate pulling a fire alarm.

I stare at their messenger icons. Both of their circles are red and their statuses read *in a meeting* like a threat. I should've hidden a camera inside Cliff's office. It would've been such a simple move and not *that* creepy if you don't think too hard about it.

Because *not* being able to listen in on conversations is actually terrible, now that I've seen behind the veil.

I attempt to distract myself by focusing on emails again. A new message appears in Rhonda's outbox.

FROM: Rhonda Staples
TO: carl.staples@livemail.ca
SUBJECT: Where in the heckin heck are you?

Honey,

I know it's not always easy, but could you please reach out here if you can?

When you were little, I used to wake up to check on you, just to see if you were still breathing even though I knew you were perfectly safe. I can't do that now. I thought you'd be my baby forever and I can't stop feeling like a mom no matter what.

Maybe it's because your birthday is coming up that I'm hoping extra hard to see you. I've been looking at cake recipes and would love to have a small party. You could spend a few nights in your bedroom too and I'll cook a bunch. Remember the R2D2 one I made when you were five?

My work is busy busy—we're making all my documents digital!

Email me here if you can get to a library. Call me, message me on Facebook.

I love you,
Mom

Shit, Rhonda's situation with her son is more dire than I thought. I search other messages to Carl's email address. There's like an email a month, going back for years—some of them begging to know if he's okay. Other times it's recipes.

If I make this tonight, will you come?

She's got more exotic Rachael Ray recipes than my mom . . .

I click my monitor off, the weight of the stack of unanswered emails drawing into my bones. I open my phone. Several messages from my mom are queued up in my texts, shamefully unread.

Mom: I'm watching a show where this ugly man is trying to put his kir in so many sister wives each week. He's not even nice guy.
Mom: During your lunch hour, you should still work so your bosses know you're serious.
Mom: I should make ashe reshteh

I should respond. But then I know she'd only use it as an invitation to ask for more—a phone call, a visit, and always the pressure to move back in with her. Exhaustion sweeps over me at just the sight of them.

So I toss the phone back where it came from. I have enough problems to take care of right now.

WHEN CAITLIN RETURNS, I watch her closely, searching for any indication of what went down during her meeting with Cliff. She doesn't immediately do cartwheels around my cube to celebrate my termination or even so much as smirk at me, which might be an encouraging sign, but her behavior is too indecipherable to be assured. She just spends the next half hour continuing to furiously type her giant email. Yet nothing appears in her sent folder.

I riffle through the emails of everyone she works with for good measure too, and still nothing.

Cliff's emails remain untouched too. What is he doing? Maybe he's working on a termination form for me right now. I think of DMing something random to him—I don't even know what—just to see if he'll respond. But that might be suspicious, so I stare blankly at my cubicle wall and wait for death.

Finally, lunch hour comes, and people begin to trickle away from their desks, marinara-stained Tupperwares in hand. Rhonda gets up and grabs her keys, declaring to no one in particular that she's going to buy a sandwich.

I stare at nothing as I break off pieces of my pathetic homemade PB and J. Normally this would be an ideal lunch hour, but I can't relax.

It feels like no time has passed when people begin to return to their desks. Armin is one of the last to come back, dragging himself toward our pod with a cloud hanging over him. Rhonda tilts her head toward the clock. "You're over twenty minutes late."

He presses his palms to his temples. "Okay" is all he says.

Rhonda squints at the ground. "Are those your new sneakers?"

Armin lets out a slow sigh. "I don't know how that's relevant."

"Is that why you were late? Did you go to the mall? Young people spend so much money on silly things. At your age, my Carl was saving for a down payment on his house."

Armin sits down hard in his chair and slides his feet pointedly out of Rhonda's sight. "First of all, I had an appointment. It was cleared by Gregory, and you were cc'd—did you forget?"

Her body tenses, clearly caught off guard by the undisguised heat in Armin's reply. I mentally take stock of all the times Armin has barbed her—but it's normally more emphasis on the passive than the aggressive.

"You have too many appointments during work hours. It's not good for—"

"Hey, it's my PTO," he cuts in. "So why don't you save your stellar mom advice for Carl this weekend."

Yikes. I've never seen him bite back this hard.

Rhonda presses her lips together and backs away. "Well, Larry is in his HR appointment this afternoon. So if EAE inquiries come, you'll have to cover for him."

Armin rubs his temples again. I wonder if the vein in his head is finally going to explode. "Why do *I* have to cover?" His gaze flicks to me pointedly.

Fuck. I realize I've been staring between him and Rhonda intensely, and the earphones I have on are not disguising it. Sweat gathers on my skin beneath my shirt despite the cool air they blast to keep us alive.

"Jolene and I are working on a *special* project." Rhonda gives me a little insider grin. "This is a busy time, so we need everyone here to pull their own weight."

Armin raises his eyebrow at me, clearly imploring me to interject. But defending him would mean going against Rhonda, who is finally coming around to liking me. So I look down at my keyboard.

I feel his stare linger, before he throws on his headphones and hunches over his computer. "'Kay."

It shouldn't be this hard to remain neutral with people. But trust Supershops Incorporated to turn a desk job into an air-conditioned version of *Survivor*, complete with alliances and betrayals.

Rhonda shakes her head and turns to her own screen.

I take a single sip of tepid coffee to calm me, and then nearly spit it out when I see the message from Caitlin to Armin pop up on my screen.

> **Caitlin:** BTW the HR guy said it's important to have multiple testimonies if there's a problem with a colleague. So I was thinking if you wanted me to also vouch for you and the creepy situation with Jolene, I'd be happy to join your meeting. Just throwing it out there that you have my support, friend. ☺
>
> **Caitlin:** Also, he's really nice, so don't be afraid to be open.

Heat rushes up my neck. Caitlin has no right to call anyone "nice." She can't recognize that trait.

My head whips toward Armin. He's drooping lifelessly against his desk. He doesn't make a move to type a response.

I glance at Rhonda again, and she notices and gives me a little secretive smile, like we're in on this together. I curdle back beneath the half wall of my cube. This lady will not make things easy for me.

I glance at Armin, trying to decipher what he's thinking, when a DM from Cliff flashes on my screen.

> **Cliff:** Hey, I'm really so sorry. Something came up, and I won't be able to give you a ride tonight. I can pick you up Monday same time?

My chest drops. Maybe it doesn't matter what Armin thinks anymore. Caitlin could've already gotten what she wanted, and my time here might be as good as done.

I will myself to hold my face steady as I type. As my insides crumble.

Jolene: *That's totally fine!*
Cliff: Thanks so much for understanding.

What a cold fucking message. Not even an exclamation mark.
A few moments later, a new email appears in Cliff's inbox.

FROM: Armin Habib
TO: Clifford Redmond
SUBJECT: Re: Employee Role Meeting with HR

Hello Cliff,
I'd be happy to meet. I've attached my availability. Also, I understand this
meeting is primarily to go over our roles, but I also have something that
veers sort of personal/interpersonal to discuss as it's starting to affect
me at work/my ability to stay focused. Just in case we need to book a
longer slot.

Thanks,
Armin

My stomach drops like a clump of lead. At this rate, I'll be packing
up my empty desk by next week.

Ungodly Hours

SUNDAY MORNING, I'M awoken in the most horrifying way known. It starts with an insistent knock on my apartment door and a screeched, "Shut up—is okay." The tone of voice my mom uses only when speaking to my dad.

What comes next is a yelled, "Jolene baby! I have brought you some ashe reshteh."

My heart stops, and I leap out of bed.

Shit! I never texted her!

Double shit—I drank some gin last night and passed out watching a documentary about cruise ships in bed. Why did I have to order all that Chicken on the Way and leave the whole mess in my living room?

I throw on a hoodie that I hope covers both my slept-in hair situation and my lost dignity, pile my garbage into the bin, throw the gin bottle and glass under the sink, and do a quick scan to make sure there are no obvious signs that the human embodiment of a bag of merde lives here. There's an empty chip bag on the coffee table, and an old take-out container that still has broth and pieces of wonton wrapper in it on the counter, but other than that, I should be able to get away with medium complaints. I shovel both pieces of garbage into a random cupboard since the bin is full and brace myself.

I barely open the door. "What brings you here?"

Mom barrels past me with a Tupperware container so huge, she had to have gotten it from a specialty store. "No need to heat this up if you get plates."

I should've known this was coming. Every now and then, she shows up with food without warning. I'm sure it's to try to keep me living under a similar regimen as when I was home, like I pretend to be, but unfortunately for us both, shit has veered incredibly off track.

Mom starts toward the kitchen, and I debate following after her to stand in front of the counters and somehow distract from how messy it is, but my dad is hovering awkwardly in the hallway. When we lock eyes, he says, "Sorry to show up like this. I told her to call, but you know." He rocks from foot to foot, as though to demonstrate he's physical standing there against his will.

"Come in, Dad."

He smiles awkwardly. "I brought my iPad. I can just watch the golf."

"Sure." I smile back as best I can.

I find Mom in my kitchen, the empty chip bag and wonton container already in each hand. "Jolene, you can't keep soup in the cupboard. It goes in the fridge."

I snatch them and say, "Thanks, that's a really good hack, but those are garbage. Can you stop opening my cupboards? I'll go through them later. I have a system."

But before I can finish, she is in the cupboard under the sink. My overflowing trash can and the three empty bottles of gin sit there like accusations.

"Are you really drinking this much?"

"No, those bottles are from months ago. And I used some for making sanitizer." My most bonkers lie to date. I scoop them up and gather them against my chest. "I'll put them in the dumpster."

She actually jumps. "Don't throw away, they give money at the depot for this! Albert, come take these bottles for Jolene to get the money."

Dad, who is sitting on the couch so awkwardly that it looks like his seat is made of Velcro, says, "I'm sure Jolene can take them in. She's in her thirties."

"Yes, I can. And yes, I *am*, thanks."

Mom waves her hand half-heartedly in our direction before setting the bowl of ashe reshteh on the counter and popping off the lid. The glorious smell wafts toward me. She's added so much goat whey and charred garlic that it almost makes everything that's happening right now worth it.

Almost.

I take a serving and slurp the first bit. This is the best hangover cure. "Thanks for bringing this."

She riffles through my other cupboards, shaking her head. "I made it so you don't have to worry about your lunches this week. You need to focus on your work. Now where is your cleaning supplies? These counters need wiping."

"Don't worry about cleaning, I'll do it later. You sit and visit."

She looks at all ten of my heads. "This place is not something I can stop worrying about. This is not how a polite person lives." She turns to my drawers next, clucking her tongue with disdain. "Why not clean after you eat? What do people say when they visit?"

There's no way I've let another human in here—the place speaks for itself.

I take a breath. "Well, normally I'd have some kind of warning. People don't just show up to other people's homes, especially when they're still sleeping."

She narrows her eyes. "You were sleeping? It's nine thirty. You could've been studying for your promotion."

"I don't think there's going to be a test." Although, given that it's Supershops Incorporated, there will probably be a non-harassment training module with a quiz at the end.

She scoffs as she wipes my counter with a cloth that is suddenly in her hands, seemingly produced from nowhere. "It's good to study your job anyways."

There's no such thing as winning when the argument is wackadoodle, so I smile and say, "How's your window garden?"

"I grow the most beautiful cilantro." Her smile is smug. "Next week, I bring you some."

I'm about to interject about her plan to return next week, but I'm just happy to hear she's gardening again. She finishes wiping and shakes her head.

"Jolene, this mess is really bad. How come you're living like this? It's like you don't care." She says this with all the severity of a doctor making a deadly diagnosis. "Are you okay?"

The crease in her brow—I hate that crease, critical and concerned all at once. I need to curl into a ball. I scramble for some excuse to make it go away. "The problem is that I care *too much* and don't know where to start."

She fake slaps the space between us in a dismissive gesture, her acrylic nails cutting the air like little claws. "Get on with you. It's very serious to be this bad." And to prove her point, she wipes the cloth under a windowsill that I'm pretty sure nobody has ever cleaned in the history of this apartment's construction. "This dust is from long time ago." She hardens her gaze accusingly, and I stiffen—she is not done with me yet. "How are you going to have a boyfriend over?"

And there it is. She's pushed the exact buttons that set me off. I look toward my dad in some useless, last-ditch plea for help, but he's already absorbed in his iPad. I want to scream.

Ever since Ellie's accident, my parents cannot stop managing my every move. And in the aftermath of a town of people sharing the same bad thought about me, all they truly seem concerned about is making sure that I fit the appearance of a perfectly functioning member of society.

But I don't want to rehash this same old argument. I say what I need to through clenched teeth. "I'm not trying to have a boyfriend over."

Mom huffs. "You have no friends?"

Normally, that kind of accusation would be my cue to curl into myself with shame, bereft with the reminder that I have absolutely no one.

Instead, I flash back to my evening drinking milkshakes with Cliff. The ease with which we were able to barb each other. The comfort and warmth between us. It's been a long time since I felt like that. Why does the only person in the world like Cliff have to be the HR guy?

In the days since he dropped me off, this world has brutally reminded me how far I am from having anything like that.

Mom watches me, her lips forming a fine line. "You can have a good life. You can find a good husband. I can help you." She lifts a hand toward my waist, and I freeze, thinking she's going to bring me into a hug. Instead, she pushes past me to wipe the next counter behind us. "This apartment is expensive, and for what? Some dirty carpet and a foozooleh mahaleh neighbor child?"

I mean, she does have a point about Miley being nosy, but I'd take her over being under Mom's roof again every time. At least here I have a door.

"I'm happy here," I tell her, the words small in my tight throat.

Her voice softens. "You should be happy. You're about to get a promotion. You just need to stop drinking and being sad about things from a long time ago."

My lips tremble. Mom's prescription for me is always just to literally *stop being sad.* I know it's not malicious. She grew up believing that depression and anxiety are controllable with the right attitude, fruit, and sunlight. She has traumas of her own that she's been ignoring, long before my pile of problems joined the mix. As an immigrant, this is survival mode.

There's only one way to put this conversation to bed. So I do what I've always done: push past every thought inside my head and every sinking feeling inside my soul, and say, "You're right. Starting tomorrow, I'm going to be better." I snatch the cloth from her fingers and pat her shoulder. "Don't worry about cleaning. I've been wanting to clean this place. I want to have people over."

Again, I'm back to the milkshakes—to Friday. Why is it every time I think I'm starting to do better, it's so easy to shift back to the wreck I became last night? How can this be me?

Mom is still staring at me with narrowed eyes, so I continue: "And drinking isn't even fun. I'm starting to suspect it might be unhealthy even."

She rests her fist on her hip. "Even drinking a little can cause wrinkles and damage to your heart."

"I don't want that. I'll be happier if I stop, I think. That's probably the problem."

She nods. "I hear it's a depressant."

"That makes so much sense."

Mom nods, placated for now. She's never one to deny an easy answer when it is gifted to her. "Make sure you finish the bowl. It's very healthy."

I smile and take another hefty spoonful of the ashe reshteh, letting the comforting, familiar flavors wash through me. "I'll put the rest in the fridge."

Once Mom gathers everything, including Dad and his iPad, she turns to me and whispers, "The girl with the dirty fingernails that let us in is still outside. Should we call her mom?"

Oh god. I peer out the window and see Miley's mousy head leaning against the wall in the hallway. "Don't worry about her. That's normal."

But as soon as I say it, she shifts, sinking lower—she's just sitting there by herself? Guilt splashes over me.

My parents smile as they open the door, passing her in awkward silence.

"Hey, Miley," I say. "How's it going?"

"It's good." She shuffles nervously from leg to leg. There's a little hole in her Toms, and it's how small her pinkie toe still is that chips into me.

"Sorry if we were being loud."

She shrugs, indifferent. "I could hear you arguing with your mom about your life inside your apartment."

I let out a sigh. "Yeah, next time could you not let her in? She needs to call before."

Miley's hands curl tightly against her chest. She must be having a terrible day, and it's not even noon. "Sorry," she says. "I thought I was helping."

I shake my head. "It's okay. It's just my mom is . . ." Actually, I don't need to go there with her. "What are you doing out here? I mean, in my hallway?"

"I came to give you this." She holds out a hand, and I notice for the first time that she is holding a mess of black and white yarn. "Your birthday gift."

I eye it warily. It looks like a bunch of loose black and white strings tied together, with two googly eyeballs glued onto the situation, seemingly on purpose. Is this a prank where I have to pretend to think it's beautiful, and then she laughs at me?

"It was meant to be a zebra," she clarifies.

Miley chews her hangnail, insecure as she waits for me to respond, and my heart tumbles like a domino. That's why she wanted to know my favorite animal. I accept the unfortunate creature from her carefully, lest it fall into pieces in my hands. "Thank you. That's really amazing of you."

She lowers her chin. "It's nothing amazing. I'm still learning."

The faint light in her eyes—I've seen it slowly begin to dim lately. "Hey, Miley, what are you . . . Is your mom around?" Her eyes shift downward, giving me the answer I don't want. I'm woefully ill-equipped for this.

"She had to work a double," Miley says to the carpet that hasn't been vacuumed in decades. "I was supposed to ask a friend to go over, but everyone was busy, so I'll just hang out." It's the insecure little fists. "Don't worry, I'm not that young. It's fine."

The little gift presses down heavily in my palms. "I know." It's technically true; she's old enough to be alone for a few hours. "So, what are you going to do today?"

"I guess I have more crocheting to do."

She looks at me—and damn it, I recognize that faint glimmer in her expression. I take an infinitesimal step backward into my apartment's threshold without thinking, and just like that the glimmer fades.

I nod. "Well, if you need anything—uh, I mean, if something happens, please knock. And if I'm not around—"

She smiles, cheeky. "You'll be home."

I press my own smile on and return to my apartment to finish the weekend out, determined that next week I will focus on my plan and not let myself be distracted by anything. Or anyone.

Milkshake hangovers are simply not worth the angst.

Bronze Medal Wife

ANOTHER MINUTE AND forty seconds until the workweek officially begins, but already the cubicles are fully stocked. Everyone hunches over their screens.

Everyone, except Caitlin.

After a weekend of overthinking everything—the night with Cliff, Caitlin's HR meeting, Armin's upcoming appointment, my parents, and my life in general, including the hour-long freakout on Saturday night after realizing I hadn't seen my birth certificate in a while—I should be relieved to be here.

This morning, when I went outside, just seeing Cliff's car there on the side of the road was a relief on its own. He's not totally avoiding me yet. But as soon as I slipped into the passenger seat, it was clear he was on another planet, hardly talking and picking up his phone to text at stoplights. Maybe Caitlin's complaints had gotten to him after all. But the worst thought hit when we passed the ice-cream shop we had the shakes at, and he tensed. What if he's been put off after that chat, reliving the conversation and all the shit I said, just like I've been doing?

Now with Caitlin's desk empty, her monitor blank, it's like a doom spiral with no end in sight.

Armin gets up and heads toward the printer room. I try not to look at him *too hard*. This morning, he emailed Cliff to confirm their appointment will be Wednesday. The air in my lungs sifts tighter.

My hand acts practically on its own accord as I rage click the meeting link. And it takes a second for my head to absorb what's on the screen. I can actually access Armin's entire calendar. None of his appointments are set to private.

Last week's appointment, the one that twisted Rhonda's pantaloons, was simply recorded as: *University Location*. I scroll back. There were two appointments the week before with identical names. More digging brings in several more, all with the same name or some that specify *South Campus.*

Is he taking secret classes? Slacking from work to attend university doesn't track for Armin, but it would explain his constant fatigue. I copy the schedule onto a sheet. I may need to use this against him.

As I slip the page into my drawer, Rhonda eases out of her chair with a creak and turns toward me and Armin's half of the pods. "Caitlin booked a last-minute PTO—can you two cover any inventory specs that come in?"

Where the hell is she? There were no emails re the PTO in Rhonda's or Greg's inbox this morning, which means she must've arranged it via text. Or in person on Friday . . .

"I'd be happy to take the lead there," I say, as I press a smile in Armin's direction. His eyes are tinged red from lack of sleep, and he merely shrugs and turns back to his monitor.

Rhonda smiles extra hard toward me as she grabs her favorite *I'd Rather Be Crafting* mug. "Jolene, you're a star."

"Thanks." I smile, as Armin pulls his headphones over his ears with a neutral expression.

I need to learn my lesson: taking on extra work for him is not the way to this guy's heart.

But then another doom-filled theory hits: What if they thought it was better for Caitlin to not be here in the fallout of her HR meeting? What if they're planning on acting on her claims today, and she painted me as so unhinged she'd be safer off the premises when they escort me out?

The only thought that sobers me is that there's no way Caitlin would voluntarily miss the chance to watch my job implode. She'd want front-row seats with popcorn.

I grin extra hard toward Rhonda. "Always happy to help. So nice Caitlin's taking a long weekend. Did she say what she was up to?"

Armin's shoulders square just a touch as Rhonda purses her lips and says, "She said she wanted to spend the day with her boyfriend. She'll be back tomorrow."

"Lovely." I smile and lock eyes with Armin, who is now staring directly at me. I try to look pleasantly unweird, but the guy keeps his expression neutral.

He's a tough egg to crack.

It's not until Rhonda gets up to head for lunch, once again announcing to nobody in particular that she's going to buy a Greek salad, that I decide to log off and head to the kitchenette in the copy room to grab the Tupperware of ashe reshteh I actually remembered to bring. I do my best to ignore the disturbing sights and smells of the other lunch boxes and long-orphaned containers that nobody will take liability for.

As I'm walking back toward my desk for my key card, I spot Armin heading toward our pods with a blue Gatorade—fresh from the hallway vending machine—in hand. And the idea trickles into my brain sudden and sharp. I've only ever seen this man do one thing with Cool Blue Thirst Quencher.

I round the corner and it's almost too perfect. I skulk toward Rhonda's cubicle just as Armin finishes pouring around three tablespoons of Gatorade into Joey's dirt, before he pulls a pen from her holder on her desk. He's so absorbed in his plant assault, he doesn't notice me as I approach the threshold of her cubicle. It's when he's stabbing the dirt repeatedly with the pen that his gaze crawls upward.

He jolts as soon as he clocks me staring at him, cross-armed. His expression falls with a thud. "Shit, Jolene. This isn't what it looks like."

I grin at him. "Oh, come on, Armin. You're talking to the girl who sent whited-out emails to colleagues. I know exactly what this is." His face pales, but I keep my smile on. "Don't worry, I'm not going to say shit. I prefer to mind my business."

The crease in his forehead smooths. "Thanks," he says meekly.

But to drive the point home, I add, "Ratting on colleagues over silly things. I'd *never* do that." I make certain we lock eyes. "Pretend I'm not even here. That's what I'm doing."

His shoulders ease some. "That's a great policy," he says, but he doesn't hide the puzzled expression on his face.

I lower myself into my seat, cool and casual, but I'm starting to doubt my ability to pretend anymore.

I SNEAK INTO the big lunchroom that is for parties only. I use this place only when I need to heat up ashe reshteh or any other food, as it's got the microwave that's far from everyone's desks, and I'm not a menace to society like Caitlin. If she'd just used this microwave like a normal person, all the email/Cliff mess could've been avoided.

The card reader for the lunchroom door beeps, and instant dread hits. I chose this remote lunchroom on purpose. My earliest anxious memories trace back to this meal—the era when having ethnic food wasn't cool, but an easy target. Laughter and gibes that I was eating a thermos of slime still ring in my ears.

But as Armin's glossy hair and frown appear, a wave of relief floods me so much that a smile falls on my lips.

The microwave beeps, and when I take out the steaming container, he eyes it curiously and says, "Ashe?" I nod, and he claps once. "It's been so long since I've smelled it. My mom hasn't cooked in forever. I didn't realize I was missing it."

I turn to face him. "I get it, it hits different than restaurant versions."

"Right!" He claps again and pulls from the fridge a doogh—a minty yogurt soda that a lot of people find off-putting, but if you're most Persians, you'd crime-spree for it.

He holds it up. "This is the sink I use to open over."

I flash a grin in understanding. The thing about doogh is, no matter how calm you try to keep the thing, the bottle will explode all over you and your children's children.

He slowly releases the lid and lets the bubbles pool down to the sink. When he finally gets it open and drained, he turns toward me. "Would you like some?"

"No thanks."

"Of course you do." He takes a cup from the cupboard and pours a glass, then slides it across the island like a bartender.

"You have to have my ashe then." And I can't help the twitch in my lips.

He shakes his head. "No, I can't—I'm supposed to save my appetite. I'm grabbing a giant burrito from Tacos Mexico after I meet a guy about a rare record, but thanks so much for the offer."

There's still a universe where Armin and I could've been friends. And maybe he and I should have an alliance, at least out there. Maybe, after everything this job has put us through, he and I should be the last ones standing. "Hey, Armin." I lean a touch closer and lower my voice. "Try not to be late after lunch. With everything going on with the HR assessments, it's best to just be good."

"True." He nods, but it's too quick, and his expression is too casual, too placating. He's thinking I'm a paranoid Larry Goodwin type.

"I mean it. You never know who's watching you or who you can trust." And before my brain even realizes what I'm doing, I fucking wink.

His eyes flash as he backs away. There's no universe where I'm not a weirdo. My entire being is about to dissolve. Every time I think to speak or do anything, I should find the nearest stock art on the wall and stare at it until I lose all inspiration.

His lips form a thin line. "Yeah, that's a good point. Well, take care, Jolene." Another step back before he full-on speeds out of the room, leaving me and my mom's ashe to pick up the pieces.

That should've been a nice interaction. But *I* was a factor.

An empty feeling flows through my chest. No matter what, I'll always be a factor. Every conversation. Every event. Every time I try to talk in a meeting.

I eat the ashe reshteh over the sink, barely tasting each bite, before dumping the rest in the compost bin.

Armin's workspace sits empty. While Rhonda plays her tile game, I angst about it all. Will today be enough to stop Armin from speaking ill of me to Cliff at the meeting? Or was my weirdness enough to void all my efforts? I pull up Armin's inbox, looking for any new clues about what he's thinking. But alas, work emails aren't always the best window into a person's personal life.

Except when I jump to his outbox, I see he sent a new email right after speaking to me in the lunchroom.

Mom & Dad,

Once again emailing from work, where I always am when not with you or Jolene. Of course I'm happy for you to come visit my office when you're up for it. Mom would enjoy it. I wish I could admire the view of the skyline from my window more often, but this week is terrible. I'll be in meetings or answering questions for my team, who rely on me for guidance.

Jolene has a very big test to study for, but she'll try and be there tonight.

Love you,
Armin Habib

Executive Accounting Manager

I have to read the email three times because most of the bananas words do not compute. Has Armin lost his bobbles?

I highlight the address he sent this note to and check for other messages; he emails his parents every few months from here. He changes his signature to have different job titles. In one note, there's a photo of him sitting in Gregory's office, feet on the table. In another, he tells them he had to miss dinner because of an accounting convention he was speaking at. Armin the executive accounting manager who is always at work? *Armin of ye old dirty PlayStation controller,* giving a damn conference to *people*? Holy hell.

And over and over again, I find my name. Apparently, it wasn't just Armin attending that fake conference; he wrote "Jolene and I." "Jolene and I can't visit tonight." "I'll be with Jolene this weekend." Most of these excuses seem to hinge on the fact that I'm in night school because "I don't want to be a secretary forever."

Even as a fake girlfriend, I seem to need improvement.

No, this must be another person named Jolene. That has to be it. My name isn't the most uncommon.

I click on another email and nearly scream when a photo of my own face fills up the monitor. It's a terrible picture of me and Armin standing next to each other at last year's corporate Christmas lunch. I remember they were handing out door prizes when someone basically assaulted us with an impromptu demand to smile for the camera. Armin sent it with the subject line: "Engagement Photo."

Wow. Here I was berating myself for being a weirdo around Armin, cringing every time Caitlin implied that I was interested in him because of that one Instagram message. Meanwhile, he's sending pics of me to his parents.

I click into his calendar again and note the address of his meeting with his parents tonight—or, I guess, *our* meeting. I recognize the location, Shiraz Bakery. It's a Persian café that specializes in preparing pastries for weddings. What are they doing there? Is this part of Armin and my engagement or something? How deep does this web of lies go?

I stare at the bakery website. It's not too hard to get there on the bus; it's actually on the way home.

I type a message:

Jolene: *Hey Cliff, turns out something came up after work. I won't be needing a ride tonight.*

His dots bounce. Then stop. And bounce again before his message appears:

Cliff: Sounds good. I'll see you tomorrow.

Armin returns from lunch with a greasy Tacos Mexico bag in hand. He averts his eyes as soon as we lock them, sliding out of sight behind his monitor.

He told his parents I'll try to attend dinner tonight. What kind of fiancée would I be if I can't take one evening off to meet my future in-laws?

Meet the Parents

I'M LEANED AGAINST a brick wall in an alleyway across from Shiraz Bakery—the front door of the café is perfectly centered in my view. I've stuffed my nest of hair into a messy bun and covered my wrinkled blouse with an oversized hoodie I found in the office. The hoodie smells about as musty as I'd expected; it had been hanging on a random coat rack in the hallway that leads to the copy room for years without anyone putting it out of its misery. Its owner has likely long abandoned Supershops Incorporated. And even though I may look sketchy AF in it, especially while I'm skulking in an alleyway, it's perfect for the incognito aesthetic I need right now.

My phone clock confirms the meeting with his parents starts in two minutes, and as soon as I stuff it in my pocket, I clock Armin rounding the corner. My heart jumps as I duck behind a car. It's almost comical that he's perfectly on time for this meeting, when his usual MO at work is to arrive as close to the end of the workday as possible.

He disappears inside the café's door. I wait a whole seven minutes—just me, the sound of my heavy breathing, and the stinky hoodie that, in natural light, shows a few crusty stains that I don't want to know more about.

Did I really stalk Armin all the way to this place? I *am* being a weirdo. Then again, this can't be any worse than using a colleague to create a whole fake life without her knowing. I'm just here to do some light reconnaissance and figure out what the heck is going on.

Finally, I head toward the bakery, take a deep breath, and pull the door open.

The little chime from the bell on the door sends a jolt through me. The place is crowded with mostly Iranian people. Nobody seems to notice me as I take my place in the back of the line, swept up by the hum of conversations and laughter and waving hands. The sweet scent of chai fills my soul with warmth.

I glance around the room and spot a mini version of myself staring back from a warped security mirror. But it's not as warped as one would hope—more that over the course of this afternoon and one bus ride, I've devolved into a weary troll. The hoodie just carries the vibe further.

My eyes skim over the tables in the back of the room, and I finally spot Armin. He's in a corner booth, a small golden samovar in the center of the table.

It's like he can feel my stare land on him. He looks sharply toward me and visibly jolts. He's sitting with an older man, but I can see only the back of his head as he talks animatedly with his hands. That must be his father.

Armin's forehead wrinkles as he sinks lower in the booth, crouching behind the bulkiest part of the samovar. Even from across the room, I can tell his complexion is paling at a considerable speed.

But Armin doesn't know that *I* know anything is up. In his mind, this is just a coincidental meeting of two colleagues out in the wild.

I wave and gesture for him to come over. I just want to know what's going on. Maybe I can even make some kind of truce with him here?

But his eyes shift away from me, and he shakes his head once before crouching even farther down into his seat, jaw set.

I do my best impression of an innocent, confused person and take a step back into his line of sight, raising my eyebrows in silent question.

He doesn't quite look at me, but his lips start to tremble. I halt in my tracks. The fear etched in his expression hits me like a flash of boiling water, and I'm back to feeling like a monster. Everything inside of me is heavy as lead.

I give him a tiny, apologetic wince and turn my attention away from him. No matter what, our personal lives need to stay personal, or society doesn't have a chance.

As I back away, the proprietor behind the counter calls out to me. "Yes, miss, what would you like?"

"Twelve danmarkis, please," I blurt out automatically. Since they're each the size of a hamburger, it's a huge order for one person, but also reasonable, if I'm being real. The guy nods, face neutral, as he pulls a sheet of wax paper out to gather my request. When he hands me my box, I thank him as quietly as possible and tap my card, bracing for this financial blow.

I'm heading for the door, danmarki box cradled against my chest—

"Isn't that Jolene?" a Persian-accented man calls behind me. I flinch at my name, at who must've said it. Armin's dad calls, "Jolene!" The gazes of the other customers crawl to me. I take a breath and turn around. Armin's dad smiles and nods in confirmation. This guy might be a spy if he can recognize me from the low-quality Christmas party picture.

I make my way to the table, arms rattling my oversized box of pastries, while Armin's jaw makes its way to the floor. This situation may be the most unprecedented moment in human history; all the words that exist have disappeared from my brain. It doesn't matter because Armin takes over as if on autopilot. "Dad, I'd like you to officially meet Jolene." He locks my gaze, a plea in his eyes. "My fiancée."

"Hello! Ah, Jolene, nice to meet you!" His dad seems to light up from deep inside. He's got the same smile as Armin's, though Armin hasn't been using his much lately. I put out my hand, but he grabs it and pulls me in for a hug.

A squeal creaks from the hinges of the little bathroom door at the back. I sense her energy before I see her. "Nice to meet you, Jolene joon!" Armin's mom's voice is airy and delicate. My chest lightens at the universal nickname of affection. That unconditional yet fully judgmental feeling of love that I get from my aunties sharpens into effect.

I turn and everything stops when I see her. Her bones jut out of thin, sallow skin. She looks like my grandma when she was undergoing cancer treatment. She embraces me, and her skin is cool and firm, her rosewater scent mixed with something medicinal like a lozenge.

Over her shoulder, I spot Armin looking as though he might break in half. And as the realization hits—I might do the same.

I break the pregnant pause. "Oh, salam! It's nice to meet you. Armin has said so many wonderful things about you."

Armin's lips curl into an uncertain smile, but he still looks like he's contemplating running through the wall next to him.

His dad's grin creases into his cheeks. "Armin had just told us you couldn't make it after all. But we're very glad you took a break from studying—even though we understand how important your exams are."

My lips wobble. "I wanted to meet you. I was starting to think Armin was making you up."

Armin's temples twitch, his gaze turning manic as it bores into me. But his parents both laugh.

I continue: "I needed a break anyway." Then I remember myself—how I look. What kind of person would dress like this to meet her future in-laws for the first time? "I'm just popping in for a few moments."

His mom nods weakly as Armin jumps up to steady her into her seat slowly. "What are you studying for this week?"

I clock Armin's look, but that tells me nothing, which means I have to say, "Human anatomy."

His dad's eyebrows weave together. "Why are you studying that if your degree is computer engineering?"

Shit. I nod, somehow maintaining composure. "Ah, yes, this confuses so many people, but it's because we are ... the original computer system. We're basically living hard drives."

They both giggle uncertainly and stare at me, assessing.

His mom's eyes glint. "So you're Persian too? That's so wonderful..." She finishes her statement in Farsi. I only understand every second word; she could be asking either where my parents live or if I'm going to move. I'm going to have to come clean that I'm an imposter.

"Well, I am Persian, but unfortunately I only know the bad words and insul—"

"Jolene doesn't have a lot of time for her break." Armin puts his hand over his mother's gently. Then he shoots me the most wild, wide-eyed expression.

It's time to put him out of his misery.

"Bye, guys—hopefully will see you soon. Excited to join the family."

Armin shakes his head infinitesimally, like he can't believe I said this. Frankly, I can't either. My anxiety is spiraling from lying to a Persian aunty so hard. A sick Persian aunty.

I turn and rush toward the door. As soon as I'm out, I round the corner to a playground, find the nearest bench, sit ugly, and stuff a danmarki into my face, ignoring the parents who are pulling their children protectively closer at the sight of me.

And the creamy comforting treat pairs terribly with my racing mind as the realization hits: Armin has a bigger house of cards to protect than me.

The Prior Engagement

THE DRIVE IN to work with Cliff the following morning feels like it could be another skit from that HR video about how to be friendly with colleagues. Cliff begins with some light conversation about wildfire smoke starting earlier than usual this year, although he doesn't remember previous years. Then we pass a shuttered storefront, and he gets sad about the record shop he liked closing forever. I ask him when the last time he went was, and he realizes it's been two years. Then we both get quiet for a bit—all fairly nice. And by the time we arrive downtown, my angst over his prior meeting with Caitlin has withered.

Only to return when I swipe into the office and head to my desk.

Armin's workstation is empty, while Rhonda sits staring at her screen, joylessly dipping a tea bag in a steaming cup. Caitlin marches in from the kitchenette, smirking in a way I don't like. We both make our ways to our seats, Caitlin just in front of me—and is there an extra bounce in her step?

Rhonda turns to greet us. "Good morning. Did you have a good day off, Caitlin?"

Caitlin's smile is too bright as she flips her hair, in the process waving her hand far too hard. "It was the *best.*"

She looks toward me but doesn't elaborate, and her smile doesn't seem right. Her smile is never a good sign.

But nothing notable appears in anyone's emails.

I'm alone in the copy room, dealing with a scanner that can't get its life together enough to know when it should beam the light across the glass, when I hear tentative footsteps approaching behind me. I turn and it's Armin, looking sheepish as he leans against the threshold, crossing his arms.

"So," he says, "studying anatomy for your computer science degree?"

My mouth twitches. "Sorry I wasn't as educated in the lie as you hoped."

He moves past me to grab a mug from the corner coffee station and turns it over in his hands, not looking at me. "I'm just... thanks."

"You're welcome," I reply. "But if you'd like to book me for more events—birthdays, weddings, and all—that comes at a price. Especially if I'm to be the bride."

His lips form a thin line. "I'm their only child, and my mom... she's not good."

The crack in his voice grates through the room.

He focuses on filling the mug with coffee as he continues. "She's been wanting me to settle down forever, and we were on the phone this one time and I just panicked and said a bunch of crap to make her feel better." His lips draw down. "My life isn't what she wanted at all."

I nod. "Say no more. I haven't lived up to my parents' expectations either. Whenever they audit my life, it takes me hours to recover."

I wince at my words—the truth of them.

"That's exactly it!" He chuckles. "I know what they want for me, but I don't know if that's what *I* want. Faking it just seemed... easier, while I figure it out."

I bob my head in solidarity. He has no idea how deeply I can empathize.

"But I'm sorry to rope you in. I swear, it was such a small lie at first. I'd been telling my parents I was seeing someone for a while just to keep them off my back, and they kept insisting on a photo, and then they sent that picture of us winning the door prizes at the Christmas lunch..."

I press my lips together evenly. "Ah, right, the day I got my Supershops lunch bag. The zipper didn't even work. I stuffed it in the freezer on five."

He chuckles again, and although it's soft, it fills the entire room. "Better than the monocular I got. Like, what kind of freaky person would want that? And why were they so certain that person works here?"

I can't hold back my laugh, and Armin grins too, but it's tinged with that weary, tense look he's been wearing as of late. Another wave of sympathy roils through my chest. "Honestly, it's fine," I say. "It's none of my business. If we hadn't run into each other at the bakery, I never would've known." I try not to flinch at my own lie.

Armin keeps a steady gaze on me for a long moment, and I wonder if he can tell there's more I'm not saying. Finally, he shifts to stare at the overflowing recycling bin and softly mutters, "It's been tough lately. She's had so much chemo, and it's on me to help, since my dad can't drive anymore..."

I pick up my uncopied paper from the printer and clutch it to my chest. "I'm sorry."

His lips press tighter. "It's looking more like we'll have to shift to comfort care. I guess I just wanted her to have some peace of mind about me." Under the fluorescent lighting, the bags under his eyes are stark. A wave of understanding seeps in: *University Location*—the U of C medical center.

"Hey, Armin. Yesterday, when I tried to warn you—you've been taking time off and stuff lately ... Maybe you could say something about helping your mom to Gregory, so he knows, or even Rhonda—she might be a good ally?"

He groans under his breath and presses his hands to his temples. "Nah, Rhonda's never going to be on my team. And this isn't my mom's first bout. Last time, Gregory knew; he even sponsored my Bike for Cancer." Our eyes connect before Armin quickly averts his. The guilt of my indifference when he was looking for Bike for Cancer sponsors grates through me. Armin continues. "But you know how it is. I could tell he was annoyed about the extra PTO. And then things got better with my mom for a while, but now ..." He sips his coffee and his Adam's apple rolls. "With all the rumors going around about layoffs, I don't want to risk it."

My stomach burns. I look down at my feet. "What if you tell the new HR guy? He seems nice."

He huffs. "Yeah, sure, HR people always act like they're in your corner. But they're just company spies. If I tell him what's going on, he'll probably just tell Gregory."

Of course Armin's right. Cliff might seem genuine, but Supershops hired him to advise about layoffs first and foremost. It's impossible to really know how sympathetic he'd be when it comes down to it.

He shakes his head. "Corporations hate this kind of shit. They feed us all this sap about being a family, but at the end of the day productivity is all that matters. No one cares what's going on in your life."

"I understand." And normally I'd completely agree with him. But my mind jumps to Rhonda, to her problems with her son. "You'd be surprised, though. Everyone has their own shit going on."

He rubs his stubbly chin, the noise scratching through the room. "Anyway, thanks again for last night. It was so cool how you figured out the situation and knew what to say, more or less." But his brow rises just so. "How did you do it? It was . . . You didn't seem all that shocked."

My skin tightens. I hold the paper even closer against my chest, and I can feel my grip wrinkling it. "I, uh, just kind of went along as it happened." I try and fail to stop my eyes from shifting. "And, you know, I get how it is with parents."

"Right . . ." Armin's heavy gaze pins me in place. I stop breathing, certain he can smell the bullshit on me. He opens his mouth, then closes it, his lips thinning into a straight line. I stand very still.

Finally, he sucks in a breath and says, "Would it be crazy to ask you to pretend to be my fiancée one more time? Maybe a dinner or something? My mom won't stop asking me, and it'd make her really happy."

My head shake is so automatic and aggressive, it makes me dizzy. "Last night was honestly a fluke. I can't pull that off again."

"I could talk you through what to say!" he insists, eyes giant and pleading. "Or I'll handle most of the talking, and you can enjoy a free meal. The hardest part would be pretending to like me for a bit," he adds with a small, teasing smile.

No way. I try to imagine myself sitting in front of Armin's parents for an entire evening, smiling and making small talk and digging myself even deeper into this bonkers hole I've fallen into. It's a terrible idea; Armin must be truly desperate. But I've got plenty of my own to deal with as is.

"I'm sorry, Armin. I can't. Even last night was too much angst for me. I'm stressed right now and really need to be focused on my job."

His eyes glint at my words. "I could help you with that! I know you and Caitlin are kind of in a battle here. She's pretty sure she's going to crush you in the multi-unit meeting tomorrow. I could find out what she's going to say and tell you."

I shake my head. "No, I don't think that'll help me. I'm not planning on talking in the meeting."

His eyes shift toward the doorway, then back to me. He takes a tiny step closer. "Okay then, between you and me, she asked me to confirm some really negative stuff about you at my HR meeting." He shakes his head quickly, holding his palms up. "I wasn't going to. That's just not my style. But I *could* deny everything, *and* I could say you're the best colleague to work with—mention how you've been helping me with stuff. Mention that she's been bullying you, even."

My jaw almost unhinges. It's almost too perfect, this deal. I should take it, I think. What's one more lie at this point? Except I can't stop thinking about Armin's mom—her kind, frail smile. Lies aren't all the same, and lying to a sick Persian aunty, on top of everything else, might finally be enough to make me explode. This was only supposed to be about keeping my job. I can't let this get any bigger than the walls of this office.

"Sorry, but no. I can't do the dinner." I take a step around him and head toward the threshold.

He nods, his entire body deflating as he stares at his feet. "Worth a shot."

I hate how miserable he looks. I hate how much I understand the feeling—the pressure to live up to someone's expectations, to make them believe you're doing okay.

I should walk away now. But his shoulders are so low, so I say, "Trust me, we don't want to push our luck. I'd definitely screw up and forget to call you the executive or something."

His eyes flash up to mine sharply. Shit. My heart drops into my stomach as I realize just how thoroughly I've put my foot in my mouth.

"Did anything about my job come up yesterday?" His brow furrows.

I shake my head. "No, no. I was just making up a random example. I mean, of the lies we tell our parents. About our love lives, and our jobs, and stuff."

"Ah." He nods. His face is completely blank. Fuck. "Got it."

He leaves the copy room first, his eyes flashing toward me one last time as he turns the corner.

I KEEP GLANCING toward Armin's desk for the rest of the morning, but he stays silent behind the cube divider. When I get up under the pretense of filling my water bottle, I spot him slumped in his chair scrolling around on his phone. Nothing out of the ordinary, at least.

Rhonda spends the morning focusing on the archive project. She makes her daily unanswered call to Carl and checks her Silver Timings daily summary email.

I spend the hour using Caitlin's password to log in to her private server folder, download the documents she prepared for the upcoming presentation, and slowly freak out. Armin was right, she could crush me. When she presents this thorough, well-researched plan and I don't present anything at all—well, I don't know if anything else I've done so far will matter.

My fingers hover over Armin's name in the chat app, tingling to message him that I'll take his deal. But even if I do, would a good word from him in an HR meeting still be enough to save me after Caitlin kicks my ass in this meeting? It's like watching myself drown through a window.

After the ten a.m. coffee break, Caitlin returns from the boardroom behind me. The chemical scent of her fresh nail polish tinges my nostrils. Deep sigh. Only Caitlin would be selfish enough to paint her nails in here. I'm about to send her a glare to mark the completion of her manicure, when I catch something glinting on her finger as she waves her hands to speed up the drying process. Is that a diamond freaking ring?

Is Caitlin engaged? Why didn't she make a giant announcement for all her 1,264 followers? She posts when Kyle makes her unseasoned chicken breast with boiled frozen vegetables, #menwhocook.

But of course, just as I am thinking this, Caitlin props her hand against the neutral wall and snaps a picture with her phone. The post appears on her feed shortly after, #4evaisnotlongenough.

Joy screeches first—from across the unit, yet loud enough to startle my internal organs. She trots toward Caitlin's cubicle, snatches up her hand, and calls, "Oh, girl! You're engaged! Why didn't you tell us?"

Caitlin's cheeks pinken. "It literally happened yesterday! Kyle booked a last-minute trip to Banff, and we had a no-phone rule!"

The office erupts in claps as more people rush toward her. Garret swats everyone away to pull Caitlin's wrist up. "Is this white gold?" he asks. She nods sheepishly while Rhonda curls both her hands together against her chest and says, "We've got a wedding to help plan!"

I try to force a smile. I should probably join the group and mutter some fake words of congratulations. But it's like I'm glued to my chair. It's like I'm stuck in place.

Armin stands up. "Congratulations, Caitlin," he says. His gaze drifts to me.

Gregory joins the throng and pulls Caitlin in for a non-consensual hug. Stu does the fingers-in-mouth type of whistle, for some reason.

"Who knew, when you started, we'd be celebrating your engagement at this very desk?" Rhonda squeaks.

Caitlin's tinkling laugh pushes through the room. "I mean, it's not *that* surprising. Years have passed and life happens." Her gaze drifts over my desk, but not at me.

More laughter and cheery congratulatory remarks all blur into a muddle. She has a whole life outside of here. They all do.

Something cold tickles my cheek, sending a shock through me: a single tear. I wipe the confusing offender away before anyone has the chance to see. But another wet mark pulls down, as intrusive as the last.

I must just be happy for her. I focus all my willpower on forcing my lips to smile. *So* happy.

I'm wiping the third and final tear with my sleeve when I catch Armin staring. He quickly diverts his eyes and turns his chair toward his screen before I can say anything to brush it off.

A message appears a few moments later.

Armin: Hey, I was thinking. You did me a pretty big solid last night when you didn't have to. So, at my meeting tomorrow, I'm going to still say only nice things about you.

He must be pitying me again. It's crushing, but also relieving in the same measure.

Jolene: *Thanks. I really appreciate that.*
Armin: Of course.

How could I forget: this job is all I have. And if there's still a chance to save it, I need to give it everything.

So I spend the lunch hour working on a plan for the conference tomorrow. Because if I can just speak, I could beat her. I have enough information sitting on my lap in these emails. I could come up with something even better if I dig through it all.

When Caitlin returns from her celebratory lunch with Marla, Garret, and Joy, I don't look up. I'll need the whole afternoon to pull something together this quickly. Maybe the whole night.

I don't pay much attention when Rhonda sends Gregory a complaint that Caitlin and Armin are on their phones too much this afternoon.

Or note that my own phone sits silent as a paperweight.

Cliff drives me home again, but I mostly just hum in agreement as he speaks, because my mind is flooding with all the information I've consumed. As soon as I get inside my apartment, I pull out my laptop and continue to prepare the presentation. I even figure out how to use a custom template to make it look nice. I read it over and over to check the spelling. Then I practice speaking in front of the mirror like I have nothing better to do. When I'm too tired to function anymore, I drop onto my bed and watch comedy skits on my phone. And I laugh without *actually* laughing. There's no point when you're all alone.

Throughout the night, I have several panicked nightmares about the conference. I hope I don't forget to wear clothes tomorrow. I need it to go perfect.

Can't Keep Meetings Like This

W E'RE ALL PILED into the big boardroom on the fifth floor, and we've sat here long enough that the sharp cologne Jean Adler's been dabbing into his neck since, like, 1984 has all but disappeared.

All the beady freaking eyes face forward; this room feels more like a stadium. I twist the metal water bottle sitting on my lap in my clammy hands and try to steady my breath.

Cliff is sitting at the end of the largest table next to mine. He's got his notepad out, and the way his pen is moving, I'd bet big money that he's doodling. But when I tried to squint and see earlier, he caught me peeking and smiled.

Armin had his HR meeting earlier today. When he returned, he DMed me: Went well for you. Didn't tell him about my mom. And as relieved as I was that he vouched for me, it hit even harder that he confided that.

Gregory is standing at the front of the room, listing off a new policy that has already been emailed company-wide several times. Rhonda nods, smiling way too hard. She's propped herself front and center at the table to take meeting minutes that nobody asked for. She'll likely file them away in some cabinet afterward, never to be seen again.

My mind feels like it's literally shaking in my skull. All the words I'm going to try to say replay over each other in discordant nonsense. I wish I could see Cliff's cat sketches from here.

Gregory claps his hands once as he shifts topics. It seems like he's close to wrapping up. "Before we go, it's time for the ideas and opinions session. I myself have been brainstorming an exciting incentive program"—he pauses to raise his brows enticingly—"But I'd love to hear any thoughts you've all been tinkering with first."

All the expressions remain neutral and uninspired by this, except for Caitlin, who nods way too hard.

We start with two suggestions from supply chain people that have already been suggested a dozen times before. With each passing comment, every tick of the clock, my skin tightens and cools. I look around the table and try to decipher if anyone will be sympathetic should I faint in the middle of the room when my brain snaps from nerves.

Larry stands, shiny sheen on his forehead, armpits darkened and heavy from perspiration.

"*Good god,*" comes from some unknown voice in the back.

My breath halts in involuntary sympathy as he clears his throat. "I think we should implement some type of town hall meeting every now and then to really form a cohesive office." He stares at Gregory, an intense smile pointed toward him like an attack. "We could share ideas and go over some of the bigger elements that affect multiple departments."

Did he just suggest the very thing we're doing? My eyes draw to Cliff, who is wincing and nodding along. He writes something down, lips pressed together.

Larry grins like he really said something there and lingers while a tumbleweed passes. Finally, Greg mutters, "Thank you." Larry retreats to his seat.

Taking advantage of the opening, Caitlin juts out her chin. "I was thinking we could sort information going to other departments into categories to better streamline." She stands up and begins passing around photocopied pages of her plan. "I've got a list of areas this would optimize and prevent lost communication."

A few people in marketing nod enthusiastically. Gregory looks at her document and does his version of a smile.

It's an unfortunate win for her. She raises her eyebrows toward Garret in silent celebration.

But Joy mutters, "What about the chain to invoicing?"

"Ah yes, well, I've designed a–" Her phone dings and she pulls it from her back pocket, tapping it. "Sorry, forgot to silence." Her brows crease together. "Where was I? I meant I've made a plan for . . ." Her eyes float across the table until they catch on me. I divert from her gaze, and she blinks several times. "That's something I'm working to incorporate as well. Thanks." Her voice is meek, her entire aura suddenly smaller as she makes her way back to her mesh boardroom seat.

Gregory clears his throat. "Any more suggestions after Caitlin's helpful one?" He looks pointedly at Larry.

I have to speak. I've prepared for it. I need to just. Do. It. I suck in a breath that is way too tight and hot.

My hand raises, shaky and sweating. Gregory's expression shifts to almost a scowl, almost offended. "Miss Smith, do you have something?"

Every single face in the room turns toward me. My stomach flips as I stand. My legs have morphed into Jell-O. I open my mouth, but all the words in the world seem to mesh on my tongue and I'm sure I'll say something offensive instead, because my brain likes to fuck me up like that.

I clear my throat, but my voice is still pitchy as I say, "I noticed several departments keep important data in silos, like supply chain and accounting regarding seasonal sales."

All the faces remain deadpan, their eyes glassy and lifeless. The only sound in the room comes from Larry Goodwin chugging his water bottle.

I may be internally dying.

My gaze pulls toward Caitlin, who is slumping in her chair with her arms crossed. Garret is sitting beside her, equally unsympathetic. My eyes shift to Rhonda, who is pursing her lips. Then to Armin, who raises his eyebrows.

I look toward Cliff. He puts his pen down and nods at me encouragingly. Now that I'm standing, I can see his notebook. He's drawn three cats in the margins.

And it hits like a rush: I can pretend. I can be good at talking sometimes. Like at the ice-cream shop, or when I was helping Rhonda, or when I met Armin's parents. Everything is so much easier when it isn't real.

What if *this* wasn't really my life?

I lift my chin. "What I mean is, several departments do all this work to reach similar conclusions from different ends. There's got to be a way to divvy this labor up more efficiently."

A breath of life washes through the room. Eyes blink. Chairs shift. Marla leans over to Stu to mutter something, and he nods, stroking his chin thoughtfully.

What if this place wasn't soul sucking?

I pick up my folder and take out the papers I'd prepared, handing them around. "As you can see here, I've created a flow chart for how certain info could be handled."

Rhonda's cupped her hands together over her chest, proud mama smile on. When I pass Cliff to give him my printout, he meets my gaze and grins. The ground below me seems firmer.

What if the people here were good humans?

I keep talking; it's like an out-of-body experience. My voice is less shaky than any of the rehearsals I did in front of the mirror last night. I manage to share more details about my idea, and I actually say what I'm thinking.

When a few people chime in with questions, I'm able to answer them. My voice has evened, my bouncing leg finally still.

Faces begin to light up as they look over my printout. A few murmurs of praise carry across the room like a song.

Gregory puffs out his entire chest and claps once. "How long have we missed that? This. This right here is why I like to have these discussions." Sure, he's basically found a way to praise himself for my thoughts, but people are smiling at *me*.

In fact, so many people are still looking at me. A nightmare.

Only it's not.

I never realized there could be a difference.

Caitlin crosses her arms. "How did you figure this out? I mean, how did you know how inventory operates while working *our* job?" She twists a brow. "Have you been spying on them?" She says this like it's a joke, but she and I lock eyes. A few others mirror her suspicious gaze, while others are more quizzical.

I don't dare look at anyone directly.

And how quickly perception can turn bad—the fickle beast. I wipe my hands on my thighs. "I'm just assuming that's how things are handled, based on what I've seen from my end. I could be wrong. In which case this flow chart will be a funny little keepsake for the bulletin board."

A fair amount of laughter for that terrible joke pulls through the room. Jean Adler says, "No, you nailed it. Thanks, Jolene!"

My mouth twitches, but I'm too shy to smile. I make my way back toward my seat. I scribble on my notepad, trying to look calm and focused, mouth twitching to smile.

For reasons I don't understand, the words I write are:

Streamline
Business
Jean: nailed it

The meeting draws to a close, and as people shuffle out of their seats they shoot me grins and nods and call out short affirmations like "nice job."

A lightness takes over.

I want to see Cliff smile at me again, but he's too busy talking with Gregory and Larry in the corner. The poor guy.

Caitlin marches in front of me with dropped shoulders as she stabs her phone. She frowns, red-faced, like she might burst.

I take a breath. I can relax now.

I SPEND THE lunch hour walking to the mall, something I've done countless times before, only this time isn't as isolated or dire as my usual ganders. Joy and Marla even wave to me from a jewelry kiosk as I pass. Aritzia is having a rare sale, so I pop in and find a perfect blazer. It looks good on me, and the discount is steep enough that I can manage it—an investment in my future at Supershops, if I can just get in a bit more mirror practicing. If I can control my thoughts enough to not freak out when I'm in front of a crowd, or sometimes alone. If I can continue being okay enough, I might just be able to enjoy this.

My size is out of stock, so the store clerk offers to ship it to me for arrival next week. That's for the best. Walking back into the office with a shopping bag is such a catastrophe. People always want to see what you bought and then have you show it off with a song and dance for our capitalist lords.

When I return, the afternoon office is mostly silent, apart from the hum of the health hazard of a fan on Jean's desk that's smudged grey with caked-on dust and human debris after years of slowly dying in this place. Water leaks from the cooler in torturously unpredictable drips, yet nobody is willing to simply stop it, myself included.

Only Caitlin isn't taking this time of rest seriously. She's been zombie-focused on her screen since the meeting, frantically pulling out folders and notebooks and clicking her mouse faster and more often than usual. As she marches toward the copy room with a document in hand, I dare a peep her way. Her jaw is set and her eyes look tired.

Rhonda marches around to my cubicle as soon as Caitlin's out of sight. "Can I come in?" she whispers.

I nod, and she sidles even closer than her visit here last week.

"So, as you know, Caitlin's engaged."

"Yes." I force myself to smile as brightly as Sir Sunny D, even as dread spins up my spine. I know exactly where this is going.

"So, us Morale Boosters should plan a surprise engagement party on Friday, when she normally goes for drinks. Just a small one with us friends at work and the happy couple."

I don't mean for my expression to shift—I really try—but Rhonda's eyes droop a bit as she notices my reaction. "It'll be small," she continues. "Nothing to outshine Gregory's work anniversary in two weeks. You won't have to do much, but could you help me on the day of with decorations? Your first assignment?"

FFS.

At face value, it's such a small ask, decorations. Only the idea of going to a party to celebrate Caitlin may make me break out in hives. But if I say no, it'll mean Rhonda has to do everything alone, yet again.

I nod and force out, "Happy to."

Her whole face brightens. "Thank you, dear. We now have two parties to plan—so fun!" She lowers her voice as Caitlin rounds the corner. "I'll go make a call in the boardroom to book the table."

My mouth twitches; I can't help the smile as Rhonda marches off. Because her steps are bouncier.

Caitlin squeaks back into her chair, and I sneak another glance her way. She's typing rapidly, yet the bags under her eyes rest heavy like flags of defeat.

Caitlin deserves a party before I beat her out for this job, at the very least.

Kidstreet

CLIFF'S DESK IS coated in paperwork and bright morning sunlight. In the middle of the chaos sit two fluffy donuts from the mall bakery. A printer on the side desk chugs out the last of its job as I tentatively take my seat across from him.

"Jolene!" His grin buzzes through me. "Apologies for the mess. I'm hoping you like the honey crullers to make up for it."

He grabs the freshly printed docs, shoves them in the stapler, and plops them on the desk in front of me. Then he tilts his screen toward me, revealing the first slide of a PowerPoint. "So you can follow along."

I slide the papers toward me and read the headline: "Communication in Business." "Can I keep this? It looks unputdownable. Maybe you should send this to a publisher, turn it into a bestseller."

He nods evenly. "In that case, I'll need to sign the first edition." He leans over me and a cloud of warmth floats between us. He bites the cap of a Sharpie off, signs the paper, and holds my gaze. "Is that bullshit out of our systems then?"

I nod. "I'm good."

"Great. We're just going through the PowerPoint together. The handout is for additional notes." He clicks his mouse and the first slide swipes across the screen.

I put up my hand like I'm a child in a classroom. "Cliff, isn't this a PowerPoint *presentation*?"

His jaw squares into quite a pleasant grump face. "What are you playing at?"

"I just meant you should *present*. I feel sort of . . . I don't want to give notes, but where's the showmanship?"

"You nail one amazing presentation, and now you're the expert, huh?" He says it teasingly, but the praise makes my heart expand anyway.

"Pretty much. You said you wanted me to do well. A student can only go as far as their teacher allows."

His nostrils flare a tad, but his lips curl up. He stands, splays his arms dramatically, and announces, "Effective communication in the workplace has three key cornerstones..."

As he continues, my eyes drift from the monitor to the yellow legal pad sitting open beneath it covered in Cliff's neat, boxy handwriting. On the top I see the words: *Employees to support.*

My own name catches my eyes like a snare. Next to it, the only words legible are *isolation, colleagues,* and *help her feel safe.*

Each word presses into me like a wound.

Cliff pauses as he realizes where I'm looking. Instantly, he is sweeping the papers together into a giant pile. "Sorry, no offense—just realized I've left a lot of my work papers on the desk." He stuffs the sheets into a folder identical to the maroon one I keep in my own drawer.

"No need to apologize." I force my expression neutral. "I didn't mean to be snoopy." The irony is not lost on me.

He shakes his head. "Nah, it's more that I don't want any distractions from the amazing show I'm putting on."

"Impossible."

His expression warms. "Hey, Jolene, you really did do a great job at the conference yesterday."

"Thanks," I say, still forcing myself not to look at the maroon folder in his arms. "I was a little nervous at first, but I'm glad I didn't fumble too much."

"I didn't notice any fumbling." He gestures toward his monitor. "But this show will help strengthen your skills. Which leads me to the second foundation of communication: body language." He swipes his hand across his body, fingers wiggling like he's in a boy band. When I don't laugh, his expression drops. "What's up? Why are you looking at the talent like they've upset you?"

I can't stop thinking about that damn folder—all the notes he makes for everyone, the individual meetings, the donuts. I swallow. "You're just... you're great at this. Your job."

He actually cares. So much. Did I lose that part of me? I definitely had it once.

Cliff's eyes widen with surprise, like he's been caught doing something other than being a total tool with a PowerPoint. "Jolene, kissing ass isn't a good look."

"I'm being serious." I look straight into his eyes, hoping he can tell how much I mean it. Cliff stares back, something strange brewing behind his expression. Then he looks away sharply toward the window.

The mood has quickly turned weird, so I say, "Doesn't it ever get to you, though? Dealing with office fucks and evaluating them on their personalized levels of bullshit?"

His mouth curls upward. "I mean, yes, I can think of times where people's bullshit in the office does annoy me." He stares at me again pointedly.

I bow my head. "Oh yes, I know I'm annoying. But anyway, it's cool you've found something you're really good at. The world needs more people who think they can save it."

It's tiny this time, but Cliff tenses again. Another look toward the window, the little golden flecks in his irises catching the light. "Jolene, I…" His eyes shift and he shakes his head, like he's physically pushing a thought away. "We should get back to it."

As he shuffles toward his mouse to wake up the monitor again, my eyes drift toward the windowsill where he'd been gazing. The glint of a picture frame sitting there catches my eye. The cars! It can't be. I'm out of my chair in an instant. There's a little boy with Cliff's same smile, hair combed back and a wash-worn shirt, sitting in the driver's side of the car.

Holy shit, it's exactly what I thought. "Cliff, is that you in a tiny car clapping with your hands above your head?"

His nod is stiff.

"Is it? Were you on–"

"Yes, that's *Kidstreet*. My sister and I got on it during some community outreach week."

"Oh my god. Oh … my god. *Cliff!* This is everything. I wanted to go on so bad, but I didn't have a sibling. I knew all the trivia. Did you win?"

His grin is all I need. "We should get back to the—"

"What did you pick? For your prize?" I hold the frame like its solid gold. It's so niche and incredible. It's unbelievable I didn't see it before.

"The Nerf gun." His tone is even, but I can tell he's glowing.

I drop the frame back onto the sill and put my face in my hands. "Oh, Clifford. You were one of the chosen few that got to scale the winners' toy mountain, and you're telling me on this day, the day of my anti-harassment training, that you didn't choose the moon boots? They were *the only* choice."

He shakes his head. "The moon boots weren't as good in person. I put tons of thought into my choice and tested everything for way longer than the producers wanted. They weren't used to that."

I detect a trace of hollowness in his tone. My chest twists as I imagine the boy in the picture carefully investigating the toy mountain, surrounded by frustrated men in suits trying to rush him.

Then I realize I've lost myself staring at adult Cliff with the same brown eyes. I clear my throat and say, "Cliff, I'm about to lose my shit all over the place right here. This is all so, soooo *cool.*"

He grins shyly. "If I'd known how heart eyes you'd go, I'd have said something earlier."

We both jolt at his words. His temples redden as a buzz rushes across my skin.

"Sorry—that wasn't what I . . . I meant as a great icebreaker. Nobody else remembers that show." He tilts his head. "What are you grinning about? Wait, let me guess. You're picturing young HR me making sure the producers form a cohesive team."

I stifle a grin and nod.

"That's fine. I'm picturing young Jolene walking around a playground rolling her eyes. And when did you master the fine art of sarcasm—high school? I'm imagining you stab-typing witty texts on your BlackBerry by the lockers."

My stomach drops. "No. I was . . . quiet in high school."

He raises a teasing eyebrow. "Really? That's hard to imagine. Did you go to high school around here?"

I shake my head on impulse. "No," I say, sharper than I intend.

There's no way I'm naming the town. Those sorts of details can stack up fast. If he looks up my high school, the article about Ellie's death always shows up. He'll wonder if I knew her . . .

I return to my seat and curl a little deeper into the chair.

Cliff's eyes flash with confusion, and the energy in the room deflates. "Sorry," he says haltingly. "I didn't mean to, like . . ."

I should've lied like a normal person. Being weird about it just makes people want to ask more questions. So I quickly paste my smile back on and say, "If you really want to know, in high school I had questionable fashion, read epic fantasy and paranormal romance like it was my job, and yes, I had a BlackBerry—but I used it for some snake game only."

He laughs. "Now that sounds like you." But there's still some tension creasing at the corners of his eyes. How can he read me so well, so often?

My eyes dart again to the maroon folder sitting on his desk, and I think of that little note again: *help her feel safe.*

I hear myself say, "I don't really like who I was back then."

I instantly regret my words. It's far too close to the bone. But Cliff nods and leans an inch closer across the desk. "Well, I don't know what you were like then—aside from that you grew up dreaming of working at Supershops, of course—but the Jolene of now is pretty great."

His words are like a warm blanket. It's not much, but it still feels like a small piece of the weight on my shoulders has been lifted.

"Want to get back to it?" he offers. "After we finish, I can draw out the *Kidstreet* studio set for you. It was way different from how it looked on TV."

"That would be lovely."

We finish the presentation without further interruption, and Cliff brings his A game to the performance. I can't help being charmed by his commitment.

But the whole time one thought presses the back of my mind: *If only we didn't have matching maroon folders.*

WHEN I RETURN to my workstation, a new email already sits in my inbox.

FROM: Clifford Redmond
TO: Gregory Hall
SUBJECT: Quick meeting?

Hello,

    After some initial meetings with employees, I'd love to meet and discuss the direction my reports seem to be heading. I also have something somewhat sensitive to discuss/an idea on how to manage an employee in the mandatory course—could prove beneficial for the company.

All the shit inside me hardens.

How could he go straight to Gregory after that meeting? What could he be saying about me? I shouldn't have been so loud, so myself, in front of him.

Gregory: How is 4 pm? I'll have Rhonda book a meeting room.
Cliff: Perfect.

So perfect.

A meeting appears on Cliff's and Greg's schedules. It's booked in the boardroom behind me. The one Caitlin just snuck into to make a call.

I rack my brain, replaying every single thing I said in Cliff's office. Did I joke too much? Did I not listen to the presentation well enough? Or did my comment about high school make Cliff decide to look me up after all?

I can feel the blood rushing away from my head. I look down at my hand, clenching my mouse in a death grip.

I *need* to know. If he's going to tell Gregory about my anxiety, or my behavior in our sessions, or anything else that will affect my life here—I need to hear it with my own ears.

If Cliff knows about what happened...

No, I can't even think about that. But what are Mr. Cliff's ideas? What after that meeting could they be discussing?

The door clicks open behind me. Caitlin emerges with her shoulders slumped, phone in hand. And an idea hits. It would be such a simple move. I look down at my phone sitting on my desk. I can't be in the room, but my phone can.

Sometimes to really play the game, you need to take a bit of risk.

Phone Plant

THERE'S ONLY HALF an hour until the meeting starts. Every muscle in my body is tense, my bones so heavy I feel as if I could fall through my chair.

I take a deep breath and square my shoulders. If I'm going to do this, I need to get into that meeting room now.

But just as I'm about to lift myself up, Caitlin huffs and bangs out of her chair, grabbing her phone and barreling back toward the boardroom.

"Don't go in there!" Rhonda calls right when Caitlin reaches the threshold.

"I'm just going to sit for a while," Caitlin says, sighing. "I need a break."

There's something off about her—she sounds worn, her lips thin and chin bent low.

Rhonda shakes her head, her hanging earrings jangling. "Not in there. Gregory's got a meeting soon and I need to set the waters up."

Fucking hell. I forgot that Gregory has Rhonda treat his meetings like he's the CEO on *Mad Men*. She'd be only too happy to wheel in a whiskey cart if the custom still applied.

Caitlin sighs again and pauses for a second like she's debating her response. "Whatever," she finally says, and returns to her desk, stuffing her phone back into her five-hundred-dollar basic black purse. I know the cost only because when Kyle gifted it to her for their anniversary, Garret held it up and announced it to the whole room.

I need to get in there. But with Rhonda keeping watch, I've got no chance. And judging from the fresh steaming cup of tea on her desk and the Excel grid I can see open on her computer, mouse hovering on the first row, she's there for the long haul.

I need to distract everyone, and fast. And I know only one thing that is guaranteed to get everyone up from their desks in a matter of seconds.

Before I can think too hard, I'm out of my chair. I head toward the bathroom, then pivot and speed walk down the hallway to the elevator. As soon as the doors open to the lobby, I race toward Artistic Coffee, the café next to our building. One only makes a purchase here out of desperation. The "artistry" from its namesake must be performative: keeping a straight face while serving diarrhea juice.

Mara, the alleged barista who has been working here since I started, doesn't acknowledge me as I walk in. I move up to the counter and call, "Are your scones your cheapest pastries?"

She nods, finally turning to look directly at me. Several piercings rise with her brows as she eyes me up.

"Great, I'll take three please."

The clock is ticking. Three forty-seven p.m. She bags them up and hands them to me with her heavily ringed fingers. The scones are hard as rocks and probably dry as shit, but that's for the best. This can't be too flashy; anything too good, like Cliff's donuts, and the entire floor would be up in an instant, marking me as the outlier.

I make my way back up to the office and swipe myself into the big lunchroom. Luckily, it's completely empty, the lights off. I drop the scones onto the center of the table and head back to the pods.

Armin is drooping so low in his chair it's a wonder he doesn't fall face-first onto his desk. Caitlin is slowly clacking away. Rhonda is taking a sip from her mug, humming to herself as she moves her icon from row 2 to row 3 of her grid.

How to get them up without alerting the entire office?

I sit down at my desk and go into my email, clicking open a blank message. My mouse hovers over my name to the option beneath it in the "From" section. I've used the admin account only to read other people's emails, not compose one of my own. I suck in air through my teeth and summon my most admin of admin voices:

FROM: Supershops Admin
BCC: Caitlin Joffrey; Armin Habib; Rhonda Staples
SUBJECT: Thank you for your great work

Dear Supershops employee,

To express our appreciation to our most hardworking employees this quarter, we've sent special gifts to lunchroom number 417.

Please collect your own gift ASAP. One per person.

Regards,

Management

I hit send, and it's instantaneous. Before I can even indulge in my dread, I hear the distinctive double tap of Rhonda opening her email. My heart is attempting to break from my rib cage and sprint across the office.

After a beat, Rhonda shrugs and stands up, heading toward the lunchroom. A few seconds later Caitlin gets up too. I'm somehow both relieved and scared shitless.

Armin doesn't go, but the good news is he might actually be dead with the way his lifeless body is leaning on the desk.

This is my chance. Through my pounding heart and dry throat, I make my way into the boardroom. Panic closes in while I'm scanning for a spot to leave the phone. It's too barren to hide anything well.

I rush to my desk, pull the tissue box from my bottom drawer, drop my phone in, and sprint back to the boardroom to leave it on the table. I'll have to hope nobody has any cold symptoms.

I emerge just as Larry Goodwin passes. I stop in my tracks in the threshold like a deer in headlights as he walks around me. A half second later, Gregory exits his office.

I'm going to shit my pants.

I put on my best neutral face and trot back to my desk. Just as I sit down, Caitlin and Rhonda round the corner, a scone each in hand.

Caitlin smiles and says way too loud, "It's so nice to have our hard work recognized."

Larry Goodwin halts in his tracks, dripping a slosh of water from his freshly filled bottle. "You guys got praised? What for?"

Caitlin speaks louder, chin jutting out. "Oh, just some of us got a little something in recognition of our hard work. It was in an email." Her eyes tilt my way as Larry's narrow on the scone in her hand.

Armin jostles awake, squinty-eyed. He clicks his mouse and views his screen.

Larry huffs; it's incredible how quickly the sweat can accumulate on his temples. "What, from Gregory?" He wipes his forehead with the sleeve of his shirt. His attention draws to Marla, who's walking from the printer room with a stack of papers in hand. "Hey, Marla, did you hear? Some people are getting recognition scones from Gregory!"

I'm dying. Sweat pools in my pits while I stare at my hands.

Marla gives him a confused look while Armin says, "Hey, Lar, if you want you can go have mine. I don't want it."

Larry lets out a disbelieving puff. "You got one too? Oh my god."

He marches back to his office double speed. As he disappears around the corner, I spot Cliff coming from the other direction. He walks right past my desk but doesn't even look up to say hi, just stares down at his phone. Heat flashes across my cheeks. Gregory suddenly turns to stare straight at me. Our eyes catch and he looks at me appraisingly. There's something mysterious in his gaze, like he's thinking something messed up, and it makes my skin prickle. I swing back around to look at my monitor.

Caitlin calls, "Oh, hi, Gregory. Thanks for the scone."

His brow twists. "What?"

I turn to stone.

I need to step in. I need to say something, do something—

A buzz suddenly tears through the room. Caitlin darts for her phone and stabs at it to turn it off. "Sorry, my fiancé's just trying to plan a weekend thing and—" Her shoulders drop as her phone starts ringing again in her hands. "I'll remind him that I can't talk during work hours."

Gregory smiles. "Young love is exciting. But it's smart to not let it distract you when you're here." And he leans closer. "Might be how errors sneak into the building."

She shrinks into herself and nods.

Cliff walks into the boardroom and Gregory follows behind him, closing the door.

My hands are shaking so hard I can barely move my mouse across my screen to fake work. It's taking so much effort to rein myself in, I almost don't notice Armin watching me.

A DM for Caitlin flashes across the screen. I can barely look at it.

Armin: Hey, didn't Jolene get a scone?

Caitlin: I guess not. Ha!

Caitlin: So the "exciting incentive program" Gregory mentioned at the meeting was . . . plain scones from Artistic Coffee? And to leave them in the lunchroom like that—what the fuck?

I blink several times, trying not to twitch or do anything weird with my face.

Armin: That's Gregory's brand. He's always giving us rewards that are secretly punishments to put us in our place.

Caitlin: I mean true. Remember the "pizza party" we "won"?

Armin: I almost punched the guy when I caught him bogarting all the microwaves to heat the shit up.

Caitlin: I guess this is better than Kirkland brand pizza pops. The cheap prick.

I stifle a chuckle. I remember the lead-up to that party that Greg kept selling us on: the printouts with graphics of *actual* pizza-shaped food—a defining moment about this place. Caitlin thanked Gregory for the pizza about a million times at the party. She sold her enjoyment so well that I genuinely worried for her.

I knew she was good with the BS, but I guess even I can't see through everything about her.

Thirty minutes pass in silence. I drag my mouse across my desktop, making grey boxes on top of my default wallpaper. I open the calculator app and type in random numbers.

Finally, the door to the boardroom clicks open. I don't turn around, but I can sense the two of them emerge. Gregory's footsteps sound behind me, heading back to his office. A moment later, I glimpse Cliff walking past. Again, he keeps his head down, eyes on his phone, until he disappears around the corner.

I can't just go and grab my phone right away. So I wait another fifteen minutes in agony.

Finally, once I'm certain that everyone is thoroughly entranced by the light of their monitors, I head to the boardroom.

When I step back out, I halt when I clock Armin watching me. His eyes shift, before he turns back to his monitor and throws his earphones back over his head.

I stand there for a beat, clutching my phone. There's no way he noticed I didn't walk in with it. I'm sure I'm just being paranoid.

Archives Aren't My Own

Back at my desk, I unlock my phone and stop the recording. Two new text notifications from my mom are waiting for me.

Mom: There's a new cheat where they sneak drugs in your luggage and another guy kidnaps you! Don't travel.
Mom: Also, Starbucks is a waste of money.

I swipe them away unread, linking my headphones to press *play*. The dead static of an empty boardroom plays.

I hit *pause*.

Anything could be in this recording. Yeah, Gregory will surely make me recoil minute one, but that's not what's tensing my butt cheeks.

It's silly. It's literally Cliff's job to talk about me behind my back. I need to get a grip.

It's this place—that's it.

As if to confirm my fears, footsteps tumble behind me as Larry and Joy pass by, matching mugs in hand and downturned mouths. They're discussing the quality of the duffel bag they each got as a fifteen-year appreciation gift from Supershops.

I can't do it here. I can't hear something that'll make me want to dissolve into a pile of dust while Stu fiddles with the angle of his desk fan. But I can't wait until I'm safely at home either. I can't sit through another car ride with Cliff if he's sold me out.

I slide my phone into my back pocket. I'm only too aware of myself and everyone I pass as I head toward the elevator, then keep going straight. The archive room at the end of the hall greets me like a dark cloak, the earthy cardboard scent beckoning me inside. The shelves are stacked so tightly with bulky file boxes they basically soundproof the room. I've actually had a few decent cry breaks in here. Turning on the lights will surely draw the attention of a passerby, so I crouch in a corner and fully settle into the sensory deprivation of the dark room as I pop in my headphones and press *play*.

I speed past the initial greetings, managing to stop when Gregory just has to say, "Let's get to the meat and potatoes then. What did you want to discuss?"

Cliff lets out a labored breath and says, "Well, I've met with most of the seventh-floor employees so far, but the most pressing thing is the employee in mandatory stress training. I think some of the resentments with the company are beyond the parameters of what we're covering. The course isn't designed to address these kinds of underlying mental health issues, and it's not in my interest to set someone up for failure or inhibit their long-term success with Supershops."

My heart drops into my stomach. Cliff had promised me he wouldn't say anything when I panicked in his office. And now he has to tell the worst fuck in the world about my issues. This is why I shouldn't have eaten his donuts or agreed to go out for milkshakes. I should never have agreed to be his carpool buddy.

He's an HR guy deep in his soul.

Gregory clears his throat. "Well, that sounds simple enough. Failing the course equals termination."

My blood freezes.

Cliff's voice comes back. "Actually, I want to propose that the company provide more mental health support."

Gregory's laugh charges through my earbuds and grates against my bones. "Mental health support." He chortles again. "We aren't running a day spa. Let's not make this too hard a puzzle. Failure in a mandatory course leads to termination. It's the easiest and, better yet, cheapest solution."

There it is. Exactly what I knew. How can Cliff be so dense? It's not right.

There's a moment of silence, filled only by my pounding heart.

"I understand that position," Cliff finally says, voice soft as a baby's bum. "But this is a long-term employee we're talking about. If we ignore systemic issues and simply terminate, it can cause more costly problems. Big picture: I've seen this in many companies I've worked with. Supershops' policies have contributed to a culture of resentment and feelings of insecurity from within."

"Insecurity is one of the most effective motivators for productivity. I'm running one of the largest retailers in the country." Gregory's laugh rips through me again, churning my stomach. "Between you and me, it's great when employees fail these last-chance courses. If all goes as expected, we may be able to terminate Larry by next week."

My heart stops. Larry! Larry Goodwin. He must be the one in a stress course! I'd thought Cliff had gotten his wording wrong.

Relief rolls through me like a wave. I sink against a stack of boxes, my whole body going slack, until I think of Larry, sitting at home in his same khakis, nowhere to go, no other marketable skills. He's a regional inventory assessor, and nobody actually knows what that means, but everyone's afraid to ask.

Cliff's voice is gentle. "We should wait to make a decision until we've completed our sessions to cover all bases."

Gregory clears his throat. "What about the other course employee? How's Jolene doing?"

I stop breathing.

"I see a lot of potential in her. She's been taking the courses seriously, and I think she's proving she can rise to the challenge."

"Hmm. Well, if she ends up failing—"

Cliff's tone sharpens. "I find that very unlikely—"

"That Armin kid is another low-hanging fruit," Gregory interrupts. "He's got a lot of unaccounted absences. If we track enough, we'll have reasonable evidence to let him go."

Cliff sighs as my tongue sours. "I met with him yesterday and . . . I've left my door open for him if he wants to discuss what's affecting his performance. I'm not sure he'll be an easy replacement."

Gregory's voice hardens. "We don't pay people to be away from their desks. Let's move on to Caitlin. She's a very pleasant gal, but she's going downhill with her errors. Last month her inventory report had three errors. Then last week there were two. If she makes any more, I might be calling you. These reports are critical."

Oh my god. Caitlin was making errors *before* I dicked with her docs?

Gregory chuckles. "That's how it goes. As soon as they get rings on their fingers, they stop caring about work, and then comes maternity leave after leave."

The room heats up. I'd eat Gregory alive if he wasn't so disgusting.

"Who exactly is the 'they' you're referring to?" Cliff's voice cuts sharper than I've ever heard. "As an HR rep that reports to head office first, I may need some clarity for my records."

Gregory's voice fumbles. "Employees. *All* employees," he mutters.

I can't help my lips from drawing up at the crack in his voice.

But the room suddenly lights up in a fluorescent flash, bright and blinding. Every one of my muscles tenses as I snag my headphones off with a tug.

I peek around a stack of boxes and find Caitlin huffing in the opposite corner, a giant stress line creasing her forehead. "I can do this," she whispers.

I crouch behind the box stack again and try to tuck myself behind it, but her eyes dart to me in an instant.

"Were you hiding here in the dark? What the fuck—are you spying on me?" Her face twists.

"No," I croak, my throat going suddenly dry. "I was looking for an old file."

Her brows twist. "Why?" she accuses.

It's just like Caitlin to think she owns the archive room when two hundred other people in this office need to file, cry, or hide.

But the line in her forehead sharpens and her lower lip trembles. It's just me and her in here, and something about that feels raw and real.

I stand up. "And what are you doing here?" I blurt out.

Caitlin's eyes widen. Then she huffs and turns away wordlessly, slamming the door shut behind her.

"Okay then," I say to the empty room. "I'll see you later."

I return to my desk just as the clock hits five. Rhonda is packing up, and Armin's things are already gone. There's a new message waiting on my screen—one that's actually meant for me.

Cliff: Did today seem longer than usual?

I smile to myself. It's such a relief to let go of the fear from earlier. If Cliff had actually exposed me, it would have been worse than I care to admit.

But now at least it's clear he hasn't been putting on an act. He cares about people.

I type a reply and hit send before I can overthink it.

Jolene: *Definitely. But in only a few mins I'll be DJ-ing in your car...*

Cliff's icon shows he's typing. Shows he's deleting. Shows he's typing again.

My breath halts with each move.

Cliff: Can't wait!

It's just an exclamation mark. It shouldn't make my heart leap.

Gutter Ball

TRAFFIC FINALLY SHOWS an opening after a painful chug of stop and go. We crawl around the pylons and past a guy in yellow coveralls who directs us through the detour. When the light flips to yellow and the guy in front halts, Cliff taps the steering wheel. "Come on, you could've made it." His gaze drifts toward the little clock under the dashboard.

"Maybe they shouldn't have broken the water main today," I joke, grabbing his phone off the console to find a new song.

"Yes." Cliff nods stiffly. A heavy sigh follows.

His phone lights up in my hands as he's taking a turn. A text notification flashes onto the screen.

Grace: Are you coming?

Holy shit. Cliff has a date.

Of course he does.

"Sorry, it's just . . . I said I'd be somewhere and it's halfway toward our neighborhood, but because we're so late . . ." He locks eyes with me. "Would you mind if we picked someone up on the way?"

"No, of course not," I pleasantly agree as my insides crumble.

A carpool buddy should have no problem letting him pick up his girlfriend.

"Thanks," he says. "That'll be much easier than heading home and then picking her up to go to the bowling alley."

Oh god, he's taking her bowling. Why does his choice of date venue have to be so *Cliff*? Something catches in my throat, and I blink far more than necessary.

When we pull up to a beautiful little century-old apartment building with a perfect red door, I blink and blink as an attractive brunette in a trendy, oversized wool jacket with clunky boots and heavy makeup trots toward the car. She walks with such a sure-footed stride that I'm half convinced she owns the sidewalk.

"I can give her my seat," I offer, my smile as delicate as a porcelain doll.

"No, don't worry, Grace's cool. Just stay put."

I don't know why I feel the urge to clarify that I'm just as cool.

This Grace opens the back door and says, "We're never going to make it unless you book it now. What, did you need them to pave the roads before you could drive here?" Grace's spicy perfume wafts toward me as she settles into the back.

"Water main. You're free to check the traffic app." Cliff rolls his eyes and tilts his head toward me, rubbing their casual bicker in. "Grace, this is my colleague Jolene."

I turn, forcing my smile to brighten—forcing my exterior to at least not crack.

Grace sizes me up, her eyes shifting across my face, before her lip curls up. "Oh, *you're* the Jolene he works with."

She sort of chuckles. And I sort of die. What the hell is he telling her about me? There are so many possibilities: *the HR problem child, the violently horny music girl, the girl with the stain on her chair.* Every possibility makes me need to crawl inside a giant hole and live like a bear during winter.

Cliff's knuckles whiten and he winces *just so.* Via the rearview mirror, I catch Cliff and her exchanging a nervous grin.

I stare forward through the windshield. Okay, so they laugh about me.

I push all my thoughts down—below the tightness in my chest, below the lead in my stomach. He just gives me rides, that's all. And maybe he shouldn't if I'm just making him late to gossip about me with his girlfriend.

I'm mentally preparing an email to let him know that three buses marinated in urine are preferable to his boorish company when Cliff says, "This is my sister, Grace."

Grace throws her hand into the front of the car for me to shake. "I've heard so many wonderful things about you."

A rush of heat flushes through my cheeks as I take her hand. Cliff looks between his sister and me again. Why am I smiling so hard? "Nice to meet you." My voice is small. What wonderful things has she heard? And how can there be so many?

Grace brightens as she settles back into her seat. "It's great you're bowling with us tonight. We need a fourth since Deirdre can't make it."

And a panic rises in me. "Oh, I'm not—"

Cliff looks at me thoughtfully as he cuts in. "We'll be dropping Jolene off first."

Grace's pink-tinted lips smack together. "Nope. There's no way we'll make it if we don't go straight there, and we're down one. Have you even *asked* Jolene?"

Cliff looks at her in the mirror and sets his jaw. "No, that's not something—"

"So, would you like to come?" she declares, bending around the passenger seat so her cheek is practically touching mine. "There's a nutritious dinner of hot dogs and nachos in it for you," she adds, raising her brows suggestively.

"You don't have to," Cliff says, wide-eyed. But he doesn't look repulsed by the idea. Just a little concerned.

"Yeah, let's do it," I blurt out before I can think it through.

Grace squeals and claps her hands with delight, while Cliff bends his chin to look at me. "You sure about this?" he says, softer.

I haven't bowled in years, probably since I was a preteen. There'll be people I don't know and weird machines I don't know, and I won't know what is what.

But it's Cliff's hesitant little grin that tugs me—I *want* to go.

"I've never been so sure about anything in my life."

Grace laughs, because it sounds like I'm joking. Not the rantings of a woman who still hasn't nailed existing in public as a skill set. Am I really going to do this?

Cliff twists the steering wheel, taking a hard left. "All right then, to the bowling alley."

My stomach tightens. I can roll some balls around for an hour. It's not impossible. I can do this.

BALLS WHOOSH AND crash into pins with violent clangs while random sirens and bells chime. Disco lights throw rainbow dots all across the walls and scuffed wooden floors. Stereos are blasting a song that probably came out when Supershops still offered one-hour photo development, and the scent of fake cheese holds the room hostage. In the corner, a rowdy group of men, all in Canadian tuxedos, pepper the corner; their head-to-toe denim is oddly comforting at this hour.

Cliff keeps eyeing me like I'm going to catch fire. To be fair, I might.

He and Grace check in, and I realize they've brought their own shoes and balls. Shit, I've volunteered to do the thing where I have to wear shoes that about a thousand other people have worn. As feared, when the bored gentleman working the rental stall proudly slides a previously white-and-green pair across the counter, I am certain the first person to have rented them died from natural causes some years ago.

While lacing up on the plasticky cup seats, Cliff shifts toward me, his leg almost touching mine. I flinch, then try to hide it by saying, "I'm fine with all of this. It's actually delightful to wear shoes that might be haunted."

He laughs, and the motion brings him even closer, whipping my chest into a swirl. "If you were dead, would you haunt some bowling shoes?"

I stare down at them in all their stained, stinky glory. "If I had nothing better to do."

His expression shifts to be more serious. "So, fair warning: my grandma is a little much. I mean, I love her to death, she raised me on hardly anything, but you know how it is with families?" He says it like it's a question rather than a universal truth. "I didn't mean to rope you into all this."

His fingers twitch nervously next to my thigh. This isn't about me.

As if on cue, a short lady with curly white hair pouring through a visor approaches in limping steps. She's got Cliff's same cheery eyes paired with a windbreaker suit so bright that the wind knows not to approach from a mile away. She shoves into Cliff and scoops him into her chest, then tilts my way while he suffocates against her bosom. "I'm Lisa, Clifford's granny. Thanks for saving us a forfeit. Do you know how to bowl?" Her eyes narrow at me, calculating.

I nod. I've bowled, like, twice in my life—as in tossed a few balls, then played on a Hulk Hogan pinball machine. I'm sure it's fine.

Cliff's granny releases him from her death grip. He takes a dramatic gulp of air like he's just been saved from drowning as his granny pinches his cheek. He looks toward me, temples red. "I'll get you a ball."

Lisa and I watch as he precariously balances three balls while walking to the seating at the end of our lane. We follow behind him more slowly since she has a slight limp.

At the lane, the opposing team—five middle-aged men with shirts that all read *Disco Dads*—sits casually. Grace is already standing over them, front and center of the group, hand gesturing to the scoreboards as she speaks. I'm the only person in this chaotic room who doesn't know what to do. I don't know where the bathroom is or if someone has a favorite seat. I stand awkwardly to the side as Lisa slowly makes her way to the lane. Cliff pulls out a curved ramp device from against the wall next to the lane and meets his grandma to set it up.

Grace motions toward me and then pats the scratched-up seat next to her. As I sit down, she says, "Grandma is so proud of him. She thinks he walks on water." Grace's smile crinkles in her eyes as she looks at them fondly.

I grin. "Cliff says she raised you?"

"Yeah . . . technically, she did." The corners of her smile waver. "Our parents weren't in the picture, so to Grandma's house we went. But Cliff was the one who kept watch." She keeps her voice light, but her words are heavy; they linger in the air between us. "Wasn't all bad, though. Cliff liked to pretend we were Luke and Leia. I'm pretty sure he still believes he carries the force."

Grace and I both turn in unison to look at Cliff. He's finished setting up the ramp contraption and is now picking up Lisa's frosty green ball and placing it at the top for her. Essentially, his grandma isn't bowling so much as simply letting go of a ball so it can fly down a slope.

Grace continues: "She's almost made a full recovery. Only eighteen months since her surgery."

I'm not sure what she's talking about, but I say, "That's great."

"Yeah…" There's an uncertain edge to her voice. "Hey, I don't suppose he's mentioned anything about moving back to Vancouver to you?"

My eyes flash toward her. "What?"

Her brows rise. "That's a no then?"

I shake my head, but my insides shatter with the sound of the crashing pins. "Sorry, I just—I didn't know. I thought Cliff said he grew up here?"

"Ah." She inhales deeply before pressing her lips thin. "He's not an open book, is he? I assumed he would have at least mentioned his last job—the life he had before he moved back to Calgary—at some point."

I suddenly feel embarrassed. I barely know him, not like his family and friends here. "Oh yeah, he sort of has … I just didn't realize it was in Vancouver." My voice tightens against my will. "What was his job?"

"So this is a huge shocker, but he used to help people—usually housing displaced or, with a less-than-stellar track record, find employment."

My jaw goes slack. "No! That's, like, perfect for him!"

"Right?" She smacks me on the thigh, like we're old friends. I stare at her waxy blue nails, still pressing into my pants, as she continues. "Yeah, he got that job straight out of college, left for Vancouver and never looked back." Her gaze shifts toward Cliff, who is whispering in his grandma's ear. "But when he heard about Grandma's surgery, we couldn't stop him. He flew back to help even though we all yelled about it." We both stare at Cliff, who's setting up the next ball for his grandma. The electronic screens above them are playing an absurd animation of bowling pins wearing cowboy hats breaking each other out of a jail cell. "He's had no luck finding anything like that here. We figured he'd go back, now that she's better, but of course he's still here helping." She chuckles, but it's hollow.

By the lanes, Lisa releases the ball and it glides straight in between the remaining pins. Cliff makes a show of wildly clapping his hands while his grandma hobbles over to swat him.

My chest caves in as the thought intrudes. He's not meant to be at Supershops Incorporated. He's not meant to stay here.

Grace nudges me. "Hey, don't worry, he's not *that* tragic. Sounds like Supershops is way better than his insurance HR gig last year. He complains so much less." Then her eyes run over my face quizzically. "Cliff mentioned you're becoming friends too, so things are good. He seems happier."

Hope bubbles in my chest. He said that to his sister? That has to mean something. But just as quickly the bubble deflates. I didn't even know about Vancouver, about his better life.

"Make sure you at least hit some pins." Cliff's granny's voice comes out of nowhere, followed by an elbow nudging my side.

"Sure thing." I smile at her and stand up.

I make my way to the floor arrows and try my best to look calm. Beside me, a ball flies back up the return machine and crashes into the row, making me jolt.

I pick up a ball that feels too big and too heavy. I toss it onto the lane in what I'm sure is abysmal form, but I do manage to get one pin down. Cliff steps toward me, a black-and-white marbled ball in hand. "Try mine, it's lucky," he says.

I put my hand to my chest. "Cliff, I'm honored you'd share your ball with me."

His lips tease out a smirk. "This *is* a great honor, thank you for recognizing that."

Our hands graze during the handover, sending a rush through my abdomen.

On my second turn, three more pins fall. Not as terrible as can be.

When I get back to the seats, Cliff is rallying the group together. "Right, what's everyone eating for intermission?" They all shout out their orders, and once he's taken them, he turns to me. "Jolene? This place boasts a lovely à la carte menu of the finest haute dogs. Would you like tapas to start? They've got nachos and cheese sauce."

"It's okay, I can get a snack myself." The last thing I need right now is for Cliff to buy me dinner—even bowling alley caliber—in front of his family.

Grace leans in and puts a hand on my shoulder. "You know you can't stop Cliff from buying shit."

She's right, of course. I do at least know that about him. I resign myself to my fate and say, "A hot dog sounds lovely." As he heads over to the food counter, I turn to Grace and say, "That's really kind of him to always treat people."

She nods and smiles, a bit wistful as she watches her brother's back. The rainbow disco lights dance across her face. "He's always been like that. Even when we were kids, he'd save me his cookies from the government lunch program. Can you imagine that? I like to tell him he's being a bitchy martyr, for balance."

My smile is wobbly. I like her, and—another rush piles through my abdomen, heavier than the last—I like Cliff.

Cliff returns with a giant tray piled high with steaming food that's been through every kind of processing invented. "There's three more trays, so hold tight," he says as he heads back to the counter.

He leaves me alone with a giant pile of French fries. I start to dig in as I look around at the other groups of bowlers. There's a teen birthday party at the far lane, with everyone singing a different part of "Happy Birthday." In the corner by the jukebox, there's a young couple looking at songs and laughing and finding little ways to touch each other. This place is so wholesome and lively.

A piercing dinging noise suddenly rips through me, sending my skin shivering with goose bumps like an ice cube landed on the back of my neck. I whip around and realize it's coming from a pinball machine, where a dad is playing with his toddler.

Reality washes over me, sharp and unbidden.

The last time I went bowling was with Ellie.

The memory pushes in, as crystalline as if it happened yesterday instead of over a decade ago. We didn't get invited to some party, so we decided to go bowling instead. We spent more time making different dirty names for ourselves in the decades-old computer system than actually playing. We were painfully uncool together, but in the best way. Eventually we gave up on the lanes altogether and ended up challenging each other to several rounds of pinball. That was only a few months before she died.

Now *this* will be the last time I bowled. A tumbling feeling hits, like sand sifting away inside me. It's like I'm writing over that memory, erasing it. I wrap my arms around my chest, looking for something to distract myself, but everyone here is moving far too fast. They're all talking, and it's so loud. Everyone in the world is thinking right now, and there's far too much thought floating in the air.

I spot Cliff turning back from the food counter, another tray full of hot dogs in hand. He grins at me from across the room. He has no idea what's in my brain, and I'll never know his. Today has proven that much, at least. These people, his family, they're all kind people. They've been through hard times, yet they manage to be calm and normal about basic things. They don't spy or send emails out of pettiness.

How would it be to lead a nice, small life with someone? To be okay?

Cliff holds a hot dog in front of my face, jolting me out of my trance. "I brought you ketchup, mustard, and, just in case, relish." He tilts his head, assessing my face. "Is everything okay? I know the hot dogs aren't—"

"I love hot dogs. Thanks." I take the silver-foiled package from him. It's warm in my hand. "Was just remembering a time I bowled with an old friend . . . one I haven't spoken to in a while."

Cliff shifts closer to me. "Ah, it's tough being away from people you care about, eh? I wish we could just force everyone we love to live in the same city as us. Like, *actually* force."

I let out a chuckle, one that's real. My mind drifts to Vancouver as I reply, "Same."

It feels like I'm on solid ground again. I open my mustard packet, and Cliff says, "I knew you'd go for mustard. I had a feeling you had taste."

I look directly at him. "Of course I have taste."

We eat our hot dogs as Cliff tells me about the Disco Dads and his granny's theories on their cheating ways. And the whole time, I'm too aware of the distance between us. When we're done, I inch a little closer to grab a napkin.

It's Her Party, I Can Hide If I Want To

THE SECOND CAITLIN slinks out with Garret at five p.m., Rhonda marches into my cubicle guns blazing—and by guns, I mean the two giant Party City bags hanging from her arms.

"You're my only decorator tonight," she announces, all business. "Garret's busy delaying Caitlin, and Marla's out sick with the stomach flu. Who gets the stomach flu this time of year? It's just a hangover or laziness."

Damn it, the stomach flu was going to be my excuse to leave the party early tonight.

Rhonda actually grabs the back of my chair and pulls it out so I'm forced to stand up. "We have so much to do. I've told Garret to give us one hour. I got these spirals at Party Plus during lunch to put up in the bar."

Part of me wonders what Rhonda would do if I just turned around and ran for the hills now, without any explanation. But her bright gaze, the lilt in her voice... her desolate Silver Timings profile she checks as often as she calls her son. She lives for this. And it's not like I can judge her for not having other things to do.

Her frosty peach lipstick that has surely been discontinued is different from her normal shade. She's paired her nylon tights with heeled sandals, and her big toenail looks on the verge of cutting itself free. She dressed up for tonight...

But it's not only that. I think of her smile when I was presenting in the multi-unit meeting. Her shy thank-you when I taught her how to use the online archive. I've always suspected that Rhonda was part evil, but maybe that part isn't as big as I thought.

I take one of her bags and say, "Just let me know what you'd like me to do."

The way she grins makes it feel like an act of mercy.

I can be the bigger person here. And it may be best to give Caitlin a nice send-off, after all.

The bar sits down the street from our building. As it's located in a corporate section of downtown, it's mostly frequented for office functions like ours. I've never been inside, but perhaps this is another thing I should start getting used to. If I'm going to be the new document lead in a few weeks' time, I may have to socialize with my team more.

We climb down the creaky wooden staircase into the dimly lit basement room that boasts hardwood floor and walls and a lot of brass items throughout. The stale liquor scent roils my tummy. I try to imagine being a regular here—one of the few who go for Friday drinks. Except the place has got all the workings of a bad time. The lighting is too bright to hide from, and there are too many standing tables so people can stare at you from all angles. Still, maybe with enough practice, it wouldn't be bad either. It could even be fun.

Rhonda finds our reserved area in the back. She somehow produces a third giant bag that reads *Dollars Plus* and crinkles with every step as she marches to plop it on a corner table. Purple streamers spill out the sides; this decor is going to be so ugly and pointless. But the fact that she went to three different party shops crushes me.

"Right." She claps her hands together. "How are you at standing on tables and making spirals with dual ribbon colors?"

"I like to think I'm pretty great at that," I mutter.

She actually squees. "Wait until you see the paper flowers I found!"

I keep my smile plastered firmly on my face. It's like she's testing how far she can pull this shit without me getting angry enough to leave something not fully dead under her desk.

We get to work tacking up weird paper shapes to the walls—me mostly standing on the tables, and Rhonda handing me tape and telling me where to put it. I'm careful to follow her instructions as best I can. When we're done, she grabs my arm. "The fund has enough for everyone to get one drink, but if we order a few bottles of wine to share instead, we can have a drink now." She winks at me, all rebellious.

"Actually, I might not stick around too long."

Her mouth puckers so small that it cracks her lipstick. "What? The party hasn't even started. Have a drink with me; you've earned it."

I stare toward the staircase. "I'm not sure..." I start to say, but she's already at the bar.

I'm not a social drinker anymore. People get in the way of real drinking. And socializing is the last thing a drunk person should be doing. Hasn't anyone else figured out this life truth?

Before I can leave with my vibe intact, she returns, bottle in hand, and says, "Oh, come on, you're not going to leave me with this bottle of rosé alone?"

She waves it in front of me, the pink liquid inside sloshing around and glinting against the bright lighting. Oh, if only Rhonda knew how familiar I am with this particular eight-dollar bottle.

I glance at the time on my phone. Caitlin & Co. won't be here for a while yet. And I can't stand the idea of leaving Rhonda to sit here, drinking all by herself, mind wandering where it always goes when a lonely person is alone.

So I resign myself to my fate and say, "Hit me."

Once the wine is poured, she clinks our glasses together and says, "Cheers! You're not half as bad as I thought."

I cough into my drink. Leave it to Rhonda to say exactly what she means. But I can respect it. I give her a small smirk and whip back, "Neither are you."

Her grin sharpens, her eyes wrinkling with mirth. And my chest lifts. She's not so bad.

And, as it turns out, Rhonda can hold her own with a bottle. She quickly polishes off her first glass and pours us both a second, then makes quick work of that too.

I'm idly listening to her tell a story about her latest knitting project when she suddenly pats me on the shoulder. I jolt, looking at her glossy plum nails against my plain black shirt.

"I know you're not one to be overly friendly with people," she says, her eyelids drooping as she stares into her empty glass. "And that's fine.

You like to keep to yourself. But I always wondered if you were mad at me for something."

I shake my head. "Not at all!" And maybe that's true, if I can ignore all the times she's annoyed me, all the white-ink emails I've sent her through the years.

Her gaze locks on to me, eyes soft and glassy. "I thought my Christmas decorations were nice."

All the air deflates from my lungs. So I'm not the only one holding on to that little tiff from six years ago when I moved Rhonda's tinsel. I really am a miserable jerk.

"Yeah, Rhonda, I'm really sorry I wrecked your decorations. That wasn't nice. I'm no fan of glitter, but I could've handled that better."

Rhonda's face goes slack, like I've just relieved her of some momentous weight. "Thank you, dear. I shouldn't have held a grudge. I just love Christmas. But maybe you don't like religion in the office. It didn't used to be an issue, but I don't like to make people uncomfortable."

I nod. "It wasn't that. I celebrate Christmas." Which, nowadays, is just an obligatory dinner at my parents' house, a small gift exchange, and a depress-y night in the apartment with whichever neighbor likes to blast *Wheel of Fortune* all evening.

She brightens and grabs the wine bottle, pouring us both another glass. "Does your mom do a big turkey?"

"An amazing one! Which is interesting since she grew up in Iran and didn't do Christmas there, yet she mastered it."

Rhonda pauses, her wineglass halfway to her lips. "You're Iranian?"

I involuntarily brace myself; I'm usually more aware of when I "come out" as Persian, but the wine loosened me up. Being white presenting, talking about my background is like playing Russian roulette. Most people are normal about it, but I've encountered enough of the type who get twitchy and start talking about their one friend or masseuse or whatever. And then there are the people who act like I intentionally tricked them into *not* being racist by holding back this crucial info—and they always make up for it.

Rhonda smiles and pats my arm. "Like Armin! Not that you're the same, but I'm sure it's nice to have someone you work with share the same culture as you."

Relief washes over me as the warmth of her hand seeps in. "Yeah," I say, and nod. So what if the majority of the total conversations we've had in our four years working together happened this week?

Rhonda twists the stem of her glass. "I know Armin gets annoyed with me, especially when I talk about Carl. But I can't help it, it's my life."

A lump forms in my throat. I take another gulp of wine to wash it down.

She follows suit, taking another heavy swig of her own. She stares at the now empty bottle sitting between us, eyes glazed over. "I know I talk about him a lot, but he made me very proud. Even when he did something disappointing, I was always so proud, so full of joy, to be his mom. It was the best time of my life."

She's speaking in past tense.

I can't help but think of my own mom—the messages she sent today asking how work was going and to tell me about the newest fucked-up show she found on Discovery Channel. That string of unanswered texts isn't much better than Rhonda's call log.

"For what it's worth," I begin, trying to keep the emotion out of my voice, "I can tell you're a great mom."

Rhonda holds up her nearly empty glass wineglass toward me. "I didn't think you were all bad, but it's good to be right."

I clang my glass with hers. "To being right."

And right when she raises her drink to polish off the last of our bottle, Garret walks in, trailed by two other guys from the finance team, Anthony Clark and Paul Chauncy. I've never spoken to them before; finance men tend to move in a pack, and the medley of cologne and hair gel odors makes me dizzy.

"The lovers will be here in ten minutes," Garret announces to the room. "She thinks we're going on a double date to meet my new boyfriend, Eduardo."

Rhonda nudges me and calls out, "Well, the party's ruined because nobody will believe that lie. You couldn't get a guy with such a sexy name. The best you could get is a Bruce. Isn't that right, Jolene?"

I try to chuckle, but more of Caitlin's friends from the office are trickling down the stairs, and all their eyes are narrowing in on me with expressions ranging from curiosity to suspicion.

"I'll get more wine!" Rhonda announces gleefully, stumbling out of her seat and toward the bar.

Garret's gaze trails from the clearly inebriated Rhonda to me, eyeing me like I'm a criminal.

And this is my cue to leave. I stand up, intending to make my way outside as subtly as possible, when—

"*Surprise!*" everyone yells at once, and I am forced against the back wall as everyone crowds forward to greet Caitlin as she appears at the top of the staircase.

She clutches a hand—the one with the diamond on it—against her chest in fake awe. "Oh god, you guys shouldn't have!"

The throng encroaches on her. A glass of bubbly appears in her hand.

"Kyle!" Garret calls, as a guy makes his way into the room behind Caitlin. From my place in the back, I can make out only the top of his gelled dark hair.

So this is the Kyle of Caitlin's Instagram, of hand and torso modeling fame. He's shorter than I pictured. He has his back to me as he greets Garret, but I can already tell that he's nothing special. His jeans are the Very Bad type—I'd almost categorize them as a red flag. Caitlin takes a big swig of her champagne and walks up to him for a hug. His arm wraps around Caitlin's shoulders and pulls her in tight against his chest, and he whispers something to her without actually moving his face toward her, in that controlling man way.

Finally, he turns to take stock of the crowd around them, and I get a decent glance at his face.

All the air rips from my lungs. I fall back against the wall like it will offer some sort of camo. But it's too late. He flinches when he registers my face too, his eyebrows shooting up into his hairline.

I'm Bambi in headlights. My head is spinning, like I've had five bottles of wine instead of half of one. I slink around the tables, toward the exit. Everyone is still crowded so tightly around Caitlin that I have to force my way to the stairs. And Kyle is standing right there, in front of the threshold.

"Jo-Jo," he calls out as I get close.

Before he can say anything else, I bolt past him and flee the room.

Curb Appeals

As soon as I'm out of the bar, I take three long strides, and that's when a hand clamps down on my shoulder and forces me to a stop.

"Jo-Jo," he says, "I can't believe it's you." His eyes are darting across my face almost manically, like he's taking stock of every detail. I turn my chin to the side and push my shoulder up to try to loosen his grip. "Every time Caitlin complained about the Jolene at work, I never imagined it was the girl from high school who—"

"I have to go." My voice sounds an octave higher, not my own.

"No, wait." He says it like an order—or an accusation. "I've wondered about you. A lot of people have." He tilts his head. "You look the same."

My skin tightens and cools beneath his touch. I nudge my shoulder again. "I really need to—"

"Hey," he says, finally releasing me so he can put both his palms up in a placating gesture. "I just wanted to—I don't know what to say. It's been a long time. But it looks like you're doing okay for yourself."

I pause, rocking on my heels. Am I doing okay? Maybe I am, if even he thinks so.

Maybe seeing him again doesn't have to be what I've built it up to be in my head. It's been so many years. I can handle it.

"Yeah," I say, crossing my arms over my chest. "Yeah, I'm doing good."

But something dark shifts across his face as I say this, curling his bottom lip. And I realize my mistake instantly. He doesn't want me to be okay. Of course he doesn't.

He laughs once, sharply. "Man, what are the odds?" He takes a step back, looking me over from head to toe. "I mean, if I'd known it was you, I would've warned Caity." He makes a cross with his fingers, laughing again as he holds it up at me.

And it's like time travel. I'm seventeen again, and I'm drunk, and we're at the party at Stanley Park. And Kyle is tormenting Ellie, holding up his fingers in a cross and shouting, "Get away, loser."

And Ellie is pulling on my wrist and saying we should go, but I shrug her off because he's not saying it to me. And because for once, before Kyle came, it felt like I belonged. Because I thought we were actually enjoying drinking random liquor from Solo cups. So I take another drink as Ellie takes off into the forest. Before I notice she left.

I glance down at my wrist, turning it over to look at the faint blue veins showing through the thin skin. I can still feel the indentations of Ellie's fingerprints there.

And I bolt. I think I hear Kyle say something behind me but don't know what. All I can focus on is the sound of my feet pounding on the pavement. I don't know where I'm going. Every step I take rattles through my chest, my heart constricting and expanding painfully against my ribs.

Eventually I stumble on a crack in the sidewalk and only just manage to keep myself from falling. I lower myself to sit on the curb. I take a ragged breath and pull out my phone and search for the *Mountain Valley Herald*, followed by Ellie's name. My heart won't stop pounding as my finger taps enter.

The article comes up, the very first hit. The one that's been burned in my brain, even though I haven't looked at it in fifteen years.

Has it changed?

I scan over the words. It talks about the senior party, but it doesn't mention how I practically forced Ellie to come. How I told her we were invited. How her face dropped when she found out I lied.

I inhale.

Ellie's underaged drinking is noted. But it doesn't mention how we drank so much that it was unbelievable we were still standing. It makes zero note of the people who encouraged us, manipulated us, bullied us... for years.

It doesn't mention that when a song started playing, Ellie started to sing along, but her voice was slurred and everyone started laughing at her.

And now that song stops me in my tracks.

The article says that she wandered off into the woods. It doesn't say that it took me ten minutes before I realized and went searching for her.

It doesn't say how raw my throat went as I screamed her name, looking for her, begging her to come back.

It doesn't describe the sound of the snap. The sound I couldn't quite place.

How Ellie slipped and hit her head on a rock and that was that.

The article says that a friend reported the incident.

It doesn't talk about how impossible it was for me to leave her body, even to get help.

But I did. I left her.

When we returned to her, she was so cold. Her fingers weren't even a person's anymore. I can still feel them. And now touching people feels impossible sometimes.

The article says it was determined that she died instantly. But how can that be? How can everything that we are disappear so quickly?

The article ends there. But there's more to the story, of course. All the whispers that followed my family, the accusatory looks. How I hid away in my room for months, thinking of all the things I could've done differently. How I felt like I had died that night too. How sometimes, when I'm drunk, I still get the urge to run for help.

I can feel the wetness gathering between my fingers. When did I start crying?

"Jolene?"

I go taut. His voice threatens to loosen the knot inside me, but I focus all my energy on holding it tight, willing myself to not completely fall apart as I lift my head to look at him.

Cliff stands under the yellow light of a streetlamp, cheeks flushed from the chilly air. His collared shirt is peeping out of the top of his zipped-up jacket.

He takes one look at my face and his eyes go wide. He rushes to close the few strides between us. "You—are you okay?"

"I'm really great," I say, forcing out the most chipper voice I can manage. I wipe at the wet tracks on my cheeks and push my lips up into a wobbly smile.

He crouches down beside me, his gaze searching mine. His hand lifts toward my face, and for a moment I think he might touch my cheek, but he catches himself and shoves it into his pocket. "You're not great. Were you at the party?"

He sounds so concerned, and I'm so embarrassed. I hate that he's seeing me like this, and I hate how glad I am that it's him.

"Yes," I practically sing. "It's a really nice little group. You go enjoy."

"Jolene" is all he says, looking at me through lowered eyelids. "Please, tell me."

Again, I force a smile. "Okay, I know how this looks. I'm just a little… Maybe something I ate."

His hand twitches in his pocket. "Then I can take you home."

"No!" I say, leaning back to add another inch of space between us. Being alone in an enclosed car with him is the last thing I need right now. I'm about to unravel. "Please, go to the party," I practically beg. "You were already on your way there, weren't you?"

His gaze flicks toward the road, like he's only just remembering where we are. "Actually, I'm pretty sure Garret invited me as a joke. It's kind of obvious, like invite the HR guy to police the party." His voice softens as he croaks, "I'd just kill the fun."

Why is the world like this? It's the clench in his fists as he tries to shrug it off—the cruelty of the invite. It's like we're all stuck in a loop. I stare at the sidewalk and blink and blink. "Yeah, sounds like Garret. Why were you going then?"

His gaze drops, a blush starting on his temples. "Don't know." He shrugs, the side of his arm brushing against mine at the motion. But I hear it in his voice.

"Why did *you* go?" he says.

I press my lips together. The answer is far too messy. The truth would mean confessing—the emails, Rhonda's secret, the hole I've been digging deeper by the day. But for a moment it feels so tempting to just tell him everything. A part of me thinks he'd try to understand. I shake that wish away. After everything tonight, I'm not thinking straight.

We both sit together in silence. Here we are, two losers outside a party no one wanted us to come to. I've been here before. Maybe this time, we can just leave.

And now his car seems like the best place in the world.

"I've changed my mind. Can you give me a ride after all?" I ask.

"Yeah, of course," he says quickly, pushing himself onto his feet. He holds out a hand and offers it to me.

I take it, letting him lift me to my feet. Heat radiates from between our palms, crawling up my neck. My mind rattles as opposing feelings swoop through me.

How long it's been since I touched another person this way.

How much I've wondered about touching him.

How messed up both thoughts are.

Together, we head toward the Supershops parking garage. Our steps echo across the gravelly lot. My knees are on the verge of buckling, but it's the soft place to land I focus on.

I slip into the passenger seat of his car and we set off. For the first few blocks, the only sounds are the hum of the car engine and the soft, melodic song playing on the radio.

We hit Seventeenth Avenue and pass a few restaurants and bars. I watch the people on the patios, talking and laughing and listening to live music. The sound drains inside, permeating our bubble.

Cliff says, "Will you tell me what happened?"

I keep my face turned toward the window. "I told you, something I ate."

I can feel his eyes drift to the side of my face. They pull me in like a magnet. It's dark outside, but the streetlights are reflecting through the windshield and casting a glow around the back of his head; the tips of his golden hair shine.

"You're lying," he says, gentle but adamant. "I know you."

I swallow. I know he does.

How can someone saying he knows me feel like everything?

I close my eyes, pressing my temple against the cool glass of the passenger-side window. "I just ran into someone at the party from my old town."

"Did they do something to upset you?" he asks quietly.

"No," I say. "I just got . . . I don't know. Can we not talk about it?"

Cliff's quiet for a long moment. "Okay," he finally says.

I peek an eye open, and he's driving steadily, staring out at the street. I watch the glare of the streetlights as they move across his face, casting him in light and shadow.

By the time we make it to my street and pull up in front of my building, the silence has become so thick and heavy. Cliff puts the car in park and his hand lingers on the gear shift awkwardly. His jaw is tight, like he's physically holding himself back from saying something.

My insides flip. I've cut so many people out. Everyone. But I don't want to do that with him.

The words tumble out all at once. "I used to have a friend, but something bad happened to her and she's gone."

Cliff's eyes shoot toward mine. He waits.

I keep going, my voice shaking. "I used to be just like I am, but worse, but also so much better. I guess I just . . . After she died, I just never really figured out how to be a person again. That's it. That's the problem."

I feel Cliff shift beside me. "Jolene—"

I shake my head, gasping. "I thought it would go away. I thought if I waited, one day it wouldn't hurt anymore. But time has passed—it's passed so much—and I've only become worse."

My words crush through me as I dare a look at him. His eyes catch me and hold me. All my skin burns. How can people look at each other in the eyes so easily? I can never look at him again.

"I know I'm not supposed to think like this. It just feels like everyone else is moving forward with their lives, but I'm trapped behind this glass dome that no one can see through."

Cliff's voice is so soft. "I can see through. I see you."

His hand lifts off the gear shift and grabs mine from my lap, pulling it down onto the console between us. The warmth of his palm cupping mine thaws my stiff muscles, and I fall slack against the car seat. This feels like I can be okay for now. Something, a word or a thought, catches in my throat.

"Jolene," Cliff begins haltingly. "You can't see it now, but I hope soon you do. You're understandable—I understand . . ."

He pauses, looking at me thoughtfully as he rubs his chin with his free hand. The scraping of his fingers against his stubble is the only sound in the world.

"Since the day you walked into the boardroom for that first meeting..." He swallows hard, his Adam's apple jumping in his throat. "Your email that was both horrible and perfect. I don't know if you noticed, but I've wanted to be in on the joke with you since the start."

I glance up and there's something behind his eyes; it's been there forever yet feels brand new. His hand tightens around mine, and for once—for the first time in years—my brain turns off. There's only feeling—a charge fluttering through me, pulsing from where his skin meets mine. It feels so good to be known by someone, to be seen, to be touched. And I want more of it.

I lean toward him, and it's so simple. His face is already angled toward me, and I slot my lips against his. Dimly I'm aware that he's not exactly moving against me, but he's not leaning away either. He's soft and warm, and I nudge a little closer. It's been a really long time since I've done this. My lips part against his slightly, and an embarrassing little sound escapes my mouth.

And then he lets out a tiny groan, and it's like a dam breaks. His hands wrap around my shoulders and pull me toward him, his face pressing harder against mine. It's hungry, and he's everywhere, hands on my back and in my hair and on my waist.

It's so good, but somehow not enough. I scramble for my seat belt and hear the satisfying click as it goes loose, so I can lean more across the console.

At the sound, Cliff suddenly goes tense, his lips freezing against mine. My whole body stiffens against my will.

He pulls away suddenly, pushing himself back against the driver's-side door. "Wait. Jolene, I'm so sorry. You're upset and I..."

I reach for his hand again, but he pulls it back against his side. I cringe at the rejection, my stomach bottoming. I can't even kiss someone properly.

"We can't do this," he says, sighing. "Not in our positions. It can be perceived as... one of us using the other."

I shake my head. Everyone in Supershops is using each other. But this wasn't about our jobs. For once, I wasn't thinking about emails or paychecks or layoffs or *anything* except how it felt. How *I* felt.

This was real. I want it to be real.

"I really like you" is what I manage to say, my voice tiny.

He drops his forehead into his hands and shakes his head against them. "This is my fault. You need to pass the course and I can't fuck that up for you."

My whole chest tightens. Every pocket of silence in the world pulls into the car with us.

It's too much. I turn and scramble for the passenger-door handle, but his hand suddenly touches my arm. Not grabbing me, just a gentle press—a silent plea for me to stop. I hold myself still and wait.

"Can we . . ." he begins awkwardly, then cuts himself off and starts again. "I'm hoping we can write this off as a momentary lapse."

Another anvil. Guilt seeps into me as I nod. "Right," I whisper. "I get it. It's okay."

"Jolene," he whispers. "I'm so sorry."

The softness in his eyes hollows me out. I want to curl back into his chest. I want to live there.

"No, Cliff. It's not you." I need the right words. Before it can end, I need to at least try to salvage some of whatever this was. "I was upset, and I wasn't thinking. Let's forget it happened. Please."

His hand drops from my arm, and the emptiness from where it was drains through me.

I open the door, catching a glimpse of his face as I turn to close it. He looks wrecked, guilt etched across his face. He shouldn't be the one to feel guilty. He doesn't know all the bad in me.

I get inside my apartment and go straight for the kitchen, grabbing one of the two Supershops mugs I own. There's a bottle of gin in the back of the cabinet, and my stomach gurgles at the sight of it. The first sip flows down my throat, hot and welcoming. My hands loosen, as do my thoughts.

Next week I'll quit drinking. It's becoming a problem, I know. But it's not my *biggest* problem right now.

Kyle probably went straight back into that bar and told Caitlin who I am. And if Caitlin knows, she'll tell everyone. Even if I still manage to keep my job, all my coworkers will see is the very worst version of me.

My phone lights up on the kitchen counter beside the gin bottle.

Cliff: I'm sorry.

I take another sip, and the thought pushes in, cruel and from deep inside my head since he found me sitting on the curb: *Cliff's going to see through me one day. And he'll look at me just like the last time Ellie did.*

Getting Mugged

MONDAY MORNING WRAPS up a weekend of spiraling—just me, my wine, and my ever uniquely anxious thoughts.

It's still dark outside when I board the first bus—the hardest bus ride because my stomach is still churning from my not-so-happy hour last night. I'd texted Cliff that I didn't need a ride. There's no way I'm going back into his car.

When I arrive at the office, I have to switch on the floor lights. My footsteps echo through the barren room. As I brew the first pot of coffee for the club, I mourn the bitter scent, the gurgle of the machine. I mourn it all because it may well be the last.

I sit down at my desk and bring my monitor to life. All the regular programs open, sitting uselessly on the screen. Cliff's little icon indicates he's online; he came in early too. We're probably the only two people in this building. I wonder if he's also looking at my icon.

Eventually, Rhonda trudges into the unit first, her big, embroidered bag heaving against her chest. I follow her movements as she walks toward her seat. All the questions I've been obsessing over all weekend scream inside my head: Does she know anything? Did Kyle return to the bar and tell them everything?

Rhonda pauses next to my desk and grins at me. "Hope everything's okay, dear. I didn't see you leave on Friday."

My smile wobbles. "Yes, thank you. I was feeling a little ill."

She nods once. "Been there."

As she sets her bag onto her desk, I add, "But thanks for asking."

And I really mean it. I guess it can be a little nice sometimes when she doesn't mind her own business. Sometimes. A little.

When she doesn't ask any more questions, I feel a minuscule beat of relief. I doubt Rhonda would hold back if she'd heard a rumor about me, but then again, she was feeling that wine pretty good on Friday. Maybe she doesn't remember. I watch as she preens Joey's leaves, lips downturned.

Armin trudges in next, hair mussed and eyes red. He nods my way before heading to the lunchroom.

Then Caitlin comes in, her cinnamon perfume wafting across the room as she heads to the fridge to stash her bland-looking chicken salad. I hold my breath and stare down at the little blinking light on my hard drive, following the sound of her routine as she reemerges to head to her desk, taking off her jacket and sliding into her chair. Every tiny motion stacks up against me. What does she know?

Caitlin gets up and walks to Rhonda's desk. "Thanks for the party Friday night."

Rhonda swivels her chair around. "Of course, dear! I'm glad you had fun."

"It was a blast." Caitlin's voice sounds slightly hoarse. I glimpse at her over the cube wall; her demeanor is stiff. Suddenly, her gaze crawls to me. I try not to look tense as I nod a greeting.

She passes behind my desk next, stopping in her tracks to look at me. Her mouth twists. "Oh, Jolene."

My life stops. All the blood in my arteries freezes.

"Thanks for decorating on Friday."

What the hell? I search her face for any clue, anything to tell me what she knows, but her expression is imperceptible.

"No problem." I smile for half a second, while her eyes shift and lock deeper into me, like she's trying to read something behind them. I try to keep still even as my heart pounds in my ears, my fingers tightening around my mouse. Then she simply turns and heads back to her desk.

I release a breath. Caitlin's not the type to be coy about using any ammo she has against me. But I can't understand it. Did Kyle not tell her? I didn't get the impression he'd take pity on me.

Just as Caitlin's sitting down, an email comes in for her.

FROM: Gregory Hall

TO: Caitlin Joffrey

SUBJECT: Re: meeting re: new ideas and info

Caitlin,

I appreciate that you are eager to workshop new ideas about the office, but there's not much time in my schedule available for this week. Not to worry, there will be other chances to discuss another day, I'm sure.

Regards,
Gregory

I check Caitlin's sent folder. She'd emailed Gregory on a *Saturday* to request another meeting with him, saying she had "new information" to discuss about her project.

My eyes flash to the top of Caitlin's head, visible above her screen. I hear the distinctive double tap of her opening the email.

And that's when it occurs to me: she didn't light her diffuser today. What does she know?

AS SOON AS the lunch hour is up, an email from Cliff arrives.

Jolene,

Hope the rest of the weekend went well. My apologies for having to do this, but a bit of an HR emergency has arisen, so I'm going to have to ask you to complete our next session at your desk. Because this is my doing, it won't count against you, and I'll be available to answer any questions. I've attached the booklet and worksheet.

I trust this will be okay?

Best,
Cliff

As I'm reading the email, about a thousand pounds of shame hits. This is how it's going to be going forward. I've messed everything up. I want to demand he see me. I want to hide in a box.

I reply:

Sounds great! Also, it just occurred to me I'm going to the gym, so I won't need a ride home. In fact, I've started a new routine where I will be going to the gym every morning and evening. It's great!
Jolene

It's for the best. And when Cliff doesn't reply, it's like a resolution. We can't just be friends.

A message pops up from Caitlin to Armin and Rhonda:

Caitlin: Have you guys noticed Jolene is a little different these days? Like she has an edge?
Rhonda: What are you suggesting, dear?
Caitlin: She's been meeting a lot with the HR guy. Maybe he's giving her tips on how to stay here. Doesn't it seem like she's getting insider info or something? How the hell did she make a flow chart THAT DETAILED by just doing our job?

My head starts to buzz as Armin tilts his gaze toward me. I pull my eyes toward my keyboard and focus on my hands.

Rhonda: I think she's just trying harder after she got in a bit of trouble. She's been so helpful lately.
Armin: Yeah, she's making more of an effort. Who can blame that?
Caitlin: But it feels like she knows things. Like she has access to some drive or something.

Armin's shoulders tense and I feel his eyes pull toward me. Again. I don't dare change my expression from the solid stone coating that I've yielded. I pretend to continue working as I slowly combust from the inside.

Armin: Nah, I get the vibe you're overestimating her. This is Jolene Smith, longtime secretary at Supershops—the girl who got in trouble for not changing the font color on an email. She's not some spy . . . she's just a bit weird.

Caitlin: I mean that's true, but I think the word you're looking for is "loser."

My heart, insides, and entire being tightens. *That* word. I blink and I blink to fight away whatever is prickling the corners of my eyes.

A new email pops up, a shipping notice from Aritzia. It's the stupid blazer I thought I'd buy myself as an early promotion gift.

I'll have to request a refund.

What a silly concept—me, speaking at the front of a meeting room, wearing a blazer. I'm so embarrassed my vagina hurts. I want to shake out of my skin and die. I stare at my keyboard as my insides twist together.

The heat of Armin's gaze burns against my cheek *again*.

To hide my reaction, I grab the Supershops mug filled with lukewarm coffee and press it to my lips.

A new message from Armin appears:

Armin: I have something to confess. I've been coming in early and taking the mugs from the lunchroom and dipping them in the toilets. I know it's bad, but nobody can stop me and it's fun to watch people drink from them.

I lean closer to the screen, mug resting against my lips—

Instantly, I recoil and drop it.

Shit. My head pounds. He sent the message to Maternity Leave Celeste, who won't see it.

The mug clatters onto the plastic that's meant to help my chair roll. Everyone in the pods, and even Garret and Stu, look at me as coffee splashes my feet.

But it's Armin's expression that halts my heart.

He's smirking.

The next message is sent directly to me.

Armin: I fucking knew it! Meet me in the archive room. Five minutes!

My skin shivers and my brain overheats. I'm busted. I'm completely fucked.

Armin leaps from his desk. "Hey, Jolene, let me get you a cloth."

I duck under my desk to get the coffee cup, wishing I could stay here forever.

How I Always Pictured My Proposal

I WAIT IN THE dimly lit archive room behind the same boxes where I listened to Cliff and Greg's recorded convo. My knees are about to buckle, but I can't move. I stare at the door like a caged animal, waiting for my captor to appear. Sweat gathers in my palms and I wipe it onto a box, marking it with my handprint. Soon all remaining traces of Jolene Smith could be filed in a box in this room to be legally shredded after seven years.

The door beeps, and my heart jumps. Armin steps through, unsmiling as he takes stock of me.

"Hey." He holds out his hand, proffering a bottle of doogh. "An offering I grabbed from the lunchroom."

I take it hesitantly in case it's some sort of rigged trick. Is it normal to present a delicious treat before selling someone out?

"Thank you," I say quietly. The bottle is cool against my skin, and I resist the urge to press it to my forehead. "I better not open it here."

He nods. "Consider it repayment for the scone."

The air goes stale in my lungs. "How'd you figure me out?" I murmur, staring at the coffee marks on my flats.

He leans against a box that reads *April 2016* in messy Sharpie. "Well, I had my suspicions something was up, but they were only mild. Then when you called me 'the executive,' it scared the shit out of me. I was certain you must have seen one of my emails." I can't stop wincing as he speaks. He continues. "Then came the day of the scones. Normally Gregory would be super braggy, but he just looked confused when Caitlin thanked him. I was wiped enough to actually get a coffee from that place later that day, so I asked the barista if anyone had just bought a few plain scones today." He shrugs, one side of his mouth curling up. "Let's just say she described exactly you."

I pull my chin toward my chest. "Is there no barista-client privilege anymore?"

Armin chuckles, the sound soothing the knot in my core. We exchange a tentative grin.

"Crap. How amateur was I?" I shake my head. "Please don't say anything. I didn't mean to let things get that far. At the time my job was hanging by a thread, and now . . . I'm getting decent at it." I lock eyes with him, expression wide and pleading. "If I lose it, I'll have to move in with my mom, and she's not just a little controlling, she's not the normal amount—it's a whole other level. And your job is in danger too, so maybe I can help—"

"I'm not going to rat you out," Armin interrupts, his brows knitting together. "I don't think I agree with what you're doing, but we're still good on me not being a rat."

Relief lifts my chest. I could swim in the surrounding file boxes, paper cuts be damned. Thank my lucky charms it was Armin and not someone else who cracked the code.

I grin. "By the way, I'm no rat either. I've kept your Joey abuse quiet for over a year."

His mouth opens, then closes, then opens again. "You've seen me mess with Joey before?"

"Um, you basically do it right in front of me." I laugh. "I know it's easy to forget I'm there . . ."

His gaze softens with guilt. "Jolene, I'm . . ." His eyes drift toward the blinds that are coated in dust, never opened for the lonely boxes. He shakes his head just a touch. "I asked you here because I'm hoping you can go to that dinner with me after all—pretend to be my fiancée again for my parents . . ."

I raise an eyebrow. "Otherwise you'll tell on me?" I finish for him.

His lips thin into an even line. "This is the favor for keeping a really big secret. That's *all*."

It's the same thing, but of course I have to do it now. I have to lie to a sick aunty.

"Fine." I nod.

His forehead wrinkles. "And what did you mean when you said my job is in danger before?"

I sigh and explain the list Rhonda's compiling of time he spends away from his desk. The total shock that crosses Armin's expression can't be real. How could he have caught on to my email ruse but missed *this*?

"Gregory's such a tool!" he grits out darkly. "But Rhonda's . . . I didn't know it was that bad between us."

"Seriously, Armin, I think you may be in danger for real. You need to stop leaving work without an excuse."

He combs his hair back with his fingers. "Yeah, you're right. I just need to keep my head down for a bit more . . . find a way to just focus in there—but that place, it's mind-numbing."

I roll the can of doogh between my palms. "Have you considered doing something else with your life?"

"Have you?"

"Point taken." I exhale, looking around at all the cardboard. "Speaking of, we should get back."

He nods and reaches for the door, but before pulling it open, he pauses. "Also . . ." He turns to look at me, eyes wide and sincere. "I'm sorry I called you weird and stuff, in the chat. I knew there was a chance you were reading at that point, and the way your eyes went . . ." He pauses, cringing. "Well, that sealed it. But I didn't really mean it."

I smile a little. "Thanks." But a niggling in the back of my mind pulls through. No matter what, there are some people who wouldn't talk about me like that—not ever. I swallow through my thick throat. At least there used to be.

We start our walk back down the hallway. Just before we turn into the communal area, I pause and I flash him a sly grin. "If I'm to be your official fake fiancée, promise me you won't fall in love with me."

He rubs his forehead. "Oh god, Jolene."

Caitlin looks toward us with a huff as we walk back to our pod together. A moment later, there's an email from Rhonda to herself.

FROM: Rhonda Staples
TO: Rhonda Staples
SUBJECT: New Occurrence

9:15 am: Spent fifteen minutes socializing somewhere with a friend

That shouldn't make me smile.

Somebody Had to Say *It*

THE PENULTIMATE HOUR of work ticks along to the beat of the ancient wall clock. Stu Wilkins has been hunched over the printer in front of his pod for the past fifteen minutes, watching sheets of paper spit out in one-second intervals like some twisted form of corporate meditation.

All these people, with their thoughts floating so close, sitting beside one another in complete silence.

Nobody ever randomly screams during these moments—a phenomenon that should be studied.

Stu's printer beeps, begging for more paper. He leans far too close, pulling on his reading glasses that hang from his neck, and rubs his head like he's trying to interpret ancient scripture. Right, it's time to call the time of death for the workday.

As if on cue, the main-floor door beeps and in walks Randal the security guard. Security personnel come to workspaces only for big issues or to let maintenance in to work on the mostly ornamental thermostats.

As Randal turns down the hall, Garret comes running across the floor. "Somebody's locked themselves in an office! Somebody that was let go!" he shouts, sounding a little too delighted by this drama.

Rhonda snaps her gum. "Oh dear."

Quiet murmurs move through the room, heads peeking up from cubicles like face cards from a Guess Who? board. A few bolder types storm toward the hallway where most of the offices are, but Randal holds up his hands and guides them to stand back. "Everyone, please stay in your workspaces until the situation has been resolved."

Randal has a sheen of sweat on his forehead; this is the event of his career. Normally this is the type of chaos I have a soft spot for, but after today, I'm just not up for it. So I stay at my desk.

Then comes the email.

FROM: Larry Goodwin
TO: All Staff—Supershops
SUBJECT: Fuck You

Colleagues,

Today will be my last day at Supershops. Regrettably, reason and morale are at an all-time low and nobody cares about each other anymore.

A lot of you have made my life wonderful here. And you know who you are.

But this message is for the absolute twats who made my life hell. The individuals who participate in blatant patterns of disrespect. You know who you are too.

Nobody notices the things I do for this office. In a couple weeks, you bitches will all have watermarks on your glassware without me to refill the Jet-Dry, and you don't care.

I may have been terminated, but I won't be leaving until the end of the day, and I thank you all for letting me have that.

Don't fear for me. Fear for you.

Larry Goodwin

The laughter comes in a stilted wave, uncertain and mumbled at first, until it takes over the floor. Olivia Espinoza, the do-gooder fire marshal, throws on her fire vest in the panic. Caitlin and Joy run over to Garret's desk even as Randal shouts at everyone to remain seated. He pulls a radio from his belt and mutters some codes into the speaker. Some staticky mess of noise comes back, and he holds it up to his ear before giving up and pulling out his cell phone.

For five minutes nothing happens, and the energy on the floor begins to lull with the anticlimax. Then a yell comes from the hallway: "No! I at least get to express myself!"

Larry D. Goodwin comes pounding out, rapidly panting, red-faced, his collar rumpled. Cliff and Gregory trail him. Randal blocks him, trying to cut him off from walking into the desk area.

Larry's expression shifts—like he's in shock as he takes in all of us silent onlookers—but then his features pinch resolutely. "This is all your faults!"

His audience watches in rapt silence.

Cliff's eyes search across the floor. They land on me and hold.

The HR emergency—it was real. He wasn't just avoiding me.

"You people manipulate each other all day," Larry announces.

Everyone looks at one another, each of them innocent in their hearts.

"Is this really the life you want?" he tries again.

Again, blank stares.

Except, alone in my cubicle, his question presses into me.

He gestures behind him at Cliff. "He's just here to fire us, piece by piece."

Cliff rolls his jaw, arms stiff. But I catch the way his eyes flash. He hates the truth of it.

Larry's face has gone the color of an eggplant. "Gregory's a fucking tool that only got scones for the cool kids!"

Gregory's eyebrows shoot up at the same rate my stomach drops. "What?"

Beside me, Armin coughs.

"All right," says Cliff. "Larry, it's time to—"

Larry grabs for his belt and it happens so fast: he turns and flashes his butt cheeks. Randal throws out his arms to shield the innocents, and Larry takes the opportunity to bend right under them like he's playing a game of limbo and starts running around the desks, still squatting. There's no doubt that it's a drive-by mooning. He makes a point to give every person on the floor a full view of the pale, freckled horror that is one man's ass. Then he picks up the Yoda plushie from Jean Adler's desk and sticks it in his pants. Randal is racing behind him and manages to pull the stuffed toy free from Larry's grasp, before whipping it to the ground in disgust.

This kind of moment is so unreal that a small chuckle escapes me. As much as a breakdown is terrible, it is also a wondrous thing to behold.

Larry straightens up, looking right at me. "Jolene, what are *you* laughing at?"

"I . . . nothing." I shake my head, pushing my chair closer to my desk.

"You're supposed to be on my team!" he spits. "We all see when Joy gives everyone but us a damn key chain from Mexico. Us office losers know who we are." That word—another bullet knocking me into myself. "We can tell when we're not wanted, right?"

I stay completely still, not daring to so much as flinch. I'm all too aware of Caitlin's smirk, Rhonda's jowls shaking with worry, and Armin's wince. But worst of all, I can see Cliff from behind Larry's shoulders. He's approaching with that same look of concern in his eyes, like I'm broken.

Larry breaks my gaze to stare at my desk. There's nothing here, save for Miley's zebra. The one thing.

We both go for it at the same time, but he's faster. He snatches it and holds it high. His forehead shines, and his clammy hands stick to the loose eyeballs.

"Drop it!" Cliff yells. He's come to stand between Larry and me, getting in his face.

Larry snorts and tightens his red sausage fingers around it. Just before he manages to get it into his pants, and right when I'm deciding I really don't love this toy enough to wrestle it back from Larry's privates, Cliff manages to grab it free, holding it high out of his reach.

Larry closes his hand into a fist and swings at Cliff, who manages to pull back enough that it only clips the edge of his jaw. Still, it makes a sound, and everyone winces in unison. Larry loses his balance and tumbles to the ground. In an instant, he's gone from office agitator to feeble old man groaning on the floor.

As he's struggling to get up—face blue, pants still at his knees—the real police arrive to relieve Randal of his duties. They manage Larry out of the vicinity with quick efficiency. Still, on his way out, he manages to advise us that a good majority of us are cocksuckers.

Not a second after they round the corner, Stu calls, "Dibs on Larry's chair! You all heard it."

As everyone races around the floor to trade commentary about the wildness that just happened, Cliff comes to my desk and hands me back my zebra. As I take it, we lock eyes.

"That was one of the scariest moments. Are you okay?" he asks, searching my face.

"Yeah." I nod, cupping the zebra gently. "And so is Mr. Barcode, thanks to your heroics."

Cliff's lips twitch. "You named it Mr. Barcode?"

"Just now. Figured he deserved a name after all he's been through."

Cliff huffs a laugh, then winces and rubs a palm against his jaw.

"Are *you* okay?" I ask.

"Oh, this is nothing," he says. Then he looks up at me through hooded lids. "Hey, uh...I know you're starting a new gym routine–but maybe you can start tomorrow? Can I drive you home?"

When I lock eyes with him, he smiles, shy and hopeful. It centers me, like coming back home. "Okay," I croak.

"Okay," Cliff echoes. "Meet you in the parkade after work."

He heads back into the hall, where the procession of Larry handlers just were. Stu is already wheeling Larry's chair across the floor.

The energy in the room is a vibrant hum. Everyone is still whispering to each other, but the excitement that was previously peppering their voices has faded into insecurity. Larry's display wasn't just about him. Nobody is immune to thinking they might be wasting their only life on a place that can toss you out without a second thought. This will be a reminder to anyone who ever suspected a company gave a shit about them. Even though we all tease that we'll quit, we know this company can more easily part with us.

I sit down at my desk and keep readjusting where Miley's zebra goes. Somehow the dire blankness of the beige and grey metal brackets has become more draining to my soul. Shouldn't I have wanted to personalize my desk before?

Larry's words echo inside me: *Don't fear for me. Fear for you.*

Cliff Hanger

A S WE DRIVE down Fifth Street, Cliff keeps fiddling with the gears, radio, and AC in complete overkill, like he's operating an airplane. But I can't blame him for being nervous; last time we took this drive, our faces ended up smooshed together.

"So," Cliff begins with a huff, breaking the silence, "the experts claim that letting someone go on a Monday leads to fewer incidents."

"It's good you did it today, then."

A tiny chortle escapes from us both at the same time. Our eyes shift together, our equilibrium teasingly close to returning.

"Wanna know something fucked up?" Cliff says, half smiling. "After letting someone go, I pretend they died. That's easier to deal with for some reason."

"That's really sweet, Cliff." And I pull his thermos from the cup holder in the console and hold it forward. "To Larry, may he rest in peace."

This time he allows himself to fully grin. But he drops it quickly. "Are you sure you're okay, Jolene?" It's the way his brows knit together, the sorrow in his eyes, that clues me in that he's not just talking about Larry.

"I'm fine." The unease builds in me, heavy and draining. I just want Cliff back. "Are you okay? I mean after *that.*"

The edge of his jaw is bright red beneath his long stubble where Larry clocked him. I lift a hand to—I don't know, gesture toward it, touch it, I'm not sure—and then pull it back down just as quickly. He notices the motion and his temples pinken.

"Yeah. It's all part of the job." He tilts his head toward me and smiles wide to show it doesn't hurt. But I can see the face he keeps inside himself.

"I don't think *all* of that was part of the job. Or was full mooning part of your HR training?"

"It was an elective," he jokes, but his knuckles whiten on the gear shift. "I've been at this for a while now and I should get used to it, but sometimes the guilt builds up and it's hard to dispel. I can't shake it off even though I know I'm supposed to."

His words pull through me like a string, tightening everything inside. "You don't have to shake it off. Guilt is heavy." And maybe it's because of everything today, or because everything feels surreal after Larry, but I say the words that I never thought I'd say out loud. "It can change you forever."

"That's the problem." Cliff's voice is tighter. "Jolene, what happened between us—what happened . . . that was unfair of me. Today it's abundantly clear that I'm an HR guy that has the power to let people go. And that means I was out of line with you."

A knot pulls taut in my chest. "What? Cliff, no. I'm an adult. And you're not just HR, remember? We're friends."

He shakes his head. "I'll get you another HR guy, have them assign you someone else."

"Are you serious?" My breath halts. "It was my mistake. I'm the one who kissed *you*. And you said we could forget it! We were doing so good just now, cheering to Larry's demise."

Cliff stares forward. "I kissed you just as much. It wouldn't be fair to jeopardize your career—"

I cut him off. "I'm only doing good in that course because of *you*." His gaze softens on me. "You're the only one who wanted to give me a chance. You know what getting me reassigned will do. It's as good as setting me up to be fired."

His eyes flash at the truth of my words. We stop at a light, the red hue painting his cheeks. He taps the turn signal and it begins to tick, counting down the seconds of our time together. "I just . . . It feels wrong for me to keep—"

I nudge him, the warmth from his arm pulling through me. "You said in this car we're friends, right?"

Cliff nods but keeps his eyes on the windshield as he continues down the street.

"So be my friend right now." My arm is still resting against his. I pull it back into my lap. "And be HR in there. We can keep things separate. You've really helped me. More than anyone."

The car halts at another light. Cliff exhales and his eyes draw toward me. "Okay," he says and nods. "Yeah."

"Thank you," I croak.

He nudges me this time. More warmth rushes through me, pulling into the tips of my ears. Will touching him ever become casual? Is there a world where it won't send sparks through me?

He stares at me like he's trying to figure something out, then shakes his head. "Thanks, Jolene. Being able to at least talk this out with you—I just . . ." He swallows. "At least we have trust going for us. That means a lot."

I want to accept the comfort of his words, but the guilt tugs at me. I'm so far from the person he sees. And between Armin and Caitlin, my house of cards is threatening to crumble.

As it turns out, being busted by Armin and seeing a grown man's raw butt cheeks aren't the worst things that can happen in a day.

Finger Food

I'M LYING ON the couch in a T-shirt and panties that are frankly ready for a demotion. The latest conga line of thoughts flash over me: Cliff—the kiss, the car ride home; Armin—his mom, the favor I owe him; Larry's face, etc.; the fucking blazer I ordered.

As a coping mechanism, I move on to binge-watching some astronomy documentary, learning how big the universe is and how we are all teeny dust. It's right as I'm having an existential crisis about the point of life when my mom's picture takes over my phone screen, the ring vibrations drilling into my stomach.

I hit silence, automatic as a bot.

But the sound of Rhonda's miserable sigh every time she gets Carl's voicemail is dredged from my subconscious.

I make like Caitlin and find the least offensive background, shoving a pile of clothes off the couch and posing the camera away from the open chip bag lying beside me. "Hello."

"You're engaged?" is what she says, her tone incredibly even as she searches my face.

The phone nearly slips out of my palm. "Uh."

Mom clucks her tongue. "I knew it was mistake. Aunty Parvin is always getting her gossip wrong."

"Wait." The hairs on the back of my neck stand up. The aunty gossip network runs deeper than any cartel. "Who am I engaged to?"

"Aunty Parvin's eyebrow-threading lady is friends with Nika, the woman who is making the best tahchin and selling on the WhatsApp, who said Babasheh congratulated her for her accounting executive son's engagement to you. She was getting a radiation therapy and told Dr. Nasseri about it."

Amazing. I can barely follow, yet I know exactly what she's talking about.

But shit.

"So it's mistake?" she says again. "I knew it."

But if I tell my mom it's a lie, that information will go all the way back down the gossip chain, back to Armin's mom. Dread curdles my stomach. If it becomes known that Armin lied to his poor sick mom, not only will he probably change his tune about keeping my email access secret, but his mom will probably freak out, and she's already frail enough.

"It's, uh," I stumble, thinking on my feet, trying not to make eye contact through the screen. "It's not like an actual engagement. We just, uh, *talked* about it, and—"

A hard-core scream sounds through the other end of the line, so high-pitched it becomes pure crackle through the speaker. "Why do you keep a man secret from me? Send me a picture. Is he handsome? Very proud he is the executive. Should I come over?"

Shit. I may have triggered a wildfire in the Persian community of the western regions.

"I don't want to make this a big deal," I begin, but Mom's camera is already turning into a blur as she moves around the house.

"Oh, my baby! Why didn't you say you have boyfriend? I was worried you didn't want to. I will get the best dress, and that ugly Minoo isn't allowed to come. Actually she can, to see how much more beautiful I am than her."

More dread sets in. What have I done?

"Mom. Mom!" I shout until she locks eyes with me through the screen. "Please, we must keep this under wraps. Our work doesn't know, and we're not allowed to date."

"Okay, okay." But the energy comes racing right back. "I didn't think I'd get to be a bride mom. I'm going to throw the best wedding."

The song in her voice. The smile. My brain doesn't have the capacity to throw another log on the shit storm in my head. "Mom, please, you can't say anything. We honestly need to keep this quiet. That's why I couldn't tell you yet."

"Yes." She throws her hand at the screen. "I never tell anyone anything. I'm very good with this and classy. I'm *not* Minoo."

We hang up, and I stare guiltily at the pile of clothes I moved.

FROM: Armin Habib
TO: Jolene Smith
SUBJECT: Is this okay?

I open the attachment and a chuckle escapes me. I quickly stifle it when Rhonda casts me a disapproving look.

The picture Armin sent me is of himself in an oversized suit looking uncomfortable at the last regional conference. It's nothing like the Armin of reality, but oddly perfect for the bullshit version we've perfected.

A message comes from him.

Armin: Thank you for making your thoughts so obvious and loud. I'm not a suit guy, okay.
Jolene: *Sorry, it's perfect—I'll use it. I needed that laugh. But FYI my mom will be sharing this with everyone.*
Armin: I somehow knew this exact picture was bound to be distributed widely from its conception, aunty network involved or not.

We both giggle in our seats, and Caitlin and Rhonda exchange a look—Rhonda confused, Caitlin salty.

Moments later, a message from Caitlin to Armin appears.

Caitlin: Are you and Jolene messaging?
Armin: Why do you ask?
Caitlin: I mean, if you're hanging with her, that's obviously fine, but just be on guard—I know I sound like a broken record, but the other night was my engagement party and she was there, but what's more is she left as soon as Kyle and I came, and guess what?

My heart stops. I stop breathing. It's now. She's going to tell them about Ellie, about what I did. How I'm not to be trusted and everyone should fear me. I'll never escape this, no matter what. Soon enough, they'll all know what I was like and who I am.

My stomach clenches like a fist as Caitlin types. The keyboard clicking is the only sound in the world.

Caitlin: She volunteered to help Rhonda with my party decorations and then took off. Isn't that suspicious?

Oh my god.
Relief swoops in and floods every part of my being. She doesn't know. Did Kyle really not tell her? I don't understand it.
I divert my eyes while Armin looks my way.
The guy needs some serious lessons on being covert.

Jolene: *STOPP looking at me!*
Armin: Are you just reading our convo? It's kind of obvious with the way you stare at your screen FYI. It's so weird having an audience.
Jolene: *Please stop looking at me.*
Armin: I'll try. You stop reading how bout?
Jolene: *Fine.*

Armin messages Caitlin back next:

Armin: Hmm that is suspicious. Have you considered dipping her mug in the toilet to teach her a lesson?

My mouth twitches. Armin is a fucking imbecile. I type while glaring at the back of his head.

Jolene: *You jerk. I'm seriously reconsidering our arrangement.*
Armin: Cheers—was just a test. Also, you know you can't.

Caitlin's reply to Armin pops in.

Caitlin: Um . . . no, I hadn't considered that. ANYWAYS. Good luck. I tried. She's sketch.

Caitlin clicks the chat shut and pulls out her hand mirror, beginning her first teeth and eye inspection of the day.

As Caitlin fiddles with her hair, it's like a rush—the realization. In about two weeks' time, she could be gone. Caitlin would simply fade into an echo of Supershops' past, and I would be free, completely. I won't have to worry about her or Kyle saying anything. I won't have to worry about anyone's emails. I can be exactly who I want.

A beeping at the door draws all our eyes.

"Does a Caitlin Joffrey work here?" The question comes from a tiny man holding a giant bouquet of chocolate-covered strawberries and mango on skewers. We can barely see his face as he tiptoes into the room, unsteady. "I'm looking for Caitlin Joffrey."

Caitlin's face goes pink and she puts a hand to her chest, a perfect picture of modest delight. "Yes, that's me."

"Oh, goodness." Rhonda stands up to examine the giant display as the man lowers in onto the worktable next to our desks. "Who is this from?"

Caitlin walks over to the arrangement and pulls out the card. "Oh, it's my Kyle." Her smile is wide, her lipstick freshly applied. "That's so sweet. Last night I was saying we should have a chocolate fountain for strawberry dipping at the wedding, and he sent this!"

She holds out the card to Marla and Joy, who've already come over for the show-and-tell portion of the morning, excited for a reason to stand around. "Oh my god!" Joy says. "The card reads: 'Until we get our own chocolate fountain.'"

"Aw," Marla and Rhonda squee in unison, while Stu, who has now joined the fray, mumbles something about putting the rest of them to shame.

Rhonda claps once. "Adorable!" When Caitlin grabs a strawberry, Rhonda tilts her head. "Oh, dear, where's your ring?"

Caitlin's gaze shifts to her empty hand. "We're just getting it resized. It didn't quite fit. Anyway, eat some of this, please! Enjoy!"

Caitlin walks back to her seat, playing with the levers to adjust it, making it creak. Her phone buzzes twice, and she picks it up to read the texts but doesn't respond. She grabs her water bottle, sips it, then drops it. We all look up as it clangs down on her desk. She picks it up, sips it again, puts it down. She pulls her hair back, twists it into a bun, then takes it out and reties it twice more. She huffs, then drops her pen and drills her hands into her temples, leg twitching under the table.

If I didn't know better, I'd say this is starting to look like an anxiety attack—except this is Caitlin, so she's probably just dopamine drained since her last Instagram post (some brunch eggs she somehow deemed grid-worthy) didn't even reach twenty likes. Still, an odd tightness seeps in. Her phone buzzes again. She hits some button that seems to kill it and stuffs it in her purse.

I turn back to my inbox, looking for a distraction. Cliff has a new notification from his LinkedIn account, which everyone knows is just a hookup site. Still, I click on it.

The notification says there is a reply to a message sent to some guy named Sanjay Singh at People Power in Vancouver, dated yesterday afternoon.

Cliff: Hey Sanjay, I can't believe it's been over a year. How are things going? I wanted to reach out. I left the insurance company and recently started at Supershops—still HR. This place is a bit of a nightmare in all the ways we talk about and it's getting hard to tolerate. Because of this, I wanted to follow up about that open offer. Would you be available for a chat this week? Definitely best to do after work hours.

Sanjay: Cliff! So glad you reached out, man. Of course I'd be game to chat. Want to have a call tonight? Things are busy as usual around here, so I'll be working late anyway. Let's connect around 7:30 PT/8:30 your time—sound good?

It makes perfect sense. This place *is* a nightmare, and his grandma doesn't need him anymore—I saw it myself. It's just like Grace wanted. He can go back to a job that makes a difference. A job that's not a living nightmare.

He doesn't owe me anything. We're just friends—if we're even that anymore.

Delightful Fashionista

Y OU'VE BEEN PRETTY quiet over there," Cliff says as he twists the steering wheel to make a left, the AC blaring but doing nothing as we turn into our neighborhood.

I force a smile. "You know, just a long day."

He nods. "Gotcha. Anything in particular?"

I shake my head. "Nothing really, just that place . . . a bit of a nightmare at times, eh?" I search him for any hint of a reaction, but nothing lands.

"Hmm, well, we're free for a few hours at least." He hands me his phone. "Please play some music. Nothing jokey."

I scroll his music app and find a current hits playlist. But as I'm about to hit play, a banner pings on the top of the screen, displaying a message from Sanjay: Great I'll call you soon!

And everything inside me feels like it's melting. It should have been easy. The department restructure is happening in two weeks, and I've done exactly what I set out to do with Cliff and more.

But it's the *more* that painted things muddy.

And before really thinking, I say, "Your sister mentioned the other day you used to work in Vancouver?"

Cliff rubs his chin. "Yeah."

"And your grandma, I heard she's doing better since her hip surgery?"

"Yes." He smiles. "Almost a full recovery."

He doesn't have to elaborate; that's his right. His plans for the future, doing what's best for himself, are none of my business. The music croons through the stereo, low and sweet. Just because I can now play music without melting down doesn't mean I've accomplished much. Not compared with anyone else.

Cliff taps his fingers to the beat, and I catch how close our arms are resting on the console. I try to swallow away the thought that rings through me at the sight: for the first time, I want to share more with someone. But no matter how small this car is, I don't know how to penetrate the invisible wall between me and the world, between me and Cliff.

A message flashes on his screen for a second time, drawing both our gazes to the phone. I don't see what's on it before he picks it up. I plaster on a contented smile and force down my useless feelings. But when we pull onto the street in front of my apartment, all my blood freezes.

She's standing on the front walkway.

I slump in my seat, trying to get low beneath the window. Useless. Cliff's gaze tilts toward me. "You good?"

I nod. "Dandy. Hey, do you think you can maybe make another loop around the block—"

But she's already at the window, crouching to peer into the car. She taps on the glass. "Jolene!" Mom calls. "Why you hiding from your mom?"

"This is your mom?" Cliff's face splits into a grin.

"Yes. But—" Before I can stop him, Cliff is rolling down my window and waving.

Mom practically sticks her head inside of the car. "I come to take you shopping." Then her eyes crawl to Cliff. "Who is this? He's very handsome."

"Mom, why didn't you call?"

Cliff's smile is too goofy, too wide. He reaches across me to extend his hand. "Nice to meet you. I'm Cliff, Jolene's . . . friend." He looks toward me with a suddenly shy expression that flips my stomach.

"You too!" Mom suddenly exclaims, making Cliff startle. She looks down at me, and I can read her mind. I know exactly what she's going to say. It happens in slow mo: "Armin doesn't get jealous you drive home with such a good-looking man instead of him?"

Cliff's temples flush, but then he pauses, looking straight ahead. He blinks and blinks as if registering the rest. If my heart wasn't pounding like it wants to break free of my chest, if sweat wasn't forming in all my creases, I'd be certain I was already dead.

I shake my head hard and look pointedly at my mom, hoping to convey "please shut up."

Her eyes flash as they shift to Cliff, who is still stiff in his seat. "Oh no, is Cliff someone from work?" Then she lowers her voice, but not low enough. "Is it still a secret at work? He said he was a friend; I didn't think work."

I shake my head—where else would he be from? I mouth, "Mom. No."

Cliff suddenly comes back to life, shifting aggressively to face forward and grab the steering wheel. "Sorry, I actually have to be off. Jolene, I'll see you tomorrow."

I slide out of the car, and as soon as I push the door closed, he's pulling away. As his car disappears, I turn to my mother. "You shouldn't have done that! Cliff is the HR guy at my office, and now he knows." My throat tightens like a vise. "That's, like, really bad!"

She pats my hair. "It's okay, he probably didn't hear. And anyways, all of work will find out soon. You can't keep a whole wedding secret." Her hand taps my cheek. "Come, I'll take you shopping! Cheer you up."

Oh my lord. "I'm tired, Mom."

"What? But I came all this way." She huffs. And even though nobody asked her to, I'm well and truly screwed. Best not to resist my fate.

I make my way to the car, and that's when I notice that my mom is the one going into the driver's seat. She almost never drives herself anywhere. "Where's Dad?" I ask cautiously.

Mom throws her hands up. "He's being annoying—not taking me for all my errands. It takes a lot to make weddings go well, so I drove here myself. I'm trying to be more *independent*." She says it with a capital *I*.

"That's great." Then my heart skips a beat. "Wait, what wedding are you planning?"

She mock slaps the air as I enter the vehicle. "Weddings take a long time to plan, we need to start now. Come, we'll get you nice things now that you're going to be a bride." Her eyes skim me over. "You didn't wear those clothes to work? Jolene, those pants are not professional with the pockets there. And you need to wear earrings, so people know you're serious."

"I don't think anybody has taken me more seriously due to what's in my earlobes."

She clucks her tongue. "You don't know." But she grabs my hand, a frown pulling between her brows. "Where is the ring? He's not cheapskate, right?"

I pull back my hand. "We're going to pick one together. When the time is right."

Mom twists the key and the car chugs on. As she focuses on peeling the car away from the road, I text Cliff:

I'm sorry about that. It's a long story, will explain tomorrow. Thanks for the ride.

I try not to freak out that an answer doesn't come right away. Or fifteen minutes later. Or twenty.

We pull into the parking lot of Westbrook Mall, which is Not Great. It's mostly a food court, two discount luggage stores, a Walmart, and a sprinkling of clothing places with names like "Delightful Fashionista," all with "fashion" from the same general supplier.

When we approach a place called Sheer Girl Designs, Mom digs her fingers into my wrist. "Come, let's go see Dorsa." She drops her grip as she runs to greet a Persian lady with a violently floral blouse and poufed-out, red-dyed hair.

Mom and the lady both jump and scream all sorts of standard Farsi greetings that, if translated directly, might sound intense. They aren't saying hello; they're literally offering to sacrifice themselves for each other. The shopkeeper takes off into the store, and Mom directs her attention back to me. "Jolene, come. Dorsa found the perfect dress for me."

This Dorsa returns holding out a puce nightmare of sparkles, and both ladies' faces shine just as bright. "I think this is respectful, yet still nice," Mom says.

I nod, a creeping sickness pulling through me. "But what is it for?"

Dorsa grins widely beside me. "Congratulations on wedding, Jolene joon! I'm excited to be there!"

My insides tumble as Mom nudges Dorsa and, from the side of her lips, says, "We will have her hair and makeup done professionally for the wedding, so don't think she looks like this."

Dorsa nods and gestures behind me. "Jolene, go to the back and pick yourself the young people trendy clothes." She winks. "For the bride, it's discount."

Dorsa goes back behind the till, and Mom pulls me by the biceps toward the back. I immediately haul free. "Mom, how many people have you told about this?"

Mom doesn't look up as she flips through a rack. "Eh, nobody. Just some that would be too happy to keep it secret from." Then she twists a brow up. "We had to make up for you keeping Armin hidden from me, your own mommy."

Shit. This is already a toothpaste-out-of-tube situation. "Like I said, Armin and I want to keep this *small*."

"Yes, it will be! Whatever you want, baby. But we need to have fun too." She pulls a blouse from the rack. "Here, put this on, is good for work."

I snatch the blouse from her harder than necessary and stick it right back on the rack. "Mom, I'm serious. Armin needs to keep it quiet; his mom isn't well, and the excitement might be bad for her."

She picks up the shirt again and shoves it back into my arms. "Yes, okay. No more wedding talk. Now put this on."

I dutifully take the top into the curtained changing room. As I'm buttoning up the blouse, my phone buzzes. I grab it from my pocket and see it's a text from Cliff.

Have a good night, Jolene.

My heart tumbles. What a terrible message to leave someone. Who does he think he even is?

Alarming Answers

CLIFF'S ALL BUSINESS, his grin stiff as I enter his office. The sun shines across his trinkets, rendering the whole situation somehow even more vivid.

"How are you doing today, Jolene?" He faces the stack of paperwork on his desk as he says this, his voice ten miles away. He nods toward the donut box. "They had a Persian donut today—pistachio rosewater. Of course I had to get it for you."

My heart breaks as I take it. It's the nicest thing in the world.

I smile and hold my voice as steady as possible. "Nice."

Cliff nods his head but doesn't look up. He hasn't looked at me once.

"Cliff, last night with my mom, that's a whole mess that I can explain. I'm not actually into Arm—"

"Don't worry about that." His gaze finally pulls up to mine, but it's indecipherable. "It's none of my business." He grins, though it's not as wide as usual. It's like a part of his smile is gone.

"But I want to. Armin's like—we're not into each other at all. Our families are just . . ." I rack my brain for a way to explain this that won't come down to me being a liar. "It's just complicated."

Cliff's blink is measured. "Sounds like it. But honestly, Jolene, I don't need to know more, as your HR."

I nod as my heart turns hard as a scone from Artistic Coffee. Our friendship could never work.

He's HR. Just HR.

His email to Sanjay this morning scrolls through my mind like a ticker tape. Thanks again for speaking with me. I'd be excited to do something meaningful again. This place got to me worse than the others.

Cliff slides one of the packets on his desk toward me without looking up. "We're getting close to wrapping up our training. Any specific questions or concerns?"

Yes: *After all this, if I save my job and everything, do I just go back to my life here? The one without you in it?*

I shake my train of thought away and ignore the heaviness that rests in my bones. "Oh no!" I force my voice to brighten. "I'm just looking forward to diving back into my studies. I have a feeling it's teaching me more than I'm teaching it." *If we can just laugh and go back to being us.*

"That's good," he says, another empty reply. His lip doesn't even twitch in that cute way it does when he's trying not to laugh—not that I notice it much.

I sink into my chair. This place got to him. *I* got to him.

Cliff pulls his packet open, and as he starts to go over internal biases, my mind wanders. I think of taking dull bus rides down the same roads I drove with him—the ice-cream shop, his bowling alley. I think of coming to work here without seeing his icon flashing as online.

Cliff stops midsentence and stares at me with a raised eyebrow. "Jolene, have you listened to a word I've said?"

I nod. I definitely did not.

He sighs. "I really want you to pass this course, so can you please focus?"

I almost nod again, but my gaze snags on the donut he got me, and I blurt, "Why do you want me to pass?"

Cliff's eyes widen, finally revealing a hint of emotion. "What?"

I lean back in my chair and cross my arms. "Why do you want me to pass? Honestly, what difference does it make to you if I fail?"

"Jolene, what?" He looks at me with an assessing tilt. "It's obvious."

"Then tell me," I demand.

Cliff looks completely baffled. He throws his hands up. "I mean, because I'd like for you to keep your job. I want good things for you. I like you."

His words fall between us and we both lock eyes. Even though there's a desk separating us, he's so close that I can feel the warmth of him radiating toward me, smell the sugar on his breath from the donut he ate. I'm again so aware of exactly how many inches are between us. It's not much, but it's the whole world.

"Cliff, I li—"

But Cliff shakes his head, his expression almost scared. "You're my friend, Jolene. Of course I like you."

His words cut through me like pellets. I'm so stupid.

His jaw is tight. Again, he won't look at me. He knew what I was about to say.

It's like falling into a pit inside myself.

Fuck him. Fuck his donuts. Fuck every trinket in his office.

"Yes, that's exactly what I was going to say." My nod is too hard. "We're friends. Such great friends." Cliff stares at me tensely, something brewing behind his eyes. All my thoughts muddle as I blurt out, "Except you're moving back to Vancouver. What kind of friend doesn't even share that?"

Cliff blinks at me, his jaw stiff, as my stomach plummets. "What?"

I found the line and crossed it.

I continue: "I saw your phone yesterday when I was picking the music."

I watch him as my words sink in. "Jolene, that's not . . . You went through my phone?" His brows twist together.

He doesn't know the half of it. Guilt tumbles into the pit inside me.

"I'm sorry," I backtrack. "I just—it was an accident."

His jaw ticks. "Yes, I was looking into it. It's complicated and actually not your business."

Of course it's none of my business. Other people know that. Other people wouldn't demand answers.

"I'm really sorry," I say through my tight throat. "You're right. You're HR. It's my job to tell you personal things, and it's your job to keep at a distance."

Cliff sets his jaw. "Our roles come with boundaries."

His words crush through the room, crush through me. I spit my next words out, like they'll release the pain. "So maybe we should stop making this so hard for ourselves, keep things simple. Stop being friends. Stop the carpooling, everything."

But as his face drops, silent for a beat, every cell in my body wants him to argue. To stop it.

But Cliff stares at me before letting out a strained sigh. "Okay," he says, and my insides knit together. "I agree that's for the best."

My brain feels like it's ringing.

Then an actual alarm rings.

The damn fire alarm—the anxious person's nemesis—has become my savior.

"We have to go." Cliff actually looks a little panicked. I'd expect no less from an esteemed HR representative.

But for three years I've been very much not evacuating for fire alarms.

"Jolene?" He's standing up, but his gaze clings to me.

"I'll get myself outside," I say, and dart past him, running for the stairwell before he can follow.

I REACH THE bathroom on my floor, slam the door shut, hide in my stall, and try my best not to inhale the wet-sponge stench that seems to come from all angles as I suck in tight, anxious breaths that mirror the clang of the alarm. I have to be ready to lift my feet if some fire marshal comes by to ensure we've all evacuated.

Eventually, all the footsteps and voices outside the door evaporate into nothing.

I finally exhale.

Just as I'm about to leave, the bathroom door swings open so hard that it bangs against the wall.

The fire alarm stops ringing.

"I'm sorry, but I can't help you." It's Rhonda, but her voice is torn up like I've never heard before. "But I love you. I really do."

She takes a wet breath. Shit, she's crying. Her sobs bounce around the tiles, filling the room.

"I only want you to be safe and okay. You're my baby." Rhonda sobs again, sudden and breathy.

I try to stay perfectly still, to not breathe, to stop my heartbeat. It's been long enough that if she catches me, she'll think it's weird I didn't make my presence known.

Then she whimpers in the worst way. "I love you, but I can't do anything for you. I can't give you any money you'll use for something that could kill you. When my credit card went missing, I was so sick with worry. I thought it meant your last breath."

The mumbled moaning on the other end of the line comes through. The cry Rhonda lets out seems to come from somewhere deeper than inside her. "Your life is worth trying to save," she begs. "You know that."

My whole body shakes. If she wasn't crying, she'd hear me.

After a few seconds, or several hours, I hear the faucet turning on, then the paper towel dispenser. Finally, the bathroom door squeaks.

I let my legs drop, and my chest heaves in relief.

"Who's in here?"

I freeze at the same rate my insides turn to stone, but it doesn't matter.

"I see your shoes, Jolene."

Shit. I open the stall door and tentatively step out.

Rhonda's face is pale in some places, red and patchy in others. She's holding a balled-up tissue tightly in a fisted hand.

I have no words.

"You shouldn't have listened in on that," she says, disturbingly calm.

"I know." I scramble for some sort of explanation. "I didn't realize you were here, then when I did, I . . ."

"Hid in a stall?" Rhonda raises a brow.

"I'm not spying on you," I blurt out.

Rhonda's stare narrows in on me, scanning my face. I don't know what she finds, but she sighs and wipes the raw spot on her cheeks. "I can tell that you're upset too." Her knuckles whiten. "It's so, so tough loving someone who is sick. Sometimes it feels like he's already gone." Her eyes widen and her skin pales a full swatch, like she's haunted by her words, by her thoughts. "He needs money for food, but . . . I can't. I can't give him anything. It might hurt him."

I take a few steps closer. It's like I'm carrying all the pain from today and my life with me with each tile I pass.

My reflection catches in the mirror behind Rhonda. It's like a mug shot—all the terrible things I've seen and done have caught up to my face. Nothing like the girl from the other day at the meeting. I'm nothing like her. I'm also splotchy, and maybe that's what does it for me. I don't start to cry so much as I finally release whatever it is that needed out. Big heaving heavy gasps come all at once.

"I'm sorry." I quickly wipe my tears and force myself to harden. Rhonda's jaw tightens. She won't look me in the eye. I'm the one crying while she's pouring her heart out. So I catch my breath and force myself to stop. Deep breaths. "I'm not going to . . . It's none of my business."

Rhonda finally moves, grabbing a tissue from the counter and handing it to me. "My son would be mortified if he knew what he was doing. He's not that person."

"I get it." The fear in her gaze dissolves a tiny bit at this. Just three words, and she's less alone.

Rhonda's voice shakes. "When they're young, we think that everything's going to be perfect, and it all seems so manageable. We can control the world they live in. Then the world gets bigger and harder and . . ." She fades out and it's as though something in her foundation crumbles. "It's impossible. I have to mourn him while he's alive. I have to wish he goes to jail. I'm not allowed to have him stay with me, help him. That's enabling, apparently. But my son's still sick, and if I don't *enable* him, then what if . . ." She lets out a gasping breath, and another.

The absolute agony of what she's been dealing with, going to her cube each day with her lonely secret—it's unbelievable. "Is there anything I can do to help? Or someone I can call for you?"

Her chin collapses. "No, there's no one, dear. My husband is gone, and somewhere along the way I lost all my friends." Her eyes are vacant, looking somewhere just above mine. "I'm going to be too old to work here soon. No one needs me anymore. I'm already useless." She closes her hands over her mouth—the shimmer in her nails puts on a depressing show against the dull lighting—as the sobs pull from her.

I need to comfort her. But what can I even say? I never know how to navigate these situations. "Can I give you a hug?" My voice comes out in a croak.

Before I even know what's happening, Rhonda wraps her arms around my shoulders and pulls me in. My arms go stiff, but as she tightens her grip on me, I soften against her chest.

My heart pinches. My mom hugs the same way.

"You're not alone," I whisper. "You're not."

The moment stills between us. She lets me go abruptly and wipes at her face, as if just becoming aware of what she's doing.

We both take a step apart, like waking from a trance, our moves slow and uncertain.

"Thank you, dear," she says, though she addresses this to my reflection in the mirror. "I'm sorry. I have to go."

She whips out of the bathroom, the door swinging in her wake, the automatic dispenser grinding as it rolls a paper towel through its gears.

I stare back at the pale mug shot in the mirror and force myself to breathe. The chemical bleach scent bleeds into my lungs.

I practically stumble onto the main floor, then beeline for the copy room. I pull a glass from the cupboard. It's impossible to ignore the water marks that cover it.

I search the cupboard under the sink, then add the Jet-Dry to the spot in the dishwasher, and it's like a farewell. A weight drills into my chest, hollow and heavy. It's like there are these pockets of sorrow waiting to be uncovered right below the surface. But we see them only sometimes, only by chance.

Otherwise, we never know.

Gregory: A Man Named Gregory
Who Works Here

I
T TAKES SIPPING a full glass of water and staring at the tiles in the copy room for an unknown amount of time before I'm ready to return to the pods. I'm not quite on solid ground as I make my way to my desk. And when I do, my inbox waits with a formally toned email from Cliff, with attached instructions to close out our session from today and a note that he'll see me next week for the next one and promises that he'll continue to support my successful completion of the course. I type: Sounds good, thanks, hit send, close out, and stare forward, willing my emotions down. Willing myself to be a desk bot.

I scan the other pods: Caitlin hasn't returned, but Armin is already back to dozing off in his seat like nothing happened. I notice that Rhonda's discreetly wiping her eyes with a tissue. We lock eyes only for a second before she averts my gaze and focuses on her screen.

Gregory marches up to the cubicle block and says to me, "Caitlin never came back up, did she? Her reports are due."

I shrug in the politest way possible, I think.

Armin pipes in: "I saw her on her phone when I was coming back. Sounded like she was pissed at some wedding vendor or something. She was telling the guy to shut up."

Gregory harumphs and stalks away toward the elevators, probably to find some intern to help him print something.

Out of nowhere, Rhonda stands up, grabbing her quilted coat and embroidered purse.

Armin looks up in surprise. "Hold up, you're not leaving, are you?"

Rhonda looks at the floor, her chin wobbling. "I'm needed somewhere. I have to go."

"Is that so? I'm not sure you've cleared this *time off* with anyone." The corner of Armin's mouth pulls up into a self-satisfied smirk, and I get what he's doing, but I want to slap him because this is not the moment. "You haven't even sent me the copy I need for Greg's party yet. I'm heading to the print shop tonight."

Rhonda rocks on her feet, her whole demeanor frail. "Right," she says slowly. "Okay, give me a few minutes." She starts to drop her bag again, and I catch moisture gathering in the corners of her eyes.

"I can do it," I announce.

Rhonda turns to me, nearly slumping with relief. "Jolene, are you sure?"

I nod. "Of course. It's a Morale Booster thing. I'm a Morale Booster."

"Okay." The corners of her lips flutter upward, barely a smile, but it's there. "Jolene, thank you ... for everything."

I gesture toward the hallway. "Just go. Your appointment is more important than anything here."

As Rhonda strides out, Caitlin returns, tapping furiously on her phone.

"Told that vendor where to shove it then?" Armin says. Caitlin looks up at him, confused. "Anyway, Gregory is looking for some report."

"Oh my god, I'll get it to him soon. He needs to calm down," she mutters. She rubs at her eye, and I catch a smudge of mascara under her left tear duct. The state of emergency in this place post–fire drill is something else.

Armin looks toward me. "Jolene, if you're really doing the write-up about Gregory, I need it by four."

"The what?" Oh god, what did I sign myself up for?

Armin raises his eyebrows, a hint of amusement in his expression. "Rhonda wanted a written toast to sit on the tables for Gregory's anniversary party. Like, a quick summary of his career and awards, a short thing about his family life, I guess."

This task is my personal nightmare, actually, but as I look at Rhonda's empty cube, I know of course I have to do it.

A GOOD WAY to not be okay is to spend a whole afternoon internet-stalking a man who every time you see his face, a part of you wants to curse your own existence because it means having to witness *his*. But the faster I finish, the quicker I can go home and drink the horrible new knowledge of Gregory away.

The interesting slash depressing thing about working for a corporation that's been around for as long as Supershops has is that a lot of things that are obvious wastes of time and money have most certainly happened. In my deep dive of the company database, I've learned that between the years 2004 and 2013, the office had a "newspaper." It was literally a weekly periodical about the people here and the things they did. There's a notice about the formation of the office Coffee Club (decades old, who would have thought!), an article about the office-wide switch to Windows Vista, and a write-up of a Bring Your Child to Work Day, featuring an old picture of Rhonda with a young child hugging her waist, who the caption confirms is Carl. I stare at their beaming smiles for several seconds, every muscle in my body as heavy as lead.

Gregory was featured in this newspaper three times.

The first was on January 4, 2005, when Gregory launched a new motivational contest for the office employees. I could've used this, but Larry D. Goodwin won, and the picture is of Gregory handing him a laminated certificate.

The second was on March 30, 2009, for winning a best tie contest. He's pictured holding up the neckwear in question to display the rubber duckie pattern—such an asshole tie to buy.

The third mention is on July 13, 2013, featuring him flipping pancakes for the annual company breakfast. It's an obvious photo-op moment: he's posing with a spatula, serving up a bullshit smile to someone holding a plate requesting *actual food*. The death glare from the person waiting in line behind them is a thing of beauty. It's nice to see like-minded people in the world.

All three of these mentions have to do with team-building programs he launched that eventually died out. Obviously, I'm not really supposed to embarrass him in his toast, but the temptation bites.

I do my best to pad the write-up with some vague sentences copied from the internet about things to say about great bosses, before moving on to the portion about his family life. I forgot his wife's name; she's that lady in the picture on his desk. But then it hits, the fastest way to find it: the Papa Bear email. I take some calming breaths before opening the message that knocks exactly six years off my life span every time I view it.

Thankfully, Gregory has the email address listed in his contacts. I finish my write-up with: "During his free time, Gregory loves to BBQ, golf, and spend time with his loving wife, Sheila." I'll play the odds that either he is a BBQ golf guy or, if he isn't, he'll be flattered that people think he is.

I shoot it off to Armin, and as I watch the email disappear from my screen, I wish that I could wipe this knowledge from my brain as easily.

Taarof-Off

THE KETTLE RINGS, signaling that the noodles I'd picked up from the convenience store near the bus drop-off are ready to be sous-cheffed by me. I'm pouring the steaming water out when my phone lights up, an unknown number ringing. I let it go to voicemail, but when it starts to ring again immediately, I decide to roll the dice by actually answering.

"Hey, Jolene, can you be a dear and get to the bakery right now?"

It's Armin, and it sounds like he's having a nervous breakdown. I'd forgotten I'd given him my number for the fake-fiancée dinner planning.

"What's up?"

"We have a, um . . . situation. Please, just get here. Now!" He practically hisses the last word.

In the background, I hear a voice say, "I want a cake that will make Minoo cry in shame!"

Oh my god. My stomach plummets. My mom's there.

"I'll be there in twenty minutes," I say, and hang up. I button up my pants, speed down the stairwell, and race to the bus station at the end of the block at record speed.

One harrowing bus ride later, I make it inside the bakery. The sweet, calming smell of fresh tea leaves pairs terribly with my mom, who is sitting in a booth looking ready to burst as she waves her hands animatedly in front of Armin's mom. Some poor bakery worker is standing in front of them with an iPad.

Both moms are screaming in Farsi, while Armin, my dad, and his dad sit facing them on the opposite side, hanging on to the edge of the table for dear life.

I'm backing away slowly, my ribs tightening around my chest, when Armin clocks my arrival and flies out of his seat to pounce on me. "Oh, hello, my dearest!" he says loudly. His eyes are wide, sweat glistening on his temples. Then he lowers his voice. "Our mothers have found each other's contact info and we're in shit."

"Yes, I see that." My insides fall to the ground as Armin's mom slaps my mom square in the arm. She does look slightly livelier than when we last met. My mom yells again, and I'm about to step in to stop someone from getting seriously hurt, when they both throw their heads back, laughing.

I'm not witnessing a mom fight. No, this is two kindred spirits finding each other.

"Our moms are thrilled to be joining families, so we're all having tea together," Armin grits out. "My mom hasn't been this energetic in a while."

"That's great?" But the look of horror on both our dads' faces indicates otherwise.

"They're already planning an engagement party for us. Your mom has decided she'd like a fifteen-layer cake."

"I literally *just* talked to her about keeping this low-key—"

"Hello, Jolene!" Armin's dad waves at me with both of his hands. "Please, come sit and have some tea. I've just met your father. He's a very good man. We both cheer for Manchester United."

My dad looks up from his lemon cake and gives me a tiny smile, a rare expression on him.

"Hi, Dad?" I say slowly as I slide into the booth, my fiancé scooting in next to me. "How's it going?"

My dad winces, apologetic. "I tried to tell your mom to wait for you before contacting the Habibs, but you know her."

Armin's dad waves dismissively at Dad's comment. "Nonsense. We're so glad to meet you. Armin has been keeping Jolene away for too long as is." He slides a cup of tea in front of me. "How are you? Have you been studying tonight?"

"Yes." I nod naturally, because the lies come too easy now. But my dad gives me a puzzled look, so I am forced to elaborate. "I'm studying hard for my career."

My dad narrows his eyes. "You were actually studying for your promotion?"

Armin's dad tilts his head toward me, curious. Why must people whom you've told lies to meet the people who don't know your other lies? I look at Armin, who is no help. He's like a cartoon character being squeezed until his eyes pop out.

"Yes," I croak, scrambling for words that will somehow cover both parents' knowledge. "I'm hoping to use my degree to stay within the company but also level up, you know?"

Armin's dad nods uncertainly. "Are there many options at Super-shops for computer engi—"

"I'm going to go order at the counter!" I feel terrible cutting Armin's dad off, but the alternative is surefire torture. I nudge at Armin for him to slide out of the booth so I can get up. "I need a danmarki, stat."

Armin's expression is stiff. "I'll come help you, love."

As we get up, I catch what the bakery worker is showing our moms on the iPad: pictures of the literal cake from the Meghan and Harry wedding. Armin sees it too and drops his face into his hands. "Why does it always end up replicating a royal wedding with our people?"

I shake my head, grabbing his sleeve and pulling him toward the front of the shop. "I'm not riding in a carriage with you. We need to stop this."

"Uh, yeah! This is the reason I called you. They're in a taarof-off."

"Shit. That's why our dads have freshly shined foreheads." Taarof is the Persian social custom of one-upping each other's politeness and generosity. It's super complex and hard to summarize and even harder to learn if it's not embedded inside you from a young age. My dad and me still don't fully understand all the nuances. Things like: You decline any payment three times minimum before accepting. If someone compliments your bracelet, you give it to them there and then, even if it's worth the price of a reliable used car. And you better think twice before walking through a door before the person behind you, especially if they're older. Basically, you need them to *envy* how courteous of a person you are.

But two Persian moms in a taarof-off while planning a party . . . Things are going to get out of hand. Our families will politely go broke. We watch the shopkeeper's eyes morph into little money symbols as he tells the worker to pull up an image of a ten-tier fruit platter, and both moms actually cheer as they lean in to get a closer look. Only Armin's mom has to use the table for support. The platter is filled with so many exotic and out-of-season fruits that it's obviously not for guests to enjoy as much as it is a status symbol—the ultimate Persian party grail.

Armin's pupils dilate. "Jolene, my parents can't afford to start putting money down on an extravagant event. Not with everything going on with my mom."

"Of course." I nod. My mom must have been the one to start this. "I'll see what I can do."

I march back to the moms, my most polite smile plastered on, prepared to use calm reasoning to fix this situation. But before I can even say anything, my mom grabs my upper arm and pulls me down into the booth, pointing at my face while yelling in rapid Farsi. Whatever she says causes the shop worker to actually bow slightly. Armin's mom leans over and kisses the air near my cheek. There's a rosiness in her complexion, but her voice strains. "Jolene joon, I'm so glad to meet your mom. She is a very kind person."

"Yes." She does give off that impression at first.

Mom pats my shoulder. "Jolene, drink your tea. We will pick a cake for the engagement party we're throwing you."

"No, Mom," I hiss quietly. "I told you. We don't want a big party."

Mom shakes her head. "I told *you* it's no problem." She turns her back to me and speaks in Farsi to Armin's mom. I don't know all the words, but the gist is she's telling her not to listen to me.

The impossible task of stopping my mom from doing this lies in my hands alone. "Mom, please listen! I'm serious. Armin and I are low-key, we don't want this. I don't even have people to invite!"

She throws her hands up like I've said something ridiculous. "You think that it will be a problem? Don't worry, I will fill the place up so it's bursting."

I stand up and return to Armin, who is looking up fruit platter prices from Costco on his phone and likely multiplying the total to the power of twenty. "I tried, but right now I don't think they can hear us. They're lost in full Persian party-planning mode."

We both share identical expressions of doom.

Armin whispers, "I think, for everyone's sake, we need to call off this wedding right now."

I cringe, because this is going to be horrible, but Armin's right. "Will your mom be okay?"

He sighs. "I don't know." He blinks several times rapidly. "Her lab results came back this week. She doesn't have much time left."

My heart pinches painfully. "I'm so sorry."

He nods, his eyes going glassy. "This is going to break her heart."

At the booth, our moms are cackling again, clutching each other's shoulders. His mom really does look happy. Even our dads are slightly smiling. But my mom—I haven't seen her face so lit up in years. It won't just be Armin's mother who's heartbroken. Will my mom ever forgive me for lying to her like this?

I look toward Armin, and he's watching them too, shoulders hunched like a soldier who knows he's about to be sent into a battle he won't survive.

"Maybe we shouldn't do this right now," I suggest. "If we can keep them from making any deposits, we can break the news gently? Build up to it. You know, fake a few arguments."

Armin knits his eyebrows together. "What would we argue about?"

"Obviously, you're too focused on your executive career. And I'm too busy studying for my promotion. It could never work."

Armin cracks a tiny smile, his shoulders sagging. "Yeah. That's probably a better idea."

"I'll talk to my mom when she's away from all this and tell her to cool it, make her feel really bad for overexciting your mom."

Armin nods. "But please, I beg of you, make her feel terrible. She needs to stop. I never would have lied if I'd known this would happen."

"Okay," I say, taking a deep breath. "So we agree, we can't do anything right now. We might as well buy them a few sweets."

The color is starting to return to Armin's face. "I'm getting a plate of latifeh, but just for me."

"I don't blame you." I smile.

"And some danmarkis too, before you buy them out. What did you order last time, like two dozen?"

I shove him in the side, and he cracks a smile. After securing our pastries, Armin and I join our dads, where we temporarily shovel all our anxieties away with tea. And I get to navigate three more awkward questions about what it is that I'm studying. And why.

Life Rated PG: Pathetic in General

I'M UNWINDING FROM my second full Cliff-free day of work by not quite enjoying a burned package of instant popcorn while checking Reddit to figure out who is the asshole, when there's a knock at my door. I run to open it in case it's my mom ready to make another scene, but Miley's eager face is waiting on the other side.

Her gaze weaves past me, jumping from the cluttered coffee table to the erratic shoe party below it. "So, this is your place. I've never seen past your shoe rack every time I try and peep."

My hand braces to slam the door—a purely robotic instinct—but I instead give her a deadpan stare. "What can I help you with?"

Her lips curl upward at the opening. "Glad you asked. I've always thought of you as someone who could think objectively about unjust rules and would fight for those harmed by them if you could."

I let out a hefty sigh. "Miley, please just tell me what I can do for you. I've had a rough week…"

She rocks on her toes, her hands clasped behind her back. "You know what's the perfect cure for rough weeks? Taking your favorite neighbor to the movies." She splays out her hands.

I back a step away from the threshold. "There's no way."

Miley shakes her head. "Please—I'm *begging* you. I need to see this movie. I'm the only one in my whole school who hasn't seen it! It's at seven o'clock, so you'll be home at a normal hour, I promise!"

I grab for my wallet, splayed on the shoe rack where I dropped it when I got home. "How much? I can loan you the money."

Miley stiffens, her wide puppy eyes turning to maximum strength. "No, it's not that. I have the money. But it's rated R, so I need someone old to escort me in."

I scoff. "So you basically need me to take a minor into a movie illegally?"

She throws her head back. "It's a stupid law. You know I've seen worse around here than anything they could put in some slasher film."

She's got a point. Just behind her, there's a punch hole in the drywall. Both Miley and I were there when the guy down the hall got pissed because his Wi-Fi broke and he yelled at everyone in the world before taking it out on the communal wall. Its twin hole is in the lobby, from when the couple upstairs broke up, and we all had to hear about the deficiencies of their sex life while personal items were thrown down the stairwell.

Miley presses her hands against the archway to prevent me from closing the door. "Pleaaaase? My mom would do it if she wasn't too busy to take me."

I turn my head and look back at my drab apartment. My blinds aren't up to the job of hiding the sun that's creeping through. And maybe I could use the company. Things feel so empty since returning to my life before Cliff.

I sigh, and it's like my resolve crumbles in front of her eyes. "Fine."

"Yay! I knew you'd do the right thing." She grabs my arms, but I keep them planted in my hoodie pocket.

"Meet me out front in ten minutes," I huff.

I THROW ON a dressier hoodie and jeans for the occasion. Miley's hopping from foot to foot out front while she waits.

We walk to the theater together. Outside the front entrance, two middle-aged men are smoking and muttering to each other. They stop mid-conversation as Miley and I walk by. I clench my fists, just waiting for them to make some creepy comment. The potential for random shit like this is what's wrong with the world.

We pass without incident, and inside security isn't exactly airport standard; they don't even look at us. Once we're seated in creaky felt chairs with vintage farts stored in their cushions, the smell of butter drizzle becoming part of us, I say, "Can I sneak out now that the mission is accomplished?"

Miley, who's busy taking a selfie of herself at the theater, tilts her phone down. "No way. You can't leave me alone with a bunch of adults." She leans closer and whispers, "What if a child predator comes?" Then she silently points at what I'm sure is probably a very nice man with a silky scarf sitting in front of us.

"Fine, but I don't like horror movies."

The whites of her eyes widen and glint in the overhead lighting. "Yeah, I don't like them either."

"Why the hell do we have to see it then? This was meant as a whole thing to let you actually have some joy."

"It *is* bringing me joy. I *need* to see this movie. My two almost friends, Sandra and Sarah, who are coming for a slumber party, have started leaving me out for not seeing it. And why? Because Sandra's creepy brother took them."

Miley squeezes her hands together on her lap. So much of the girl I once was bounces in her seat.

I lean in, voice softer. "Miley, I haven't forgotten what it's like to be your age—how hard it is."

She shrugs. "Good, then you understand why."

"Yeah, but . . . a real friend wouldn't care about the movies you've seen. They'd include you anyway."

She rolls her eyes. "Thanks, Hallmark Channel."

"I'm serious. Just this week I was, um . . . admiring the zebra you made me." I flash back to poor Mr. Barcode being handled by Larry, to Cliff saving him, to *our kiss*. How could things have gone so bad since then? I push that thought loop down—my angst down—for the hundredth time today and continue. "That was so thoughtful of you to make that. You're a good friend."

"My crochet sucks, Jolene. Everyone knows that. No matter how many YouTube tutorials I watch."

There's a hint of hardness in her eyes. There's no way to stop the world from getting to her. "Well, to me your crochet is charming, and my actual point is that anyone would be lucky to have a thoughtful friend like you. Take it from me; it's better to be a little picky and hold out for real friends, 'cause the fake friends can crush you."

"But who wants to be that picky?" She leans in conspiringly, the tang of soda on her breath, in the orange on her lips. "Now that you're old, aren't you, like, allowed to do whatever you want without asking? But you never do. It's like you've grounded yourself."

I stiffen.

She keeps going. "You don't even drive with that friend from your work anymore. Picky again?"

I fully turn to stone.

Unacceptable behavior. And as I'm about to defend myself from her vicious attack, my heart stops in its tracks.

Because somehow, some way, Cliff has stepped into the theater. Cliff the *actual* person. Not an illusion. Not a wish. The HR guy. He's sporting a fitted hoodie and crisp baseball cap.

But my blood pauses in my arteries. Because there's a very attractive young brunette walking next to him who is definitely not his sister.

"Oh my god." I stiffen and crouch in my seat. This isn't a dream. It's a nightmare.

Miley looks at me, raising an eyebrow. "What's gotten into you—"

I squeeze Miley's shoulder and pull her down with me. "Shh!"

She follows my gaze and practically screams. "We were *just* talking about him! Is he your boyfriend?"

"No!" I almost yell. I squeeze her arm a little too hard. "Keep your voice down. I don't want him to see me."

Our gazes turn back to Cliff, who has taken a seat a few rows ahead. He's chatting easily, picking pieces of popcorn from the bag sitting in the woman's lap. He's so casual and happy looking.

The attractive brunette leans close and whispers in his ear. I crouch farther.

I want to disappear into my bones. Instead, I have to sit here, watching Cliff on a date. Oh god, am I going to have to watch him kiss her?

While the trailers start, Miley whispers, "If he's two-timing you, he's a piece of shit."

I shake my head, even as my stomach curdles. "No, he isn't. We're just friends." But I know that's a lie. I stopped us being friends. And now it's official. He's moving on. And that's okay.

Miley gives me a lingering look that is way too knowing. "Sure, Jolene."

I WAKE FROM the nightmare as the lights finally come on and the theater begins to empty. I have no idea what we just saw. I spent the entire time watching the dark outline of Cliff's head, analyzing every inch of space between him and that woman.

They start to stand up, and so does Miley, but I pull her back down. "Let's give them a buffer."

She nods, and we let them pass. We wait a full five minutes before she finally tugs on my sleeve and says, "Come on, let's go! I have to pee!"

I'm waiting outside the bathroom door for her when the men's room door opens and, for fuck's sake, it's Cliff who comes out. He glances up and physically stops in his tracks, his jaw dropping. He looks as horrified to see me here as I am to see him.

"Jolene!" There's a hesitation to the way he says my name, like he can't quite believe this is happening.

I take a step backward without meaning to.

Then that brunette appears and sidles next to him, all cozy, and smiles at me.

Cliff's whole demeanor remains tense. He won't look at me directly.

"This is Silvia," Cliff says, gesturing at her awkwardly. "We play Warhammer together. Silvia, this is my colleague Jolene."

Silvia's kind smile makes me want to crush into myself. She's pretty, really pretty, with the kind of gentle curls that look effortless but probably took her three hours to perfect. *And* she likes Warhammer.

Miley pops out of the bathroom, and her eyes instantly go wide as she takes in the drama. She runs up to me and grabs my arm.

"This is Miley," I say, looking anywhere but Cliff.

Silvia's grin turns even warmer. "We were just about to get some food. Would you and your young friend like to grab a ton of tacos from next door with us?"

Cliff's head starts to shake, but it's Miley who pipes in. "You mean me and Jolene? We're not really friends. She just snuck me into an R-rated movie. I'm only twelve."

"Oh?" Silvia's smile falters.

My insides turn to stone, yet Miley doesn't stop. "But we can't go for food with you. My mom doesn't even know I'm out, so I should get home."

"Miley," I whisper, "could you kindly shut up?"

I smile through my teeth. And why doesn't this theater have any fainting chairs? My eyes dart to the exit as I back away, legs as heavy as bags of sand. "I'm sorry, but Miley's right. We've got to head back."

Cliff doesn't say anything, just looks at the carpet. I wave and pull Miley along.

I'm walking really fast, and her breath hitches as she keeps pace. Once we're clear of the theater, Miley finally yells, "Jolene, what the hell?"

"I never should have brought you here. Why did you say that?" I spit my words out. "I'm so embarrassed. Look at me, just hanging out with you while he's on a date."

Her face crumbles. Shit.

"No, Miley. What I mean is—"

Miley takes a step backward. "No, it's okay. I'm sorry I said we weren't friends. I just figured that's what you'd want."

The look in her eyes, the slouch in her shoulders. I recognize this girl.

"It's just . . . Miley, we shouldn't hang out like that anymore. One day you'll understand."

She shakes her head, the crush in her gaze still there.

The world seems so simple for some people.

We walk the rest of the way back in silence. I leave the building door propped open but don't wait for her as I walk in.

Please Excuse My Wine

THE NEXT WEEK comes and goes, and nothing much happens. I continue replacing my commute with Cliff with shaky bus rides. My evenings are no longer interrupted by bowling, Miley, or anything else. I even stop checking Cliff's icon to see if he's online. Or I at least do it a lot less. I submitted some course material to him yesterday, and it was all so formal, with phrases like: "I hope this finds you well" and "Best regards."

After a few sleeps I like to think I've come around to our new dynamic. It's for the best that he moves on from this place. From me.

The only notable events this Friday: Rhonda spent fifteen minutes comforting Jean Adler, whose daughter did not make it into the same law school Carl went to (I averted my eyes the entire time as she did this); Caitlin spent the morning giggling while she presumably texted Kyle and spent a whole hour standing by Joy's desk talking about wedding stuff; Armin spent the day zoning out while twiddling his mouse to keep his screen active. It's all so typical.

But tonight, we're being held captive longer. Even though we've already contributed forty hours of our waking lives to this cursed place this week, we must donate an additional two hours of our Friday evening to celebrate the fact that Gregory has wasted the most time here.

There's no way to duck out unnoticed because the entire office decides to walk over to the bar together. Armin ends up between Caitlin and Garret, so I sidle up next to Rhonda, who is telling Marsha all about Carl's latest false victory.

The party's on the main floor of the bar this time. Rhonda's spirals and balloons hang from the ceiling. They've set up tables with plastic tablecloths and folding chairs. The banner hanging above the oak bar reads: *For He's a Jolly Good Fellow*. A sad little buffet of cold cuts and oily cheese is set up on a table in the back of the room, but the email invite made sure to be crystal clear: drinks are not included.

The piece I wrote for Gregory sits on little stands in the middle of each table. Armin did a top-notch job printing on the cardstock. The picture they selected is of a much younger Gregory, his hair poufy and jolly-good-fellow-y.

As we file in, everyone seems to find someone to chat with. I realize I should do the same so as to not stand out as abandoned. I see Armin, but he's in a conversation with Chris Fernando in IT. The guy is like an eccentric artist about software—every time someone contacts him for help, he gets accusatory and unhinged. Best to avoid him, given my current deceptions.

I slink into a seat at a table in the corner, where some other seventh-floor people are lingering. They seem as unhappy about the life decisions that landed them at this party as I am.

But then Caitlin and Garret settle into the chairs across from me, seemingly without noticing me—they're leaning so close together, having a hushed conversation, that it's impossible to listen in.

A server comes around to ask for drink orders, coming to me first since I'm the only one not talking. I'm not hyped by the idea of consuming alcohol in front of all my colleagues, but at least I can get something to hold in front of me and press my lips to, so I don't look too weird by myself.

I say, "Glass of red wine," which is, of course, a mistake. Next thing I know, the server is listing off an endless variety of wines and asking for my preferences in body and dryness. My only method for picking wines is the price. At my baffled expression, the waiter pulls a written wine list out of his apron. Wow, one glass costs eleven dollars. But that's the cheapest, so I go with that. Except the wine is called Revinionvissino or something. I try to say it, and the waiter tilts his head and asks me to repeat that.

By now, all the conversation around the table has died out as everyone is checking what's holding the waiter up. I take the menu and point, my finger shaking over the tiny print. "This one."

He leans down to look. "Sorry, which one is that? Are you pointing at the Montepulciano?"

The Montepulciano costs eighteen dollars for six ounces, so I panic and say, "No, no, the eleven-dollar one."

Beside me, Caitlin laughs out loud.

Well, fuck her.

"Oh, that sounds good," a voice says behind me—Cliff—and my skin flushes, the splash of heat instant and gripping. I didn't think he'd come here, but of course he would. He's HR, after all. "I'd like to try that too," he continues.

He smiles at me, a small plea in his eyes. I blink, but I'm too frozen to do more. We haven't been this close to each other since the movies, the fire alarm—all our recent half-finished messy conversations—and I don't know what to with any part of my body. I'd been planning to call in sick on the day of our next session, hoping that I could somehow pass the course without seeing him again. I should say at least one casual thing to him, but I don't know what, and more relevantly, I *can't*. The idea of showing any human emotion, especially in front of the entire office and *especially* Caitlin, makes me want to actually dissolve into the blender that's mixing margaritas in a loud drone at the bar.

So I grab my phone and pretend to read a text.

Cliff takes the hint, and when the drinks are served, he takes his glass, smiles a little sadly, and takes off to the other side of the bar without saying another word.

I watch him over the top of my phone as he speaks to a few of the reception and intake staff members, then makes his way to the supply chain people. After a few minutes, he takes off his hoodie, revealing a checkered shirt I've never seen him wear before. Then he chuckles really loudly and claps Robin Winters on the shoulder. What did Robin even say? I'm tempted to advise Robin that Cliff chose his death for a billion dollars just weeks ago.

And that's when I realize I should pay attention to my own table.

Armin and Rhonda have sat down near me, talking about the shredder guy and how he hasn't shown up on schedule lately. Marla, apropos of nothing, starts telling us about her ex-husband's intimacy issues; I'm fairly sure this party isn't the place to share this, but who knows. Rhonda suggests that it might be fun to start a book club for the singles in the office. I'm beginning to zone out when suddenly the whole table erupts in laughter—a joke I've missed.

And again, I'm alone.

If we were in the office, I would just click on their messages, read them back to figure out what they're all discussing. But I don't have the cheat codes to real life.

Finally, Gregory comes bouncing into the bar, arms wide as he greets the room like he's a prized pig. His wife is beside him, wearing a perfect A-line dress in signature Supershops blue—the same one she wore to the Christmas lunch last year. I can barely look at her, now that I'm holding on to the knowledge of Papa Bear. I shudder down a sip of my wine.

Gregory takes a seat at the head table that Rhonda prepared with a sash that reads *20 Years*. He grabs the card stock and reads it. A smile pulls across his face, crunching the corners of his eyes—he must like the bit about BBQ and golfing, and that reassures me more than expected. Following my instincts to write the most generic praise possible seems to have worked on his simple mind.

But then his eyes widen, nearly popping out of his skull, before narrowing hard.

He flips the card facedown and slides it under the table. His eyes dart to Mrs. Gregory, who's busy getting hors d'oeuvres from the sad buffet.

Rhonda gets up and passes by his table, holding her glass of the same rosé she drank last time we were here. Gregory stands and taps her arm to stop her. I can read his lips as he asks, "Who wrote this?"

My heart drops into my feet. I don't catch Rhonda's answer, but Gregory's eyes dart in my direction and my heart plummets.

I've stood up without realizing it—some fight-or-flight survival instinct. Maybe Gregory is actually terrible at golf and I've roasted him by mentioning it.

Gregory rubs a hand over his mustache hard, his eyes still on me. I hear him say, "I need all of these taken away immediately."

Rhonda's expression drops. She places her glass on the table. "Will do."

His wife appears next to him. "Nice to meet all of you again!" she says brightly. "Thanks for throwing a great party."

"I'm not sure you've met all my colleagues here. Let me introduce you." Gregory's gaze crawls back to me, slow and sharp. When he clocks my weak smile, he looks like he wants to spit on me. "Jolene," he calls out in my direction. "Come over here."

Everyone at my table goes quiet, their eyes trailing to me. I take teeny steps, drawing out the six-foot walk as long as possible.

"Madeline, this is Jolene. Jolene, this is *Madeline*."

He watches me register her name.

Shit. Shit. Shit.

I got her name wrong. How did I get her name wrong? Then, two seconds later: the email got her name wrong. Nope. Finally, it hits me—Gregory catches my face when it does, and my blood turns to ice.

"Madeline, Jolene's work has been very visible this quarter. We're going to meet soon to discuss her *future* at Supershops." Then he leans toward me and whispers, "We'll discuss this later."

He takes his wife by the elbow and walks away, leaving me to deal with my heart attack.

I stumble back to my table on wobbly legs.

Caitlin is holding a frozen margarita just beneath her lips, her huffing breaths creating steam on top of the glass.

I grab my wineglass and force down a big gulp. No relief follows. Instead, my stomach curdles. I think I might be sick.

I run into the bathroom and lock myself in a stall.

IT'S BEEN ALMOST two hours.

Before today, I would've thought it impossible to hide inside a three-foot-square stall this long without feeling messed up after, and I'm unfortunately right. I listen to the sounds of others coming and going from the three other stalls, experience all the awful smells. There shouldn't be anything worse than this. But going back out into that party, being either glared at or ignored, depending on the person, or trying not to look at Cliff, to have him see me, would've been worse.

The bar was reserved only until seven p.m. for Gregory's party. By now, everyone should be clearing out.

I steel myself. It's time to make my exit.

But as soon as I open the stall's door, I curse the universe for its terrible timing. The bathroom door swings open and in walks Caitlin. She walks right past my ajar stall and stands in front of the mirror, checking herself. And holy shit, she hasn't noticed me.

"Oh, you're so lucky," she says to her reflection, voice slurred. "You're going to have so much good stuff. You're perfect."

This would normally be a blessed, magical occasion, and I'd enjoy this image for decades, but the door I'm still holding half open creaks, and Caitlin whips around, locking her eyes on me—as best she can. One eye is like the half-mast flag that has surrendered for the night.

She gives a limp point in my general direction.

"I don't know what the fuck you think you're playing at, but I know you're up to something," she says—or at least that's my best guess, as her voice is so garbled.

I try to keep calm. The most important thing to remember is that she's wasted. I was on my way out anyway, so I slowly back away toward the exit. Because when it comes down to it, I'm nothing but a coward.

But Caitlin's not done. "I mean it. I know *all* about you."

I freeze mid-step. The glossy tile squeaking under my shoe is the only sound in the room.

She wobbles in front of me, a predator zeroing in on its prey. "Kyle told me what you did."

My stomach drops through the floor.

She lets out an ugly cackle. "Are you messed up?" Then she points and, even though it's actually nowhere in my direction, I physically flinch away. She laughs again. "It's actually true? That's *horrible.*"

My anxiety can sometimes be painful, words banging around in my head, my ribs tightening around me like a vise. But the worst kind of panic is numb, almost peaceful. My brain starts to swim away. I'm afraid I'm going to actually pass out or lose control of my voice and scream.

I need to get out of here.

I push past her with an elbow, but she grabs my arm, her grip surprisingly firm. "Hey, you can't assault me! You're like that, I guess. I'm adding all this to my email." Her eyes shine like twisted marbles. "I'm telling Gregory all about you next week. It's a matter of safety!"

She releases me with a shove, and I stumble backward into a stall, almost fall into the toilet. My vision is clouding. My hands have closed tight. All the bones in my fingers have fused together, hard as stones. My brain might burst any second.

I close my eyes, take one long breath, and run for it, sidestepping Caitlin. I make it back into the barroom. It's pretty much empty now, a few staff members clearing used plates and glasses from the tables. I rush outside onto the street. The cool air nips at my skin, affording me a second of clarity. But my earlobes feel tingly and numb, and my temples pull tight. I'm having a panic attack, and I need to go somewhere private.

On autopilot, my feet carry me back to the office.

THE OFFICE IS completely empty when I make it to my floor. I don't bother to turn on the lights, heading straight to my desk and slumping into my chair. It says a lot about my mental state that as soon as I stepped into the elevator, I could feel myself calming down, soothed by the familiarity of the stale air.

But Caitlin knows about Ellie—*has* known, probably, since the day of her engagement party. Why didn't she use this information sooner?

She mentioned an email.

I log in to my computer and check every single item she sent in the last month. Nothing.

Unless... she didn't send it yet.

I go into my bottom desk drawer and pull out the maroon folder. Scrawled on a Post-it note are her passwords.

I look around the barren room. The only sound is the rhythmic dripping of the watercooler, echoing through the space like a drumbeat.

I have to know.

I go over to her desk chair and pull it out gently. Her diffuser is sitting to the right of her monitor, unplugged. On the left are several photos of her fluffy white cat, who looks as miserable as a Ben Affleck meme in its tutu.

I move her mouse across her purple mouse pad and her screen comes to life. I type: Iamagoddess.

And there it is, sitting in her drafts folder. The one folder that I can't see with my admin privileges.

TO: Gregory Hall
FROM: Caitlin Joffrey
SUBJECT: Information about an Employee

Hello Gregory,

I've been thinking about my future with Supershops. As you know, I've been with the company for a few years and (LIST THINGS DONE HERE THAT SHOW HOW GREAT I AM). I'm aware there may be some departmental restructuring soon, so I wanted to bring to your attention (FIND A WAY TO PROFESSIONALLY EXPRESS: Jolene is a loser by definition, and she's ruining the company with her vibes and messed up attitude).

I do feel that if opportunities for progression are to come down to me and a colleague that may have been here longer, I'd be the stronger choice. I assure you that my dedication to this company, the pride I take in every project, my education and ability to represent myself within this office, is unmatched compared to any other potential candidate for this role.

I believe my reputation within Supershops speaks for itself. As does yours: you're someone I admire, and your career is impressive. I view you as a mentor figure and honestly a super boss. I'd love to continue to grow within this company and continue to build on the impressive machine you've managed to run so smoothly.

I pause. Even as I struggle to comprehend everything I am witnessing, I have to wonder: Who hurt her to be able to say such kind things to Gregory?

I have an idea what the final paragraph will say before my eyes even reach it. It's like years of this specific dread have developed into a sixth sense within my soul.

(MENTION HER DEAD FRIEND AND THE THEORIES). I thought you should know. Given Jolene's pattern of aggressive behaviors toward colleagues in the office, I feel it's a duty and a matter of safety to voice all relevant concerns about this employee's past.

Respectfully,
Caitlin

All my blood heats up and pulses through my pores. It's exactly what I feared, yet worse with its vagueness.

She hasn't sent it—she hasn't even finished it—but she will. And it will all be over for me. Everything will have been for nothing.

My breath is pitchy, and it's like the world is shrinking around me. My fingers twitch to delete it. I *need* to delete it. Except another wave of doom hits. She can always write another one. There's nothing I can do to actually stop her from emailing him.

It's pure survival instinct. My only plan is to make the part of the email about Ellie disappear into the ether. I need to silence it. Except as soon as I delete the last paragraph, I realize I need to fill it in with something. I type: Jolene sucks. Might be helpful to have her credibility challenged just a little these days. I'm scheduling it to send for when I'm long out of the building. I'll make sure to scan out with my card to solidify my alibi—

"What are you doing?"

I jolt so hard in Caitlin's chair it rolls into her cabinet. I swing around and Cliff is standing behind me.

"Cliff!" I blabber. What the hell is he even doing here?

His expression twists as he takes in the scene before him: me in Caitlin's chair, an email sitting up on her screen. I'm about as guilty looking as they come.

"Jolene, what the fuck are you doing?" he repeats, his voice darker than I've ever heard it.

Everything inside of me is shaking. I try to say something, but all the words die in my throat.

He raises an eyebrow at me. "Are you reading your colleague's emails? That's a fireable offense."

A stilted chuckle comes out before I can stop it, like my brain has finally snapped.

Cliff's mouth falls open.

And everything I've done lately twists like a spiky corkscrew inside my stomach. This is who I am—despite everything I've tried, I'll always be the same person.

"Jolene." Cliff's voice cracks. He's standing a few feet away from me, holding himself very still. "I need to know what you're doing. Please tell me the truth."

The truth. I shudder a breath, shallow and wheezy through my dry lips. There's no other way.

"I was altering one of Caitlin's emails."

Cliff flinches backward like I've slapped him. "I can't—you can't do this, obviously. I have to report this."

I nod. "I know."

And that certainty, the knowledge that it's *finally* over, breaks the dam. A sob pulls from me before I can stop it.

They're big, ugly tears. Old tears, like they've been waiting inside me for months—years, even—and now that they've been released, there's nothing I can do to stop them. I bury my face in my hands and bend my head toward my knees, a futile attempt at hiding what's happening, because my entire body is shaking.

"Jolene . . ." Cliff says, voice so small I can barely hear him over my weeping.

"I'm sorry," I try to say through the lump in my throat. "I lied. I didn't tell you—I didn't tell—"

I hear his footsteps on the padded carpet. They come to a stop right in front of me. From my bent-over position, I see the tips of his shoes in front of my own. I hoist myself up in the chair and he's looking down at me, devastated.

"What didn't you tell me?" he asks carefully.

Everything, I want to say. A million things—a million lies. But it all comes back to one thing. The biggest lie of all is the one I've been carrying for years.

"I told you my friend died in high school. Her name was Ellie," I start, wiping at my face with my sleeve. "I didn't tell you why I moved away."

He nods, silently allowing me to continue.

And it's just like the tears—once the story starts, I can't stop it. "It was horrible, the way she died. We were at a party, we drank too much, and she got hurt. It was an accident. I—I couldn't save her." That part, at least, finally feels true. "But I was the only one who was with her when it happened, so there were rumors. People started to say I hurt her. It got out of hand. Everywhere I went, it was like all anyone could see was that version of the story. After a while, I started to believe it too."

Cliff's jaw ticks, but he doesn't say anything.

I continue. "Caitlin's fiancé knew me, back then. He used to terrorize me and Ellie. He was at the party too when she died. I'm pretty sure he's the one who started those rumors in the first place."

Cliff's fingers ball into little fists at his sides, but still, he says nothing.

"Caitlin told me she's going to email Gregory about ... deeply personal things." I swallow. "About Ellie. And I just—I know it has nothing to do with work, but it would ruin my life here."

Cliff's head shakes. "You don't know that."

"I *do,*" I push back. "I've been here before. It doesn't matter what's true. No one will look at me the same. I just—I don't want them to—"

"Did you hit send on the email?" Cliff's voice is firm.

I shake my head once, staring at my feet.

"Okay, then I didn't see anything. Just close the draft and walk away."

My face juts up. "Are you serious?"

He looks up at the ceiling. "What am I going to do, go to Greg about you?" He shakes his head. "I just can't do it."

My breath halts halfway in my throat. I can't believe it. "Thank you."

A few beats of silence pass. He grabs a tissue off Rhonda's desk and hands it to me, and I gratefully wipe it over my already drying tears.

"What were you doing here?" I finally ask.

His lips tick downward. "Well, I came to get my car from the building, but my tongue was still wine dry in a way that only blue Gatorade can cure." He gestures toward the back hall, where the vending machine is. "Can I get you one?"

And I let out a welcome chuckle, relieved to have the energy shift. "No thanks."

Cliff steps closer. The scent of his soap warms my cheeks. "Jolene, I know things have been weird and we're still keeping our distance..." His gaze draws to mine and my chest loosens just a bit, hearing his voice. "But I'm sorry I was so awkward at the theater—"

"You don't need to apologize for *that*," I interrupt.

He swallows heavily. "Right..." His gaze lingers as his fists clench. "That's the thing. Between Larry's breakdown and what happened with us... everything... I'm like the worst HR guy."

More heat flashes across my skin as I remember our kiss, but I force a teasing grin. "Yeah, I mean you were doodling when we first met, during a disciplinary meeting. That was a red flag." His lips twitch into a half smile, and I look at him with sincerity. "Cliff, I need to apologize to you, though. I'm sorry I read your texts. And I'm sorry I overreacted about that message to your old boss. That wasn't my place."

The slight clench of his fists seems to loosen. "Thanks."

His reply does nothing to ease my guilt. I wish I could go back in time. Would I have stopped myself and my email plans if I'd known him just a little earlier?

"It makes sense," I say, "going back to Vancouver, if that's what you want to do." The truth of my words hollows me out. He deserves so much better than this place.

Cliff's eyes soften. "I don't know..." He presses a hand to his temple. "I've been thinking about my career a lot lately. Honestly, you've made me realize some stuff."

I huff a laugh. "I should be an HR person."

Cliff throws back his head. "Please don't." Then his lids drop, more serious. "I'm taking it day by day, but I'm trying not to lose myself to this job. Who I am and what I do in this world are more important than where I work. Even if it's Supershops."

I put my hand to my chest. "Cliff, I think you've just said something illegal in this office."

His mouth twists with amusement: a tiny smile for just me in this dim room. "You know, you're the only person here that's been real with me, right from the get-go. I can tell when someone's kissing ass or faking nice. But you were giving me shit about my cat doodle from day one, asking me who I'd kill for money by week two. It was nice to have someone see me as a person."

"Same, with you," I say—the most honest statement I've made to him.

Cliff bends toward me, holding out his hand to help me up. "I miss my carpool buddy. Can we be friends again?"

My heart squeezes when I look at him. I can definitely be fine with him as just my friend. I have to be.

It's all we get.

"Friends," I agree, and take his hand. We both look down at our palms, slotted together, for a second too long before he tugs and I lift myself up.

He smiles. "All right. Let's just walk away from the computer that you haven't touched and get out of here?"

We leave the dim office together. The whole drive home is spent in emotional silence, but not the uncomfortable kind. Occasionally we catch each other's eye and smile. It's good to be back in here in this car that smells like happy dog.

When he pulls over on my street, he finally speaks. "Oh, Jolene. Please don't do that kind of thing again. I can't fire you. Like, I don't think I actually could." He looks at me again, his gaze heavy with unspoken words. Finally, he settles on: "I like you . . . like more than anyone else there."

My heart bursts like electric sprinkles inside my chest.

I smile but can't manage any more than "Thanks." I step out of the car, pathetic as can be.

When he drives off, I whisper into the space where his car was, "I like you too."

More than anyone else.

But in my head, the thought that's been fighting its way to the forefront since I ran into that bathroom at the bar finally surfaces. *I'm a liar.*

Gold-Plated Dinner

ON SATURDAY, MY carefully curated day of nothing is interrupted by heavy pounding on my door.

"Mom, what the hell?" I say as I open it, taking in her frustrated expression. She's all dolled up with thick eyeliner and glowing pink lipstick.

She puts a hand on her hip. "It's almost time for dinner. You're in your pajamas?"

"It's loungewear," I say uselessly. "Why are you here?"

"We're going to dinner with the Habibs," she says, like I should have known this the whole time.

"What?" I sputter. "No, we're not."

I've been peppering her with little comments about Armin being annoying all week. How does that translate into unplanned group dinners?

"Yes, Armin's mom and I arranged it. Get dressed, don't keep them waiting. We're not a rude family."

She herds me toward my bedroom with shooing hands with the efficiency of a border collie. As soon as I'm inside, I grab my phone and text Armin: We're having dinner?!

The reply comes almost instantly: They didn't tell me either until a second ago!

When my mom ushers me into the car, my dad is sitting in the driver's seat. He at least has the decency to look apologetic.

At the restaurant, the table holding our party shines like a beacon from the foyer. The Habibs are already sitting down, Armin looking miserable beside his parents.

My mom nudges me into the chair opposite Armin and then takes the seat beside him. He's sandwiched between moms. I pull my phone out underneath the tablecloth. Shit. They have us separated.

Armin's jaw clenches. His reply comes a moment later. It's okay, just don't say anything too specific. **Then a second text:** We can do this. Just keep chill.

My mom calls, "Isn't it nice to be a big family together with the bride and groom!" And she and Armin's dad stand up and clap, loud and hollow through the room. It's like dominoes: the servers and some patrons build on to their claps, drumming a surprisingly loud vibration. Even the guy eating alone at a table in the corner smacks his thighs.

So far so chill.

My mom tugs at Armin's sleeve and goes in to kiss both his cheeks while his mom grins widely. A drink is placed in his hand, and a giant pot of lamb stew is spooned onto his waiting plate, appearing as if by magic—only really it's by fawning middle-aged mothers.

"So, baby, how is work going?" Armin's mom asks him.

Armin's eyes flash my way as he takes a long sip of his water. "Very good. We're going to have one of the best Q2s I've ever seen and are forecasting a lot of returns on investments."

I almost spit out my own water. Damn, that was believable.

The moms look at him with absolute glee. "Here," his mom says, tearing a piece of bread and adding it to his plate, then pushing over the bowl of eggplant dip I was just eyeing for myself. "You need to eat."

Holy shit, of course! How did I not realize before? Armin is a doodool tala. Direct translation: "golden penis" (because of course). Basically, he's a mama's boy who can do no wrong and must not lift a finger in the process.

Even worse, he's a doodool tala who hasn't become a doctor or lawyer—or accounting executive—even as his mom is ailing. It's a wonder his bullshit isn't wilder.

I smile toward Armin. "All the bosses ask Armin to lead their projects. He's the most precise and efficient." Two impressive buzzwords.

"Ahhh," all the parents hum.

Armin shoots me a grateful smile. "Well, Jolene has the best ideas. I was talking to Gregory—my second-in-command—and apparently head office was so impressed by her suggestion at a recent meeting that they may implement it across Canada."

My face flushes because Armin doesn't sound like he's lying this time.

"Jolene's always been a very innovative thinker." This comment comes from my dad, and it's his proud grin that hits me the hardest. He continues: "When she was a kid, she helped design the shelves for her mom's spice rack."

Mom claps. "And I made so many good meals because of this." She pats Armin's hand that's sitting on the table. "Don't worry, I'll teach Jolene to cook better. Is that the problem?"

Armin opens his mouth in surprise, but before he can respond his mom cuts in: "Jolene is so beautiful. Did you notice her right away?"

Armin grins. "Absolutely. I couldn't help it. Tried asking her to go for poutine, but she shut me down."

"Good girl," they all chant. My gaze draws to Armin again. The poutine story really happened too. Was he actually doing that when we first met?

My skin flushes, and the room is suddenly warmer. Obviously, we're not *like that* now, but how many things—how much—have I missed?

It's an odd type of melancholy that washes over me as they all laugh around me. I think of the girl I was when I first started at the office, all the experiences and chances I've denied her. My throat dries.

"So why are you fighting?" my mother suddenly says. "You are very in love!"

What? Armin and I lock eyes, twin looks of horror creeping onto our faces.

This isn't a celebratory dinner. This is an intervention.

"You are both very busy," Armin's mom says, "but once you are married you will see each other every day."

"We're fine, Mom," Armin says. "Work has been very hard lately, but we're still in love."

I widen my eyes at Armin. What happened to letting them down gently?

"Good!" my mother says, clapping her hands in delight. "Now drink some tea!"

As the teacups are passed around, I can't help but admire the way my mom glows, the joy she's taking in serving Mr. and Mrs. Habib. There's a world where she's completely made for this—if I'd just given her daughter a chance.

The conversation across the table shifts as my mom starts to comment on how the food at this restaurant compares with others'. She starts to break down her recipe for ashe reshteh and promises to cook it for Armin. "Of course, I can make you best stuff just like your mom."

Armin smiles. "Only if it's not too much trouble."

"No trouble. I'll send with Jolene for you at work."

Armin seems to relax into the idea. And there is a part of me that would really love for it to all be true. I mean, obviously not the Armin part—the ship that was my ability to find him even remotely attractive sailed away a long time ago. But it's the way our families are meshing, the comfort of being with a group of people who all like one another. My mom's high shoulders, the rare softness in my dad's expressions. I haven't thought about the mess at the office once since I sat down.

If this were real, it would be kind of . . . wonderful.

I swallow over the lump in my throat as more food is served family style, and we all attack it, but politely. No tense questions arise like they normally do when it's just me and my parents. They cling to Armin's every word, but I even get the golden treatment of a second helping without having to do it myself.

Maybe I can live in this world just a little bit longer.

I'm a liar, my brain reminds me.

"Now, kids," Mom says, looking between us at each end of the table. "Our families have made very good friends in a short time, and we are both very proud you found each other."

Armin and I smile, the unease cracking our grins.

"It's fast because when you get older you know time is less," she says. "It's sad that Armin's mom is sick, but she has a good idea."

Armin's mom nods. Her husband puts a supportive hand on her thin shoulder. "I know you don't want to plan a party now, but I'm afraid I might not be around for the wedding if it takes too long."

Crap. My chest tightens as Armin's eyes flash toward me, his lips downturned.

My mom shakes her head, her expression overly sad.

His mom takes a big breath, struggling to speak at full volume. "Because I'm so sick, would you please have the party early? Maybe in two weeks?"

Armin's eyes nearly pop out of his skull.

We absolutely can't do this.

"Armin's busy with tax season," I start to say, at the same time he begins, "Jolene's working for her promotion."

Armin's mom nods. It's quiet and small, and what the hell am I doing to this lady?

I stare at Armin—he needs to be the one. But his face is too crushed.

"We can do it." Armin smiles in my direction, his lips so stiff it looks painful. "Jolene's just being conservative. She knows how much these things cost." He squeezes his mom's hand. "Please, Mom, you have to let me help with the expenses."

"Good man," my dad says.

But the cost is not what we should be focusing on. This can't *actually* happen!

Armin is looking absolutely everywhere except me.

When the bill arrives with all the mints, a wrestling match between the dads threatens to ensue. Armin snatches it away, insisting that his executive salary can cover the cost.

With the bill taken care of, Armin's dad begins to help his wife out of her seat. My parents come around to help too, my dad pushing over the wheelchair and my mom making sure the Habibs have plenty of to-go containers with the extra sauces.

I slide into the empty chair next to Armin. Before I can speak, he says, "I know, *I know*. But she's so happy."

We both look toward our parents, who are now moving toward the door together, laughing at something Armin's mom said.

Without really thinking, I say, "Is this really what she needs?"

My heartbeat picks up when Armin's eyes lock on me. "What do you mean?"

And truthfully, I'm not exactly sure. I get what he's doing. And I'm not exactly in a position to judge. But I shake my head, and it's like I'm not connected to my body. "I guess . . . I just think your mom loves you no matter what. Like, to her, you're Carl. To my mom, *I'm Carl.* You know?"

"Fuck you."

His laugh has a manic tinge. A wave of relief hits as the laughter pulls through me too.

He gets up. "Okay. Yeah, I get your point a little. Even though I could've lived without the Carl comparison." He looks toward his mom again. "Just give me a little more time. I just want her to know I'm okay."

I smile.

At least his lies are for someone else.

Extortion Portion

THE MOMENT I log in for the day on Monday—before Caitlin or Armin are in, before I've even poured myself a coffee—an email from Greg pops up. Come see me now.

Shit. I peek toward Gregory's office. His light is on, but his door is closed. He's *never* here this early. The tiny hairs on the back of my neck rise; he must have been waiting for me to come in. I stare at the email for a solid minute, mind racing in all the wrong ways.

"You all right, Jolene?" asks Rhonda, who is standing up to wipe her desk trinkets with a sharply chemical-scented Lysol wipe.

I nod, broken from my trance. "Just haven't had my coffee yet."

Rhonda smiles and says, "Oh yes, the most important meal of the day," as she wipes down the yellow Yankee candle she's had on her desk for years but isn't allowed to actually burn.

I make my way toward Gregory's office; my legs are bags of sand. By the time I reach the doorway, my blood is made of pure cocaine and dread. I open the door, and Gregory is sitting at his desk tilting a Pepsi toward his mouth and licking his mustache. "Shut the door when you come in," he says, casual as can be.

The hollow click as his door shuts stiffens every muscle in my body.

I take a seat without being asked, the alternative being standing until my knees buckle.

He stares for a moment, and I blink back at him in a silent standoff. Finally, he weaves his fingers together and speaks. But his words completely throw me: "What do you want?"

I stare at the crease between his eyes, the question not fully seeping into my brain.

"Is it money? Job security?" he continues.

I nod. Because . . . yeah?

"I can't offer you a lot of money, but I can make sure you keep your job."

"Uh" is all that comes out, because his words are the exact opposite of what I braced for.

He taps his fingers on his soda can. "You're a lot more cunning than I imagined. But I suppose I'd do the same if I were you. I still can't figure out how you found out about Sheila." Then he holds up a hand, even though I haven't tried to say anything. "No, wait. We shouldn't go over any more details about my personal life."

Relief hits like a fire hose. I nod a little too hard. Details are not my friend here.

Gregory's chin juts upward. "It gets to be tough when you're the boss—a lot tougher than people think. I have a target on my back, sure. But being extorted is a first—by an assistant, no less." He gives me a coy grin.

I lean back in my seat and look around his office. Every object—the signed baseball in a glass case, the nail clippers on the desk, his special golden Supershops mug—compounds and lowers my spirit. On the wall behind him are framed awards, all meaningless, the kind designed by corporate to keep employees like him—like all of us—in line. It's all so useless.

Yet *he's* the upper echelon of this office—and more broadly, the world.

For once, I'm able to stare at him longer than a few seconds without shuddering away. He holds himself proudly, his sausage fingers woven together confidently. Gregory's below average in every facet one could evaluate a human on. He acts boastful and controlling, but really, he's paranoid and insecure.

It's so obvious now: people show most of who they are up front. It just takes someone to really watch.

So why can't I take advantage of this man? He's made so many assumptions that he basically extorted himself, and I'm just along for the ride. He's used his sad sense of power to control everyone in this office for years. Just this once, I can control him.

"Could I be off probation? My job security guaranteed?" My voice is solid and clear.

Gregory's jowls shake unpleasantly. "Unfortunately, you still have to go through the motions. That HR guy takes his job far too seriously, so you'd be raising an alarm. But I assure you, even if he recommends your dismissal, you no longer have anything to worry about."

My lips quirk. I can't help it. Even if I fail now, I'm going to be okay.

Gregory smiles back, like we're equals in this situation. "In fact, it was getting too hard to warrant, with your improved performance. I'm not sure what your secret is to getting the IEC forms completed so quickly or the innovative ideas you've had lately." Gregory pauses, staring expectantly. I shrug and try not to shift my eyes. "In any event, we likely would've had to keep you, without all this trouble. Nevertheless, come layoff time, you won't need to worry."

My heartbeat skips. It's official. After all of it, I get to stay.

It should be a relief. It should. But an odd feeling, like my arteries have switched directions, bubbles in me.

I don't have to even be nice to them anymore.

A hollow spot opens in my chest. I swallow through it and stare at my new colluder.

Gregory grins. "But please know that if you mention my affair to anyone, I will figure out a way to ensure your position here is terminated."

I nod steadily. That horrible knowledge is staying in my vault forever. The end to human suffering needs to start somewhere.

"We're done here." He gestures toward the door.

As I walk out, the distinct click of nail clippers and ricocheting nail debris sounds behind me.

Outside Gregory's office, I can see Armin and Caitlin are just arriving. Rhonda eyes me as I pass and seems like she wants to say something, but I don't have to worry about her anymore. I don't even have to be nice. And that's freedom.

I sit down and see that an email from Gregory to Cliff has appeared.

Hello Clifford,

After our discussion, here are my recommendations for the new office arrangement. If all looks good, let me know if we're clear to proceed next week.

I click open the attached file. It's the same document as the one I printed out when this all began, with everyone's names and possible consolidations, but this time people's names are highlighted.

My eyes zoom in on my name first. My row is yellow, and beside it, new text: "Promote to Document Lead." Beneath it, Caitlin has been marked to be let go. I take a moment to internally celebrate.

But I can barely take joy in it, because underneath Caitlin's name, Rhonda has also been marked as a layoff. I close my eyes. She's retirement age, and I doubt she'll find another job. This is going to devastate her.

Armin's name has been highlighted in a different color, though. I flip back to the email and read the rest.

> Also attached are the latest reports on Armin Habib. This past month he's been spending more time away from his desk and he is lacking a sense of urgency about his work. Are we able to move forward with a termination, as discussed?
> Greg

My chest tightens. Since I'm off the chopping block, Gregory must be desperate to fill his quota of firings with cause. Anything to save the company more severance payouts. This man is truly management material.

I want to yell at Armin, who is currently away from his desk, going through the boardroom and testing the chairs to assess whether he should steal one for his desk. He can't lose his executive accounting manager position before the wedding. If our fake universe falls apart, so will our real one.

Armin finally returns to his workstation with a new chair, letting out an audible huff as he mutters, "This fucking place with the cheap-ass chairs causing us all to need chiropractors."

I send him a DM.

> **Jolene:** *Armin, stop messing around. Rhonda is literally reporting your every move to Gregory, who's fucking looking for a reason to terminate you.*

He clicks open my message. His face remains blank as he looks at me, then to Rhonda, and back to his screen as he types.

> **Armin:** Don't know if you know, but last night I prevented our moms from booking a belly dancer.
> **Armin:** Also, maybe you should stop reading everyone's emails, Jolene.

He gets up and wheels the chair he was testing back to the boardroom.

Anxiety crawls up my spine with every squeak of the chair wheels. What's happening in his head?

Rhonda shakes her head and logs his every move.

JUST AFTER LUNCH, I'm working through some charting for next month, when Rhonda heads to the boardroom, notepad and water bottle in hand. As soon as she's out of sight, Armin grabs his coat and marches toward the elevators.

Shit. This will absolutely be the last straw for him.

I beeline toward Armin and cut him off just as he makes it into the hallway. "Hey, what are you doing?"

He takes a pointed step around me. "I'm just going to make some copies at the color printer on eleven."

"Don't do it. You've got your jacket."

Armin's gaze flashes toward Garret, who is emerging from an office with his ears perked toward us, before he pulls closer to me. "Okay, fine—I'm going to pop out. Was trying to be subtle, but you're blowing it for me here, Jolene."

He takes another step toward the elevator, and I return the favor by stepping in front of him again.

"Come on, Jolene." Now he's getting loud.

"If you leave, you'll lose your job. Gregory is setting you up."

Garret's eyes widen as he pretends to look at a folder while standing in the middle of the hall.

I turn his way. "How's that folder coming, Garret?"

He snaps it closed and stalks off to his desk.

I make myself tall, getting in Armin's face. "Rhonda is going to notice."

He lets out a huff. "Well, everyone's watching us now anyway. So I guess that's that. I'm going regardless." He takes a step closer to the elevator, then stops. His eyes soften as he turns back to me. "You know, this weekend at dinner, when you asked me if lying was the right thing to do, you were right."

I shake my head a little too hard. He's going to ruin everything for himself. "No, I wasn't," I say. "I was just thinking out loud. It wasn't even about you; I was projecting!" My voice has a panicked hitch in it I could do without.

Armin shakes his head. "I'm starting to wonder if any of this matters anymore. My mom is sick, and I'm tired of lying. Every day, all she wants to talk about is the wedding. This isn't how I want to spend the rest of our time together."

My hand darts out to squeeze his wrist, automatic and abrupt. "You're not thinking straight. We can still help your mom." Both our eyes dart to my hand grabbing him. I quickly retreat as flames radiate up my face.

Armin says his next words lower. "Jolene, are you … Is lying, reading people's emails, everything, maybe getting to you?" He tilts his head. "This job might not be worth what it's doing to you, you know? Life is—"

"I'm *fine!*" My voice takes an unfortunate squeal. "Things are finally going good now." Armin drops his eyes to the floor as words scramble on the tip of my tongue, as I will myself to find the right thing to say. "The truth isn't always the best policy. You knew that when you chose to lie."

Armin's shoulders drop, but it's the plea in his gaze that stops me in my tracks. "You know what appointment I'm going to today?" he asks. "We're talking to a lawyer about afterlife things. I *have* to be there. It's more important than this crap job." His words come out in a choke.

"Oh." My chest constricts. What am I doing? "I—okay. You're right. Go. I'll cover for you."

The realization is like a deflation. He doesn't need this job like I do.

"Wish your mom well for me."

"We'll talk later." He half smiles as he walks away.

WHEN I MAKE it back to the pods, Rhonda's emerging from the board-room and heading to her desk. Her gaze shifts to all the empty cubicles before zeroing in on Armin's.

She has no idea that the only job she should be worried about is her own.

What's going to happen to her? She doesn't have a son who can look after her. Her Silver Timings matches always come up short. Just like me, this job has always been all she had.

And it's like a reflex. I don't know what I'm going to say as I walk over. "Knock-knock," I murmur, tapping on the wall of her cube. Rhonda jostles in her chair to look at me, smiling. "Can I come in?"

"How can I help, dear?"

It's an excellent question. I stare blankly at her before blurting out, "I'm just thinking about the next Morale Boosters event."

Rhonda's face drops. "Unfortunately, it looks like things are quite slow for a while on that front." Her cheeks pull down, the empty week-ends and evenings stacking up against us.

"Maybe we can come up with something to do then? Like I heard you talking about a book club?"

Rhonda's voice is hollow. "I don't think anyone was interested in that idea." Then she tilts her head toward me, curious. "Do you read?"

"Not really. But I don't think *reading* is, like, the main point."

"Of a book club?" Rhonda looks at me with sincere confusion. Then her shoulders drop. "I know what you're trying do." It's the meek way she holds herself that tugs at me. "Don't worry. I'm not that lone—"

"Do you still know how to crochet?" I nod at the plush coaster sitting under her mug.

"Of course."

A light bulb goes off. "Rhonda! I have this neighbor girl. It's sort of a long story, and she's really awesome and so interested in learning to crochet but having trouble. Would you come teach her? And me too? Maybe this weekend?"

"Jolene, you don't have to…" Again she seems to shrink into herself; her fists curl in.

"I'm not *doing* anything." I march to my cubicle and hold up the zebra, only partially aware of the curious onlookers. "She made me this. She's really trying to learn." Rhonda blinks. Her stare turns wistful as I march back toward her cubicle. "Do you think you could help her? Even teach me too?"

I hand Rhonda the zebra. She flips it over in her hands and mutters, "The stitches are pulled too tight. That's why she ran into trouble."

"So you'll do it? We could meet this weekend."

"This weekend?" Rhonda blinks—the edges of her eyes shine. Finally, she nods.

"And maybe we can get coffee after? Weekends are pretty open for me these days."

It's Caitlin's chuckle that breaks it. Our eyes both draw to her. She's watching us with her twisted smile.

Rhonda's expression turns to stone in an instant. "Unfortunately I'm all booked up. Carl visits me on weekends."

I rest my hand on her wrist—the second time I've been compelled to do that to someone today. "Rhonda, you know I'd appreciate the company too."

Rhonda's expression softens. Her posture weakens.

"Where was Armin going before you talked to him just now?" Caitlin pipes in.

"To the eleventh-floor printer," I mutter.

The shift in Rhonda's expression would be imperceptible if I didn't know her so well.

But I do.

"Sorry, dear, but I'm too busy." Her lips purse as she turns toward her computer. "Maybe when my son slows down at work and has more than weekends for visits."

A shaky instability thrums through me as I reluctantly step away. It's the same feeling as when I first walked into the boardroom the day the email that I forgot to white-text for Caitlin was discovered.

I won. I should be thrilled right now. But Mr. Barcode keeps watching me with his beady eyes. I swallow an empty feeling down. It would've been nice to crochet a friend for him.

Irregular Business Hours

A T THE END of the day, I return from a bathroom break to find Gregory, Rhonda, and Garret all standing around Caitlin's monitor. The first thing I hear is Caitlin saying, "Jolene's job."

My stomach plummets. This is it. They're going to know I violated them. They will all know I lied.

I take a breath to steady myself. As soon as Caitlin spots me, her smile twists around me. "Jolene, did you not change the format for the JMS forms?"

I take a tentative step forward. "I did."

Her gaze hardens as she clicks her mouse. "No, no. The newest one—the one I issued you on May fourth. Corporate needed us to all start using them."

"That was the day you had the meeting with HR. I didn't get the update the following day either."

Gregory's pompous nod, his side-eye—all of it churns my insides.

Caitlin's eyes widen. Her flustered breath snatches through the air. "I sent it, I swear. Let me look at my outbox again." She frantically taps her keys, and the same mania seems to tap inside me. "Crap."

Caitlin looks at me with, to be frank, misguided anger. Garret's eyes are wide and scandalized. Rhonda seems weary. Gregory pulls his belt up into his belly. "This has to go out tonight. Corporate will need them by tomorrow morning."

Garret and Rhonda effectively scurry away. The excitement of a big error has obviously been replaced by the need for the team to pull together to fix it, and nobody is having that.

"I'll stay late. I'll fix it," Caitlin whimpers, her lip quivering.

Gregory just nods. He's going to fire her next week, yet he's still happy to let her bend over backward pulling extra hours to keep this company afloat. Of course.

I should leave it be. It's Caitlin's screwup, and the lady wouldn't hesitate to let me drown by myself if the roles were reversed. But then Gregory looks at me and asks, "Are you the only two that can do the forms?"

Caitlin and I lock eyes. There's a silent plea in hers.

"Yeah," I whisper, as if saying it quietly will make a difference.

"Well then, can you stay too? We need to meet this deadline."

I stare at him, baffled. Did we not just agree in his office that I was the one with the power now? This has to be some form of retaliation.

Then the worst thing that has ever happened in the exact location I'm standing happens. Gregory winks. "Jolene, helping fix a colleague's error is just the kind of dedication we look for here at Supershops."

For Donkey Kong's sakes, Gregory, this is terrible acting.

Caitlin's face pinches, stress lines pulling through, but I can't enjoy it. "Thank you, Jolene," she practically whispers.

Gregory smacks his hands together like a baboon. "Great work, ladies. This is what a team really feels like." Then he's off to violate someone else with his presence.

I sink back into my chair and pull up the new JMS form. Everything needs to be done from scratch.

Cliff messages me: Are you ready to go?

I doubt I'll be leaving this office before midnight. So I message back: Work emergency. Caitlin and I have to stay late.

Cliff: I can wait.

Jolene: *Oh, please don't wait up. I don't know how long it'll be, and that kind of pressure will kill the project.*

Cliff: Okay. Have a good night. I'll pick you up tomorrow, same time?

Jolene: *No, after tonight I'm going to sleep in. I'll see you for our appointment at 11am.*

Cliff: Wow, you're willing to take three buses tonight and tomorrow for this company. You're a dedicated employee.

Jolene: *Isn't that what I've been saying the whole time?*

Cliff's little icon switches offline, but I'm still smiling.

—————

IT'S JUST ME and Caitlin, working in the dim lighting since most of the motion sensor lights have gone out. Only she's not working; she's texting on her phone. That's fine. I will do my half and leave, no matter what.

Her phone rings. She sighs and smashes some buttons until it goes silent. She won't make eye contact with me. Passive-aggressive silence is fine with me.

Her phone rings again. She grabs it with a frustrated huff and slinks into the boardroom, shoving the door shut behind her violently—so violently that it ends up bouncing back and doesn't quite shut.

I hear her whisper, "Hello?" There's a long pause as she listens to whoever is on the other end of the line. Then she grits through her teeth, as softly as possible, "I told you, I have to work."

I'm not really paying attention, until she suddenly shouts at full volume, "Seriously? Look for yourself! I'm turning on my camera."

Then a male voice yells back, now on speaker: "They can't keep you there. You're needed at *home*."

Kyle.

"There was a mistake I need to fix." Caitlin's voice is gradually getting higher. "You'll have to come up with your own dinner tonight."

"Caitlin, what the fuck? They're going to lay you off anyway. Just leave. You've got other obligations."

Her voice cracks. "Kyle, please calm down. My colleagues will hear—"

"Are you with another dude?"

"Oh my god, no. Can't you see I'm at work?"

"Never know with you anymore. Can you blame me? I apologized a hundred fucking times, even sent an apology to your office, but still you're ignoring my texts. Now you won't even come home!"

"Just stop," Caitlin hisses. "I told you I forgave you."

"Doesn't feel like it," Kyle replies. "This feels like you're still mad at me, and you're trying to make me suffer—"

"You're right, okay? I was being dramatic. I'm sorry. Can you please pick me up tonight?" Caitlin sucks in a sharp breath.

"I need to get dinner sorted now, so figure out your own ride. And if you're home too late..."

The air in my lungs starts to burn. My bones twist tighter in my body as everything comes into sharp focus. I pull up Caitlin's emails, heart pounding, running on pure instinct and adrenaline. I search his name in her *deleted* folder as I think of the incessant phone calls, the texts, even the gifts. I scroll quickly and find one in an instant, but it's benign enough. I click on another he sent over two months ago, before I had email access. And it's enough to know for sure that I didn't mishear—what I already knew in my gut.

FROM: kyle@electriciansplus.com

TO: Caitlin Joffrey

SUBJECT: Wow

Blocking my number? So tired of playing these stupid games. I can do so much better than you...

I click it shut and pull up another from March:

I'm sorry. I picked up your favorite wine. Love you.

It's like the final deflation: Kyle is fucking abusive. It shouldn't surprise me. It doesn't. Kyle made my life hell for years, and he's still a bully. All the time I spent watching Caitlin... I just didn't properly look. I didn't *see*. All her recent anxious moments shine differently, in a way I know too well.

I didn't *want* to see.

Silence seeps from the boardroom for far too long. I think maybe I should go check on her, but I don't know what I could say. My throat scratches each time I swallow.

After fifteen minutes, she finally emerges. I watch her hand linger on the doorknob as she registers that it wasn't completely closed. She looks devastated and so small. It's like she's looking for permission to exist. An impossible thing to find.

Then she takes a deep breath, pushes her shoulders back, and it's gone. Like she's compartmentalized away everything that happened in the span of a few seconds.

She glances at me and catches me watching. Her eyes widen—she must know I heard. Then her eyes narrow into slits. "What are you looking at?"

I can't keep up with the change of vibe. Whatever she did to switch gears so fast, it's a skill nobody should need to have.

Caitlin needs to get away from this man. I need to do something.

"Are you—" I begin to say, but she drops into her chair and cuts me off.

"Can we not waste time talking? I'd like to get out of here before daybreak."

It's like a part of me has shut down. I watch as she clicks her screen awake, the glow of her monitor casting a stark white light across her face, highlighting the shadows under her eyes.

I turn back to my computer, but I can barely see the screen.

IT'S ALMOST MIDNIGHT by the time we both finish our halves of the grid. Caitlin's mascara is smudged from rubbing her tired eyes, and we're both sallow from the unnatural amount of hours spent beneath the fluorescents. My breath is sour from too much unauthorized Coffee Club coffee.

No more words were exchanged after her call with Kyle. The only human interaction I've had since then was a text from Cliff, asking me how the project was coming along. Slowly was my single word response.

I'm packing up my access card and phone when Caitlin says, "Should we stick together since it's dark?"

Her voice startles me after all the silence. I glance up and she's watching me carefully, her face a little guarded.

"Right, yes, murder is a thing," I say. "Are you taking the bus?"

Caitlin sighs. "I'm in Sundance. An Uber would be like a hundred bucks. I'm supposed to be saving money for my . . . Yeah, the bus."

I nod. "Same. I'm in the other direction, but just as far."

An awkward smile emerges on Caitlin's face for a second before it drifts away. "Let's hope our buses come at similar times so neither of us have to give witness statements tomorrow."

It feels like an olive branch. I chuckle.

We make our way down the stairwell to the bus stop just in front of our office in polite silence. Ever since Kyle yelled at her, it's like a layer of skin has been lifted. I thought I knew who Caitlin was, but now I finally see her.

But the idea of her going back to Kyle is like a corkscrew drilling into my brain.

"Caitlin," I blurt out, "are you going home?"

Caitlin stiffens and her hands clench. "Yeah . . ." Her eyes flicker to mine and then away. "Is this about Kyle? It's fine. Just stay out of it."

She's right, of course. This isn't my problem, and Caitlin isn't my friend. I shouldn't have listened to that phone call. There's so much I shouldn't know these days.

But I do know Kyle. I know that he is a terrible person—dangerous even. It's like a scream is stuck in my throat, causing a phantom ache as it begs for release.

It's too much. I open my mouth and the words tumble from me. "Caitlin, if he's willing to talk to you like that when others can hear, I'm really worried about what he says when he thinks nobody can."

Caitlin tucks her hand into a fist against her belly. Both our eyes slip to the ring on her finger. She shakes her head. "No, it's not like that. Things have just been stressful for both of us with work. That was a one-off."

I wish I could believe her, but I saw the emails. And I know Kyle. I speak softly: "But things sounded so heated. Are you sure you want to—"

"Jolene, can you honestly drop it?"

It's not like Caitlin isn't capable of taking care of herself. But the corkscrew twists inside, sharp and urgent.

"It's just—" I swallow, hardly able to believe what I'm about to say. "I actually know Kyle from—"

Caitlin throws up her hands. "Enough!" Then her gaze locks directly on to me, her lips curled with disdain. "You think you know Kyle? He told me all about *you*. I know all about your friend. How you left her to die."

I stop breathing as her words splash over me like boiling water, hot and painful. Her lips turn into a smirk, taunting me.

This has always been my worst nightmare—even worse than losing my job was someone knowing.

But this isn't about me. She's the one who needs help right now.

I inhale and look directly at her. "It was the worst moment of my life." My breath hitches despite myself. I push down my panic and keep speaking. "Ellie was my best friend."

Caitlin's gaze shifts down to the sidewalk, her nose wrinkling.

"I don't know what Kyle told you, but I really was alone with her when she slipped and fell. Everyone said I left her there, but I stayed for a long time. I tried screaming for help. Eventually I had no choice, I had to leave her."

Caitlin's eyes flash back to mine, but she doesn't speak.

"You know what happened when I finally got back to the group? I was begging for someone to call for help, but Kyle laughed and said I was just a drunk loser trying to get attention."

Caitlin's fingers squeeze into little fists at her sides. I wipe my cheeks with the back of my hand.

"Weeks later, he would taunt that we had some squabble and I killed her for fun." My throat is raw and broken as I keep going. "Whatever Kyle says I am, I've thought worse about myself. So think whatever you want about me. Nothing is worse than what happens inside my head."

I choke down a sob, turning away from her in a last-ditch effort to hold it together. But then Caitlin's hand darts out and squeezes my wrist tight, and I fully break.

"I'm sorry." Then she says, "I believe you."

Her voice is shaking as much as mine.

"Caitlin, it's none of my business. I just—I spent years wondering if I could have done something different. And I have that same feeling—that fear that I'm watching another bad thing unfold, and I need to be sure I tried my best."

She covers her face with her palms. She's so silent and still. Then a sob rips through her, like it's being pulled straight from her core. She wipes her palms over her eyes, pushing at the tears that are flooding from them, urgent and visceral. Finally, she whispers, "I've gotten so good at managing him. And myself, because of him, even though I don't want to be good at that." Another sob crumbles through her words. "But I can't lose him." She looks up, her eyes wide and desperate. "This is going to sound fucked up, but he's the only stable thing in my life. My job here has not been going well lately. I've cut out my friends, my family. And he's not always like this. Sometimes he's so sweet. He takes care of me."

Guilt seeps into my muscles, making my legs buckle. Next week Caitlin is going to be let go. She'll be alone with him. Everything I've been doing to fuck with her job has been driving her closer to danger.

I put both my hands on her shoulders, letting her lean some of her weight on me as she straightens herself. Her warmth from being alive, from being a human being, draws into me.

"I'm so sorry, Caitlin. I hate this."

Then it's like a switch is flicked. She stops crying mid-sob, rolls her shoulders back, and says, "I have to leave him."

The wave of relief that hits me is sudden and sweeping. "If you need anything—any help—I can—"

She shakes her head. "It's okay. I'll be okay tonight."

I nod uncertainly. I wish she wasn't in this tough position. I wish I could take back everything I did to mess with her.

She tucks her chin into the collar of her jacket and says, tentatively, "I'm sorry I've been so mean to you." Then she smiles, soft and sad. "I've been trying so hard because . . . this job, it's the only thing that's mine. It means everything to me."

A reel of memories plays behind my eyes of us through the years, sitting a few feet across from each other, both angry about the other person, both ashamed of ourselves. It's hard to believe how similar we are.

"I know exactly what you mean." Then I let out an empty chuckle. "I can't see how this company could lay either of us off when we're the only two that could fix this bullshit tonight."

"Yeah. Good point." She almost laughs, though it dies in her throat.

The distinct squeal of a bus approaches and rounds the corner, casting its headlights over us. "I think that's the twelve," Caitlin says, looking at me guiltily. "Will you be okay out here?"

I check my phone. "Mine's three minutes away."

She gives me a solemn smile. "I'll see you tomorrow."

I watch through the windows as she takes a seat in the dimly lit bus cabin. She looks back at me, waving her hand as she goes.

As soon as Caitlin's bus peels away, a car rounds the corner and slows right in front of me. The headlights are blinding, and I suppose that's for the best if I'm about to get murdered.

"Get in the car, Jolene."

The Day Is Still Going

MY CHEST SWELLS at the sound of Cliff's voice. The golden wonder that is his car pulls up toward the curb beneath the streetlight.

I pull the passenger-side door open and slump inside, grateful for the rush of warmth from his heater. Then something wet pushes into the back of my neck. I flinch, whipping around to find a hound dog nudging his wet nose at me from between the seats. So this is the mysterious dog I've been smelling for weeks. When I turn around to say hello, his tail starts to fly at full speed and he jumps up onto the console, practically flying onto my lap.

"Get down, Biscuit! You're coming on too strong for a first meeting."

Biscuit doesn't listen, just licks the salty part of my cheek. Nothing gets past dogs.

Cliff pushes Biscuit into the back seat again, then looks my way, bashful. "So believe it or not, I wasn't stalking you that much."

A grin tugs at my lips. "Sure. I believe you."

"Really! I was wrapping up playing you-know-what at a place nearby"—he points at his Warhammer hoodie—"when I got your text that you were still working, so I thought I'd swing by, just in case."

"Thank you," I pretty much whisper. After everything tonight, all I want is to collapse into my bed and sleep for a million years. Taking the bus would've taken me out.

He holds out a paper box. "I smuggled one before the vultures emptied it. It's lemon custard."

I accept his offering and pull open the lid. Inside, there's a single donut with pale yellow icing and white sprinkles. I want to cry when the decadent scent pulls toward me. But I think I'm out of tears for this quarter. "This donut might save my soul."

He laughs and gazes through his windshield toward the office building. "Where's Caitlin?"

I swallow the first glorious sweet-and-tart bite. "She just caught the bus, right before you pulled up."

He taps his steering wheel. "Ah."

I let out a breath, thinking about what might happen when she confronts Kyle tonight.

But there's nothing else I can do. I have to believe that.

I lean toward Cliff. "So, did you score any great Warhammers?"

"I . . . may as well just say yes."

"Oh, it's like that?" I can't help my smile. "Do you really paint the little game pieces yourself? How do you do the eyeballs?"

He turns to face me, brow raised. "You googled."

"I did."

"I have painted many a game piece, but the eyes are a whole other layer to get into. I'll need five hours of your focused time as a starting point."

"Probably for the best we leave it for another day, then." I drop my head back against the seat. "Tonight was long."

Cliff's eyes are soft under the car's faded overhead light. "That bad, eh?"

"We got the work done. It was just . . . hard."

He nods. "Then let's get you home."

I watch through the windshield as the car pulls away from the curb, turning onto the street.

"Thank you for picking me up," I tell him. "I know you said you were nearby anyway, but I'm glad you checked."

"No problem." We stop at a red, and he nods toward the digital car clock. "It's really late to be taking the bus."

Before I can stop myself, I nudge his arm with mine. "Aww, you do care."

He looks toward me and says, with too much feeling, "Very much."

And it's like an anvil has dropped between us. All the air in the car feels charged. A palpable urgency crawls into me.

"I care too," I whisper.

Cliff's voice softens. "I know you do."

The words float in the car between us, neither of us daring to say more.

We spend the rest of the drive home in comfortable silence. I stretch my hand into the back seat and let Biscuit lick it, laughing a little because he's really going to town.

Finally, we pull up in front of my building. I look out at the darkened street, the flickering flood lights.

Cliff inhales. "Hey, Jolene, I want to tell you something. Off the record."

I nod so, so casually. "This sounds intense. Should I be scared?"

His jaw hardens. "Very."

I turn toward him, raising an eyebrow.

"Tomorrow I'm going to submit my final report on your training." A grin draws across his face. "I'm very sorry to tell you this, but despite your best efforts, it looks like you'll be staying at Supershops awhile longer."

Of course, I already knew this. And I wish I could be excited. But his words just remind me of all the people who, despite their best efforts, won't be staying.

His grin wavers. Shit. I should look happy. "That's great!"

"You must know you deserve it," he says. "You've done amazing work the past few weeks."

"But what about the layoffs?" I ask. He tilts his head, a hint of curiosity in his stare, and I remember I'm not supposed to actually know about that. "Everyone's heard the rumors."

He sighs. "Between us, I have to begin the process of letting people go early next week."

"What about Rhonda and Armin and Caitlin? Are they staying?"

His chin falls toward his chest. "You know I can't discuss individual cases."

His brow wrinkles. He looks completely wrecked. Because firing people isn't Cliff. He made individual meetings with everyone in the company. His desk is covered with ideas about how to help employees thrive. He tried so hard to help Larry, right up until the end. He's done everything to help me.

And I've been selfish, wanting him to stay.

The words burst free. "Cliff, I think you should quit."

Cliff's mouth falls open. "What?"

"Letting people go next week? That's miserable. You're going to hate that."

"I . . . I can do it."

"So what? I *can* eat a Subway sandwich, technically, but I'm never going through that misery again."

Cliff's lips press together into a thin line. His knuckles tighten on the steering wheel. "This is part of my job."

"Seriously, Cliff. Remember how torn up you were about Larry? You told me about your coping mechanisms. How many people will die in your eyes next week? You know this isn't the place for you."

If I can just be honest from now on . . . if I can help Cliff.

His head shake is slow, uncertain. "Larry was a tough case. The rest won't be that bad."

"'That bad.' That's not how someone should feel about the job they do every single day." But more uncertainty rattles through me. "Let's be real. You *hate* this job. Your grandma is doing better now. You were speaking to that guy, Sanjay, about going back to work for him. So what's honestly keeping you at Supershops Incorporated?"

Instantly, our eyes meet—and in that single flash, I realize exactly what he doesn't want to say.

I didn't mean for this to happen. I didn't mean to like him so much.

"I don't need you to stay here to look out for me," I beg. "I don't need to be saved. You're not your fucking Warhammer thing."

"Okay, I think you've missed the mark on what happens in War—"

"You need to help yourself," I plead. I hate that it's my words that are making his face drop like this, but I need him to *see.* "Cliff, you're giving up on an amazing opportunity in Vancouver, and for what? To work at Supershops, defending us assholes, even though the place is a nightmare?"

His expression tugs down, startled by my intensity. "That's not it! That was never it." He inhales, looking down at the steering wheel. The car's overhead light bounces over his skin, highlighting the shadows under his eyes. "I need to be honest here. At first, yeah, I was trying to help you out. I liked you; I didn't want to see you get fired. But it became clear pretty fast that me being here was what could've screwed you. That's why I was looking into going back to Vancouver."

I try to process his words, but they don't add up. "Then what's still holding you to this job?"

He looks down at his lap. "When my grandma got hurt, I wasn't there. I don't want to go through that again. I like being back here with her and Grace. That's more important than the crappy jobs I take to earn a living."

I shake my head. "Feeling good about what you do is important too. Taking care of yourself is important."

"I'm not as brave as you, Jolene."

I almost laugh at the absurdity. "Me? Brave?"

"Are you kidding me? You're fucking brave. If what happened in the boardroom that first day we met happened to me—to anyone—they would've run away." His eyes tug toward me, a current flickering behind them. "But that first day, when I adjusted your computer and everyone stared at you, you somehow managed. You kept going. And it's not just that. You've helped other people too. Greg told me how you helped Rhonda with the Morale Boosters and taught her all the computer stuff."

"Please, stop." It's like he's laying out a play-by-play of all my deceptions—all the times I could've chosen a more honest path but didn't.

He huffs. "I'm just saying, I'm not staying to try and save you. You can do it yourself." Guilt swaddles inside me, but Cliff keeps his gaze on me. "And when I thought you might like Armin—when you wanted to stop being friends—of course it hurt, but it was also a relief, because that meant I could get over my feelings for you." His fingers twitch on the console. "I went all in on my mission—even tried going on a date..." We exchange a sheepish stare as I remember the theater and Silvia. "Because if I didn't have feelings for you, I wouldn't have to leave."

My breath hitches. I look up sharply. The air between us feels charged, like tinder about to ignite.

"And were you able to get over them?" My voice is tiny. I don't know if I can handle the answer.

But he doesn't have to say anything. The answer is in the heat of his gaze. The answer is in the swoop of my chest.

"I have to, Jolene," he finally says. "For now, I'm still HR."

I nod, leaning an inch backward. He leans back too. We both look straight ahead, sinking into resignation.

"Jolene," Cliff says, gently. "Maybe if one day our circumstances are different—when one of us isn't at Supershops anymore . . . Maybe we can get shakes again then? I mean, only if you want to."

I want that, so much. But it's too late to start over, at least for me. I'm still a liar.

I try to sidestep it with a joke. "Cliff, that's never going to happen. We both have excellent jobs at a wonderful company."

I think I feel his eye roll more than see it.

Biscuit barks, cutting through the tension. We both look toward him in the back seat, where he's happily panting. I give him a little scratch on his chin, silently grateful for the interruption.

"I should get inside," I say.

Cliff nods. "Big day tomorrow. You'll finally be free of me and all the HR propaganda."

"I'll never be free at Supershops." I force a smile and reach for the door handle. Starting tomorrow, I'm not going to read a single email that isn't in my inbox. I'm going to be perfect.

As I'm stepping onto the street, Cliff leans toward the passenger side to look up at me. "Jolene," he calls, "if I'd never met you, this would've been the worst job I ever had."

My neck flushes as I lock eyes with him. "Cliff, of all the anti-harassment courses in the world, I'm glad I stumbled into yours."

His chuckle breaks my heart.

When his car pulls away, I say out loud, "I like you so much."

I take a few steps toward the foyer when Miley calls, "Little late there! I knew he was your boyfriend."

I slam the door to my apartment closed a little too hard.

Party in the Boardroom

I

T'S ALMOST ELEVEN by the time I make it to the office. I pass
through the rotating lobby doors and my heart stops. Because
standing in front of the security desk is Kyle. He's red-faced, his
phone pressed to his ear as he has a heated conversation with the front
desk worker.

It's impossible to know what happened between Caitlin and him
last night, but his presence here cools my blood. I should call the police. No, I can't report him for just standing in the lobby and being
generally horrible.

If he's here, that must mean Caitlin's here too. She's probably upstairs. I should warn her.

But I can't walk past him without him *seeing me*. And that makes my
knees wobble. I take a few steps onto the freshly glossed tile before I
feel his gaze land on me. I don't pause to acknowledge him, just take
off running to the elevator. As soon as I'm inside, I repeatedly press
the door shut button. Kyle appears right in front of me at the threshold as the doors start closing. His stare bores into my pores. "You're
still crazy," he spits, voice low so only I can hear. "You shouldn't have
messed with Caitlin." The door closes.

His words bounce in the elevator, hitting me again and again until
they eventually rest inside me. As soon as I'm up on my floor, I rip
toward the pods, rapidly scanning the area. Caitlin's not at her desk.
Adrenaline pumps through me with every beat of my pulse. I charge
toward Garret. "Where's Caitlin?" I demand.

His stare flickers across my face, and he leans back like I'm a wild
animal. "She had to step out... But what are you doing?"

And maybe I really have gone feral, because I ignore Garret and
zero in on Rhonda next. She's picking at something in her hair. My
ribs tighten.

It's like I'm not in my body as I make my way closer. I step toward the edge of her cubicle. Her chair squeaks as she turns toward me. "Hello, dear! Caitlin said you guys were here until almost midnight."

"Have you seen her?" My voice is hoarse and foreign on my lips.

Rhonda's eyebrows knit together. "I'm sure she'll be back soon. In the meantime, could you help me with this document? I'm trying to change the color . . ."

But Armin pulls my arm from behind and says, "Can you come here a sec?" Something in his expression catches me enough to follow him to the quiet corner near the watercooler. His jaw ticks. "We need to tell our moms the truth. *Today*. My mom just texted me. They're on hold with the Palliser to book it as a wedding venue. Do you know how expensive that's going to be?"

Shit. "Okay, we'll do it. Just give me a few—"

"No, Jolene," Armin cuts in urgently. "We have to do it *now*. I can't hold them off anymore."

I nod aggressively and practically yell, "Yes—okay, okay, we'll just—"

Anna, the office manager, appears out of nowhere and pushes past him. Her expression is blank beneath her blunt bangs. "Miss Smith, you need to come to the boardroom right away. We need to have a meeting with HR."

Oh man, my final HR report is due from Cliff today. "I'll go as soon as I can. I just need to talk to Caitlin."

Anna shakes her head. "I really meant *now*."

Suddenly I realize that Randal the security guard is standing behind her. I should've known something big was happening for Anna to come to our floor. Randal's eyes droop like he hates what he's about to do. "Jolene, can you come with us, please?"

My nails squeeze against the flesh of my palms, and I'm afraid I'm about to snap from everything. "Yes. But I have to let someone know something. It's a matter of safe—"

"*Now*."

The whole room freezes. *I'm* a scene. Everyone in the office is peeking up from their cubicles at me like little gophers from their holes. How had I not noticed them?

I follow Randal toward the boardroom, a cloak of tension surrounding us. Nobody bothers to even whisper to each other as I pass them by.

Entering the boardroom is like delving into a stiff and dry cave. Gregory sits at the end of the table, clearing his throat. Cliff is beside him, focusing on his notepad, not a doodle in sight. A rock forms in the middle of my stomach, because in the very last seat is Caitlin.

"Are you okay?" I ask her. "Kyle's in the lobby." My words come out in a croak.

Caitlin stares through me, arms not crossed so much as curled around herself. My stomach twists. Whatever happened between us last night, the switch has been flicked.

I stumble toward the chair Armin tested yesterday, eyes focused on the floor.

Cliff speaks first. "We've had some concerning information brought to our attention that we're hoping to clear up." His voice is firm, but he sounds a million miles away. And when I draw my gaze to him, he won't look directly at me, staring instead at my forehead.

Gregory's lips tease a smile. He quickly covers his mouth by pretending to rub his mustache, but not that quickly.

Cliff continues: "Caitlin reported that last night you interfered with a private correspondence between her and her partner, and that you tried to convince her to leave her partner?"

Caitlin perches in her chair, her gaze soft and distant, staring through me like a porcelain doll. Her hands rest neatly on the table, but her lips quaver, and she's so far gone from the person I spoke to yesterday.

A wave of fear flashes. Kyle is still in the lobby. I address her directly. "Are you safe? Is he forcing you here?" My voice is shaky, my throat tight.

Instantly her eyes gain focus, her chin rises. She turns to the others and says, "This is what I'm talking about."

Cliff winces and his jaw tightens, yet he won't look at me—or speak up. Anna, who took the seat between Caitlin and Cliff, scribbles on her notepad, and Gregory mouth breathes from his perch in the corner.

Everything inside me starts sinking. Caitlin dabs the corners of her eyes. My thoughts speed past me, rapid and broken. I speak to Caitlin before thinking: "So you're not leaving him?"

She curls farther into herself, like a turtle into a shell. I can't catch up to all the stillness and silence in the room.

Her shoulders shake with a silent sob. I may not have spoken to her much over three years, but I've watched her almost every day. The fear in her eyes is real, but when her gaze flashes toward me, it's the remorse that drills into my core.

Cliff adjusts the papers in front of him. "Jolene, after a conversation last night between you and Miss Joffrey regarding her fiancé, Kyle, Caitlin had reason to believe you were interfering in her—"

"I knew my draft email was messed with! You sabotaged me! We know what you're really like." Caitlin's voice is stilted and pitchy. "I had to tell Gregory everything."

My skin goes taut. I flash back to the night Cliff busted me at Caitlin's computer. Me typing *Jolene Sucks* could've been my demise.

"Miss Joffrey! That's enough." Cliff still can't look at me. His knuckles are firm fists, his lips a thin line.

This was always going to happen. I knew this was going to happen with him one day.

He continues: "Due to the concern, Gregory had authority to check your desk."

"It's company property," Gregory just has to say. The joy in his heart is an ugly thing.

Of course Gregory was all too happy for *any* excuse to riffle through my things—extorting the guy probably didn't help my situation. I picture Gregory pawing at my desk, going through my papers . . . My stomach turns to acid. Cliff gestures toward Gregory. "Unfortunately, there was concerning material inside."

Gregory puffs out his chest, just thrilled with his existence.

Cliff adjusts the papers under his hands. My heart tumbles and tumbles into the ground. "You can't do that! That's my private stuff! That's my life!" But as the words tumble from my mouth, I know I'm not the one to speak.

Cliff nods frustratingly, but still, he won't look past his hands. He pushes a folder toward me. I keep my hands tucked into myself. "Several printed documents that are undeniable were recovered from your desk."

He props open the folder. A piece of paper has been clipped to the top with a list:

Caitlin's passwords
Phone number for Rhonda's son(?)
Armin's schedule vs. PTO days
Office consolidation materials
Emails from other units

The tightness in Cliff's expression is like a betrayal.

"That's not what it looks like." I stare at him in a silent plea. "I was trying to help."

"Were you?" Cliff's jaw ticks in unison with the drop of my stomach. He breaks our stare first. "The primary concern is that there are documents printed that weren't sent to you containing sensitive management materials." His voice is growing increasingly airy and distant. His eyes flash to the paper he's holding out. "And a plan detailing your deceptions."

My list I'd written just a few weeks ago:

—*Do everything better and faster than Caitlin*
—*Win over Gregory via his tolerable proxy, Rhonda*
—*Convince Armin I'm normal/give him no reason to talk to HR*
  about me
—*Get Cliff to like me*

His fingers halt on the last line.

My simple plans bang around and crush in on me. Cliff's expression is not one of anger but of indifference.

"That's not . . ." I fumble with no words left. "Cliff, you know me. It was all real."

Cliff's stare is cold before his gaze drops from me toward his hands. It sends a stab through my chest, sudden and hard.

Caitlin pipes in. "I wasn't sure when Kyle first told me . . ." Her shoulders square. "But Kyle was protecting me. She has a history of obsessing over people and hurting them."

It's like I'm falling down, but I'm stuck in my chair. I search Caitlin's eyes. I search for the girl from last night, but it's like there's no light left inside here.

"My fiancé is worried because he knows what Jolene is capable of when she has an unhealthy interest in someone." Her eyes squeeze shut. Her shakiness, her fear. Surely she sees how utterly fucked up this is? Surely she sees.

All the blood drains from my head. I'm losing control. I'm only partly aware of the words that spill from my mouth. "He's going to hurt you! I heard how he talks to you! How he emails!"

Everything stops as the room pulls into sharp focus.

"Is it true, then?" Cliff's eyes are wide when I come back into focus. "Miss Smith, you accessed Caitlin's email without her consent?" We lock gazes for a second, because he knows this, but—oh my god—I'm so stupid. The realization punches me in the gut. His stare is stony and distant, and it's like he's looking at me for the first time. A stranger. I'm an idiot. An imbecile. I trusted him. But he trusted me.

And I hurt him. Like always.

Caitlin strengthens her stare. "She was trying to get me away from Kyle. She wanted me isolated, I think. She's always watching me. I didn't want to share this, but I feel I must."

Everything I never allowed myself to think runs in my mind right here. Right now.

I *was* alone with Ellie that night. I made her stay at the party—did I convince her to leave the group? Was I jealous of her? Of Caitlin? I *did* order that Caitlin-esque blazer.

I should say something to defend myself, but when my gaze inevitably draws to Cliff, I'm done. Everything there is to say seems ridiculous now. Every single word there is. It's like I'm tumbling down a hole.

Cliff lets out a sigh, all the stress in the world stored in the wrinkles in his forehead. He wearily nods toward Caitlin. "The rest of this meeting will be just with management and Miss Smith. Caitlin, please feel free to take the day for personal time as our office handles this matter."

Caitlin and I exchange one final look. There's so much floating between us. So many times we've exchanged venom with just our eyes.

She breaks the stare first. I swallow audibly.

This is how it all ends for us. It's too much and not enough.

Once she clears out of the room, her cinnamon scent lingering in her final wake, Gregory nods toward Anna and Cliff. "She's also been reading *very* intimate emails of mine." It's my cringe that gives me away. Is extortion not even sacred to the guy?

Finally, Cliff locks eyes with me. I'm trapped by them. I need to get as far away from him as possible. I want to touch him.

Anna peers up from her notepad, adjusting herself higher in her chair. "We're going to ask you quite formally. Have you been reading people's emails?"

I nod once. "Yes, but I can explain it."

That's all it takes. They all shift in their chairs while Cliff gathers the papers and handles the final blow. "Miss Smith." He clears his throat. "Due to your extreme misconduct and personal breaches with your colleagues, we're going to dismiss you from your position within Supershops Incorporated, effective immediately."

Something in me breaks with the words "personal breaches." I have no fight left. This was always going to happen. I shouldn't have spoken to anyone. I stare at my lap and give a small nod.

"Security and I will escort you to your workstation to clear your belongings and ensure your safe exit from the building. Please turn in your access card and ID card to me."

I pull the lanyard from my pocket and slide it over. Our fingertips touch for a second.

I immediately pull my hand away. There's something broken behind his gaze. He broke his promise too.

Good for him after all, I suppose.

I step out of my chair and straighten my shoulders. I won't let my legs buckle.

Now it's time to start the final procession of shame to my desk.

Walk of Shame 2.0

ANDAL, CLIFF, AND I round the corner. My eyes dart across the office—everything in the space seems ornamental, surreal, like it's from a dream.

A whole room of muffled voices falls silent as we approach. Some stare directly at us. Some refuse to turn away from their screens, like I don't exist. In a way, I no longer do. Heat crawls up my neck as we pass the watercooler, our footsteps in time with its incessant dripping.

A dizzying pulse rushes through my head. I might faint in the middle of the floor, in front of everyone. And it wouldn't even matter.

I flash back to my first walk of shame. I fought so hard. Broke everything.

I lock eyes with Rhonda as she shuffles through her desk. Her expression crumbles at the sight of me. She knows. Somehow, she knows.

I take a step back as my gaze lands on Joey. And all the frustration that I was bottling deflates. An emptiness takes its place. I blink a few times, fast. I'll never see Armin water it with Gatorade again. I'll never suffer Rhonda's Christmas decorations. These are just facts, just words. Just the truth.

I stare at the faces around me. *I've* made them hurt. My throat is like a vise holding back the sobs that won't come.

After all of it—these people were never nothing. This is my whole life, right now.

"Armin's killing your plant," I say to Rhonda. "Actually, I don't know if you remember, but it was my plant first."

Rhonda's head shakes. Her jowls rattle as she pulls Joey closer, protective as a mother. Protective as she's always been.

But they hurt me too.

I stumble to my desk and grab Miley's zebra. The three pushpins stay in place.

Cliff mutters behind me, "You can go through your drawers and take any material that wasn't confiscated."

I shake my head. "Irrelevant now. You can toss it."

I step away and my gaze snags on the chair stain. I choke up when the realization hits. The wrong I did is too vast, too much.

I have nothing left here.

As I'm turning around, Armin exits the bathroom, headphones around his neck. He rushes toward me, not even noticing the procession flanking me. "Jolene, my mom just call—"

"It's over, Armin."

"The party's off?" His brow creases. "Thanks. It's for the be—"

"It's all over." And I step away, leaving him staring after me.

Cliff and Randal walk me to the elevator bank. As we wait for it to arrive, Cliff squares his shoulders. "You accomplished at least one goal on your list. You nailed it."

My stomach curdles. "It's not a Monday, Cliff. What are the stats on letting someone like me go today?"

"I don't know. I've never fired someone like you." His voice is hollow, distant. Hurt. His gaze falls away from me with finality.

The elevator doors open. Randal and I step inside. Cliff turns from us, not even waiting for the doors to close.

In the elevator, Randal stares at the floor. I say goodbye to him in the lobby, even though our relationship was, of course, parasocial. I'm not sure he even knew my name before today.

I step out of the building for the last time. The wind tickles my cheeks. It's a sunny day. And I am jobless, with no prospects.

I promptly make work of getting completely destroyed.

My plan involves liquor. I stop at the store and buy as much as I can carry. I won't have enough for next month's rent anyway.

When I make it back to my building, Miley's seated on the bench in the communal area.

"You're home early," she says, eyes floating from the bags of booze dangling from my arms to her zebra, clenched in my grip. "What's going on?"

I push past her without saying a word.

Important to Keep a Schedule

I PEEL MY CRUSTED eyes open, wiping the residual tears away. It's not quite dark in my living room, but the sun has given up for the day. I remember putting on *Schitt's Creek*, pouring alcohol into me, and letting the bitterness creep in. Bitterness about everything that's ever happened until my brain and body couldn't take anymore.

I pull myself up from the musty couch that has been soaked in misery, every muscle and joint sore from my void slumber, from the heaviness in my chest. I'm still in my stiff work pants. I somehow managed my shirt off but not my bra, so it's all twisted.

I push the half-empty wine bottle onto the far end of the couch, where it'll stay put for later. I slide out of my pants and leave them on the floor as I stumble to bed.

My eyes fall closed and heavy as I wait for the void to give me mercy and take me away again.

They were right about me.

The next time I wake, I check my phone and see a few messages from my mom. She's talking about some DJ she's booking for the party at a steep discount that her third cousin says is best. I guess Armin hasn't said anything yet. I text her, That sounds good, and toss my phone on the floor.

I peel back a curtain to check the time of day. Outside my window, Miley is sitting on the stoop. Her gaze shifts to my window as she notices the curtain move, but she stays in place.

I'm too numb, too distant, to feel anything.

"Go inside," I say to my closed window. "Nobody's coming to talk to you."

My phone chimes several times as I disappear under my covers and drift into another dreamless slumber.

DAY TWO, I have instant coffee and search for jobs from bed. There's no market for a socially fucked-up administrator anymore.

I could never do an interview anyway. I can't leave this apartment. Maybe I could live here until the money runs out and they send me away somewhere in the countryside.

I order fried chicken and wash it down with gin.

Outside my window, Miley is tying two balloons to the streetlamp. Beside her sit two of her demented crochet figures.

There she sits, still not broken from it all.

I should do something for her birthday.

LATER, I'M DRINKING and watching another early 2000s comfort show from the same spot on my bed, when I hear a commotion outside. I check through the window and see two girls Miley's age standing by the streetlamp. Miley runs out and talks to them, a bounce in her step. I pull the windowpane up an inch.

The girl on the left's voice carries. "This place is gross. I don't want to sleep over here. Come on, let's go."

Miley mutters something, but they walk away anyway.

She walks over to the bench and collects the crochet figures she placed earlier. Her shoulders drop in a way I recognize too well.

Finally, she turns toward the stairs, the bounce in her step gone, face torn.

A hallway door slams as I take another big drink. I should say something. I should *want* to hug her or to comfort her in some way. But all I keep thinking is: *Finally, you see what it's like. It stays that way forever.*

But tears fall from my eyes for no reason, confusing and foreign. I don't need them. I can't feel them in a way that matters.

My phone chimes over and over. I never check it, and eventually the chiming stops. I fall asleep and know that there's nothing inside me. I'm a hollowed-out void.

THE NEXT DAYS are the exact same. Nothing at all happens, and I am alone. I'm only pretty sure I'm disappearing.

White-Text Conversations

O N DAY . . . WHATEVER, I wake up and go to pour myself cereal, but the box is empty. I manage to find a package of oatmeal I'd purchased years ago when I really thought I'd be a wake-up-early-and-chop-bananas-into-things kind of gal. I manage it down despite its uninspired texture. And I even manage to brush my teeth and change from one pair of sweats into another before a loud knock sounds on my door. I tiptoe toward the peephole. The large *Warhammer* is clear on his hoodie.

I groan.

"Hey, Jolene?"

What the hell is he doing here? After the last devastating look he gave me, I never thought I'd see him again, certainly not in my hallway.

I click open the door but keep the chain intact, lest he see the mess of clothes, food wrappers, and undies. Even before I became a goblin, the state of my apartment wasn't winning any prizes, but now it could probably be featured on Investigation Discovery.

He's balancing a precarious two-coffee-and-two-donut-bag situation. There's a hesitant softness in his gaze. "Your donut is root beer float."

I clear my throat. "I'm not sure why HR is making house calls. But I'm not one of your subjects. I'm extremely fired, so I think that makes me dead in your eyes."

Cliff almost smiles, before he clocks my crossed arms and it falls flat. "I'm glad you're still *you*. And I'm sorry to show up like this. I tried texting first. I just came to drop off some letters. A few people at work wanted to get in touch with you."

"I'm pretty sure getting fired means I'm not involved in Supershops business anymore," I remind him.

"But I'm not here on official Supershops business." His gaze shifts down. He lowers his voice. "Could you let me in? Your neighbor Miley is listening."

He has no business being here, seeing the shit show I worked so hard to keep exclusive.

But I'm not the one who deserves to be mad. I was the one who hurt him.

"You get used to it." I stare Cliff down but pull the chain. It clatters against the door before opening fully.

He's being very careful not to look at anything but my eyes as he makes his way around the clutter. Some coffee spills onto his wrist from the overfilled cup and he winces.

"I can take the coffee off your hands, lest you get more hurt," I say. He pretty much jumps over himself to give me the cup. It's too apparent how shaky my hand is as I take it.

He pulls a manila envelope from his hoodie pocket. "The letters."

A wave of opposing feelings crash inside me. Flashes of his cold tone after firing me. His face when my list was revealed, when he found out everything I did with him was a lie.

I keep my face even as I take the envelope and toss it onto my shoe rack. "Thanks."

He reaches into his hoodie again. "Also, you left a lot of stuff at your desk. The stuff I determined is more personal—"

"Is that all?" I interrupt, and look pointedly at my mess of boots and junk on the floor. "I'm pretty busy here."

"I won't take too much of your time, but... can we talk for a minute?" He locks eyes with me, splitting me in half. I nod and he continues. "Jolene, I was shocked when I realized you'd been reading my emails." His jaw ticks, proving the hurt I caused. "When I saw your list ... My head was so screwy. I was hurt and pissed."

Guilt tugs my gaze down toward the floor.

He catches his breath, and his expression softens. "But after you left, when I was at that office without you, cleaning your desk in front of everyone, I realized I *know* you." He closes his eyes briefly. "I did what I had to do as an HR rep. But I'm here to let you explain. As a friend."

But I was the shittiest friend.

"What is there to say?" I almost laugh. "It's all true. I did what I did. I'm a horrible person. I'm finally accepting that."

Cliff lowers his eyes. "I know you care about people." His gaze tilts to the letters. "And people care about you."

I squeeze my hands together, willing my heart to stay as solid as wood. I can't do this.

But at least I can finally dispel myself of some of the guilt that's been roiling in my belly. I can give him the apology he deserves. "Look, Cliff, I'm really so sorry about the spying. It was terrible of me. I really mean that. Like, what kind of person does that?"

He nods and waits.

"That day you changed the settings on my computer, I tried to tell you at first. But I was embarrassed, because people were saying things about me I didn't want you to see. And then I realized the layoffs were coming and I thought, *Why not, if it's already there?* Everything was already so screwed up, I figured it wouldn't hurt to give myself a tiny leg up."

I hold in a breath. But he doesn't respond, just watches me, face blank. So I push myself to go on.

"And then it just got so out of hand. That list I wrote—it became moot as soon as I started talking to people. For the first time, I felt like people were starting to notice me, like we were becoming friends, even. But I couldn't say anything, because they'd hate me."

Cliff nods.

"And you firing me—all of it was the right thing to do, obviously." I stay very still. "But you need to know, you weren't part of a list. It was all real. I really cared about you."

I exhale. There. Done. Now we can close things out on neutral terms. But the softness behind his gaze pours into me. I let out a breath, willing my heart to keep quiet.

"I know . . ." Cliff swallows. "Jolene, I care about you too."

I clench my teeth together. I won't let his words sink into me. It's not worth the pain.

The look in his eyes threatens to make me feel it all again.

Cliff's shoulders square. "You were right about me too, what you told me in the car. I was scared to leave Supershops. I still am."

I want to tell him to stop it—to stop reminding me of the conversations we shared, of feeling understood.

"You helped me see what I couldn't about myself," he continues. "I deserve to choose a life that makes me happy. So I'm going back to my old company."

I was doing a pretty good job at not letting myself hope, but as soon as he says this, I realize I've failed utterly.

He's really going.

"Cliff, that's wonderful." Both my smile and my words are real. He deserves this.

His eyes widen. "I know things are messy, but we brought out a lot of good in each other too. I don't want to end things like this. Maybe we can stay in touch?"

"You still want to be friends?"

He rubs his beard, and the scent of his soap carries toward me. It would all be so blissful to just be there with him, instead of alone here forever. But he continues. "We could try. As long as, this time, we're completely honest with each other."

But all the flutters come crashing down—it hits like a brick wall. He's leaving, and I'm a mess. I'm no good for anyone right now.

I stare at my floor, not wanting to say the words I know I need to. Finally, I speak. "Cliff, I don't think that's a good idea."

The words settle between us, heavy. I gaze around at my mess and wonder how I was ever able to exist in the world as the person that I am.

"But thank you," I mutter, voice tight. "For the donuts and for showing me there's good in the world."

"There *is* good in the world, Jolene. You deserve the good—you deserve happiness."

His words tug at me and tighten my throat.

Cliff tilts closer. "Promise me you won't punish yourself forever?"

I nod and hold it all in. After a beat I say, "How about I promise to try?"

His smile is sad. "In that case, I wish you the best in all your future endeavors."

I smile back. "You too."

And as he walks toward my door, away from me for good, I know I mean it.

I want the best for him.

Cleaning Up

AFTER CLIFF LEAVES, it's like a closed chapter: nothing from that job or those people can hurt me again, not if I don't want it to. The last gin bottle, taking a break on the coffee table, stares me down.

Is it already time to start drinking again? I've had my coffee.

It's not normal to think like this, but it must be a *start* that I'm realizing that. And I *do* want to start somewhere. It somehow feels like things can be okay, now that they're so broken. Now that there's nothing left to hold together, I can just deal with what's in front of me. Where I'm going, I don't know, but I can put some garbage away. That's all I have to do.

Next, I have to shower. That's only standing somewhere where water happens to be falling. Nobody can blame me for that.

Once I manage to get myself washed and into a clean pair of sweats and less dirty hoodie, I find a way to gather the trash and the bottles and take them out. I spend about six hours tidying, and it isn't anything like I'd built in my head.

After I make myself a can of soup, I spend a good half hour looking at my face in the mirror. Mostly, I try to look myself in the eye.

I find my phone. It's been out of battery for days. I plug it in before I go to bed.

I GET OUT of bed at the respectable hour of eight a.m. I shower and manage to take some laundry downstairs. I go to the store and get groceries and buy a new vacuum that is a pain in the ass to assemble. I'm heating up a bowl of vegetable soup when I finally make eye contact with my phone.

Tons of messages plaster my screen, sent days ago. I take a heavy breath—best not to put it off forever—and dive in.

Armin: Okay, so our moms are freaking out. Apparently, your mom's guest list is at 111?
Armin: I'm going to have to come clean. Wish me luck.
Armin: Mom collapsed today. In hospital. Please cancel the party.

Fuck. I should've checked earlier.
The next few are from my mom.

Mom: I have invited a few cousins you don't know, but they're family.
Mom: Also, when Hassan calls, tell him you want discount because you're giving him good business.
Mom: Hassan is the dessert maker.
Mom: Are you okay? Ey Jan.
Mom: Armin's mom is in hospital. Please call.
Mom: You broke up? Oh no. Maybe we can still have party to celebrate you were engaged?

And the last message, sent yesterday, is:

Mom: Please answer. I'm worried.

Worried about *what* is the question. Because a party that's basically in her honor being ruined might be the biggest tragedy of them all.

I need to call her. But as I grab my empty glasses from the bedside table, I hear Miley say from outside my window, "Sorry, but Jolene asked me not to let you into the building anymore."

Then my mom says, "This is very disrespectful . . ."

I sprint to the front hall before things get bad.

"Mom, come in. I was just getting some tea made."

Mom's face is pinched as her gaze searches mine, the disappointment already apparent. "Jolene, what are you doing? Armin says you broke up, and you don't tell me? So many people have asked me if things are still okay for the party. Why aren't you answering my messages?"

"Sorry, I wasn't feeling good." I pull the door wide to my thankfully cleaner abode.

"Drink some tea and eat fruit." She storms through my apartment and straight to my fridge. She'll be angry that I don't have something like pomegranates on hand.

"I just ate a bunch of melon," I lie. "Hopefully I'll feel better soon."

She nods, satisfied for now. "Why did you and Armin break up?"

I shake my head, bracing for the terrible Band-Aid I'm about to rip. "No. That was all a lie—we were never dating . . ." Her face drops. "Or engaged."

She stares almost through me. I expect her to drill into me with a million questions about it, but instead she says, "But are you okay? Would you still like to have a celebration. One for your promotion?"

A chuckle escapes through the hollow part of my chest. I'm so far away from the person she thinks I am. I inhale, and it's like the words come flying out of me. "I'm really not doing good."

I fall onto my couch and put my head in my hands. After a beat, I feel the cushion beside me sink.

"I haven't been good since Ellie—or even before that. I know you've been trying to help me move on and lead a good life, but it's not happening." I gasp for air, peering at her from between my fingers as her eyes widen. Her lips press into a line.

"You are doing good," she says. "Men aren't as important as your career. Just because Armin didn't work out, your promotion is still a big deal."

I lose my breath and gasp for air. "I'm not getting promoted. I was fired last week and I don't know what I'm going to do."

The sob pushes through as soon as the words are out. My chest tumbles—it's like something inside me is falling.

My mom's expression is as solid as stone.

Finally, her face breaks, and so do I.

I'm crumbling into her lap, another silent sob stuck in my throat.

Just before I land, she holds me and hugs me and it feels like everything. "It's okay, baby."

"I'm sorry I cut you out. You don't even know me anymore because I hide *so* much. Mom..." I reach for her wrist. The same wrist I'd grab for safety my whole life. The same wrist that's always been there. "There were days—there *are* days—when I'm not sure why I'm here."

Her chest shakes, and she whispers into my hair, "Oh, baby, I love you no matter what." She tightens her hands around me. "So much of the things I was hoping to protect you from I couldn't. But I will always be here for you."

And it's that, just her assurance, that feels like enough. I crouch into her. This is the first time something has felt like home with her in forever. She squeezes my hand. She's my mom. I'm her Carl.

We break apart. There's a moment of silence that shakes reality back into my bones.

And so I continue through silent tears. "I might have to move back in for a bit, until I get back on my feet."

My mom nods. "Of course! This way I can help you."

I shake my head. "Mom, it has to be different this time. I need to be able to eat what I want and grow without control. I need to be able to heal, otherwise I'll be back here again."

She nods silently, while her gaze catches on a dark smudge under a light switch. "Okay."

I don't know if I believe her, but I don't have a choice. So I continue. "Also, I think I need professional help from someone—a therapist maybe. I need to deal with my issues, my trauma, the drinking, and everything I never tried to address. Could you help me with it? It might cost more than I can handle."

Every single thing in me clenches. And even though I'm on the couch, it feels like my knees will buckle. Finally, Mom says, "I would have paid for you to have a fancy party to make you happy. I will pay for this."

I grin. "Thanks, Mom."

Her gaze shifts downward. "Now, I have something."

"Is it about the cake? Because I don't know if the owner of the bakery can even pull it off. I was kind of hoping to see what would happen."

She mock slaps me. "I know. I felt like he was bullshit too, but his prices are good." Her gaze softens. "I want to ask one thing."

"Yeah?"

Her lips form a line. "Even though you don't have to do what I say, can you invite me to do things with you? It will be hard living with you again if you never want to hang out with me."

I look directly at her, but she's burying chin in her chest. "What do you mean?"

"My sisters always have lunch or go shopping with their daughters. I moved here for you, and I wish I could know you better, but every time I come visit, you get mad at me for coming over and touching your special garbage in the cupboard."

I laugh, but a sob presses through. Because my god. "Yeah. If you change the venue of the Monday aunty dinner, I'll even come to that."

"Why change? That's the best kabob."

"The waiter rejected me, and I'm humiliated."

"Pssh." She shakes her head. "I found out he's not very nice to his mom and he thinks with his kir. Good thing I stopped that before it got serious."

After we clean our faces, she grabs her purse and heads to the door. "I need to go cancel more party things. I might need to threaten Hassan for my deposit. He's always ugly about these things." And she's muttering curses in Farsi. Hassan the baker is now comparable to a donkey's dong it seems—a far fall from grace.

After she leaves, I'm not as settled as I'd like. One niggling thought keeps eating at me.

Before I think too hard, I send the text.

Would you like to have lunch, just us, next week?

As soon as it's marked delivered, I stop breathing. But the answer doesn't come. I need to unsend. I want to throw my phone into a garbage can and forget I ever sent it.

Ding.

The relief is too much.

Dad: Yes, that sounds good! I'll pick you up.

My eyes well up, but I'm smiling.

Small Talk

I'VE COMPILED AN embarrassing amount of recycling after finishing the last of my apartment clear-out. It took me four whole days, but I'll never get off track again, maybe. It's when I'm gathering all the old mail—some realtor flyers from those delusional enough to send them to us and menus from restaurants that seem heartbreakingly desperate—that I spot the letters Cliff left, and my stomach flips.

I pick the first one up and recognize Rhonda's handwriting immediately.

Honey,

First, I'm sorry about the way things happened on your last day. When I heard the mutterings you'd been spying on us, I was so miffed. I had some big secrets you were seeing and that wasn't okay. But one thing I'm good at is forgiveness and understanding desperate situations. That's why I want you to know one thing: I was always proud of Carl, never ashamed. I just didn't think the world would understand, so I did what a mom does, I protected him.

You were proving yourself to be a true friend during your last month, and I appreciate all the things you did to help me keep up with the office and the time you spent helping plan parties. My loneliness hurts me and even scares me at times. But it was worse knowing you saw that.

I have mixed feelings about what you've done. It's complicated, but when I think of you, I remember that day in the bathroom. I remember you talking to me before Caitlin's party, and I remember you inviting me to teach crochet.

You're a kind person, Jolene.

We never know what somebody is going through and I'm no different. I never saw you, Armin, or even Caitlin how I should've.

Something I've been pondering since the day in the bathroom is: acceptance. I'm never going to have the life I thought I'd be living at my age, and the hardest thing I must face is that I might never see my son again. I might never see the person he was before he got sick.

But I can still have a life worth living. I can still hope my son heals. I can accept what has happened, but I don't have to accept what will be. I've included my home phone number. I hope you reach out to this lonely lady when you're ready.

More importantly, I hope you find your place in life. I know you can ;) (that means winking).

Rhonda

My throat squeezes, but I'm also smiling.
The next letter is from Armin.

Hey Jolene,
The first thing I should say is: sorry. I was a shit for getting mad at you after forcing you into my scheme and blaming you for selling the lie too well. I was not the ride-or-die cubicle mate turned fake fiancé I should've been, and for that I'll never forgive myself.

The second thing I should say is: thank you. You warned me that my job was on fragile ground, helped me, and called me on my bullshit. I hope you got to see your own bullshit that way. I mean that sincerely and kindly…

We put my mom in hospice a few days ago. Her cancer is too far gone, so we're just making her comfortable now. All the doctors were surprised she held on this long. I truly believe she did because of the joy meeting you and planning something with your mom gave her. I came clean. About everything. And you were right. She said that she was still proud of me and would always love me.

Also, you'll be happy to hear that I told Gregory to shove it. He told me I couldn't take more PTO to be with my mom due to the staffing shortages as they enact layoffs. Motherfucker really tried it. I walked out. I'm interviewing for a better job at VCV Games (been searching since the day we made our deal). It's a bit of a pay cut, but there's room to grow. I wasn't happy at Supershops for a while. But you were right, I should have told people what was going on with my mom. Rhonda was really supportive when she found out. She was the only one to send flowers to the hospital, and she even stopped by with muffins.

If you ever want to grab a latifeh or whatever as ex-fiancés and real friends, let me know. Message me on Instagram. I promise I'll answer this time.

Armin

I put the page down as tears well. I blink and they fall. They fall for all the good in the world that found me—the goodness in people I got to see. I was lucky, and I took too long to realize it.

But there's a tinge at the back of my mind that presses.

It's curiosity. A wondering.

I've had only two therapy sessions so far and still haven't quite worked through all the mess that's woven so deep inside of me, so maybe it's natural I still wonder about Caitlin: if she's posted some bullshit from the office, gotten that document lead promotion, went for eggs with Kyle . . . if she's okay—any of it will help.

I pull out my phone, open Instagram. And Caitlin hasn't posted shit. And a tightness builds up. It's like I need to see some proof she still exists.

But watching people without them wanting me to doesn't work. I know what I really need.

I hit *block* and close the app. It feels like a tidy ending for her and me after everything.

I exhale and gather the colleague letters back into their envelope and toss them into a box that is destined for my parents' house. The envelope lands right on top of the yearbook. The realization is like a rush. I need to close another door.

I pick up the yearbook and take it to my bed. I haven't opened it in years. I'm not even sure why I took it with me when I moved out of my parents' house. But when I flip it open, it automatically falls on the only page I ever looked at. The faded picture beneath the words "In Memoriam" stares back.

And I speak.

"I'm so sorry I've kept you in a box. That was messed up of me." The tears tumble as my voice shatters. "But what else did we expect? Your death was too awful. Where was I supposed to put the pain? Where was it supposed to go once it filled me up?" I take a heavy breath. "I should've said goodbye. I'm so sorry I never could. But I can't keep holding on to you like this forever."

A heaving sob pulls and twists from the deepest part of me. I stroke my hand over her face, but it's just a picture.

"Goodbye." I close the book, crumble into my mattress, and finally, I let the pain flow out of me.

I let it drown me.

HOURS LATER, I peel myself up, fragile but standing. I'm finally taking the flyers down to the basement recycling center, when Miley's mom comes marching up the stairs in a rush. She's typing on her phone and barely registers me, standing there in my partially marinated sweats. I was planning on showering *after* going to the dumpster room.

We don't even make eye contact as she approaches the doorway, and that should be that. It really should.

Which is why I'm so confused when I step closer and the words that come out of my mouth are "How was Miley's birthday?"

She stills as her head turns to me. "Sorry, what?"

A legitimate question. None of my business. Except I think of Miley's shoulders dropping. I think of her alone on her birthday, and I just want to make sure she got a cake or something.

I lighten my tone. "Miley was super excited to be turning thirteen. Did you guys do anything fun?"

She looks directly at me. "Yes, I got her a—I'm getting her a toy she wanted."

Maybe it's because it's too vague an answer, or maybe it's because I still don't know how to keep to myself—a recorded fact—but I say, "Glad her day was special. She's such an awesome kid or I, guess, teenager."

But the tears form in my eyes. I try to blink them away and choke down whatever kind of sob presses my throat. I'm freaking crying at a neighbor in the hallway. I should've stayed in—I'm still too fragile.

"Sorry," I mutter.

Her smile is pure discomfort, but something behind her eyes shifts and she says, "No, it's true. She is." She then passes me, making a show of stepping around me more than required—which, fair.

Maybe what I said will make no difference, but maybe when Miley comes home, her mom will greet her. If they see each other just a bit today, then it has to be worth it.

AS I'M MOVING the last of the boxes into my mom's car, I finally spot Miley on the stoop. I'd been avoiding her and mostly leaving the house when she's in school. Terrible.

She doesn't look up, even when I'm close enough to cast a shadow over her. I deserve that. But I hold out the little package for her anyway and say, "Happy birthday."

"What's this?" Her voice is distant and closed.

"A present slash apology slash goodbye."

She eyes it suspiciously before tearing into the paper. "Why are you apologizing to me?"

"I . . . just haven't been the greatest friend lately."

She stops unwrapping and her face juts upward. "Jolene, I thought we weren't friends?"

"Well, we could be."

"Aren't adults who are friends with kids kind of weird?"

I shrug as she pulls the last of the wrapping paper away from the T-shirt. It's from the movie we saw.

"But thanks. I love it."

"I'm really glad we did that," I say.

"Calm down, Jolene. I just used you to get me in." But her cheeks are flushed all the same.

I crouch closer. "And I never apologized for storming off that day, for avoiding you after. I'm sorry about that."

"Thanks." Her face scrunches. "But what's the goodbye about?"

"I'm going to have to move away today. I won't be around anymore."

A surprisingly impossible thing to say. Miley's face droops instantly. "Where are you moving?"

"I have to stay with my parents for a bit." An easier thing to say. Moving home doesn't seem so scary. It simply feels like going home. But Miley's face stays low. "But, I mean, we can keep in touch."

She flips the T-shirt in her lap. "Yeah, yeah. People always say that kind of thing."

I crouch lower, so I'm eye level with her. "Well, I mean it. I'll give you my number. I have to go do some things now. But I'll see you around before I leave? Sorry your present was weeks late."

Miley swipes her hair back and I notice it's less knotted than usual. I think she even got a trim. "It's okay." She shrugs. "My birthday celebration with my mom is tonight too."

My chest lifts like a helium balloon. "Fun!"

Her eyes round out as she looks at me. "You were always my easiest mark when I was looking for someone to talk to. And when you didn't want to talk, you were at least funny to watch." She stares at her worn Toms insecurely.

"Miley . . ." There's so much I want to say, so much I need her to remember about herself before she starts to doubt. "I know things can be hard at your age. But I'm proud of you for coming out here every day and trying to connect with the world. You honestly are so cool to me."

She shakes her head. "Um, yeah, the adults that are friends with kids are freaks."

I let out a chuckle. "I guess that's true."

I shift the box in my arms and start to walk to the car again, when she calls out, "Jolene, wait." Miley turns to run into our building. "I forgot! I have something for you."

I put the box down on the cracked pathway and wait as I stare at the various types of weeds that poke through. Finally, she comes trotting back with a plain brown letter-sized envelope. "Your boyfriend gave me this a few weeks ago. He said he forgot to give it to you, but you'd already said goodbye."

I stiffen instinctively. Cliff's already gone. Every time I've exited the apartment, I've been doing a double take at cars that look like his, at people walking dogs. Checking behind me at the grocery store.

A rush swells in my chest as I reach for the envelope, but Miley pulls it back. "I didn't even open it, but the way you're looking at it like it's a bomb, I'm thinking *not* snooping was a huge mistake."

She hands it over and I peek inside. Of course it's not a note. It's just the desk crap he tried to give me when he came over. For the best, of course. A clean break is honestly the best way.

I drop it into my box. "I'll catch you around, Miley."

She blinks up at me and gives a rushed but sincere smile. "Bye, Jolene."

No Outside Food Allowed

MY MOM GAVE my room a thorough deep cleaning before I arrived, and the chemical fresh scent from the products she'd sprayed over every surface lingers.

I threw out most of the stuff from my old apartment. I don't want to surround myself with those things, those memories, again. Everything I was afraid would happen happened. Yet relief is what rules me somehow. I inhale the lemon disinfectant and let it cleanse my lungs with carcinongens.

I pull the lid off one of the few boxes I've brought upstairs. Inside sits Miley's zebra and the envelope from Cliff she'd given me as I left. *Things forgotten in your desk* is printed in his writing on the front.

Recycling it would be nothing at all. If I do that, I can move on to all the things I've actually planned to do this afternoon: setting up my room, going with my mom to the store to get new things, researching programs at local universities. If I open this now, it would mean going back to that cubicle, back to that person.

I stare at it for too long. Finally, just as I've decided to take it to the bin, my mom calls my name from downstairs and I whip around, my arm hitting the envelope and spilling its contents onto the floor.

I bend down to gather it. It's just napkins, Post-it notes that have lost their stickiness, old receipts. But my heartbeat halts as I pick up the first item: the Post-it note I'd grabbed off the donut box Cliff brought for the whole office that reads *Not Poison ;)*. Next is the sketch he made to show me the set of *Kidstreet*. The napkin with the name Robin Winters written on it, from when we got milkshakes. The receipt from my bowling shoe rental. The ticket stub from the movies.

Why was I such a pack rat? I put all these things in that bottom drawer because they didn't feel like garbage. They all meant so much to me. It's so obviously laid out here.

Undeniable.

He knew when he came to see me. He knew when he left.

He knew.

I clock a Post-it note I've never seen before. There's a doodle of a cat. Underneath is written: *You're brave.*

Instantly my phone is in my hands. It's urgent and ill-advised and impulsive.

He's probably in Vancouver by now. He probably has moved on from our last conversation.

But it's *Cliff.*

I bring up his number and type one line: I miss you.

I throw my phone on the bed. I don't deserve an answer. Last time we spoke, he was reaching out to *me*—despite everything I did—and I turned him away. Why would he give me another chance?

After watching my phone obsessively for a full hour, I accept that no reply is coming. It's time to move on. So I go downstairs to join my mom and get on with all the errands we planned for the day.

But late at night, as I'm brushing my teeth, my phone buzzes. Only one word sits on the screen, but I exhale with relief. My favorite word. Milkshakes?

I CAN DO this. I just need to breathe through the tightness inside as I open the ice-cream-cone-shaped door.

This is Cliff. It won't be bad even if it goes terribly.

The place is mostly empty, and the only sound is the buzz of the refrigerators. One bored-looking teen in a retro all-white creamery uniform stares at his phone behind the counter.

Cliff's already sitting at the booth in the back, two Tiger-Tastic shakes waiting. He's got a collared shirt on and a fresh haircut with just a bit of gel. So perfectly Cliff.

His gaze draws to me as I shakily make my way over.

"Hey, Jolene," Cliff says when I reach him and lower myself into the seat across from him. He gives me a tentative stare, like he's not sure what I'll do next.

"Hey, Cliff." I return a wobbly grin. There's so much to say. But being near him . . . his eyes . . . my insides whoosh, and all the words I'd mapped out in my head leave me.

"I got you a donut," I say, pushing the yellow box I'm holding across the table toward him.

He opens it up, taking in the rainbow-colored icing and sprinkles. He puts a hand to his chest and his lips part just a little. "This is amazing."

"I think I owe you at leas–"

"No outside food!" the tired teen shouts from behind the ice-cream counter.

"Honestly, I did not expect them to care," I say, and we both chuckle as Cliff closes the lid and pushes the box to the end of the table.

"So," I start. "It's official. You're off the Supershops books."

Cliff brightens. "Now we can say what we really think of that place." The curl of his lips, the brightness in his eyes–they feel like home.

"Did you end up changing your pick for who you'd kill for a billion dollars?"

Cliff quirks his lip. "Oh, definitely Gregory. And I think he knows it too. We didn't exactly part on great terms. Sent quite the report to corporate before I put in my notice."

A satisfied thrill races through me at the thought of Gregory getting beat down by his own beloved corporate machine.

"When do you start the new gig?" I ask.

He swallows a sip of shake before answering: "Next week." His face is bright and his passion comes through as he speaks. "I'm really excited about it. Nothing like Supershops. This time I'll be focusing on large corporations that don't yet have structures in place for employees to advocate for themselves." He raises a brow in my direction. "I'll be empowering them to organize and negotiate."

"Amazing," I say. It's perfect for him. He'll be so much happier at his old place. I take a sip of the shake to smother the empty feeling swirling inside.

Cliff continues. "In fact, some of the people I'll be meeting with are employees at Supershops Incorporated." His grin turns teasing. "Seems like the mass layoffs made some people recognize a major need for more employee protections."

"Clifford!" I pull my hand to my chest. "Are you being a hero?"

His sheepish smile, I missed it—and I'm going to miss it *so much*. "I can't help it," he says. "That job was the wrong fit, but it helped me find the right one."

He's right, and a deeper part of me is genuinely happy for him. "That's really great."

I look out the window, toward the gas station across the street. The one he told me his grandma used to work at. "Is Grace happy you're moving back to Vancouver?"

Cliff shakes his head. "Jolene, I wasn't clear. I'm working for my old company, but the projects will be here."

"What?" My chest swells, afraid to hope.

Cliff lets the straw hover beneath his lips before answering. "Sanjay and I talked. He's expanding the company, and I convinced him he needed a guy in Calgary."

He's staying. A million emotions race through my brain. I want to say so much, but when I open my mouth, all that comes out is a puff of air.

"I couldn't leave my family again," Cliff says, leaning closer. "But I need to be happy too."

My heart does a somersault as the hope rushes higher in my chest. "I'm so happy for you!"

"So," Cliff says carefully. "I'm not moving, we're not at Supershops. What do we do from here?"

"We can try to be friends again?" I ask.

His gaze shifts to the donut box on the table before locking back on to me. "We agreed to be completely honest from now on?" He says it like a question as he leans closer. "Are we okay just being friends? Has it ever worked for us?"

I swallow down the lump in my throat. It feels impossible, but I've wanted to tell him for so long. I thought I never would get the chance. "Cliff, I like you more than anyone else."

His smile is instantaneous, so bright it hurts to see. "I know." His lips quiver with emotion. "I emptied your desk drawer, remember? I know *exactly* how you feel. You're maybe a little obsessed with me?"

I mock flick his straw. "You're the one who showed up at the office at midnight, who came to my apartment—and that was all sweet, but I'm just saying…"

He leans farther across the table, and I'm like a sunflower to my light as I tilt to meet him halfway. The sugary shake scent lingers on his lips, and a rush pulls from where we meet, shattering through every part of me, replacing any thought, any worry, with this moment. This kiss. Us—

The employee behind the counter coughs loudly. Pointedly.

We pull apart, exchanging sheepish grins. "Okay, but let's be real," Cliff says. "I bet way worse things have happened in this shop." He reaches out and takes my hand on the table. We both look down, staring at our fingers as they entwine. I want to stay right here forever.

But then the hollowness sets back in.

"Cliff, I … I need to say this," I say, turning serious. He leans back, and my words are already in his eyes, in the pause of his breath. But I continue. "I'm not in a good place to date right now. I'm still pretty much a mess." I let out a sigh, but the next part feels easier to say. "I'm working on myself."

He doesn't let go of my hand as the words settle between us. "Yeah, that's … that sounds like the right thing." He lets the hurt in his voice slip through a crack. "I'm really happy for you."

I know he means it, but this can't be it for us. I can't let him go again. So I say, "But maybe we can meet up again? I might need advice from an HR professional about finding a part-time job, college courses, career things. Is that what HR does?"

"Yes. You finally got one right." A small spark lights in his eyes. "But for good measure, we should plan to meet up more than once. We might need a few sessions."

I nod. "Sounds reasonable."

He pulls out his phone. "I'll circle back with my availabilities."

"Great. I look forward to working with you." I release his hand on the table and hold mine out for a handshake.

He takes it, and as we shake hands, we both smile.

Deal made.

One Year(ish) Later

I SPOT THE RED balloons tied to the pole and yell, "The party's in that building! Those balloons mean party! Pull over."

Cliff claps his hands on the steering wheel. "Thanks for cracking that code there."

I smile shakily. "Sorry. I'm a bit nervous. But not the bad kind of nervous! But *some* kind. I want everyone in the room to think I'm so cool and humble and wonderfully funny. Just casually, though: the winner ex-employee prodigal daughter doth return to the motherland Supershops retirement party."

Cliff gives me that special look he reserves just for situations when he's truly tired of my shit but in a good way. "So, okay. Just reasonable stuff then?"

I fall back against the car seat, looking out the window at the giant brick building with all its big windows. It looks kind of like a high school. "I kid, obviously. But I haven't seen them in so long, you know? And even though none of this will matter, it also *does* matter."

Cliff nods, putting the car in park. "I totally get it. But you'll do great."

He reaches for my hand that's sitting on the console and gives it a squeeze. I squeeze it back.

I keep his hand in mine as we go through the double doors of the community center and follow the glossy signs on the wall toward the gymnasium. As we approach, I hear tinny music blaring from speakers. There's a hand-painted banner strung over the door that reads: *Happy Retirement, Rhonda.*

When we walk in, the unfortunate first thing I see is Gregory salivating over the buffet table, hands in pockets. He's wearing the same Supershops-branded polo and khakis as always. After everything that went down at the office and Cliff's scathing report to corporate, there was a formal investigation, and Gregory was sent to mandatory harassment training. Even still, he's holding himself with the same Big Boss energy he used to. I guess some things never change.

The urge to turn around and run right back through the doors tugs at me.

Cliff runs his thumb over my wrist. "You good?" he whispers.

"Yes," I say, nodding. And I take another step into the room. A poorly taped spiral streamer falls from the ceiling and lands before my feet. I shake my head. "My Morale Booster replacement needs to get their shit together, I see."

"Jolene!" a voice calls. And Miley comes barreling over, mousy hair bouncing against her shoulders. She's getting so tall these days; she's wearing the shirt with the movie logo I bought her last year, but already the hem is looking a bit high on her. She tilts her head to Cliff, eyes wide and excited. "Hello, Jolene's boyfriend." Then turns to me: "Rhonda just told me you started a war on Christmas one year."

Cliff guffaws.

"We found peace." I shake my head, slapping his shoulder. "How are you?"

She flips her hair back. She looks so confident, her head held high. "Oh, you know, the stoop is good. It misses you. But otherwise, fine."

I grin. "We need to catch another movie soon. You around next weekend?"

"Ooh, yes!" But then she frowns. "But next weekend I've got a sleepover party. And the week after, Rhonda asked if I can help set up early for crochet club." She pulls out her phone, looking disturbingly like Anna the office manager as she taps at her screen with pursed lips. "Let me get back to you and I'm sure we can schedule *something...*"

Just as I'm coming to terms with getting stiffed by a teenager, two arms tug at me, pulling me around and scooping me straight into a generous bosom. "You came!" Rhonda's arms hold me tight against her chest, rocking me from side to side. "It's so great to see you!"

She releases me, and it's amazing to see how bright her face is. Another year has gone by, but somehow she seems younger.

I nudge her shoulder. "So, retirement. Never thought I'd see the day."

After I was fired and Armin quit, it was determined that Rhonda's position was necessary. I was so relieved when I finally called her and found out she was still employed. Her smile reaches the corners of her eyes, creasing the bright green eyeshadow. "Things have gotten so busy. I just couldn't be bogged down by work anymore."

Miley pipes in. "She's running three classes now."

"And training my star pupil to teach one," Rhonda says, her whole face glowing as she looks at Miley. "We just got approved for a permanent spot at this community center. We submitted all the applications virtually." A blush tinges her cheeks.

"That's amazing. I'm really happy for you Rhonda."

That's when Gregory comes stomping up to us, hands jiggling his junk until his very marinated fingers emerge from his pockets and find their final resting point on Cliff's back to thwack it. "Who let this guy in? I've got half a mind to get some bouncers in here. Damn thorn in my side." His voice has that aggressively amiable tone that only he can pull off.

I can't help the huff I let out. I'm trying to grow as a person, but there are exceptions when it comes to certain people.

"Not a thorn." Cliff smiles stiffly, and his fingers twitch against mine. "Just helping some employees get their basic rights met."

Gregory's attention draws past him toward me. As much as I thought I'd evolved past caring about this horrible man's presence, I curl away. "Jolene! All right there? No more *issues*?" A glint of spit is caught on the corner of his mouth.

Just a little bit louder than a whisper I say to Cliff, "Too bad you quit before Greg got put in those HR sessions. That would have been fun!"

Gregory's face turns into a pomegranate as he backs away and spots Robin Winters. "Robin! You got your steps in there?"

Cliff shakes his head with a small grin. "Chaotic of you."

I lean against his arm, resting my head against his shoulder. "You're going to have to clean that shirt where Gregory patted you. He touches his penis a lot."

Cliff's nose scrunches with disgust. "I'll find us some drinks. Grapefruit soda?"

I fight the instinct to stop him from ditching me and nod, releasing his hand.

Just as he walks off, I realize I'm doing pretty okay so far, standing right here, alone in a room with people who are looking at me, even though I'm still not sure what to do with my hands.

I search for a familiar face and spot Armin talking to a group of people in a corner. I take a step in his direction—only to realize I recognize the back of the blond head standing to his right. My skin pulls tight. Cliff had warned me that Caitlin might come today. I've overthought what I'd say if I saw her about a trillion times—had several chats with my therapist, asked Cliff every detail about his union work interactions with her—yet nothing has prepared me for the flash in her eyes when she turns around, like she can sense me watching her. She was always good at that.

Armin turns too and sees me. He whispers in Caitlin's ear before coming toward me. "Jolene! Great to see you! How's everything going?"

I grin politely while keeping one eye on Caitlin, who's already moved on to chat with Gregory. "Things are decent, a little stressful. I've got finals next week, so my whole life is basically studying right now. But I'm enjoying it."

I mean it. Training to be a youth counselor has fulfilled me more than anything else in my adult life. It's the perfect combo: I can genuinely help people and know I'm doing something that matters, which is what I was so desperately craving for *so* long.

"You'll do amazing," he says. Then the slightest wrinkle forms under his eyes. "And thanks for sending the latifeh last month."

My throat dries. Last month was the anniversary of his mom's death. I pull him into a side hug, and he leans against my shoulder. "Of course. How's your dad holding up?"

He pulls back, rubbing the back of his neck. "Eh, he's mostly good. Asked about you recently. I told him you're in school for counseling, and he's more confused than ever."

I slap my hand onto my forehead. "The poor man."

I don't notice Caitlin sidling toward us until she's directly in front of me. The song on the speakers fades away, a beat of silence falling around us, and my hands clench against my will. I shouldn't be scared of her.

She taps Armin on the arm. "Do you mind if I have a word with Jolene?"

Armin nods, giving me an encouraging nod before he walks away.

My skin flushes as I look toward my feet.

I feel her take a step closer. Her pointy heels enter my vision. My gaze trails up to her floral skirt and then to her French-manicured hands, twitching against her hips. But it's the lack of ring on her finger that snags me.

Caitlin speaks first. "I left him about a month after."

I keep my eyes down. "That's really good."

There's a long, uncomfortable beat where we just stand there. But I don't know what to say.

Finally, she breaks the silence. "I'm sure you don't want me to say sorry or to thank you, after everything, I should probably leave you be, but anyway—sorry, and thanks."

As I let the words sink in, I release a relieved breath. Not because I needed to hear this, but because I realize I didn't. I look up and meet her eyes. She's shorter than I remember her.

"Caitlin, it's okay."

She nods and looks down, a small tremble in her fingers.

So I continue: "It must have been hard, not to mention scary. I can understand why you did what you did. I can understand feeling like you had no choice." She nods again shakily, but I can tell she's holding herself together. "And I'm so sorry about reading your emails and messing with your job. I truly am."

Moisture shines in the corners of her eyes. She dares a tiny smile as she quietly mouths, "Thank you," then dabs her eyes with a tissue from her purse.

"Congrats on the promotion, by the way. Cliff told me." My smile is genuine.

Her eyes lock on to mine, a little steadier. "I appreciate it."

"Also, I should thank you too."

"For what?"

"For helping me lose that job."

She blinks at me, then a high-pitched cackle escapes her. It's the same cackle that set me on edge for so many years, but now it's kind of nice to hear.

"Truly." I look around the community center, at all these familiar faces. "I never would've left otherwise. And for me that would've been tragic."

She smiles again shyly. "I'm happy you're doing well."

"Caitlin!" We both turn to spot Garret waving a hand at her from across the "dance floor" that I'm worried people will start using. "Come try this and tell me if it tastes like the wings from the Unicorn!"

I laugh. "See you around."

She smiles once more and walks away.

Alone with nobody to talk to at a party once again, I fall back against the bleachers. I sit down and pull out my phone to stop from appearing too tragic.

Three messages from my mom popped up in the last ten minutes.

Mom: Are you sleeping at Cliff's again? When are you going to move in with him?

Mom: They say don't give the milk for free but we need to sample it too. But still save your money just in case.

Mom: Mind you he's tall and not cheap so he's good.

I grin and throw my phone back into my bag. I kind of adore her texts now. It's easier to see the love—it's clearer now.

Cliff squeezes through the crowd and sits down beside me. He's managed to balance two red Solo cups and a plate filled with snacks. "The donuts are decent. They're not, like, premium quality, but for a community center party funded by Supershops, they're pretty good." He pauses. "Why are you looking at me like that? Everything okay?"

"Yeah," I whisper. "I really am."

I stare at the entire party, at these miscellaneous work weirdos. I know too much about them in the absurd way that basically living with people in an office for forty hours a week always is. It's incredible. And awful. Yet deep affection for every single one of them swells in my chest. I was so lucky to have crossed paths with them for a time.

Except it's more than that. I take a breath and the smile comes easily. I think about the person I was when I worked there, but I can't find her. And that feels like power, after all.

Somebody in this crowd might be saying something bad about me behind my back. I'll do something, somewhere, out of pettiness soon. Somebody might be keeping a secret from me, and it might hurt to find out. But I'm more interested in the parts that people want to show me.

And right now, that's all I can see.

Acknowledgments

GETTING HERE TOOK a lot of help, but I'm glad it did, because the real book was the people I met along the way.

First, thank you, reader, for spending your time with these pages and for taking a chance on a debut. I appreciate you very much.

To my incredible agents, Melanie Figueroa and Taylor Haggerty, for helping make my dream come true. Thank you for your infectious enthusiasm, passion, and guidance from the first call. Working with you is both magical and a pleasure. Special thanks to Jasmine Brown, Stacy Jenson, Holly Root, and everyone in the Root Lit Fam, including my talented and welcoming agent siblings.

To my foreign rights agent, Heather Baror-Shapiro, and everyone behind the scenes at Baror International. To my film agent, Alice Lawson, and to Olivia Handrahan, Eren Joyce, and everyone behind the scenes at Gersh. You are all amazing!

To Julia Elliott, thank you for loving this book from the start and never once making me doubt that, for your keen insight every step of the way, and for being an incredible editor and champion. Thanks to everyone at William Morrow, including Rachel Berquist, Jes Lyons, Kaitlin Harri, Eliza Rosenberry, Jessica Williams, Emily Krump, Jennifer Hart, Liate Stehlik, Leah Carlson-Stanisic, Michelle Meredith, and Kerry Rubenstein. Thanks to everyone else behind the scenes for your very valuable work.

In the UK, thank you to Amy Perkins for your incredible enthusiasm toward me and this book. Thank you to the team at the Borough Press, including Emilie Chambeyron, Emily Merrill, Sophie Waeland, Bethan Moore, and Harriet Williams. Also Simeon Greenway, for the cutest cover. Thanks also to Carla Josephson.

To Julia McDowell, for your incredible insights, brainstorms, enthusiasm, and guidance, and to Iris Tupholme, Jennifer Lambert, Michael

Guy-Haddock, Cory Beatty, and everyone else at Harper Canada for championing my book at home.

To Jesse Q. Sutanto and Grace Shim. You went above and beyond as mentors and became true friends. It's a wonder how kind and giving people can be. Thank you for inspiring me, helping me, and seeing the potential. Thanks also for the DM screams, for sharing so much of yourselves, and for being all around delightful.

To my critique partners, Ashlyn Cramer and Kira Quan, for your valuable perspective. It's been so satisfying seeing our projects evolve. I love our team! To anyone who shared any group chat or server with me where we met through writing but truly came together to share disturbing content and gossip—that's been one of my favorite parts since pursuing this. To my fellow talented mentees and everyone at Pitchwars and AMM, thank you for all you did and the programs you provided that helped so many. I will always be grateful to Dana Mele and Aimee Salter, for seeing potential in my earlier writing. To my fellow 2024 debuts, thanks for being such a genuinely supportive group as we navigate publishing. Also, for your incredible books.

To the writing community at large, thanks for sharing so much info and encouragement. Special thanks to Leah Jordain for about a trillion things, but especially for encouraging me to pursue this project at just the right time.

Over the years of querying and through my journey to debuting, I've had the pleasure of crossing paths with wonderful people in the industry. To anyone I've met with, anyone who offered feedback, or anyone who guided me: I remember every kindness and kind word. Sincerely, thank you for your time and consideration.

To the miscellaneous weirdos (affectionate) who I worked with at an office some time ago, thank you. Special thanks to Cassandra Madsen and William Tran.

Thanks to my amazing supportive extended family and friends. There are too many to name as I'm very lucky despite myself. If we've ever shared a meal or adventure, I mean you. Special thanks to Emery Eden for the support (and the Warhammer help).

To the people of Iran, to those who lost their lives and those who continue to fight for freedom: you are the definition of bravery. I hope there comes a time when you don't need to be brave, and you are able to follow the dreams that everyone deserves to have.

To Christina, thank you for being the best sister. Your support has been a constant in life, so much so that I'm used to it. Thank you for never making me have to be *not* used to it.

Mom and Dad, thank you for everything. You gave me more and have done more than I could ever sufficiently thank you for, and you still do. Also, for basically being a personal catering service at times and being the best grandparents. Thanks for handselling to extended family and friends, and for all the material both of your actions provide in general.

To Ken, thank you for all the ways you've supported me in this pursuit and in life. It takes a special person to support a writer. For your undying belief and for treating it as an inevitability. For saying it's probably funny before hearing it. I save my worst jokes for you.

To Vada, it's a privilege and joy to witness the world through someone as smart, interested, and funny as you. I wouldn't have written this book without you the most.

About the Author

NATALIE SUE is a Canadian writer of Iranian and British descent. She spent her formative years moving around western Canada with a brief stint in Scotland, where she discovered her passion for storytelling as a means of connection and reading as a means of comfort. When she's not writing, she enjoys bingeing great and terrible TV, attempting pottery, and procuring houseplants. She lives in Calgary with her husband, daughter, and dog.